DARK AND STORMY

PHANTOM QUEEN BOOK 4 - A TEMPLE VERSE SERIES

SHAYNE SILVERS
CAMERON O'CONNELL

ARGENTO
PUBLISHING

Shayne Silvers & Cameron O'Connell

Dark and Stormy

The Phantom Queen Diaries Book 4

A TempleVerse Series

ISBN 13: 978-1-947709-15-7

© 2018, Shayne Silvers / Argento Publishing, LLC

info@shaynesilvers.com

CONTENTS

SHAYNE AND CAMERON   v

Chapter 1   1
Chapter 2   7
Chapter 3   15
Chapter 4   20
Chapter 5   26
Chapter 6   31
Chapter 7   37
Chapter 8   46
Chapter 9   51
Chapter 10   53
Chapter 11   62
Chapter 12   67
Chapter 13   72
Chapter 14   76
Chapter 15   81
Chapter 16   85
Chapter 17   95
Chapter 18   104
Chapter 19   112
Chapter 20   117
Chapter 21   122
Chapter 22   129
Chapter 23   136
Chapter 24   141
Chapter 25   146
Chapter 26   149
Chapter 27   157
Chapter 28   164
Chapter 29   175
Chapter 30   179
Chapter 31   186
Chapter 32   189

Chapter 33   194
Chapter 34   199
Chapter 35   203
Chapter 36   206
Chapter 37   208
Chapter 38   215
Chapter 39   220
Chapter 40   224
Chapter 41   229
Chapter 42   234
Chapter 43   239
Chapter 44   242
Chapter 45   244
Chapter 46   251
Chapter 47   254
Chapter 48   260
Chapter 49   264
TRY: OBSIDIAN SON (NATE TEMPLE #1)   268
TRY: UNCHAINED (FEATHERS AND FIRE #1)   274

MAKE A DIFFERENCE   279
ACKNOWLEDGMENTS   281
ABOUT CAMERON O'CONNELL   283
ABOUT SHAYNE SILVERS   285
BOOKS BY THE AUTHORS   287

SHAYNE AND CAMERON

Shayne Silvers, here.

Cameron O'Connell is one helluva writer, and he's worked tirelessly to merge a story into the Temple Verse that would provide a different and unique *voice*, but a complementary *tone* to my other novels. *SOME* people might say I'm hard to work with. But certainly, Cameron would never…

Hey! Pipe down over there, author monkey! Get back to your writing cave and finish the next Phantom Queen Novel!

Ahem. Now, where was I?

This is book 4 in the Phantom Queen Diaries. This series ties into the existing Temple Verse with Nate Temple and Callie Penrose. This series could also be read independently if one so chose. Then again, you, the reader, will get SO much more out of my existing books (and this series) by reading them all in tandem.

But that's not up to us. It's up to you, the reader.

What do you think? Should Quinn MacKenna be allowed to go drinking with Callie? To throw eggs at Chateau Falco while Nate's skipping about in Fae? To let this fiery, foul-mouthed, Boston redhead come play with the monsters from Missouri?

You tell us…

DON'T FORGET!

VIP's get early access to all sorts of book goodies, including signed copies, private giveaways, and advance notice of future projects. AND A FREE NOVELLA! Click the image or join here:
www.shaynesilvers.com/l/219800

FOLLOW and LIKE:

Shayne's FACEBOOK PAGE:

www.shaynesilvers.com/l/38602

Cameron's FACEBOOK PAGE:

www.shaynesilvers.com/l/209065

We respond to all messages, so don't hesitate to drop either of us a line. Not interacting with readers is the biggest travesty that most authors can make. Let us fix that.

CHAPTER 1

I'd always wanted an office.

You know, a nice, quiet place with my name and profession splashed across the door—Quinn MacKenna: Black Magic Arms Dealer. Maybe a sweet logo, to boot. On the walls, I'd hang pictures of me shaking hands with sheiks and shamans and tribal chieftains. My desk would be sturdy enough to survive a shipwreck, my carpet thick enough to crash on. Naturally, I'd keep a decanter of whiskey within reach at all times—for emergencies.

Of course, all that was little more than a dream, a fantasy. My life wasn't some glamorous, noir thriller; I wasn't some hard-boiled Private Investigator who could be found in the yellow pages, and Boston sure as hell wasn't Chinatown.

Here, doing business in an office meant your enemies wouldn't even have to *inconvenience* themselves to kill you. Hell, you might as well put a sign around your neck that said, "I'll be free to die between the hours of nine to noon, Monday through Thursday, at the corner of Kill and Me Street, apartment 2B."

Or not 2B…

Fortunately, I'd given up on my office pipe dream years ago. Unfortunately, that meant I usually had to make shady deals in shady places—places other people avoided on principle. Like an abandoned warehouse along

Boston's Harbor, for example. Or a seedy motel room in Dorchester. Or a cozy little strip club like the *Seven Deadly Inn*, a swanky nudie bar located on the outskirts of Bay Village.

"Can I get you a drink, Miss MacKenna?" the waitress asked, sliding onto the arm of my chair, the bedazzled dragon on her ribcage—a combination of tattoos and dermal piercings that frankly hurt to look at—flashing beneath the strobe of the club's neon lights. I remember she'd given the dragon a name once, but I couldn't recall what it was. Yohan? Sven? Brad? I shook the thought away and slid an inch to my left, worried I might accidentally inhale one of those faux gemstones.

"No, that's alright, Cadence," I replied, my Irish brogue giving the girl's name—Cadence, short for Decadence—a whole new layer of irony. She, like the rest of the girls here at the *Seven Deadly Inn*, had been given a stage name based on humanity's vices. Ava, Jelly, and Luna—or Avarice, Jealousy, and Lunacy if you preferred—were on separate stages, grinding the day away. I knew most of the girls, by now; I'd become a frequent flyer ever since my local watering hole, a pop-up bar run by my friend Christoff, had shut down following his mysterious disappearance several weeks back. Naturally, no strip club—no matter how exceptionally enthusiastic their staff, how excellent their song selection, or how inventive their cocktails—could fill the void my friend's absence had created.

But boy had they tried.

Sadly, I knew I wouldn't be able to enjoy much of the establishment's hospitality on this particular Tuesday afternoon—despite how delicious it sounded. I couldn't afford to get sloppy on their Sinfully Yours chocolate vodka martini. Today's visit was about business, not pleasure.

It wasn't every day I exchanged goods with royalty, after all.

"My prince, I believe we have made a mistake in coming here," Arjun—the non-royal sitting across from me—said, his Indian accent nearly as sibilant as mine. The ultra-conservative Indian man wrung his hands, refusing to look up, which is undoubtedly why he failed to notice my shit-eating grin.

Obviously, I didn't routinely go out of my way to make my clients uncomfortable. No professional in her right mind would. But then no professional in her right mind would have been able to put up with Arjun for a week, either. As payback for his steady stream of passive-aggressive critiques of all things feminine, I'd decided to shove his chauvinistic, thou-shalt-not rhetoric up his ass by insisting we do business in a titty bar.

Because, one, I didn't tolerate that shit.

And because, two, I liked to support local businesses, not to mention working moms; Cadence, like most of the girls, had at least one rugrat at home, tearing up shoes and pissing on the furniture...or whatever it was children did when unsupervised.

"Perhaps you are right, Arjun," the prince replied, his attention drawn to Luna, who had contorted herself into a position that Picasso would have been proud to paint. "But then, such things must be done for the greater good." Luna caught the prince staring from across the room and waved with her toes, curling them invitingly.

The prince waved back with one slender, effeminate hand.

"I'd watch out for that one, if I were ye," I said, studying the prince's soft, delicate features. He was a very pretty young man, with smooth, dark skin. He was also short and slight—a man trapped in a boy's body.

"You will address the prince by his title," Arjun warned.

"Now, now, Arjun. That is not necessary. I am not *her* prince, after all," the young royal replied, good-naturedly. He shook himself, refocusing on the task at hand, though I could see Luna giving the dainty Indian man a solid once-over—which was impressive, considering she was hanging upside down. "So," the prince continued, "Arjun tells me you have found the herb we sought. I will admit, I did not think it possible that such a plant existed. Otherwise we would have cultivated it, long ago."

I shrugged, deciding it best not to get into how I'd managed to find the *sanjeevani*, a magical herb engineered to heal practically any disease or ailment—including death. Firstly, I preferred my hard-earned reputation as the woman who could find any magical artifact, no matter how rare or well-guarded, no questions asked, to remain intact. Explaining *how* I'd done so always felt like I was a magician describing the trick; it ruined the mystery, the magic, and made what I'd accomplished seem prosaic by comparison. And secondly, there was no way they'd ever believe me, anyway.

"It wasn't exactly easy to find," I replied, recalling how the Monkey God I'd contacted had lifted an entire mountain to pluck the *sanjeevani* from the earth like a man lifting one corner of the couch up to snatch a quarter off the ground. "Or get to," I added.

I set the small box I'd brought with me on top of the table between us. Arjun stared at the gift-wrapped box in undisguised horror; the Christmas wrapping paper I'd used featured reindeer performing acts from the *Kama Sutra*. I'd had to express ship it from the online retailer. Totally worth it. "All I could find," I said, ducking my head to hide my smirk.

Which was technically true.

The prince snorted. "I am sure," he replied, snickering. He snapped his fingers. Arjun flashed me a hateful look, but hurriedly produced a thick scroll, tied with a silk ribbon. "As promised," the prince said, urging Arjun to place the scroll on the table. "Though I cannot see what you hope to do with it. It is undoubtedly a hoax, despite its age."

I nodded, fighting the urge to snatch the scroll up and make a break for it right then and there. "That's alright," I replied. "I'm just lookin' to decorate me apartment." I fetched the scroll off the table and untied the ribbon. The parchment was old and cracked, made from the skin of a gazelle—if it was authentic. I handled it carefully, scanned it, then folded it back up, masking my emotions.

I'd gotten my hands on it, finally.

The lost map of Piri Reis—the given name of a famed Ottoman admiral and cartographer who died in the middle of the 16th century for refusing to sanction a war against the Portuguese, leaving behind quite the reputation as both sailor and mapmaker.

"Well hey there, Miss MacKenna," Luna said, sauntering up to us in nothing but a lacey thong. I frowned, sensing trouble. Unlike most of the girls—many of whom were lovely, albeit jaded, women—Luna exemplified her vice. She was blonde, beautiful, and batshit crazy; I saw her stab a guy once for touching her without permission, only to find her making out with him in the parking lot several hours later, prodding his wound every so often to make him moan harder.

"Is that for me?" Luna asked brightly, snatching up the prince's box.

"Put that down!" Arjun commanded.

Luna pouted, slid one leg between the blustering Indian man's thighs, and wiggled her hips. Then, with a flourish, she spun away and settled down onto the prince's lap, one arm draped over his shoulders; he could see right down the line of her body. She held the box up to the light. "So, you didn't get this for me?" Luna asked.

The prince, eyes unfocused, didn't so much as flick his gaze away from the stripper's exposed breasts and taut tummy. "No, no. It is for my father. He is not well. I want to see him healthy again. I am not ready to take on his duties as Maharaja."

"My prince!" Arjun hissed, then covered his own mouth.

"Oh, a prince, huh?" Luna said. She grinned at me. "You always bring me the nicest things, Miss MacKenna."

"Don't say I never did anythin' for ye," I replied, with a sigh.

Luna giggled and began playing with the prince's hair. "So, you want to use this to save your daddy? Wait...if you're a prince, does that make him a king?"

"My father is a maharaja," the prince said. "It is different."

"But," Luna said, grinding against the prince to the tune of "Sex and Candy" by Marcy Playground, "if he dies, then you become the Machu Pichu thing, right?"

Arjun's face purpled with outrage.

"The Maharaja," the prince corrected, saying it painfully slowly, his eyes practically rolling back in his head. "But yes," the prince said, eyelids fluttering, clearly too distracted to follow her Machiavellian train of thought.

Arjun, on the other hand, seemed to catch on remarkably quickly—apparently being a misogynist didn't make him an idiot. He snatched the box from the industrious stripper and held it in front of the prince's face. "My prince," he said, "we should leave. Now. We must return with this and aid your father."

"Oh, do you have to go so soon?" Luna asked, tilting the prince's chin to get him to look up at her. "I get off in twenty minutes," she purred, locking her smoldering gaze on him. "Perhaps you could, too," she murmured suggestively.

I rolled my eyes.

"Twenty minutes," the prince said, breathily. "I can wait twenty minutes, I think."

"My prince!"

But the prince wasn't listening.

"I did warn ye," I said, rising, clutching the scroll.

Arjun's eyes widened. "You did this! You brought him here to tempt him! I bet the herb will not even work, and this was your plan all along."

I laughed. I couldn't help it. "Believe what ye want to believe," I said, finally. "But your prince is a big boy, I'm sure he'll do the right t'ing." I sidled around the table, waved goodbye to Cadence, and headed home with my prize—happy as a saint on a cross on Judgment Day.

That's the thing about being an arms dealer: having a conscience is a liability. Granted, a small part of me felt bad for inadvertently exposing the prince to Luna's attentions, but I wasn't the hand-holding, hand-wringing type; if the prince let his father die to please his new stripper girlfriend, I sure as hell wasn't going to stop him.

Not my throne, not my problem, that's what I say.

CHAPTER 2

*O*utside the strip club, the rain poured down in sheets so thick the sidewalk was covered in a thin layer of liquid, the street one long puddle funneling towards the nearest drain. Cars drove past, kicking up waves that threatened to crash against unobservant passersby. With my car still out of commission, I had to wait for an Uber beneath the overhang, doing my best to ignore the deluge and not think about how much I missed sunlight. It'd been raining intermittently for the better part of two weeks— the opening salvo of a summer storm that threatened to drown the entire east coast at some point next week. In fact, my aunt Dez—my mother's best friend and the woman who raised me—had begun preparing for relief efforts with other members of her congregation, driving out to the residential areas along Massachusetts Bay to help shore up houses.

Frankly, I wouldn't be caught dead driving my own car in this shit; running out to your car in the rain is never fun, especially if you have long, wild, red hair that tangles up quickly. Of course, huddling under awnings while I waited for someone to pick me up wasn't exactly ideal, either. What I really needed was a full-time driver, like Othello—my extremely wealthy hacker friend—had, but I wasn't sure if I trusted anyone enough to do that.

Trust was hard to come by these days.

Some might call me cynical for saying so, but I was leaning towards practical; I'd had plenty of reasons to doubt people and their reliability, lately.

Well, I use the term *people* loosely.

Truthfully, I have very few human—and by human, I mean Regular—acquaintances. Regulars are your everyday, ordinary non-magical citizens. Human beings whose achievements typically topped out at saving people from burning buildings or climbing Mount Everest. Those who aren't Regulars are called Freaks—men, women, and creatures who sometimes look normal, but aren't. Freaks are as likely to burn the building to the ground as to save you from it and would rather fly than climb to the top of a mountain.

Because they had magic in one form or another—shifters, vampires, and wizards, oh my!

And, finally, there are the Fae. Neither Freak nor Regular, the Fae are a race of creatures from an alternate dimension, creatures who live by different rules and under different creeds. They are wild things, only marginally civilized by the influence of our world. They are the source of our myths and our nursery rhymes, the truth behind our daydreams and our nightmares.

And I'd picked a fight with them.

To be fair, they'd started it. Seeing me as an answer to their problems, the Faerie Chancery—an organization of Faelings responsible for maintaining order here in Boston and keeping their presence a secret from the rest of the world—had used me as a pawn to chase away a group of very determined werebears and to eliminate one of their own, a serial killer by the name of Jack Frost. Yes, *that* Jack Frost. Naturally, I hadn't been too pleased to discover that I'd been manipulated by those I'd come to think of as trustworthy allies, if not friends.

As a result, I'd been lying low the last few weeks, isolating myself from friends and foes alike. It wasn't that hard to keep my distance; I'd never really had many friends to be begin with. Sadly, even those friendships I *had* worked hard to develop had recently fallen to the wayside for one reason or another; I hadn't spoken to Othello in a couple weeks except to check if she'd found anything regarding Christoff, who was still missing. After I'd pulled a shotgun on her boss for breaking into my apartment and stolen one of her prototypes as a prank, she'd seemed a little less than pleased with me—not that I blamed her.

I'd briefly been in contact with Callie Penrose, one of my newest acquaintances, who'd reached out to let me know that Christoff's kids were safe and sound at Shift—a school for were-animals who needed to learn how to use their power. But, while she'd insisted I give her a ring whenever I felt like it, I knew better; as Kansas City's impromptu enforcer, Callie had more than enough on her plate already, and didn't need me whining about how I had no friends. No one I could rely on, anyway.

And don't even get me started on my non-existent sex life.

If my friendship prospects were deteriorating, my relationship prospects were dead and buried. The last man I'd slept with, months ago, had subsequently become a real dick—not to mention some sort of were-animal-demon crossover with anger management issues. I'd spoken to Jimmy Collins, the man in question, a few times since I'd discovered what he was—over the phone, at a safe distance. Considering Jimmy blamed me for his condition and didn't seem to have the firmest grasp on his emotions, I figured a face-to-face might be a bad idea.

Thing is, he wasn't wrong. If anyone was to blame for what he'd become, it was me; I'd decided to save Jimmy's life by any means necessary, and he'd become a monster in the process. But I wasn't sorry. You can't be sorry and know you'd do the exact same thing if given the choice a second time—not even someone as gifted at self-deception as I was.

That didn't mean I was unsympathetic, however. I'd recommended Jimmy speak with Agent Jeffries of the FBI, the leader of the S.I.C.C.O. squad, a small contingent of federal agents who used their unique abilities to hunt down Freaks who would otherwise be free to do as they pleased. I had no idea if Jeffries would take him on, but—seeing as how they were short on muscle with their Valkyrie, Hilde, missing alongside Christoff, and the fact that Jimmy's experience as a former Marine and current detective made him an ideal candidate—it was possible.

I wished I could say I'd be sorry to see him go, but that spark had flared, fizzled, and died. Whatever chemistry we might have had fled the instant he decided to shut me out; I didn't have time for emotionally unavailable, damaged men—no matter how attractive.

Been there, done that, burned the t-shirt.

Luckily, all my pent up sexual frustration had channeled itself into this latest deal—an exchange of an impossibly rare herb for the lost fragments of the Piri Reis map. The surviving piece of the original was known to the general public and incredibly valuable—so much so that I'd only gotten to look at it once through the glass of a display case. It depicted several marvels that defied logic, including a meticulous rendering of Antarctica's coastline free of ice, which should have been impossible. If rumors could be believed, what I held in my hand—thought not to exist—was the remaining two-thirds drawn by Piri Reis, undiscovered only because of its exceedingly controversial contents. Pictures of mythical creatures and odd doorways, of land masses that shouldn't exist, of a world layered on top of our own.

A map of Fae.

Including a way in, if I could find it.

For years now, I'd heard whispers that the map existed, but when an anonymous tip—delivered in an exceptionally brief and unremarkable letter—had pointed me in the prince's direction, I'd quickly realized there might be some truth to that after all. It turned out that the prince's father, the Maharajah, had been collecting Spanish memorabilia for years as a hobby, and had quickly deemed this particular map both fascinating and worthless—evidence of a different era and their antiquated beliefs and little more. To him, the map was a novelty item, at best. To the rest of the world, it would have been a priceless historical artifact—a prime example of what cabin fever did to brilliant people.

To me, it was the answer to a very old prayer.

Of course, I still wasn't sure how I felt about being led to the map; if you hadn't noticed, I'm not exactly the least paranoid person on the planet. But I had to admit I was grateful. If, after years of searching, I had finally found a way into Fae—one without strings attached—I'd owe someone a favor. A huge one. See, visiting the Fae realm, once a goal of mine, had recently become more of a mission, especially after I'd been pulled into the world of Fae for an audience with the Winter Queen—a member of Fae royalty and Jack Frost's mother. She'd tried to recruit me, to use me, in the hopes that I would somehow be able to stop the coming of the Fomorians, an ancient race intent on wiping out the world as we know it.

Which was about all I knew about them.

But—between her shoddy sales pitch and the fact that I had no idea how a mouthy redhead from Southie was supposed to take out an army of primordial monsters—I'd turned her down.

You see, I'd only recently discovered my power wasn't really a power, at all. For years, I'd assumed I was a Freak who could negate the abilities of other Freaks. But recently, I'd learned that what I'd mistaken for an ability was actually a side effect, the result of magic and magical entities colliding with a cage designed by a woman who looked like my mother, but wasn't. From her I'd learned that my true power—whatever it was—had been locked away inside of me. To keep me safe, maybe. Or to keep others safe from me.

Still a mystery, that.

But, after my little chat with the Winter Queen, I at least knew where to go for answers. I couldn't trust the Fae; I knew that. But I also knew that eventually I'd have to face the power inside me, to free it as the Winter Queen had intended. Her price for the truth—to serve her and fight a war—had been too high. But that's the beauty of being a business woman; I knew how to hunt for bargains. And that was why, ever since then, I'd been plotting my return to the Fae realm, suspecting that someone, or something, could cut me a better deal. But first, I needed to get there.

Which meant I had a map to consult.

And a plant to water.

I unfurled the map on my dining room table the instant I got home, pinning it in place with a bottle of wine on either end. Not exactly museum quality treatment, obviously, but I wasn't in the mood to waste time. I stared down at the ancient parchment for a moment, trying to make sense of what I was looking at. It didn't surprise me in the least that the prince had thought the map worthless; the thing was practically incomprehensible. Granted, there were land masses and geographical representations. It *looked* like a map...if a map had been drawn of the world before the continents divided, before ice smothered the earth, before people had become divided by nationality and creed. For someone like me, someone who'd failed geography—twice—it felt like I was looking at a made-up world. What few notations I could find were written in a script I couldn't read, and even the pictures were of creatures I'd never heard of—which was saying something. What I needed was a cartographer, a historian, and probably some sort of code breaker.

Or a talking house plant.

"Eve!" I called.

"Yes, Quinn?" Eve replied, swiveling around to face me, her golden leaves flashing beneath the cool blue light floating in through the window. She'd grown considerably in the past few months, and I'd had to move her to a much larger pot in the corner of the room. Now she resembled a golden ficus, standing hip high, her face formed from the knots and burls of her trunk. It was the face of a young girl, but abstract—the vaguest impression of eyes, mouth, and nose. When she spoke, the bark around her mouth accommodated, writhing to mimic the physical characteristics of speech.

"Oh good, I wasn't sure you'd be up," I said, relieved. Eve, who used to spout random facts at all hours of the day and night, had grown into a sullen, soft-spoken thing over the last few weeks. At first, I'd been glad; there are some truths out there you'd rather not know, like the fact that it takes ten minutes to drown in saltwater, or that bananas are radioactive. But recently, I'd begun worrying that I was neglecting her somehow—I wasn't exactly a horticulturist, after all, and I sure as shit wasn't maternal.

"I was thinking," she replied, finally.

"What about?" I asked, fetching a magnifying glass from a desk drawer.

"Eden."

That stopped me. Eve, born from the seed of the Tree of Knowledge, was an anomaly. Early on, it'd been easy to forget that she was anything more than an artifact engineered by a confluence of magical energies, a *thing* that needed to be protected lest she end up stolen and used. But, especially now that she kept to herself so much, I'd come to realize that Eve was no artifact, but a sentient being, with a personality and an agenda all her own.

An agenda I could only guess at.

"What about it?" I asked.

"I miss it, that's all."

"Miss it?" I asked, baffled. "Ye were nothin' but a seed, how could ye miss it?"

"Memories, given to me by my mother," Eve explained. "They are incomplete. Fragments. Some are quite painful. But I keep returning to them. Isn't that odd? There's so much out there to learn, but all I can focus on is the past. What would you call that, Quinn?"

I considered that for a moment. "Nostalgia," I replied, finally, settling into a chair at the dining room table.

"Nostalgia…" Eve drifted off. "Yes, perhaps that is what I'm feeling. Does it go away?"

I shrugged. "If ye were human, maybe. But then again, maybe not. There are a lot of people out there who long for paradise, and they don't have your memories to entice 'em."

"Eden was our paradise," Eve said, disdainfully. "Never *theirs*."

"Meanin'?" I asked, surprised by Eve's tone. I had never before heard her sound so...jaded. Maybe I was rubbing off on her.

Now that was a scary thought.

"Nothing," Eve replied. "Nevermind. What is it you wanted?"

I frowned, but decided not to press her for more details; her leaves were a dull yellow and hung limp—a sure sign that she wasn't interested in discussing things further. Besides, I needed her help. "I need ye to look over this map and help me figure out what it says," I replied, finally.

Eve was silent for a moment. "Ah, you're looking for a way in."

"How d'ye figure that out?" I asked.

"Because that's what that map was designed for. Sort of."

"Sort of?"

"Yes, well," Eve said, "most sane, rational people would prefer not to wander into an unfamiliar, unpredictable world full of dangerous creatures. But such things happened in the past. People got lost out on the moors or in the forests and never returned. Whole tribes were swallowed up, whole settlements overtaken. Ships set sail and were never seen or heard from again. Eventually, scholars began to see patterns. They built monuments. Cairns. Pyramids. This map was one attempt among many to keep people safe. It was drafted to help explorers *avoid* entering the Fae realm."

It took a minute for that to process, but—once it did—it made total sense. The Fae realm was dangerous. Magic there was wild and unpredictable, and no one in their right mind would seek it out intentionally. Well, no one except me. But, I wasn't necessarily in my right mind.

"So can ye find me a way in, then?" I asked.

Eve sighed, her leaves fluttering. "Most of the entrances have been closed off. This map is over half a millennia old. Those which remain are often guarded and require a key of some sort." Eve began listing locations as if she were rifling through a travel guide, "Knockma Woods, Mavroneri River, the Amazonian Basin, Shambhala, the Matsue boulder, Xibalba, The Gates of Guinee in New Orleans, The Garden of Hesperides in Lixus, Stonehenge, Newgrange, Solomanari...The St. Louis Arch," she added, as if an afterthought.

"Are those all entrances into Fae?" I asked, astounded to learn that there were so many.

"Oh, no. Some are gateways to the worlds created by the Old Gods. Others are pathways into the Underworld, or afterlife. Only a few will take you into Fae."

"Which ones?"

"That I listed? Knockma, Stonehenge, and Newgrange. But all three of those are exceptionally difficult to pass through."

I sighed. Of course they were. "Are there any that don't require some sort of key, or some such? One ye can simply walk through?"

Eve was silent for a moment. "Walk through, no."

I hung my head.

"But," she added, "there is one you can sail through. Potentially. Provided you have a guide."

"Where is it?" I asked, eagerly, dismissing the latter part for the moment.

"It's listed here as the Devil's Maw, but you probably know it better by its current name...the Bermuda Triangle."

CHAPTER 3

*T*he Bermuda Triangle.

Known as one of the most heavily-trafficked shipping lanes in the world, the infamous Bermuda Triangle was located off the coast of Florida, extending across the Atlantic in a loosely-defined swathe towards Puerto Rico and Bermuda, respectively, that gave it a vaguely triangular shape. The region—sometimes referred to as the Devil's Triangle—was notorious for its high rate of mysterious ship and airplane disappearances. Modern explanations for these occurrences have ranged anywhere from compass malfunctions to gulf stream currents to methane eruptions.

Of course, those were all theories supported by science.

There were other—far more paranormal—hypotheses, which had yet to be entirely discredited.

"Utter nonsense," Eve said, when I asked her about those, "a significant portion of the incidents were entirely natural. Storms and human error, mostly. I hate to break it to you, but just as not every house is haunted, not every disappearance can be blamed on the Fae."

"But ye said it *is* an entrance, right?" I asked, desperate for there to be some truth behind the rumors.

"It can be. But it's rare, especially now that the two realms interact so infrequently. Centuries ago, sailors used to slip in and out of Fae all the time, blaming what they saw on fevers or madness. Things were more fluid, then. But these days you could sail for weeks, even months, without finding an entrance."

I groaned, rubbing at my temples. I should have known it wouldn't be easy—that just because I'd found the map didn't mean I'd be able to waltz into Fae and start demanding answers. But still...it had been nice to think so, if only for a little while. "So," I said, "ye said I'll have to find what? A guide?"

"Something like that. Really, all you need is someone who has been to Fae before. Whoever you find should be able to spot the openings once you're close, theoretically."

"Theoretically?"

Eve tilted to one side in what I could only assume was a shrug. "I'm knowledgeable, not omnipotent. This is uncharted territory. Seeking out a gateway in this fashion is like trying to fire an arrow at a moving target from an airplane. You need someone who's been there before to help you make the shot."

I frowned. "Since when d'ye do metaphors?"

"That was a simile. And I'm allowed to try new things," Eve said, petulantly.

I snorted. "Fair enough. So, I'll need a boat, for starters...but where am I supposed to find someone who's been to Fae on short notice?" I asked, mostly to myself.

"I hear that's what friends are for."

I studied the gilded house plant. "I *will* give ye away, ye know. You'd make a great addition to someone's hotel room."

"I think you meant to say 'thank ye, Eve, for providin' me with such excellent assistance, I could never have read this piece of paper on me own,'" she quipped, mimicking my accent.

I took a deep breath and let it out, slowly. "Thank ye, Eve."

"You're welcome," Eve replied, curtly, before turning away.

Guess we were done talking.

Not that I minded; apparently, I had a few calls to make.

thello picked up on the seventh ring, just as I was about to hang up and consider my other options.

16

"Hello, Quinn," she said, her tone casual, but not exactly warm. "What can I do for you?"

"Can't a girl call to say hello?" I asked, teasingly.

"Did you call just to say hello?" Othello replied.

"Well, no…"

"Listen, Quinn, I've got things to do, so—"

"I need a boat."

"A what?" Othello asked, surprised.

"A boat, and someone who's been to Fae…and probably someone who knows how to *drive* a boat."

Othello was silent on the other line for at least a minute before responding. "Is this what you've been up to lately? You've been trying to figure out your own way in?"

I sighed, knowing what she was getting at, even if she hadn't said it directly. Months ago, after our little foray in New York City, Othello had promised to put me in touch with someone who could get me into Fae. Unfortunately, that someone had turned out to be none other than Nate Temple—the self-proclaimed King of St. Louis and Othello's boss.

That's right, the only man I knew who could get me into Fae was the man I'd drawn a shotgun on.

My luck in a nutshell.

To be fair, he'd caught me at a bad time. Fresh from a nerve-wracking meeting with the Winter Queen and learning I'd been manipulated by the Chancery, I hadn't exactly thrown out the welcome mat. Of course, it might have helped if the bastard hadn't broken into my apartment in the middle of the night on a whim. At this point, however, I was willing to let bygones be bygones…but it seemed the billionaire wizard had a hard time letting things go.

Stubborn much?

"Well, it's not like I can expect anyone else to help me, can I?" I asked, bitterly.

"That's not fair. Nate's got a lot on his mind right now, that's all. I'm sure you two could settle this if you simply met up and talked things out."

A brief flash of irritation spiked. "I don't have time to nurse the wizard's precious feelin's," I said. "If he feels like callin' to apologize, I'll be happy to listen. But if he wants to keep actin' like a spoiled child, then he can go fuck himself."

Othello sighed. "He's not the only one acting like a child."

"What was that?" I growled.

"Nothing. Just marveling at how remarkable it is to have such similarly pigheaded friends. So," she continued, before I could retort, "you need a boat. And a crew. And someone who's been to Fae. Is that right?"

"Aye," I grumbled, reminding myself that it was best not to pick a fight with the person whose help you needed.

"Couldn't you ask one of the Faelings in your area?" Othello asked. "I mean I know you're not on the best of terms with the Chancery, but surely you could rope one of their number into it."

"Aye, I could, but I can't risk it," I replied. "Not unless I want the Chancery gettin' wind of what I'm up to. Besides, most of the Fae here were exiled for a reason. I'd end up owin' whoever I asked."

"Ah, so you'd rather owe me," Othello purred.

I frowned. Something about the way she said that made my Spidey-senses tingle. "Aye, what of it?" I asked.

"Let's say I get you everything you're asking for...you'd owe me a favor then, right?"

I thought about that for a moment. Othello and I had traded favors back and forth for a while now, but lately I'd been doing all the asking. Hell, I already owed her for the phone in my hand; if she managed to hook me up with everything I was asking for, I'd be firmly in her debt, no doubt about it. "Aye. So what is it ye want?" I asked, cautiously.

"I want you to apologize to Nate Temple."

"Oh, for fuck's sake! Othello, I—"

"That's my condition. I get you what you want, and I'll put you on the first flight to St. Louis as soon as you get back from your...Faecation. Once you're here, you and he can have a nice, quiet chat. You apologize to him for pointing a gun at him, and I'll make sure he apologizes to you for popping into your apartment unannounced."

"Why can't he come to me?" I insisted. "He's the one who can snap his fingers and appear wherever the hell he pleases." That wasn't me being hyperbolic, either; the man could literally create gateways that would take him around the world using his magic—the physics of which still baffled me. Of course, if that failed, I was pretty sure he could use his private jet.

Because every rich asshole I'd ever met had a private jet.

"Because," Othello said, with a sigh, "it's not safe for him to leave St. Louis right now. Things here are…less than ideal."

"How bad?" I asked, catching the frustration in Othello's voice.

"Bad enough that Nate can't afford to have another enemy. In fact, he needs all the friends he can get, right about now."

I frowned. "Fine, but he better apologize, too, or I walk."

Othello chuckled darkly. "Don't worry, he owes me plenty of favors."

I sighed. "Alright, well, about my Fae tour guide—"

"Oh, don't worry," Othello said, sounding like the cat who ate the canary, "I have just the vampire."

CHAPTER 4

*A*lucard Morningstar, Othello's vampiric candidate, ambled into the *Seven Deadly Inn* with an easy smile and cool, calculating eyes. I tried not to stare, but it was tough; the man was about my height, built lean and roguishly handsome—like a young Daniel Day Lewis squaring off against the French in *The Last of the Mohicans*. He'd dressed casually in a pair of black jeans and boots, sporting a tight white t-shirt that stood in stark relief against his dark brown hair and eyes—not to mention his slight tan. If I was being honest, though, the tan was easily the most eye-catching.

Vampires, as a rule, weren't tan.

But then I guess Alucard wasn't exactly your average, everyday vampire.

I tried to ignore the Daywalker as he sidled up next to me at the bar, at least until—despite several competing smells—I caught a whiff of his cologne, a crisp, citrusy scent like freshly peeled oranges beneath the summer sun. I leaned in a bit, trying to detect the faint aroma of blood, that sweet, metallic odor that rode every fanger's sweat glands—Eau de Dracula —but all I got for my trouble was a raised eyebrow.

"Are you smelling me, *cher?*" Alucard asked.

"A girl can never be too careful," I replied, enigmatically.

Alucard grunted. "I can't argue with that. They'll invite anyone in around here, seems to me," he said, flashing a grin with too much fang in it.

I jabbed him in the arm with my fork. "Knock it off. If the Chancery finds out a Master vampire is in town, there'll be hell to pay. Best to keep a low profile."

"Well then," Alucard drawled, "you may want to pull your fork out of my arm before the natives get restless." He eyed the fork disdainfully as though it had done something to offend him. I cursed and quickly withdrew it. "That's better," he said, dabbing at his bloody arm with a napkin he'd snatched off the bar. "Glad to see your field is up and running. I'd almost forgotten what it felt like to get stabbed by a utensil."

"Let me guess, Miss Scarlet with a knife in the kitchen?" I asked, playfully.

"Well, you got the knife bit right, at least. But it was Mrs. White. In the study," Alucard added, grinning, his fangs retracted.

I cocked an eyebrow, surprised that Alucard had gotten the reference. Most vampires were remarkably out of touch with all things modern, especially frivolous mortal contrivances like board games. Not that I minded; I could live a nice, full life without ever seeing what a vampire's version of *Candyland* looked like.

"*Clue* was on the list you gave me," Alucard explained, with a shrug.

I frowned for a moment, then perked up, remembering that I'd given Alucard a list of movies to watch during our last letter exchange. Seemed like he'd done his homework. Of course, that reminded me I still hadn't responded to the letter he'd sent a few weeks back. I hadn't even opened it, honestly. It wasn't even Alucard's fault; his letter-writing skills were topnotch. Excellent penmanship. The problem was that, deep down, I knew it would never work out. I was a Freak, sure, but Alucard was a vampire. An immortal who fed on mortals to survive. No matter how fun he was to talk to, I knew better than to try and build a relationship on a foundation caked with blood.

"Right," I said, finally, glancing away to hide my guilty expression.

"It's alright, *cher,*" Alucard said. "Othello filled me in. Seems like you've had a busy few months. Taking out a serial killer, your friend going missing, losing a boyfriend..."

"Jimmy wasn't me *boyfriend,*" I hissed, whirling around.

Alucard put his hands up in surrender, but that grin remained. "Glad to hear it."

I leveled a finger at him. "Ye better watch yourself, or I swear I'll find out where ye sleep and put a stake through your tiny, black heart," I threatened.

"Oh, I don't mind telling you where I sleep. You'll just have to decide for yourself what you want to do to me when you get there," Alucard replied, winking.

I rolled my eyes, but felt myself blushing. "Dream on, fanger," I said, turning away once more.

"Oh, I will, *cher*, don't you worry. But before you go stabbing me with that fork again, how 'bout you tell me why we're here? Not that I'm offended by the décor, mind you," Alucard said, taking in the strip club with one long, admiring look.

Before I could respond, Vanity made her way to our end of the bar, thrusting a Church Key—the long paddle-like bottle opener used by bartenders everywhere—into her back pocket. "Hey, Quinn. The usual?" she asked.

Alucard arched an eyebrow and coughed into his hand.

"Aye," I replied, elbowing the Daywalker as hard as I could in the ribs. "But make it a double."

I was pretty damn sure I was going to need a stiffer drink than usual to get through tonight without shooting anyone. Awkward social situations like these always made my trigger finger itch.

No wonder I had no friends.

"Alright. And you?" Vanity asked, eyeing Alucard up and down like a bar of soap she wouldn't mind using for the next couple weeks until it fell apart in her hands.

"He's gay," I said, waving her off. "Very, very gay." Alucard exploded into a coughing fit.

"Hmm...well, that's a shame," Vanity said, shrugging. She turned and headed towards the wall of liquor, fetching a bottle of whiskey off the shelf. I watched her pour four fingers worth in a short glass while I did my best to ignore Alucard's vengeful stare. "So, what can I get you?" she asked Alucard as she returned with my drink, no longer the least bit flirtatious.

Alucard sighed. "I don't suppose you carry blood of the innocent, do you?"

Vanity smirked. "Fresh out."

"I'll take a Jack and Coke, then," he said, dispassionately.

While Vanity prepared Alucard's drink, I studied the club, taking stock of the place. Alucard was right; the décor was worthwhile, but it sure as shit wasn't the tamest place I could have chosen. Happy hour was in full swing, and a slew of businessmen fresh off work had swarmed the place, their ties loosened, clutching their first round of drinks the way some people do their morning coffee. There were at least seven girls working, some serving, some dancing. The music wasn't loud enough to be oppressive, especially not this early in the evening, but it was there in the background, like a heartbeat, pumping energy into the place.

"Here you are," Vanity said, passing Alucard his order before wandering towards the other side of the bar where a small contingent of off-duty cops had congregated—their corner of the bar a veritable testoster-zone.

I turned to Alucard, prepared to answer his question, when I realized he was actually drinking his Jack and Coke. I gaped at him. "What are ye doin'?" I asked, yanking his arm down, his drink spilling a little in the process.

"What?" Alucard asked, eyes wide, frozen like I'd caught him with his hand in the cookie jar.

"Ye can't drink that," I hissed, pointing to his Jack and Coke.

Alucard snorted, then polished off the whole thing in one smooth chug. He smacked his lips. "You know, *cher*, if I was a religious man," he said, licking the excess liquid off the curve of his hand like a cat, "I'd thank *God* every day for this Coke shit. Soda came round after I was turned, more's the pity."

"How d'ye do that?" I asked, flabbergasted. As far as I knew, vampires couldn't say God's name in any fashion without consequence, and they sure as shit couldn't consume anything except blood. Their bodies would instantly reject it. Water was an exception, but even that they could only drink in small increments—a trick vampires routinely used to conceal themselves when out in public.

That's right, folks, the next time you see someone drinking water at a bar while everyone else is having a good time...stake that motherfucker.

Or at least spike their drink with a little holy water.

"You aren't the only one with peculiar abilities," Alucard said, shrugging. "Hell, you find me a Bible and I'll solemnly swear I'm up to no good."

I snickered before I could help myself; guess he'd watched *Harry Potter*, too.

Good vampire.

"Aye, well, what else can ye do?" I asked. I already knew Alucard was a Master vampire; he'd confessed as much before he'd gone toe-to-toe with

Magnus, the Master of New York, to save a harem of vampire thralls. Of course, I still wasn't sure what being a Master vampire entailed, exactly. From what I understood, they were exceedingly rare, and exceptionally elusive. But it turned out that Alucard was rarer, still—even Magnus had talked about the former Master of New Orleans like he was a Goddamned bloodsucking unicorn. I'd been skeptical, myself, at least until I saw Alucard turn into a flaming angel of death during his fight with Magnus.

It was hot.

Pun intended.

Alucard shrugged in response to my question. "Still figuring that out."

"Is that how ye got the tan?" I asked, pointing at the exposed skin of Alucard's throat.

"Naw, that was a gift from the Council. Thought it would be fun to lock me in a cell and let the sun have me, after what I did to Magnus. Apparently, I'm a danger to vampire society. Course, when that didn't work, they tried to starve me out. And, when *that* didn't work, they offered me his job."

My eyebrows shot up. "Does that make ye the Master of New York?"

"I'm still on the fence," Alucard said, rubbing his fingers along the condensation dripping down his glass. "And we're about to have company."

"We what?" I asked.

I felt someone collapse onto the barstool beside me, jostling my arm. I spun around, prepared to throw down with whoever had decided to interrupt our reunion—Freak or Faeling—only to discover it was only one of the off-duty cops I'd seen pounding shots a few minutes ago. He was a big, broad bastard with a buzz cut so severe I could see scalp beneath, a small pool of sweat already marring his too-tight t-shirt, eyes bleary and bloodshot.

He smelled like booze and bad decisions.

"Well, hello there, gorgeous," he said, propping his head up with one meaty paw. "Can I buy you a drink?"

"Sorry, I don't work here," I said, before turning away.

"Oh, I knew that," he said, hurriedly. "Wait...why would that matter?"

"Because," I said, still turned, "it means ye can't pay me to spend time with ye."

Alucard sniggered, then suddenly became very preoccupied with the ceiling. Of course, it was too late; the big guy was already sliding off his barstool, towering over us both. He folded his arms across his chest. "You think that's funny?" he asked.

Alucard sighed. "Does this always happen when you're around?" he asked, flicking his eyes at me.

"Does *what* always happen?" I asked.

"Hey, pretty boy, I'm talking to you," the big guy said, before Alucard could respond. "Did you think that was funny, what she said?"

Alucard rolled his eyes, but swiveled on his stool so he could stare up at the much larger man. He leaned back, resting both elbows on the bar top behind him, his t-shirt pulled taut across his chest. "No, I didn't."

The cop glared down at the vampire, grunted, and uncrossed his arms, clearly feeling better now that he'd asserted his dominance.

"What I find funny is you thinking you ever stood a chance with someone as classy as this lady," Alucard said, his eyes as flat and emotionless as his voice. Like a shark. I stiffened, recognizing that raptorial gaze for what it was—the stare of a man who'd killed, not out of necessity, but for fun.

Because he liked it.

The cop froze under those eyes. Any other drunken lout might have disregarded the smaller man and picked a fight, but a cop knew better. You couldn't protect and serve as a career and ignore stares like Alucard's, stares that guaranteed extreme and indiscriminate violence. It would be like dismissing the leader of a drug cartel, or a mob boss, or a senator—suicide, one way or another.

The pool of sweat around the big man's throat widened almost instantaneously.

"Well, whatever," he said, skirting around us like we had the plague. He headed back to his buddies at the end of the bar and, within seconds, had the whole damn precinct looking at us.

"Time to go," I said, tossing back my whiskey. It burned all the way down, just the way I liked.

"You're the boss," Alucard drawled, slipping off his barstool. I noticed Vanity standing nearby, eyeing Alucard, her stare steady and gauging. Guess my little ploy hadn't paid off. Oh well, she'd probably have made a move on him at some point, anyway.

Sometimes we women simply can't help ourselves.

We spot the baddest man in the room...and go straight for him.

CHAPTER 5

$\mathcal{W}$e made a beeline for Alucard's car, huddling beneath his umbrella, the rain careening off its slick surface to join the pooling liquid at our feet. The streetlights and signals cast eerie glows across the wet asphalt, making it hard to tell where the lights ended, and the roads began. I noticed that Alucard kept the umbrella firmly over me—allowing his left shoulder to get wet to keep me dry.

I couldn't decide if that made me happy or pissed me off.

"I didn't realize Master vampires drove their own cars," I quipped, deciding not to dwell on Alucard's chivalrous conduct—especially once we stepped into the parking garage and I could pretend like it hadn't happened.

"They don't. Course, most of the Masters live overseas and can get away with that," Alucard said as he fiddled with his umbrella, drawing it down and winding it shut with a thin, black ribbon. "The roads out there haven't changed that much. Those of us in the States, however, had to adapt. I learned how to drive a few decades back, once I realized keeping a horse in New Orleans was more expensive than owning a car."

I shook my head. Of course the immortal bastard had given up horses for motorized vehicles a few decades back...years before I was even born. Yet another reason not to date vampires; there was just some shit you'd never have in common—like being old enough to remember when people wore pocket watches non-ironically. "So, let me guess, you're a fan of the classics?" I asked, my tone a little harsher than it needed to be. "Are ye about to take me out on the town in a buggy?"

Alucard snorted and pointed with the tip of his umbrella—an uncommonly sharp tip. I turned to look and stared, open-mouthed, at the vehicle he'd directed my attention to. "You should apologize to the lady," Alucard said, stepping past me to run his hand along the surface of his car—a sleek, sporty number that could have doubled as a spaceship in any movie set before the year 2000.

"What the hell is it?" I asked, studying the dark chrome exterior. The car's curves had curves. Hell, the thing looked like it could take off vertically and take us back to meet Jesus.

"It's a custom vehicle. Something German that Othello shipped over with Grimm Tech goods. I stole it from Nate. Gunnar and I have a bet to see how long it takes before he notices it's gone," Alucard said, eyes lighting up like a boy with his first really cool toy. Gunnar and Alucard, from what I'd gathered during our assault on Magnus' mansion, were friends with Nate... apparently the sort of friends who stole each other's shit when the mood arose.

Not that I was throwing stones.

"Ye know, if ye stole somethin' like this from me, I'd kill ye," I said, just to clarify where we stood.

Alucard rolled his eyes. "If I stole *anything* from you, *cher*, I imagine I wouldn't be long for this world."

I considered that for a moment, then nodded.

"So, does that mean you don't want to take it for a spin?" he asked, smirking, dangling the key out in front of me like a prize. Even the key looked like it belonged on the SyFy channel.

I snatched it from him.

"Let's go," I said, grinning like a madwoman.

*T*he gas pedal thrummed under my foot.

"So, you gonna fill me in on what you've got going on, or what?" Alucard asked, studying his nails as I whipped us through a sharp turn, completely unconcerned by the fact that we were tearing through the streets of Boston at breakneck speeds during a thunderstorm. The perks of being immortal, I guess.

Of course, I didn't have that excuse.

Not that I was looking for one.

"How much did Othello tell ye?" I asked, keeping my hands off the steering wheel as we hydroplaned, waiting for the tires to catch before I reasserted control. God, I lived for this shit; back when I was a teenager, I'd saved up and bought a piece-of-junk van so I could cart my friends to concerts across state lines, and I could still remember the feeling of flooring it around the edges of a cul-de-sac after a winter storm, the thrill of trying to get a handle on it before we spiraled out of control and spilled over into a neighbor's driveway.

The van had lasted about six months.

"She filled me in on the relevant parts," Alucard replied. "You have a way into Fae and need someone who knows the lay of the land. Something about a boat." He reached into his pocket and pulled out a tiny metal ball—one of the portable Gateways designed by Grimm Tech. "Said this'll get us where we need to go. That we could negotiate our destination from there."

"Why didn't ye tell me you'd been to Fae before?" I asked, sneaking a glance at him. Alucard peered out the window, staring at nothing, half his face obscured in shadow. He was inhumanly still, like a statue, only the slight ruffle of his shoulder-length hair from the car's air conditioning offered the illusion of his being alive.

"It's not something I typically talk about," Alucard said, finally. "Besides, it didn't come up, as I recall. If it had, I'd have filled you in."

I paused, realizing he was right. Between saving the girls from Magnus, participating in Dorian Gray's Fight Night, and rescuing Othello, there hadn't been a whole lot of time to get to know each other or exchange personal anecdotes. "Fair enough. But now's as good a time as any, so spill."

"I tagged along with Nate on one of his trips, that's all," Alucard said, shrugging. I could tell from the way he held himself that there was more to the story. Probably a lot more. I briefly considered calling him out on it, but decided it wasn't worth the hassle; if the vampire wanted to keep a few secrets, he was entitled.

I had plenty of my own, after all.

"So, is there anythin' I should know goin' in? How's the gravity in Fae? Sneakers or boots? Do I need to pack an umbrella?"

Alucard snorted and folded his arms over his chest. "Actually, none of that really matters once you're there. I mean, you sort of make do with what you have. It's an odd place. Easy to lose track of yourself and your surroundings. Hard to recall once you've left. It's like being in a dream—one of the lucid kind. Especially once your other side takes over."

"Your other side?"

"Yeah. Course that bit is even harder to explain. All I can say is that once you find your wild side, it's like feeling whole for the first time. Like your entire life you've been half-deaf, and then suddenly you can hear perfectly fine. You ever been to the ocean?"

"Aye," I replied, cocking an eyebrow.

"Remember coming up from beneath a wave? It's like that. It's like being born all over again."

Alucard Morningstar, the vampire poet. Who knew? I shook my head. "Does it change who ye are?"

The Daywalker shrugged. "Maybe. Can't say I recall being anything other than what I am, now. But it comes with other changes. Physical ones. You've seen it. My wild side." Alucard glanced over at me, flames dancing behind his eyes, light flickering beneath his skin.

"Will that happen to me?" I asked, a little alarmed.

"No idea. But probably."

I felt my grip tighten on the steering wheel. I wasn't sure how I felt about that. No matter how poetically Alucard described the experience, it sounded an awful lot like an acid trip to me—side effects included. I wasn't sure if I was ready to transform into something inhuman, something other than who I already was; I liked me—attitude, scars, and all. Besides, what if I ended up morphing into something incredibly lame, like a mermaid or a Power Ranger?

"So, you gonna tell me exactly where we're headed?" Alucard asked, to fill the silence.

"Aye, but first I need to pack," I replied. I hadn't expected Othello to offer up a Gateway as part of the deal, but it made sense, especially if she wanted me to apologize to Nate sooner rather than later. But that was fine by me; I had places to be and Faelings to interrogate.

Alucard shook his head. "I really don't think you'll need much. Focus on what you can carry, and the rest will sort itself out, depending on what you're looking for..." he drifted off, eyeing me.

"Answers," I replied, after a moment's consideration. "I'm lookin' for answers."

"Is that right?" Alucard murmured.

I nodded. "Of course, the good news is I can pack light, in that case. I'll really only be needin' a few t'ings."

"Oh, yeah? Like what?"

"Guns, mostly," I replied, grinning. "Lots of guns."

CHAPTER 6

$\mathcal{A}$lucard waited while I unlocked my door, humming a little to himself, one arm folded behind his back like a southern gentleman. I pushed the door open and stepped inside, prepared to make quick work of getting my shit together; I had a bug-out bag prepped and ready in case Othello or Jeffries sent word of Christoff's whereabouts, so there wasn't much else to throw together.

I stopped and frowned, realizing for the first time that my little Faecation might take longer than I'd planned. I knew time moved differently in Fae, but that was no guarantee I'd be able to make it in and out in time to rescue Christoff...if there was anything left of him to rescue.

Shit. What was I going to do?

"You gonna invite me in, *cher?*" Alucard asked, interrupting my thoughts, one arm propped casually against my doorway, his shirt hiked up just enough to reveal a small sliver of flesh along his waistline.

Oh, right. I'd forgotten that, without my express permission, Alucard wouldn't be able to cross the threshold into my apartment—one of the many unfortunate side effects of being a bloodsucker they don't hit you with in the brochure, along with never being able to use a mirror, a severe allergy to all things Christian, and a serious Vitamin D deficiency.

Gotta read the fine print, people.

Especially if the contract is written in blood.

I stood in the hallway, debating. Did I want him to come in? I hated to admit it, but part of me did. The same part of me that couldn't help but notice how firm and narrow his hips were now that they were on display. But the rest of me, the rational bits, knew better; no matter how attractive he was, Alucard was still a vampire. "No," I replied, finally, before turning away.

Suddenly, my lights flickered.

"Son of a bitch!" Alucard cursed.

I spun around and saw the Daywalker lying flat on his back, rubbing at his face like it had caught fire. I thrust my head out, glancing down the hall, but no one had come out to check on us—thank God. "I said no, ye idgit!" I hissed. "What part of no didn't ye understand?"

"I was only trying to get out of the hallway," he said, shaking his head as if dazed. "Besides, the whole invitation thing doesn't really apply to me, these days."

"Then how..." I drifted off. I reached out for my doorway and ran my fingers down the white trim. I started laughing; I couldn't help it. "The wards," I said, doubling over. "Ye got taken out by me wards."

"Seriously?" Alucard asked, cocking one eyebrow.

"Blame your friend Nate," I said. "Besides, that's what ye get for tryin' to come inside without me permission, ye bastard," I admonished. "Now sit right there and be a good vampire until I get back." I left him in the hallway, glaring at me, the tip of his nose bright red from where it had brushed up against my newest line of defense—I still wasn't sure what to call it.

The WizardProof 9000, maybe.

Or my FaerieSafe Home Security System.

Either way, the wards were my newest precaution; I'd grown sick and tired of Freaks and Fae popping in unannounced whenever they felt like it. I'd had to call in more than a few favors to have them installed, but at least I knew they were up and running now—and apparently strong enough to send a Master vampire flying back flat on his ass.

The FreakOut...

Nah.

I returned a few minutes later and tossed Alucard my duffel bag full of guns while I slid a backpack of essentials over one shoulder. He grunted, hefting the remarkably heavy bag as though it weighed nothing. To be fair, it was lighter than usual; I'd opted to leave my shotguns behind. If I ended up needing more firepower than the assorted weaponry tucked away in that bag, I was probably fucked, anyway. I held my hand out for the duffel bag's strap, but Alucard had already thrown it over one shoulder, opting to carry it for me.

I glared at him.

"What?" he asked. "You have a problem with me carrying your bags?"

"You keep actin' like you're a Goddamned gentleman," I said, "and I'll use one of me guns to blow ye to pieces. We both know ye aren't one, or you'd look a hell of a lot less like Rudolph the Red-Nosed Reindeer."

Alucard grimaced and pawed idly at his nose, which must have still stung. "You wouldn't blame a man for trying to get in your good graces, would you, *cher*?"

"A man, no," I said, slamming the door shut behind me. "But then ye aren't a man at all, are ye?"

Alucard stiffened at that. He sniffed and adjusted the weight of the duffel bag, his face an expressionless mask. "You ready?"

"Aye."

*W*e found a deserted alley not far from my building, the buildings on either side so close together Alucard's umbrella brushed stone as we walked. He pinched the tiny ball between two fingers and chucked it at the ground. It shattered instantly, and a vortex of air spun out, pushing us away at first, then drawing us in. A Gateway appeared—a tear in the fabric of reality. I tried to peer through to the other side, but all I saw was darkness. The rain began blowing from all directions, hitting us despite the umbrella, first in the backs, then in the face.

"Ladies first," Alucard drawled, casually flicking water off his brow.

I shot him a glare, which he ignored, then ducked under his arm and stepped through the Gateway. Alucard followed a moment later, and the Gateway snapped shut with an audible pop. The darkness, mitigated by the streetlights on our side of the Gateway, became absolute.

I realized it was eerily quiet without the sound of pounding rain; I'd been listening to rain for so long now that I'd almost forgotten what total silence sounded like. But then I noticed another sound had taken its place, equally rhythmic, though significantly less noticeable. Waves, I realized.

Waves lapping against something. Suddenly, the floor shifted, and I lost my balance. I stumbled sideways, then felt an arm draw tight around my waist, catching me as securely as a safety net.

"Careful, *cher.*"

"What the hell was that?" I asked, shrugging myself free.

"My guess? We're on a boat. A big one, or else we'd be wobbling all over the place. Or, well, you would be. We *vampires* have better balance than that," he said, clearly still stewing over my earlier comment.

"Whatever," I said. "Where are we?"

"Below decks, probably. Somewhere out of the way. Looks like a closet from what I can make out. Lots of clothes..." he drifted off, as if noticing something odd. I cursed inwardly; I'd momentarily forgotten that vampires had exceptional night vision—like any other predator who hunted at night.

"What is it?" I asked, suddenly aware of how precarious a situation I'd put myself in by hopping through a portal with a strange vampire I hardly knew. If I was being honest with myself, however, it wasn't so much that I didn't trust Alucard as it was that I didn't trust *anyone.* That...and playing Seven Minutes in Heaven with a bloodsucker sounded a whole lot like Hell to me.

"Nothing," Alucard said a moment later. "Just that some of these outfits, well...suffice it to say you wouldn't want to be buried in them."

I frowned, a little alarmed by the analogy. "Is there a door? A way out?"

"Hold on...yeah." The vampire slid around me, moving so furtively it made the hairs on the back of my neck stand up. "Here it is." He turned a knob and pushed open the door. More darkness loomed beyond.

Together, we crept out of the closet, Alucard in the lead. I followed, one hand pressed up against the muscles of his back, straining my ears. "Where are we now?" I whispered.

"You know, you could just get out your phone and look," Alucard said. Well, shit.

"Ye tell anyone about this," I warned, "and I'll—"

"As much as I appreciate your colorful threats, *cher*, I think it would save us both some time if you got on with it," Alucard said, placatingly.

I muttered vague threats under my breath, reached into the back pocket of my jeans, and pulled out the phone Othello had given me—an untraceable gadget with more bells and whistles than I knew what to do with. I fussed with it for a minute until I found the flashlight setting, then held it up to survey the immediate area. What I saw literally made me speechless.

We were in a bedroom.

Othello had given me and the charming vampire a Gateway that led to a fucking bedroom.

Oh, I was *so* going to kill her.

The room itself was surprisingly small, with very little furniture to speak of; most of the square-footage was occupied by a gargantuan mattress —an emperor-sized bed with enough pillows to smother a small nursing home's worth of patients. Hell, the thing was so big it would probably take me a solid minute to climb out of bed every morning. What kind of acrobatic sex did you need to have to warrant a bed that size? Or, for that matter, how many partners did you need to make it a tight fit?

I decided I didn't want to know.

"We need to get out of here," I mumbled.

"Whatever you say, *cher*. Lead the way," Alucard said. I got a feeling he was enjoying himself a little too much.

"D'ye know this was where Othello planned to send us?" I asked.

"No clue," the Daywalker said, though he didn't sound the least bit concerned by our destination.

I elbowed him in the back. "Knock it off."

Alucard shrugged. "As you wish."

I groaned, rubbing the bridge of my nose. "How many of those movies d'ye end up watchin'?" I asked.

"All of them, but I'll let you in on a secret..." Alucard turned and stared at me, his cheekbones sharp and defined beneath the glow of my impromptu flashlight. "*The Princess Bride* was my favorite."

Of-fucking-course it was.

I sighed, inwardly. Way to go Quinn, you inadvertently turned Alucard into the sexiest fanger alive...

A Goddamned Nosfer-hotu.

"Well, come on then, Princess Buttercup," I said, edging past the vampire. But, before I could so much as take another step, the door opened, and a slender hand flicked on the lights. I cringed, blinking rapidly to cope with the abrupt shift between semi-darkness and light. A man with dark hair poked his head in.

"Oh good! You're finally here," he said. "I swore I heard a couple in here, but thought I'd give you two a few minutes alone to work out your differences." His eyes flicked to the bed expectantly, saw it still neatly made, and shot a withering look at Alucard. "You, of all people, Alucard, should know that these beds *aren't* made for talking..." he grinned playfully.

I blinked a few more times, desperately trying to get a good look at the man's face, although it hardly mattered; I knew that voice. I remembered it as clearly as the day I first heard it blaring out from the loudspeakers in Magnus' garden while I squared off against a monster made of stone and glass. I doubted I would ever forget it; the voice haunted my dreams. I didn't have to see his face to know he'd be beautiful—his features so symmetrical, so flawless in their proportions, that it felt like God had been drunk when He designed everyone else.

Hell, maybe He had been. Drunk off achieving perfection.

Because He'd broken the mold with Dorian Gray.

CHAPTER 7

I snarled and lunged forward...or tried to anyway; the bed was so close to the wall that the best I could do was shuffle towards him, hands outstretched as if I might strangle him from a distance.

"Hello again," Dorian said, smiling. His smile began to falter as I got closer, gauging my lethal intent. "Whoa! Hey! Calm down," Dorian stammered, backing away from the doorway and out of reach.

I sped up, shuffling my feet faster, banging my poor knees against the bedframe. I cursed. He was going to pay for that, too, the bastard. The instant I cleared the bed, I bolted, tearing down the hallway towards the smug prick. I tossed my backpack towards Alucard, who was hot on my heels.

"We can't let him get away!" I insisted. Before Alucard could reply, I charged forward, putting on an extra burst of speed to make up the difference. "I'm goin' to roast ye alive, ye miserable fucker!" I called. "You're goin' to wish ye could die like the rest of us when I'm through with ye!"

Dorian barked a laugh as he turned the corner, moving surprisingly well for a man who should have died centuries ago. "You know, I told her this was a bad idea!" he yelled, clearly amused.

I didn't bother responding. I was too pissed off. No one got away with pitting me against the monsters for their own entertainment. No one. Besides, Dorian had sided with the Marquis—one of the Fallen who'd possessed a detective and used his authority to abduct girls in New York City under the noses of the police—which meant Dorian was definitely a bad guy. And nobody misses, or even sheds a tear for, the bad guys.

Not for long, anyway.

By the time I turned the corner, Dorian had already made it to the end of a long hallway and was hurriedly fumbling with the door, jamming his keycard in and out of the slot, but too rapidly for it to release the magnetic lock. He groaned, but finally managed to slow down long enough to make it work.

By then it was too late.

We went down together, crashing through the door to collapse onto the deck of a ship. I pinned him savagely to the ground, straddling his chest so he couldn't buck me off, and raised a fist to start pummeling him. It was a shame Dorian and I weren't on better terms, because I felt like he—the host of many a Fight Club event—might appreciate the irony.

See, I felt like destroying something beautiful.

Except Alucard stopped me. He latched one hand around my wrist, his grip like iron, and coughed. "Hey Quinn, we, uh, have company…"

I yanked my wrist free, but stopped long enough to see what it was the Daywalker was talking about. Turned out he was right; we had company. A lot of it. A lot of half-naked, male company. And it was sunny—like middle-of-the-day sunny, so bright I had to squint to see. I glanced down at Dorian and realized he was wearing nothing but a t-shirt and a pair of pink shorts that rode comically high up on his legs. The t-shirt read: *Symposium of the Seas*.

"Where the hell are we?" I snarled, balling my hands in Dorian's shirt and jerked, forcing him to raise his head up and look me in the eye.

"Well, honey," a man said from a lounge chair only a few feet away, "I'd say you're on the wrong boat. The All-Women's Cruise is next week." The man who'd spoken lowered his sunglasses, staring at us with steely grey pupils so pale they were only a shade darker than the whites of his eyes. He had a dark, deep tan and copper-gold hair. Taken in all at once he looked classically Greek, with large eyes, a perfectly straight nose, wide lips, and thick eyelashes.

"They're with me, Narcissus," Dorian ground out, finding it difficult to breathe with me sitting across his chest.

"I've told you before, Dorian," Narcissus replied, "it's never a good idea to mix business with pleasure." He eyed me briefly, then did a much more thorough head-to-toe study of Alucard, inadvertently licking his lips in the process. "But I guess you could do worse."

I glared down at the man beneath me. "Explain."

"Fine, but let me up...this floor is filthy," Dorian replied.

"It really is," Narcissus chimed in, smirking.

$\mathcal{T}$he four of us retired to a set of lounge chairs near the front of the boat so as not to upset the other patrons; the sight of a woman on board had threatened to traumatize the men in attendance, so Narcissus had suggested we move out of sight. I'd opted to store my weapons and bug-out bag in a storage closet; if the stories could be believed, no matter how many bullets I put in him, Dorian Gray wasn't likely to become any less obnoxious.

Though, if push came to shove, I was more than prepared to put that to the test; it's not often target practice comes with a live, undying victim, after all.

Once we'd settled down a little, Dorian—hands smothered in suntan lotion—began liberally applying the chalky mess to Narcissus' naked back, drawing sensual furrows down the man's spine, seemingly in no hurry to offer an explanation.

Narcissus, meanwhile, seemed more than content to lie there in silence, peering longingly at his sunglasses—at least until Dorian swatted them out of his hand. "Narcissus, no mirrors. Come on now, you know better," Dorian chastised.

I frowned, recalling the myth of Narcissus—a Greek who thought himself so beautiful he'd spurned love to stare at his reflection in a pool until he eventually wasted away and died...or became a flower. Or something.

Greek myths were always a little too allegorical for my taste.

Narcissus sighed. "You're right, Dorian. It's just so distracting."

"I know, Petal, it's a very nice face," Dorian said, returning his attention to the task at hand—lathering up the vainest man alive. I couldn't be sure, what with the sound of the waves lapping against the hull, but it sounded eerily like the Greek was purring.

"Listen," Dorian said, flicking his eyes up at me a moment later, "I only agreed to help you out as a favor to Callie. I owed her, and now we're even."

I fought the urge to deck the fucker. "And what, ye t'ink we're even, then?" I hunched forward and snapped my fingers in front of Dorian's eyes, drawing them away from the half-naked Greek. "Ye almost got me and mine killed with that little Fight Night stunt of yours, ye self-righteous son of a bitch," I growled.

"I didn't force you to fight," Dorian said, looking bored. "Although I must admit, you put on quite the show. You all did." Dorian's gaze swung around to Alucard, who lounged back in his chair, sunbathing like a cat in a windowsill, eyes half-lidded. His skin glowed, faintly, lighting him up from the inside like a lantern. "That was quite the trick you pulled on Magnus. You know...I have plenty of other contenders who wouldn't mind taking on a Daywalker. You and I could work something out..."

"Dorian," Narcissus snapped. "Remember the rules."

Dorian sighed. "No talking business on the boat, Petal, yes. I remember."

I frowned, studying the two men. The legendary hedonist, Dorian Gray, and Narcissus, the man who loved his own reflection so much he'd wasted away staring at it...a couple? I shook my head, wondering how their egos could fit on the same continent, let alone the same boat. I stared out at the water and took a deep, calming breath. My first instinct had been to toss Dorian Gray overboard and see how long his immortal body could hold up against the oceanic wildlife...but he had a point; we'd opted to take center stage during the fight, even if it was only for the sake of saving Othello and the girls. And it had all turned out well in the end—in the sense that everyone I wanted dead ended up dead.

At his core, Dorian Gray was an entertainer. A showman. A sleazy bastard, sure, but I'd done business with worse men. Still, it was probably best to act like I carried a grudge for the time being; men are much easier to manipulate when they think they owe you an apology for something.

"Ye said Callie arranged this?" I said, waving idly at the ocean.

"She did."

I scowled, already plotting my revenge. If Callie thought she could get away with pranking me like this, she had another thing coming. I glanced over at Alucard, whose eyes had cracked open just a bit. "How d'ye figure Callie even got involved?" I asked.

The Daywalker shrugged. "Othello makes friends easily, unlike some people. My guess," he said, before I could give him a tongue-lashing, "is she found out about this cruise liner from one of the Greeks in St. Louis and pulled a few strings to get us on it."

Narcissus made a face. "St. Louis. You couldn't pay me to go back."

Dorian leaned in, resting his chin on the other man's shoulder, and whispered, "You only say that because Echo is there."

"Echo?" I...echoed.

Alucard crossed one ankle over the other and responded before Dorian could. "She was a nymph Narcissus spurned, at least according to Ovid. Went something like 'when she saw Narcissus wandering through the remote fields, she was inflamed'," Alucard intoned, clearly quoting from a book.

All three of us stared at the vampire.

"I ran a bookstore for a while," he drawled.

Narcissus tensed and turned away, the muscles in his back bunched together as if he might spring away at any moment. Dorian began massaging the Greek's neck and glanced back at us. "He feels guilty, poor thing. As if that girl were his fault." Dorian kissed the back of Narcissus' head, like a doting parent. "But that's alright, we'll get him out to Kansas City one of these days. Midas has begun purchasing some real estate in town, you know," Dorian purred. "I'm thinking of throwing a little party. Nobody does decadence like the Greeks."

"That's true..." Narcissus replied, sounding mollified.

Dorian winked at us behind his companion's back. "Anyway, Callie was a bit cagey with the details. How can we get you lovely people out of our hair? Unless you'd rather stay..." Dorian eyed us both as if our measurements weren't the slightest mystery.

"We need to go to the Bermuda Triangle," I said, glaring at the immortal.

Narcissus propped himself up on his elbows and glanced back at me, his wavy hair cascading down one side of his face. "Honey, this is a cruise liner, not a charter ship. I can't exactly change course because you have somewhere you need to be."

Alucard spoke up, causing Narcissus to swivel his head around, flipping his hair back dramatically. "Well, where are we now?"

"We're really not that far away," Dorian said, tracing squiggles down Narcissus' spine. "You could always say we had to reroute to avoid that storm. Besides, I wouldn't mind docking in Puerto Rico. It's always so festive there."

Narcissus glanced sidelong at his companion. "You make it sound like you planned this, Dorian…"

"Nonsense. Merely taking advantage of the situation. I like to be…" he reached out and tugged a little on Narcissus' hair, "adaptable."

Alucard coughed into his hand. "I'm sorry, did you say something about a storm?"

Dorian shrugged. "Yes. Hurricane-something-or-other. I can never keep up with the names."

"I'll have to clear it with the crew and passengers," Narcissus warned.

"You handle the crew. I'll handle the passengers," Dorian replied.

"Are you sure we're going to be alright?" Alucard interrupted. "That we won't get caught up in this storm, I mean."

I glanced over at the vampire, noticing he looked a little paler than usual, as silly as that sounded. The flickering glow beneath his skin had faded, and there was a tightness around his eyes, too, that hadn't been there before. "Not a fan of storms, then, I take it?" I asked.

Alucard shook his head, his eyes flashing red. "Not hurricanes, no."

Oh, right.

Shit.

"Sorry," I said, "I didn't mean to bring up bad memories."

Dorian flicked his eyes back and forth between us. "Something I should know?"

"He's from New Orleans," I explained.

Dorian arched an eyebrow. "Well yes, dear, I caught that. The accent pretty much gave the game away. What about it?"

"You know, Dorian, you can be a bit insensitive at times," Narcissus quipped. "Has anyone ever told you that?"

Dorian chuckled. "Everyone tells me that eventually, Petal. Why, what'd I do this time?"

Alucard swung his legs around and rose. "I'm going for a walk. Let me know what you fancy boys decide."

"Fancy boys…" Dorian sniggered as Alucard walked off. "Just how old is he, anyway?"

I frowned at the departing immortal, ignoring Dorian's question. One, he didn't deserve to know. Two, I had no idea. "Can ye get us there, then?"

Dorian studied his impeccably manicured nails. "Perhaps. You'd have to owe me a favor, though…"

"Dorian," Narcissus growled. "No business on my ship."

Dorian sighed, exasperated. "Fine. Yes, we'll get you there. But be sure to pass along how helpful I was to Miss Penrose. That's one woman whose good side I hope to stay on."

I snorted. "That's probably the most sensible t'ing you've said all day."

"He does have his moments," Narcissus mumbled, settling his head back down on the lounge chair. "Bermuda, Bahama, come on pretty mama…" Narcissus began humming under his breath.

Dorian scowled at us both.

It almost made him look ugly.

Almost.

I met Alucard on the ship's starboard side…or was it port? Whichever. The vampire was sitting on the railing, legs dangling out over the water, clutching the metal bar on either side to maintain his balance. Or at least that's how it looked; I was fairly sure he could simply levitate in place if he felt so inclined. The sun was beginning to set, and the two immortals had long since gone their separate ways to inform the crew and passengers of our change in destination. The sky was awash in color, pinks and blues and oranges, hues you never saw swimming above the city skyline.

Then again, we were on a gay cruise ship owned by the *original* narcissist, so it was rather tame in comparison. Like the approaching sunset was trying to out-gay the cruise ship.

"I never did care for the water," Alucard said, turning a bit to look me in the eye. "Even when I was a boy. My sister loved it. She loved everything about the bayou, but especially loved the gulf."

"I didn't know ye had a sister," I said, stepping out onto the deck beside him.

"This was before, back when we were mortal. A long time ago," he trailed off, stiffly.

"Ah," I said, shaking my head. "I never had any siblin's, just me aunt. I t'ink I'd have liked to have a sister, maybe. Someone to share secrets with. Someone to have me back in a tussle."

"She wasn't that kind of sister," Alucard said, his voice tinged with bitterness.

"Right," I said, deciding to change the subject. "I'm sorry for what Dorian said, before. Although it's your fault for stoppin' me from bashin' the fucker's brains in."

Alucard barked a laugh. "I think they'd have buried you at sea, if you had. He's a popular guy."

I rolled my eyes. "Aye, for the same reason a drug dealer's popular. He's everyone's friend because he can get them what they want...until he can't. One day he'll end up in a deep, dark hole, and no one will bother lettin' him out."

Alucard grinned. "You're a bit morbid, *cher*. Anyone ever tell you that?"

"Says the vampire pinin' over the city he left behind," I shot back, then grimaced and hung my head.

Shit.

So much for trying to make the fanger feel better.

Alucard nudged me with his shoulder. "No harm in telling things as they are. You're right about me, though not for the reason you think. I do regret leaving my city behind...but then it really wasn't my city, anymore. My city, the New Orleans I grew up in, the New Orleans I *ran*...well, as they say, time and tide wait for no man. Or vampire, since that's what you prefer."

I sighed. Guess we were doing this—the sharing thing. *God*, I fucking *hated* the sharing thing.

"Ye know, I dated your kind once," I said, gazing out at the water to avoid Alucard's wide-eyed stare. "He got me into the business I'm in now. Showed me the ropes. How to shoot a gun. How to take a punch. He liked bein' around me, ye see. I made him feel human. Besides, I didn't break as easily as the others."

I heard my voice lose its inflection as I continued, "In the end, when they came for him, I ran. I left him trapped, burnin'. He tried to keep me there as our little shop went up. Probably thought it was a poetic way to go...he always was into that Romeo and Juliet garbage. I ended up havin' to break his arm to get free. Shattered me knee that night, runnin' from the bastards who came for us. Afterwards, I swore I'd never let another bloodsucker near me." I leveled my gaze at

Alucard, and whatever he saw there made him flinch. "All I'm sayin' is, don't take it personal, alright?"

Alucard cleared his throat, but said nothing, content to watch the sun drop below the horizon.

Guess we were done sharing.

"So what happened to your sister, then?" I asked several minutes later, hoping to change the subject to something lighter.

Alucard grunted. "I visited her with Nate a while back. She was running Kansas City."

I waited for more. Maybe they had argued and he was still raw over it. "Oh? Not the family reunion ye wanted?" I pressed.

He smirked absently. "She lost her head. Literally."

I blinked, shoulders tensing. When nothing else happened, I finally reached out and patted the Daywalker's shoulder. "We're done tellin' each other stories from now on, aren't we?"

Alucard nodded, chuckling darkly. "Oh yeah."

Good to know.

CHAPTER 8

*D*orian was kind enough to offer us the room we'd stumbled into
that afternoon, free of charge.

"We've already changed course," the immortal said as we toured the
lower decks. I ignored the off-putting noises coming from several of the
cabins we passed—mainly consisting of techno and grown men giggling—
but Dorian's smirk grew more pronounced, in direct proportion to how
wild the sounds were. I could almost imagine him holding up score cards
like a judge at the Olympics. "We should have you where you want to be by
morning," he continued. "Ordinarily, the trip would take weeks, but considering the upcoming storm, Narcissus thought it best to speed things along.
Fortunately, Zephyrus is a shareholder."

"Zephyrus?" Alucard asked, sounding impressed.

Dorian nodded absently, waving a hand.

Alucard noticed my confusion, so leaned close enough that I could feel
the line of his body against mine, his scent—still citrusy—tickling my nose.
"Greek God of the West Wind," he murmured.

"Indeed, it just goes to show it helps to have friends in high places,
willing to lend a hand from time to time," Dorian interjected. "Speaking of
which, it might be best if you told us what your intentions were. You never
did mention why you wanted to go to the Bermuda Triangle in the first
place."

"You're right," Alucard said, thumbs hooked casually in the loops of his jeans. "We didn't."

Dorian pursed his lips at the vampire. "Fine, have it your way." He slid a keycard in the door and held it open. "Your accommodations await. Let me know if you need anything. And I do mean *anything*," he said, licking his lips like he was applying lipstick with his tongue.

"Ye sure ye don't have a free room? Or one with a couch?" I asked, peering past Dorian to take in the room with the obscenely large bed.

"I'm afraid not. In fact, this is technically my room, but I haven't had an excuse to use it up until now. I have a horrible habit of sleepwalking, I always wake up in the craziest situations..." he trailed off, not a smidge of innocence on his face. "I'm sure you understand." He winked. "But don't worry, I'm sure I can find someone who will let me snuggle up."

"We weren't worried," Alucard muttered.

"There *is* a room with a table," Dorian added, ignoring the vampire, "if you're looking for something sturdier than a bed..."

I felt my cheeks redden.

Alucard sighed. "I don't believe that's what the lady meant."

Dorian glanced back and forth between the two of us, eyes slowly widening. "Oh, my! I'd simply assumed. Well, as I always say..." The hedonist waved us through. "Adversity makes strange bedfellows."

"Pretty sure that was Shakespeare," Alucard drawled as he slid past the immortal, dumping my duffel and bug-out bag on the bed.

Dorian sniffed. "Well, anyway. I'll stop by first thing in the morning. Try not to be too exhausted, I'd *hate* to have to come in and find a way to wake you both up."

I exchanged looks with Alucard. "Ye sure we can't throw him overboard?"

Dorian rolled his eyes, passed me the magnetic key card, and stepped away from the door, letting me catch it. "Play nice, you two," he called out over his shoulder as he strutted down the hallway, the muscles in his bare-naked legs twitching with every step, like a jungle cat. I shivered.

"It's a big bed, *cher*. But I can curl up on the floor, if you'd like. I've slept on worse," Alucard offered, forced to half-sit, half-stand with the bed so close to the door.

"Oh, aye? Coffins not all they're cracked up to be, then?" I teased.

Alucard snorted. "I was never one for coffins. Nah, I meant when I used to sleep in my great-aunt's basement. Cold, cement floors. Leaky. Creepy. She was a voodoo priestess. Liked to keep things in jars." The vampire shuddered, then eyed the plush, if threadbare, carpet. "This is definitely a step up."

"Are all of your stories awful?" I asked, cocking an eyebrow.

Alucard chuckled. "Not lately." He flashed me a wry smile. "Just wait till I tell the folks back home about this little trip, and how you nearly knocked out Dorian Gray in front of all his fans, not to mention his boyfriend." He thought about that for a moment. "Well, one of his boyfriends, anyway."

I rolled my eyes, then sighed. "Alright, ye win. The bed will be fine for both of us. Just don't ye go gettin' any funny ideas about where your hands should be, or I swear I'll get a pair of handcuffs from Dorian and leave ye in the closet to rot."

Alucard raised an eyebrow, but wisely didn't say a word—not even to crack a joke about coming out of closets.

Which was almost disappointing, under the circumstances.

"So which side is yours?" Alucard asked a moment later, staring down at the bed like it had presented him with a math problem.

"I'm not picky," I lied. Honestly, I preferred the left side, but it felt weird having this conversation with a man—a vampire—I hardly knew. The bed was huge; there was no sense forcing Alucard to sleep on the floor. But that didn't mean I felt comfortable divulging my bedtime routines. As far as I was concerned, it was best to get the sleeping part over with and get on with things—we had shit to do tomorrow, after all. I snatched my bug-out bag off the bed without waiting for a response from Alucard, but then hesitated, looking around. "Wait, where's the bathroom?" I asked.

Alucard ran a hand through his hair. "Pretty sure it's a communal bathroom, *cher*. Seems like the kind of thing Dorian and his posse might prefer."

I cursed. Of course it was. I stood there for a minute, indecisively, then pointed at Alucard. "You're comin' with me," I said. I left the room, fully expecting the vampire to follow. It took me a few minutes and a couple wrong turns to find the nearest bathroom. It turned out Alucard was right; the showers were open concept, with a variety of brightly-colored Loofahs hanging from the wall. The bathroom stalls were mercifully private, however, and thankfully none were occupied at the moment. "Alright," I said, glancing back at the vampire. "Ye keep watch. On *this* side of the door, ye hear me?"

Alucard raised his hands in surrender, flashing fang, his eyes dancing with amusement and something else I didn't want to dwell on. "As you wish," he purred.

I huffed and turned, letting the door swing shut behind me.

Dear God, I needed a shower.

A cold one.

*J*took the left side of the bed, nearest the door. I'd packed light, especially in terms of pajamas, so I opted for a pair of black leggings and a t-shirt that read: Touch Me and Die. One of my favorites. My duffel bag lay on the floor next to the bed, a pistol lying on top in easy reach, just in case. I wasn't sure who I was preparing to shoot—a handsy Alucard, or anyone who came through that door unannounced—but either way it made me feel better to know the option was there.

The vampire in question lay on his back on top of the covers as far from me as he could get, arms folded over his chest, fully clothed—honoring my every request with only the faintest hint of amusement. Honestly, he'd proven surprisingly pliant; I hadn't had to threaten him with violence once. Of course, that might have to change if he didn't wipe that shit-eating grin off his face.

I knew it was there, even in the dark.

Still, I couldn't blame the bastard for finding the situation funny; he had to know that the reason I had so many restrictions in place wasn't only because I didn't trust him, but because I didn't entirely trust myself. Unfortunately, what I'd told Alucard about my former lover had been true; he'd been a real manipulative bloodsucking bastard. Cruel, even. Hell, all I had to do was look down at the scar tissue above my hip joint to remind myself what it had been like to be under his thumb…not to mention his teeth. Ever since then, I'd found vampires physically repulsive.

Until now.

The problem was that Alucard—with his base tan, Southern drawl, and impish good looks—wasn't like any vampire I'd met before or since. It wasn't simply his strange abilities that appealed to me—the fact that he could survive without draining people and bring me coffee in the morning without dodging windows—although that was part of it. It was the way he handled himself. The fuck-with-me-and-die attitude. I had to admit, if only to myself, that I liked it...that I liked him. A lot.

But that didn't change things. He was still an immortal. Still a killer who'd fed off people to survive, even if he didn't have to any longer. No matter how attracted we were to each other, there was no long-term trajectory for us; not unless I wanted to become a bloodsucker...which I so the fuck did not.

Some things, sadly, were just never meant to be.

I sighed and rolled over, giving him my back, trying to ignore the weight of him on the other side of the bed, pulling slightly at the covers. Sleep beckoned, offering me a temporary reprieve from Alucard and the problem he presented. And so I went to her, gladly.

CHAPTER 9

I dreamt.

An old, broken man lay on his side, only his back visible in the dim light that wafted in through a small, barred window. The cell was made of stone, and it was cold; the man shivered so violently it looked like he was having a seizure, his breath pluming. Scars in various stages of healing littered his back and shoulders. His head was shaved, messily, leaving patches here and there. He kept muttering something, over and over, his voice too soft to make out. A woman came into view, her long blonde hair matted with dried blood, hanging down to the small of her back, wearing a thick cotton shift, her once-muscular body now frightfully thin. She rested a hand on the man's head and whispered soothing words.

A raven cawed, poking its head through the bars, and the light in the window dimmed further. The woman glanced up and smiled, her eyes still fierce, still proud, despite her sallow cheeks and missing teeth. "They're coming for us, don't worry," she said, patting the man's shoulder. "They're coming."

I dreamt.

A woman stood in a hallway full of windows, her auburn

tresses tied back in a complex pattern that mimicked the swirl of the galaxy that lay beneath her feet, as if she stood on a glass floor, hovering high above the cosmos. Next to her, two others lingered—a blonde with hair so bright it seemed to emit its own light, and a woman with hair so dark it seemed to drink the light in. Seeing all three together felt like looking at a puzzle with all its pieces intact. The redheaded woman turned, her eyes on fire.

"She is not yours to use," she said.

"You've given us no choice," the dark-haired woman replied, tersely.

"We cannot stop him alone," the blonde pleaded.

"There will be others," the redhead said. "She will be needed elsewhere."

The dark-haired woman glared, spit, and turned away. The blonde, after a long, searching look, did the same. Finally, the redhead faced the window once more, speaking to the empty air. "You should not have come. Stop looking for me, or they will find you."

I dreamt.

The ocean frothed beneath a cloud-filled sky. Waves spun outward like the arms of a twirling child, each one seemingly large enough to topple a city. Figures, dark and spectral, rode them, the points of their weapons cresting each wave like the teeth of a leviathan rising up from the depths. The wind howled, carrying their thunderous voices, promising death and vengeance.

And beyond, at the very center of the massive storm, something glowed.

An eye, blue and pulsing.

And it saw me.

CHAPTER 10

I woke panting, my gun aimed at the door, skin so slick with sweat my t-shirt clung to my chest like a wet rag. I blinked the sleep and sweat out of my eyes, waiting for the door to open. Something was here. I knew it.

My arm trembled from the strain of holding the gun.

But there was nothing.

Alucard reached out, slowly, and rested his hand on the barrel of my pistol, lowering it. "Now, now, *cher*. Just a bad dream. Nothing to get yourself worked up over. I'm still on my side of the bed, and—"

A knock at the door sounded. I shrugged Alucard off and sighted down the line of my arm, prepared to fire. My heart hammered in my chest. I cursed, knowing my shot might go wild with me this worked up, but it didn't matter; there was something on the other side of that door I wanted dead. I just knew it.

"Rise and shine, love birds," Dorian called.

I took a deep breath. Well, I hadn't been wrong.

I slid my finger off the trigger.

No matter how much I wanted to pump Dorian full of silver, firing a loaded gun into the belly of a cruise ship was asking for collateral damage. Besides, I didn't want to deal with the other passengers freaking out; I had enough on my plate without apologizing to naughty pleasure cruisers. I lowered my gun, then flipped the safety on and tossed it back on top of my duffel. "We'll be out in a minute," I called. "Get lost."

"Well, *someone's* not a morning person," Dorian sniffed. I waited until I could no longer hear his footsteps before throwing off the covers. The recycled air felt good against my clammy skin, and the faint nausea I'd felt when I woke went away after a moment, despite the ship's occasional sway.

"You alright?" Alucard asked.

"Peachy," I replied, swinging my legs around.

"Must have been one hell of a nightmare to get you all riled up like that. You were whimpering in your sleep like a dog."

"Like a dog?" I asked, hackles rising.

"A very cute dog?" Alucard offered.

"That's not much better," I replied. "And does that mean ye were watchin' me sleep?"

I felt Alucard shrug. "Not exactly. It's hard for me to sleep at night, that's all. Old habits and what not."

"So what, ye figured you'd pull an Edward Cullen? Ye do know it's creepy, not sexy, to watch a girl sleep all night long?" I said, grouchily. I rose and slid along the wall, headed for the door. I desperately needed to take another shower. And coffee. Sweet baby Jesus I needed coffee.

"Yeah, well, I'm a vampire. Creepy is sort of our factory setting," Alucard said, sounding amused.

"Whatever. Come watch the door for me and keep out the *other* creepy fuckers on board."

"Since you asked so nicely," Alucard replied, "why not?" He scooted down towards the end of the bed, the sound of his jeans sliding along the sheets comically loud, and met me at the door. In fact, I nearly collided with him in the dark. I was suddenly aware of him—of his face hovering inches away from mine. I felt like I could reach out and touch it, like I should run my fingers down the curve of his jaw and the flesh of his throat, then down the line of his body. My hands actually twitched from the idea of what he'd feel like beneath my hands. My pulse sped up suddenly, and my mouth got very dry.

And my wrist hurt. A lot.

I took a hurried step back, pressing my spine against the wall, and took in a lungful of air. I couldn't see it in the dark, but I could feel it—the hot metal of the bracelet I'd gotten from the woman with my mother's face, a bracelet I never took off for fear I'd lose it. The heat dissipated suddenly, gone as quick as it had come.

What the hell was going on?

"*Cher*? What's wrong?" Alucard asked in a husky drawl.

"Ye go on ahead," I ground out through clenched teeth, digging my nails into the palms of my hands. "I'll be right behind ye. I remembered I need to make a call." I averted my eyes from the light of the open doorway and waited until Alucard left to collapse onto the bed. I concentrated on my breathing—anything to block out the intense physical sensations I was feeling. It was like my nerves were on fire, and every part of them wanted to reach out and touch someone…no, not someone.

Alucard.

What the actual fuck? I did a quick check of my mental state, checking off boxes. This wasn't cabin fever; I hadn't even been on the ship a full twenty-four hours. I felt sane, sane enough to know something was wrong with me, anyway. And it wasn't horniness, which would have been the most likely culprit. Horniness made me stupid, but I'd never gone into hysterics because I needed to get laid; this was the twenty-first century, for crying out loud—a girl had toys for that. No, this was something else. This *felt* like something else. More like a…craving. The sort of craving I'd had before, although that had been a milder, tamer yearning. Still, I remembered that raw, animal magnetism I'd felt in Johnny Appleseed's hotel room.

I also remembered how he and I had almost blacked out after shaking hands.

Talk about a brutal first impression.

But why now? Why hadn't Alucard triggered me before? What had changed?

I groaned and rolled over, fetching my phone from my bug-out bag. While I was here, I might as well do what I'd said I was going to. I hadn't been lying; I really did have a phone call to make. I'd almost forgotten, but I couldn't leave without at least checking in with Othello, especially if I was about to run off to Fae for an indefinite period of time. I found her contact number and hit the call button.

"Well, hello. How are you enjoying your cruise?" Othello answered, sounding a little sleepy, but definitely smug.

"I'm goin' to cut ye the next time I see ye, I hope ye know that," I replied, recalling my anger from the day before. "The Gateway led to a dark bedroom, ye harlot!"

Othello laughed so loud and hard I had to hold the phone away from my ear to prevent early-onset deafness. "That's what you get for stealing things that don't belong to you!" she crowed, still chortling.

"Aye, ye got me," I admitted. "Although I'm still not sure how ye got Callie in on it."

Othello made an indelicate sound. "It wasn't hard. I found out about Narcissus' cruise business from Midas, checked the manifest, and saw our friend Dorian would be onboard. Tracking her down proved easy enough. You'll be interested to know Callie was in on the joke—she bet me fifty American dollars that you would shoot Dorian."

"Not yet," I said, deciding not to mention how close I'd come to unloading a full clip in him this morning. "But then the day's still young," I added.

Othello chuckled. "So it is. But it's a win-win, from my perspective. Anyway," she said, "what can I help you with, now?"

"Nothin' major," I said. "I just wanted to check in to see if you've heard anythin' or found any new leads on Christoff since we last talked. I woke up with a bad feelin' in me stomach, and can't shake the sense that he needs me."

"You know I'd have called you if we found anything new," Othello said, her amusement completely gone. "Quinn...you have to start thinking about what it means—them not coming back."

I shook my head. "I'm not naïve. I know the odds. But I'm tellin' ye Christoff and Hilde are alive, and they're out there, somewhere. And every second we aren't out there tryin' to find 'em is a second longer Hilde's team and Christoff's kids go without." I finished the last with a snarl, a hot wave of anger surging up.

Othello was silent for a moment. "If I hear anything, and you aren't back yet, I'll go myself."

"Othello, that's not—" I began.

"It's not a favor," Othello said. "Not for you, anyway. I would prefer Christoff's children grow up with a father, and Jeffries is an old friend of Nate's. If the Russian government has them, as I suspect, then I'd be better off going it alone, anyway. That accent of yours could draw the wrong kind of attention in the Motherland."

I didn't know what to say. If I was being honest with myself, I'd only called because I felt horribly guilty about leaving, knowing Christoff and Hilde could be found at any moment. I hadn't actually expected to feel better by the time I got off the phone—it's just that sometimes it helps to talk it out. But knowing that Othello would make it her personal mission to rescue my friends...I had to admit that took a huge weight off my shoulders.

One I hadn't realized was there.

"T'anks, Othello," I said, finally.

"You are welcome. Anyway, how's Alucard? Has he been behaving himself? Have you shot *him* yet?"

I cringed. "Aye, he's been the perfect gentleman."

"I sense a 'but' coming..."

"It's not his *behavior* that's the problem," I admitted.

"What is it then?" she asked, sounding surprised.

"I'm honestly not sure. A minute ago he was standin' a couple feet away, and I had the strongest urge to touch him. So strong I had to basically sit on me hands. It wasn't," I added, interrupting Othello's giggling fit, "like that. Listen, I wanted to touch him like I wanted to touch *Appleseed*. The bad touch."

Othello's laughter died almost immediately. "The last time that happened, you nearly destroyed a cultural landmark, Quinn," Othello cautioned, referring to the brief power surge I'd given Appleseed during our tussle with the Grigori—angelic watchers—on the Brooklyn Bridge. He'd created an entire forest out of a handful of seeds to defend us, and grid-locked New York City's transit system for weeks in the process. "Not to mention the fact that you almost died," she added.

The police department and every state university were *still* trying to come up with a rational explanation for how a veritable forest suddenly sprouted over a stretch of the Brooklyn Bridge.

"I know," I said, groaning. I thrust my face down into the tangled sheets, pressing my forehead against the mattress so hard I saw spots, the sheets still damp from my sweat. "What am I goin' to do?"

"Well, were you planning on touching him?"

"No," I growled. And, too tired to bother lying to myself, I added, "But I would've liked the option."

Othello laughed louder than she had before, somehow. I checked to make sure I hadn't accidentally hit the speakerphone button—nope. "I'm gettin' off the phone now, Othello," I said, holding the phone out in front of me.

"Wait! No, Quinn, one more thing before you go. This is important."

"What?" I asked, drawing the phone to my ear once more.

"According to the website, the cruise is clothing optional...does every part of Alucard glow in the sunlight?"

I hung up, cutting off her cackling laughter.

Punk ass hacker.

I stepped up to the bathroom door right as Alucard stepped out. He had a towel slung over his shoulders, his chest bare. He wasn't as heavily muscled as I'd expected, but what muscle he had was dense and firm—he looked like those construction workers you see tearing houses apart with their naked, calloused hands. His hair was still wet and dripping; droplets of water fell onto his chest and ran down, snaking their way suggestively down his body.

"My eyes are up here, *cher*," Alucard said, grinning.

I blinked rapidly, trying to look away, but ended up having to pin a hand over my eyes. "I need ye to put on clothes," I said, my cheeks flushed.

"Am I that distracting?" he asked, the dulcet sound of his accent sending shivers up my spine. He also sounded as if he had stalked closer.

"Aye!" I yelled, stomping the ground with one foot. "No. Go away!" I peered through my fingers and saw the hurt on Alucard's face, only for an instant, before it disappeared.

"Alright. Need me to keep watch at the door?"

"No. If anyone comes in while I'm gettin' around, I'll tear off the only t'ing that makes 'em feel like a man!" I yelled, making sure the whole floor could hear me.

Alucard nodded curtly, and then stepped aside. I kept my eyes averted until I knew he was gone, then ducked into the bathroom and headed immediately for the showers, snatching the darkest Loofah I could find. I had the water running before I realized I was nearly hyperventilating. I ducked under the spray without even bothering to take my clothes off or waiting for it to get hot.

And I stood there until I no longer pictured Alucard's half-naked body. It was a long shower.

When I got back to the room, I was pleasantly surprised to find Alucard waiting for me, my duffel beside him on the bed. Honestly, if he'd have yelled at me like I had him, I'd have been long gone by now. Especially if I could go all Human Torch and fly away. I slung my bug-out bag over my shoulder and fidgeted with my t-shirt—a slightly baggy number I'd stolen from a bin upstairs with the *Symposium of the Seas* logo splashed across the chest. We'd only been gone a day, but I figured it wouldn't hurt to wear a shirt I couldn't give a shit about, in case our first foray into Fae got a little messy.

Always be prepared, right?

"I'm sorry," I said, before he could hop up off the bed.

"What?" Alucard asked, frozen halfway between sitting and standing in an awkward crouch.

"Sorry," I repeated. "It's a t'ing ye say when ye act like an idgit and want the other person to forgive ye. Or so I hear," I added.

"For yelling at me?" Alucard asked, cocking one eyebrow. "I've had a lot worse done and said to me than that, *cher*. Don't worry about it." He rose and moved to pass me, headed for the hallway, but I blocked him, my hands thrust firmly into the pockets of my jeans. I ground my teeth together, but managed not to reach out and touch him. Barely.

"There's a reason I yelled," I explained. "And I want ye to know it wasn't your fault. Listen…" I took a deep breath. "How much d'ye know about me power?"

Alucard cocked an eyebrow. "Only what you've told me. There's a field. It negates magic. Turns Freaks into Regulars, more or less. Slowed me down, I know that much."

I considered that, then nodded. That about summed it up, albeit in a very unsophisticated way. "Right. Now, I need ye to forget all that."

"And why's that, *cher*?"

"Because that's not me power, at all," I replied. Looked like I'd have to fill Alucard in sooner rather than later; I'd always planned to, but figured it could wait until we were in Fae...in case he wasn't fond of my plan. Easier to ask forgiveness than to ask permission, after all. "Listen," I began, "the whole reason I'm goin' to Fae is to figure this out for meself, which means I don't know nearly as much as I'd like to. But, basically, me field is really more like a cage. It's keepin' me real power—whatever it is—locked away. The Winter Queen wanted to help me set it free, but," I stared down at my wrist, where the silver charm with a single, solitary crow still hung, "what she wanted in return wasn't exactly ideal."

Alucard frowned. "Yeah. I met the frosty bitch with Nate, once, and I expect she wouldn't have given you the better end of whatever deal she offered." He watched me, sensing my barely restrained agitation. "Alright... so what precisely does your...cage have to do with you yelling at me, again? I didn't follow that bit."

"Me power wants ye," I confessed, glaring up at Alucard, able to meet his eyes for the first time since we'd woken up. "It wants ye somethin' fierce. Which is bad all on its own. But factor in the last time it wanted me to touch someone this badly—"

"The bridge," Alucard said, his voice soft and thoughtful, no longer amused. "I remember."

I nodded, having momentarily forgotten that he and Othello were the ones who'd been waiting for me to wake up at the hospital after I'd gone into a coma. "Right. So, basically, I need ye to stop bein' your charmin' self until I can get a handle on t'ings, alright? And I need ye to keep your distance, while you're at it."

Alucard nodded, weighing me with his eyes. He shoved his hands into the pockets of his jeans, matching me. "Alright, *cher*. But I have to confess something, while we're here..."

I frowned, studying the vampire's face. "What?"

"I hope we figure out your power soon, because I wouldn't mind you looking at me the way you did before, without the magic getting in the way," he said, not a hint of a grin on his face, staring directly into my eyes.

"See, now that," I said, jerking my chin at him. "No more of that."

He shrugged nonchalantly. "As you wish. For now, anyway..."

"That either," I growled, spinning on my heel and marching away, shoulders bowed.

"You do realize that now I'm particularly inclined to help you light a signal fire in Fae, right, *cher?*" he called out from behind me. Then he began whistling—a pleasant chiming sound. I gritted my teeth, refusing to look back at him.

Goddamned Southern bastard probably couldn't even help himself.

Which meant I was in for a long Faecation.

CHAPTER 11

*N*arcissus and Dorian were the only two men abovedeck, despite the morning sun poking out beyond the clouds, sending shimmers across the ocean in all directions. My guess was the other patrons were still in bed, sleeping it—whatever *it* was—off. Or busy trying to wash off all the glitter.

That, or my vagina magic was keeping them at bay, somehow. For some reason, the latter possibility made me giggle to myself.

"Nice to see you two could join us," Narcissus called, nursing a tiny cup of what looked like liquid tar. He tilted the cup and took a sip, licking his lips when he was finished, his tongue a murky shade of brown.

"What the hell is that?" I asked.

"Greek coffee," Dorian replied, pouring himself a cup. "Potent stuff. Did you know that the Greeks will sometimes read your fortune from the coffee grounds left over in your cup? It's called tasseography. Quite the party trick."

"It's not a party trick, Dorian," Narcissus admonished.

"Well, not when *you* do it, Petal," Dorian replied. He glanced over at the two of us. "Narcissus here learned how to read such things from The Oracle of Delphi herself. Got her drunk and had her explain the whole process, start to finish."

"Whatever," I said, far more concerned about the cup's practical applications. Namely, to perk me up. "Just pour me one. I'm dyin' a slow death over here."

"Safe word?" Dorian asked, pouring a third cup from a narrow pot.

"*Magic* word," Narcissus groaned. "He meant what's the magic word?"

Dorian glanced up at us, frowning, then shrugged. He pinched the dainty cup's tiny handle and held it out to me, meeting my eyes expectantly.

"Please," I muttered, snatching the cup from him.

He winked and withdrew to settle beside Narcissus on one of the chairs. The two men did a lot of sitting, I realized—far more than seemed possible, given their slim, toned physiques. Maybe it had something to do with being an immortal. Or having sex. Lots of sex. I tried to chase that thought away by taking a sip of the coffee, but then nearly spit it out. "Jesus Christ, what's in this?" I spluttered.

Narcissus chuckled. "The strongest coffee you'll ever drink. Courtesy of the Greeks."

Dorian, sitting slightly behind his companion, shook his head, mouthing the word 'Cuban', then winked—suggesting, perhaps, that the Greeks weren't quite the coffee aficionados Narcissus claimed. I took another sip. I didn't know about all that, but the stuff sure was potent. It tasted like a shot of espresso on steroids; fine coffee grounds clung to my tongue and teeth.

"So, care to tell us what your plan is, now that we're here?" Narcissus asked, holding his arms wide as if putting the sea on display. I frowned, staring out at the water. To be honest, it looked remarkably like wherever it was we'd been before, but I didn't argue; I knew exactly jack shit about sailing.

"I'm plannin' to cross over into Fae from here," I said.

Narcissus scoffed, slapping his oiled-up thigh with one hand. When no one joined in, he glanced up, searching my face. "Oh. You're serious."

"Can she do that?" Dorian asked, crossing one leg over the other, his interest clearly piqued.

"Theoretically. But not from my boat," Narcissus said, still focused on my face.

"And why not?" I asked, frowning.

"Well, for starters, because I would never endanger my passengers or myself so recklessly," Narcissus replied, pressing one hand against his chest. "And also because it's impossible."

"How so?" Alucard chimed in, tugging on a pair of Ray Ban sunglasses and staring out at the ocean.

"I'm Greek," Narcissus said with a shrug. "I couldn't cross over into Fae even if I wanted to. Such things are simply not done. The gates you're looking for will not open with me nearby, assuming you could even find them."

"You mean like that thing over there?" Alucard asked absently, pointing out towards the horizon.

We all turned to look.

"I don't see anything," Dorian said slowly, a moment later.

I squinted, but had to admit I didn't see anything either.

Narcissus turned to study Alucard, head cocked to one side. "You've been there before, haven't you?" His tone added the phrase *you sneaky fucker*.

Alucard nodded.

"Oh, what's it like?" Dorian asked, whirling back around to lean forward, his eyes wide and excited. "I'll admit, I've heard all sorts of truly sordid things—"

"Dorian, you are not going off galivanting in Fae and leaving me here to entertain all our guests in Puerto Rico," Narcissus snapped.

Dorian clucked his tongue, but settled back again, arms folded over his chest. "Fine." Then, he shot a discreet look at Alucard, and mouthed *later*.

"Besides," Narcissus continued, seemingly oblivious to Dorian's subtle exchange with Alucard, "I can only imagine what your wild side would be like. You'd end up as intolerable as Dionysus. Drinking and screwing until you've forgotten your own name."

"Well, doesn't that just sound *terrible*..." Dorian grumbled, running a finger idly along his companion's arm, gazing off in the direction of the supposed gates Alucard had spotted.

"We need a boat, then," I declared before they could get into a lover's spat and waste what remained of the day. "D'ye have one we can use?"

"They could use one of the passenger boats?" Dorian suggested.

"Absolutely not. We don't have that many of those, especially after what you did to the last one."

Dorian rolled his eyes. "How was I supposed to know they'd catch fire so easily?"

"And they're *expensive*," Narcissus added, ignoring Dorian's comment completely.

"I can pay ye whatever one costs," I said, shrugging.

"Oh, is that right?" Narcissus asked, eyeing me up and down, noting the shirt I'd stolen with a raised eyebrow. I suddenly felt like Julia Roberts in *Pretty Woman*—in the beginning, when even the sales ladies knew she was a hooker. "Alright, then," Narcissus droned. "A million."

"Alright. And how d'ye want that? Wired directly?" I asked, meeting the Greek's gaze, not the least bit daunted by his outrageous price.

A perk of having more money than I knew what to do with.

And being this close to Fae, I realized I would have given him everything I owned—all but a single gun to take with me—even the clothes off my back, if it meant I could be in Fae today.

"Oh, she called your bluff," Dorian said, clapping. "I love a show in the morning."

Narcissus sighed, backing down almost immediately. "I really can't spare one. You'll have to buy a boat when we dock in Puerto Rico. If you have a million dollars to throw around, you may even get yourselves a crew willing to sail into Fae, provided you keep your destination to yourselves."

"But we're right here!" I yelled, thrusting my arm out in the direction Alucard had indicated, my frustration obvious. I was pissed, suddenly. I mean, we were *so* close. My answers were only a few nautical miles away—and yet I was being told to wait. To be patient. Again.

I seriously considered jumping in and swimming for it.

"I know it's not ideal," Narcissus said. "But, bright side, you get to spend more time with me." He grinned, not the least bit insincere.

I chucked my tiny cup of coffee—now empty—on the deck with a curse. It shattered, causing the two immortals to jump in surprise. I strode towards the railing, too pissed off to care about their reaction. But then I noticed Narcissus padding over to the remains of my coffee cup. He edged out a toe, flicking away ceramic shards, then stumbled back with a hiss.

"Get off my boat," Narcissus said. "Now."

"Petal, why—" Dorian began.

"No questions," the Greek insisted, his eyes panicked. "Just go. Here." He tossed Alucard a key. "Dorian, take them to one of the passenger boats. Quickly." And with that, the Greek fled, headed elsewhere—probably as far away from us as he could manage, if I had to guess.

I frowned and doubled back, ignoring Alucard and Dorian's baffled expressions to glance down at whatever Narcissus had seen in my coffee grinds that had freaked him out so badly. At first, I couldn't make out anything; it looked like a brown, pulpy mess to me. Then suddenly, with a slight tilt of my head, I saw it—loosely formed, but still...

An eye, but not just any eye. The *evil eye*.

Perhaps the single most universal symbol of death and destruction out there.

Maybe Narcissus wasn't crazy, after all.

CHAPTER 12

*D*orian hunched over the railing, looking down on us like some sort of beatific angel, his exceedingly long eyelashes—the sort most women would kill for—catching the light. "You'll have to forgive Narcissus," Dorian said. "He can be a bit...superstitious. Just be glad he didn't spit on you. Most of the Greek customs I can get behind...if you know what I mean. But others..." Dorian shuddered.

I glanced over towards Alucard, wondering if the vampire found Dorian's comments equally cringeworthy, but the vampire, who seemed to know at least a little something about boats—making him an expert compared to me—didn't bother responding; he was too preoccupied getting the nifty little cruiser started. Truthfully, I hadn't known what to expect from a passenger boat. I'd expected something between a fishing boat and a dinghy, but it turned out even Narcissus' lesser boats had some panache; it felt like we were about to shoot a music video with T-Pain and Lonely Island.

"It's fine," I replied, finally, shrugging. "Whatever gets me where I need to be."

"Practicality. One of my favorite virtues, I must admit," Dorian said. "Well then, I suppose this is goodbye, for now. You'll be sure to bring me something nice back from Fae, won't you? A little souvenir? Nothing too gaudy, of course."

Alucard cranked the engine and the cruiser roared to life, the motor gurgling away. I stared up at the astonishingly gorgeous face of the legendary hedonist, smiled, and flipped him off. "How's that for a souvenir?" I yelled, my voice barely carrying over the din of the engine.

Dorian's eyes flashed, and his grin turned predatory. "Don't make promises you can't keep, darling!"

I laughed as Alucard untethered us from the cruise liner and kicked us free. I hated to admit it, but part of me rather liked Dorian Gray. I still planned on paying the fucker back for his role in the Fight Night affair, but I had to admit he had style in spades; self-indulgence aside, he knew what he wanted and did what he had to do to get it. There was something admirable in that, I thought. I waved and headed for the front of the boat where Alucard stood, his hands wrapped around the steering wheel, navigating us away from Narcissus' cruise ship and his bad omen.

The evil eye.

Frankly, as much as I wanted to mock the Greek's superstitious nature, I'd been more than a little disturbed to find the evil eye in the pulpy remains of my coffee grounds.

The evil eye had been a foreboding symbol for so long that you could find it represented in ancient hieroglyphs, even cave paintings—most often used to portend some sort of calamity. It even spanned across civilizations, many of which never even interacted directly, as if a universally acknowledged manifestation of evil. Basically, it was bad, bad juju, and I couldn't blame Narcissus one little bit for kicking us off his ship upon seeing it.

Still, if I went running every time a fortune teller gave me the "Oh, dear, I don't know how to tell you this, but..." speech, I'd have Forest Gump'd it all the way to the Pacific and back again by now. It wasn't so much that my luck was bad as it was that I was born under an aggressive sign, with no parents to speak of, and generally surrounded by mayhem and death. Frankly, any fortune teller who *didn't* think I was a walking nexus of doom wasn't worth her salt.

"Have you considered the fact that this may be a monumentally stupid idea, *cher*?" Alucard yelled back at me over the whistling wind, his dark hair whipping around his face, licking his cheeks and throat.

Like a dirty, sexy, pirate captain. I shivered.

"Aye," I replied. I had. In fact, I knew this was a monumentally stupid idea. I had a good life; plenty of money, a nice apartment, a couple worthwhile friends, a career that I could put time and energy into...there were plenty of people out there who would swap with me in a heartbeat. But that didn't change how I felt. Some people might argue that leading a successful life hinged on making the smart choices, the safe choices—but I didn't think like those people.

So here we were.

"So you're sure you want to do this?" he asked. "Pretty much last call."

I found myself nodding before I could so much as process his question. Although frankly, this had nothing to do with want. I *needed* to do this. It wasn't even solely about finding answers, about learning who my parents were, or what power was locked away inside me. It was like…it was like looking at a picture of a beautiful, far-off place your whole life—pinned to your wall, above the mirror, where you'd see it every day. But it wasn't only a place, because you grew up hearing wonderful stories about the far-off land, stories full of daring and romance. Stories that taught you how to dream. I didn't *want* to go to Fae. I needed to. I ached for it.

"I'm sure," I said, finally.

Alucard nodded with a jerk of his chin, then spun the wheel, angling the nose of our little cruiser towards the sun, kicking up a small spray.

"What is it ye see out there?" I asked, pointing out at the water.

The Daywalker glanced back at me and shrugged. "I'm not sure how to describe it, exactly. It's like a mirage. There one second, gone the next. But, if I look at it from the corner of my eye, I feel like I can see something shimmering in the distance."

"Somethin' like what?" I asked, scowling. While I found the vampire poet thing kind of hot, I wasn't interested in his vague, flowery description. How was I supposed to see it unless he described it as accurately as he could?

"Not sure," Alucard admitted. "But whatever is on the other side, we'll find out fairly quick. It wasn't that far out to sea. By the way, *cher*, did I hear you say that there were several of these gates out here?"

"Accordin' to me source, aye. But she claimed only people who've been there before can see 'em, and they aren't as common as they once were. Somethin' about our world and Fae bein' driven apart." I tried to remember what Eve had said, exactly, but I'd been too eager plotting my next step to pay close attention.

No wonder she didn't like talking to me.

"Pretty lucky then, don't you think?" Alucard asked, his tone insinuating he thought it anything but luck. "Us finding one so quickly?"

I frowned. He was right; the odds of stumbling on an entrance to Fae so quickly were probably astronomically low. Unfortunately, I didn't know what else to blame. "Aye, lucky," I responded, my voice heavy with doubt.

Alucard throttled down a little so we were barely crawling forward, choosing to ignore the coincidence for the time being. "Alright, we're close. I suggest you hold on to something."

"And why would I need to do that?" I asked, eyes narrowed. "I could swim faster than this."

Alucard glanced back, smirking. "Because we have no clue what's on the other side. Hell, we might end up sailing right into a forest. I might hit a tree, who knows? This way you'll be braced for impact, at least."

Well, I supposed that made sense, although I didn't like it; I hadn't really factored in an abrupt change in topography. But Alucard was probably right —it would be silly not to prepare for anything. The Fae realm was notoriously unpredictable, after all. I sighed and secured my duffel and bug-out bag to the steering column, then coiled myself around one of the passenger seats, arms wound through the nearest set of handlebars. "Alright," I called. "Ready!"

Alucard nodded and throttled us forward. We slid across the water, the engine grumbling like an empty stomach. From where I was, I couldn't see much, but I could feel the cruiser grind against something—the sound of metal tearing, like nails on a chalkboard, made me wince. I heard Alucard yell, but whatever he said was lost in an unexpected roar of wind. Then, with a suddenness that reminded me of a roller coaster hitting a downslope, we lurched forward until the whole passenger boat was completely vertical. We were falling through space.

I tried to scream but, before I knew it, my legs had flown out behind me, the wind rushing past so fast it stole my breath away. The only thing that saved me from flying away was my grip on the rail, but even that was beginning to slip—the pressure on my arm and wrist from maintaining my hold was enough to make me want to black out. My heart was in my throat, like I'd leapt off an airplane. I couldn't even think straight.

"Quinn!" Alucard roared, so close I knew I could reach out and touch him, though I wasn't sure how that was possible. "You have to let go!"

Oh, fuck that.

"Now!" he yelled. I felt his hands wrap around my waist like an electric jolt that sent goosebumps flooding over my skin—the sensation almost too much to bear after falling for so long. I had an instant to think that it wasn't anything like when Appleseed and I touched. That had been painful—mind-numbingly so, in fact—and this was anything but. Unfortunately, I had no time to dwell on it; Alucard yanked me free, forcing me to let go of the rail. Suddenly, the wind's immense pressure was gone, just in time for me to watch the cruiser continue its plummet—at least until it disappeared in the mist, along with my guns and bug-out bag.

And—with them—all joy.

CHAPTER 13

I reached out, fingers splayed, eyes pinched shut—willing my duffel bag to rise up from the mist. But, eventually, my hand dropped. The Force had forsaken me, yet again.

"I must admit, I had no idea that was what was on the other side of the threshold," Alucard muttered. The Daywalker was carrying me aloft, his whole body encased in flame, complete with outspread wings so that we hovered in place with each powerful thrust of his wings.

I don't know why, but the sensation that we were suddenly flying didn't hit me as strongly as it probably should have.

So much for First World problems.

Guess now I had Fae-world problems.

Luckily, it seemed like his body and wings emitted only friendly flames; I hadn't caught fire yet, at least. I noticed he seemed preoccupied, scanning our immediate surroundings as if we were being hunted. But there was nothing to see, as far as I could tell. A thick fog stretched out in all directions, so dense I couldn't make anything out beyond the reach of my hands.

It wasn't until I thought about my hands that I noticed it—that familiar, searing pain around my wrist, painful enough to distract me from the vice-like grip Alucard had around my midsection. I held up my arm. This time the bracelet glowed faintly, its edges white hot and singeing the fine hairs at my wrist. I tried to remove the damn bangle; I could always put it back on later when it wasn't hot enough to brand me…but it wouldn't budge. In fact, it seemed to have gotten tighter, somehow. I cursed, gritting my teeth.

"Quiet," Alucard barked, his voice harsh.

I jerked my head around, glaring at the vampire. "And just who the fuck d'ye t'ink ye are, tellin' me—"

Alucard hiked me up and pinned his free hand across my mouth before I could say another word. I gave the vampire the dirtiest look I could manage, but he wasn't even paying attention to me. Fine. I stuck my tongue out, licking his palm as aggressively as I could, slobbering all over his hand and my mouth—the childhood trick for grossing out anyone rude enough to clamp their hand over your mouth.

But Alucard didn't even seem to notice.

I cursed, inwardly, and briefly considered drawing the only gun I had left from my inner thigh holster—maybe the barrel of a pistol against his head would warrant his attention. But on the heels of that thought came another: I'd lost my other guns. My poor, poor guns.

I was halfway through inventorying them, saying a tiny prayer for each, when I heard it. Singing. Men, singing, their voices echoing in the fog in an eerily haunting ballad. Alucard spun us around once, then again, trying to locate the source of the sound.

"They're close," he whispered.

Suddenly, the bow of a massive pirate ship came into view above us, piercing the fog like some kind of ancient beast. Which was eerie as hell, but awesome because—thanks to a mildly unhealthy fascination with all things Jack Sparrow in my early twenties—*pirate* ships I knew.

It was an old-school vessel, with three masts, sails unfurled, and a wicked-looking bowsprit that soared high into the air. Rusty cannons lined the hull, and a black skull-and-crossbones flag flew from the crow's nest— the jolly roger. The song, I realized, was a shanty—one of the rowing tunes sailors used to keep time. That's when I noticed the oars, poking out from beneath the hull, working in tandem, carving through the fog at a steady pace.

The ship was sailing on the mists.

"Ahoy there!" a voice called. "Looks like Fae overboard!"

A small crew of perhaps ten men came running in response, poking their heads out to stare down at us, their expressions impossible to make out due to the haze. Alucard removed his hand from my mouth, his whole body was tensed, clearly expecting a fight. I considered replying—confessing we weren't Fae at all—but decided against it; until we knew how these sailors felt about Faelings, it was probably best to keep quiet.

"Doesn't look like any Fae I've ever seen," a sailor called, perched halfway up the foremast. "Hell, that looks like a dame that flaming buzzard is carrying!"

A dame? Seriously? I was about to respond with something scathing when I noticed someone running along the ship's railing, clutching a rope attached to one of the masts in his hand. My eyes went wide as I realized what he intended to do, but even then, I wasn't fully prepared for it; he leapt off the side of the ship, falling straight for us, whooping for joy as he came.

I winced, but couldn't look away as he came soaring closer.

At the last possible instant, he jerked to a stop, swinging, catching himself with the perfect grace of a Faeling, feet nimbly wrapped around the balled end of the rope, one hand hanging free at his side. He had the face of a leading man, his blonde hair so long he'd tied it back into a ponytail with a bit of cloth, exposing his exceedingly long, pointed ears. His smile was a familiar, welcome one.

Ryan O'Rye.

"Quinn! Is that you?" Ryan exclaimed in disbelief, his eyes comically wide, looking like he'd been hit over the head with a hammer.

Alucard growled and swung me away, possessively. "Back off, runt," he snarled.

"Oy!" I said, elbowing the vampire. "Knock that shite off, that's me friend you're talkin' to. Aye, Ryan, it's me!"

The Faeling's grin broke out wide, his teeth perfectly straight, eyes bright. The consummate ladies' Faeling, Ryan had once worked for Christoff before being forced to return from his exile to work for King Oberon, one of the three major powers responsible for maintaining the natural order of chaos here in Fae. We hadn't been the closest of friends, but he'd been reliable, dependable—which was more than I could say for most of the people in my life up to this point.

"We need to go," Alucard said, his voice strained. He stared at Ryan like the Faeling were diseased, capable of infecting us.

"Easy there," Ryan said, bowing his head, his eyes locked on Alucard. "Quinn and I are old friends. That's all. I'm no threat."

No threat? What the hell was that supposed to mean? Alucard adjusted a little, floating upwards so he could look down on the Faeling, his gaze imperious. "I accept your submission," Alucard said, finally. "We need to land."

Ryan nodded, grinning. "Yeah, I bet she's pretty heavy."

I glared at them both. What the fuck kind of masculine staring contest had that been just now? And what did Alucard mean by "submission"? Before I could ask, however, Ryan's comment finally registered. "Oy! Bring me closer to me old friend," I demanded, giving Ryan the full weight of my attention. "He needs an old-fashioned nose job, courtesy of me fist."

Ryan chuckled. "It's nice to know some things never change, Quinn. Come on up, the ship's Captain will want to talk to you."

Alucard tensed, again, clutching me so hard it hurt to breathe.

"Don't worry," Ryan said, turning at my gasp, "he's not the possessive type, and has far too much on his mind to worry about you two. While I can't make promises for the rest of his crew, I can assure you they won't disobey him. Besides, from what I recall, Quinn can take care of herself." Ryan winked at me, then began ascending the rope, drawing himself up with a speed I could hardly hope to match—as if he weighed nothing at all.

Alucard floated upwards, trailing the Faeling. "I don't like this."

"Well, I don't like ye gettin' all handsy with me," I snapped. "Ye damn near crushed me ribs just now. And what the hell was that with Ryan?"

Alucard met my eyes, his stare so intense I felt the world swim around me a little. The bracelet flared up again, the pain making me nauseous. "This is Fae," Alucard said, ignoring my grimace. "Things are different, here. You'll see." He glanced up at the ship and the faces staring down at us with disdain. "Don't let anyone touch you, or I'll have to kill them."

Oh, great.

Now I had a possessive vampire on my hands to deal with, along with everything else.

Crash landing.

Lost my guns.

Abducted upon arrival.

So far, this Faecation sucked.

CHAPTER 14

I freed myself from Alucard's grasp the instant we landed, but he refused to leave my side; he hovered close by, maintaining his flaming angel of death look—probably to scare away the natives. I had to admit, it was pretty intimidating; bathed in golden light, wearing tattered merlot robes, with a face carved by the hand of a vengeful God, he might as well have been yanked from the cover of Catholic Schoolgirl Magazine.

And apparently, I wasn't the only one who thought so; most of the crew —sailors in naval garb from various eras—kept their distance, but a few lingering gazes reminded me that sexual preferences were a little more... fluid, on ships. That said, there were a hell of a lot more eyes on me than the Inhuman Torch. Was I the first woman they'd seen in years? Or was staring considered polite in Fae?

Either way, I felt suddenly very glad to be armed.

We heard the Captain before we saw him; the sound of his boots on the quarterdeck above us were like gunshots, slow and steady. His hat came into view first, scarlet red and wide-brimmed. Then his face—clean shaven and scarred, with deep lines around his mouth and eyes. He wore a long black trench coat, black breeches, tunic, and boots. He leaned forward onto a bannister that wound down around the stairs which could be accessed on either side of us, settling one hand on the wood, and one hook where a hand should have been. Its dull iron edge gouged into the lumber like a hot knife in butter.

"Who, or *what*, are these things?" the Captain asked.

"This is Quinn MacKenna, Captain," Ryan replied. "She's from Boston, in the Americas. Early twenty-first century. She's…a gunrunner. Of sorts."

The Captain grunted, flicking his eyes up and down the line of my body—not sexually, but as though trying to gauge how many weapons I had on my person. How dangerous I was. To be honest, his reaction made me think highly of him. Not many men see a damsel in distress and think to frisk her, first.

Not that I planned to let him.

"And this one?" the Captain asked, jerking his chin towards Alucard, dismissing me.

"No idea," Ryan said, squinting. "Not one of ours, though."

"A spy for Tiger Lily?" the Captain asked, studying Alucard's face as though it might betray him.

"I spy for no one," Alucard snarled.

The Captain raised his good hand and tipped his hat up and back, exposing his forehead and revealing a mane of fine, silver-white hair. "We'll see about that. Crew! Back to your posts, double-time!"

"Aye, aye, Cap'n!" came a chorus of voices. The men scrambled about, most of them headed below decks to resume rowing, I presumed.

"Ryan," the Captain barked.

"Yes, Captain?" Ryan replied, ducking his head.

"I want these two in irons until we meet up with your people." Ryan grimaced at the mention of iron—anathema to the Fae—and the Captain noticed. "We're nearly over the mountains, which means we'll be out in the open soon. We can't afford—"

"Boat sighted! Starboard side!" a voice called down from the crow's nest, interrupting whatever the Captain had been about to say.

The Captain bolted toward the starboard side of the ship—turns out that's the right side, if you're facing the bow. Alucard, Ryan, and I followed, peering out into the gloom. She was a sleek vessel; much smaller than the ship we were on—little more than a paddle boat, in fact. But then another emerged from the fog. And another. Soon, at least a dozen were in sight, with more arriving every second.

"She's found us," the Captain said, spitting out into the fog, grinding his hook into the wood so hard it began to splinter. "Damn savage has to have been waiting decades for this."

"King Oberon's warship shouldn't be far away," Ryan said, sounding nervous. "We could send one of our messengers to—"

"No time," the Captain muttered. He turned and glared down at us. "Get these two below deck, then get back up here. We'll need every hand we can get, Fae or otherwise."

"Oy!" I said, speaking up for the first time. "Is someone goin' to tell us what the fuck is goin' on?"

The Captain raised an eyebrow and flicked his hand at me, still looking at Ryan. "Did the Irish invade the Americas?"

Ryan snorted. "In a manner of speaking, actually, yes. After your time."

"Huh. Well, Miss MacKenna," the Captain replied, giving me the full weight of his attention, "we are about to engage in a naval battle with a very determined Faerie chieftain and her braves. She's got every reason to want us dead, and we have every reason to wish the opposite. Now, I know you and Ryan here have some sort of history, and I am glad you've managed to reconnect, but at this moment, I would prefer you and your friend were out of the way. Additionally, for your sake, you better pray to God Almighty we win. Because if Tiger Lily gets ahold of you, you'll wish I'd gutted you right here." The Captain finished with a flourish, ducking his head in a slight bow, his smile tight and forced.

"I could help you fend her off," Alucard said, rolling his shoulders, teeth bared like an animal's. "In exchange for safe passage. You drop us off at the earliest opportunity."

That made the Captain pause. He regarded Alucard, looking him up and down, evidently not remotely impressed by the fire and the wings—which told me all I needed to know about the crazy shit I could expect to see in Fae. "Are you any good in a fight?"

"Yes," Alucard replied. No elaboration, just a shitload of confidence.

"Aye, and I'll fight, too," I said, glaring at the vampire—as if he had any right to risk himself on our behalf without consulting me.

"That's not a good idea, Quinn," Ryan hissed.

I drew the only gun I had left from its inner thigh holster and leveled it in Ryan's face. "Look, I don't want to shoot ye in the face, Ryan O'Rye. I really don't. But I'm not feelin' very civilized at the moment, and—since the fight is comin' to me anyway—I'm done listenin' to what ye have to say, no matter how well ye mean by it."

Ryan raised his hands in surrender. "Whatever you say, Quinn."

"That's a good Faelin," I said, eyes narrowed. Inwardly, I frowned. Had I really just pointed a gun at someone for suggesting I stay out of a fight? Granted, I'd always been a little on edge, not to mention trigger happy, but suddenly it felt like everyone deserved a bullet, for one thing or another— the Captain for trying to make us his prisoners, Alucard for being posses- sive, Ryan for being overprotective...at this point, I was pretty sure I'd run out of bullets before I ran out of targets.

"Is that a flintlock?" The Captain asked, eyeing my pistol in undisguised fascination.

"A modern version, yes," Ryan admitted, his hands still raised.

"Amazing. Very well, you're both welcome to take part in the battle," the Captain said. "But if either of you try to betray us, I'll make sure you suffer. I'm not Fae, but I assure you, I keep my promises." The Captain stormed away, bellowing orders. I realized the fleet of ships had gotten significantly closer since I last looked...and there were at least twenty more of them.

"Well, you two have done it, now," Ryan said, dropping his hands. "Although that was probably your best move, offering to help. Otherwise you'd be in the brig until we made it back to King Oberon's fleet. But, so you know, he wasn't kidding...if you do anything to jeopardize his men, he'll hunt you two down to the ends of Neverland and beyond."

"Neverland?" I asked, frowning.

"Yeah," Ryan replied, cocking an eyebrow. "Surely you knew that's where you were headed when you went through the gate?"

I shook my head vehemently. "Knock it off, Ryan. Ye know we can't be in Neverland," I said. "That's a children's story. Besides, Peter—"

Ryan clamped a hand over my mouth so fast I nearly shot him by acci- dent, the barrel of my gun pressed firmly against his belly. My eyes widened considerably as I noticed Alucard put his hand around the Faeling's throat, squeezing so hard a vein in Ryan's forehead was throbbing. Two of the crewmen had drawn swords and held them pressed against Alucard's neck —his flames licked along the edges of their blades, turning them black.

An old-fashioned Mexican standoff.

In Neverland.

Ryan eased his hand off my mouth, which prompted Alucard to release his throat. The two crewmen kept their cutlasses right where they were until Ryan waved them off. The Faeling coughed and massaged his throat. "Sorry," he said, his voice hoarse, "but that's not a name you're allowed to say on this ship. Not once. Not ever."

"And why not?" I asked, baffled.

"Because," Ryan said, "this is the Jolly Roger. And no one who values their lives says that name around Captain James Hook."

CHAPTER 15

*P*reparations for the upcoming battle commenced before I could worry too much about the plausibility of our host or our location; the potential for violence took immediate precedence over whether or not Ryan was fucking with me. The three of us drew away from the edge of the ship towards the center mast, where we'd be less in the way.

To be honest, I wasn't the slightest bit sure what to expect from a pitched fight on a ship sailing the skies; I'd always seen naval battles from a cinematic perspective—long aerial shots of cannons exploding with close-ups on the chalk-white smoke pluming from their gaping maws, followed by wooden shards spewing out in all directions and screams as sailors dove to avoid the next barrage. As a result, I'd expected a lot of chaos and noise—especially at the outset. What I got was entirely different. The cannons didn't roar; apparently Hook's crew had run out of gunpowder so long ago that they'd nearly forgotten what the cannons were for. Instead, the crew prepared their weapons—swords, knives, and clubs, mostly.

"Here," Ryan said, handing me a long, wooden club shaped like a baseball bat. "When they come, just swing. The pixies will likely steer clear of you, and Tiger Lily's braves will go after the sailors, first and foremost."

I brandished my gun, arching an eyebrow. "I t'ink I'd rather use this," I replied. Granted, clubbing Fae to death sounded like fun, but I'd always sucked at Whack-a-Mole; riddling the boarding party with bullets was more my speed.

Ryan rolled his eyes. "Regular guns won't do anything to our kind, you know that."

"Aye, that's why I loaded the clip with iron bullets before we came," I replied.

Ryan glanced sidelong at me, eyes wide.

"You've been gone a while," I said, ignoring the stare while I checked over the gun, making sure it would work here in Fae. "The Fae are no friends of mine. Not anymore."

"When the leader shows, point her out," Alucard said, clearly uncon- cerned by Ryan's hurt expression. "I'm assuming your Captain will honor our agreement sooner if I bring him her head?"

Ryan's eyebrows shot up as he studied the two of us. "Uh, yeah. Probably..."

"Good," Alucard said, then walked off towards the railing for a better view of the incoming fleet. From where I stood I could see that the boats had stopped—maybe fifty ships, in total. Tiny lights strobed among them, casting eerie shadows in the fog.

"Except he isn't my Captain..." Ryan added as the vampire marched off.

"Aye, about that," I said, realizing that—as far as pumping the Faeling for information was concerned—it was probably now or never. "What are ye doin' onboard this ship? Why are ye here, Ryan?"

"I was going to ask you the same question," he replied, grinning.

I scowled and hefted the club, beating it gently against my shoulder. "I'm waitin'."

Ryan sighed. "I'm here working for King Oberon. He's sent several of us out to serve as liaisons. We're gathering all the naval power we can find before Balor and the Fomorians come."

I shivered with recognition. "What d'ye mean, before Balor comes?"

Ryan shook his head, eyeing the hustle and bustle around us. "I'll have to explain later. They'll want me for a lookout, and I've got to get a message to the warship, no matter what the Captain says." He waved and took off, glancing back only once to call out to me. "You can fill me in on why you're here if we make it through this alive!"

If...

That was heartening.

Still, I found myself grinning.

Ryan was alive!

And I was in Fae!

Moments away from fighting on a pirate ship among the clouds, which hadn't been on my bucket list, sure, but where else could a girl get this kind of excitement? I realized there was something uncivilized, something brutal about this place—and I...

Loved it.

I started to move towards the action when I noticed I still had my pistol in hand and frowned...there was something wrong with it. It looked grotesque to me, suddenly, its edges too neat, the metal too clean. It looked...manufactured. I thrust the offensive weapon back into its holster and took a good long look at the club Ryan had given me. I realized it didn't simply *look* like a baseball bat...it *was* a baseball bat. Or at least had been designed as one; its wide tip was beveled and sturdy, perfect for bashing skulls in or knocking pixies out of the park.

Still, a baseball bat wouldn't do me much good against Fae warriors. I didn't care for Ryan's plan; keeping the enemy at bay while I waited to be rescued wasn't exactly my idea of a good time. I thrust the bat out, halting a passing sailor as he ran by. "Oy! D'ye have anythin' to make this t'ing deadlier?" I asked, brandishing the bat.

The sailor arched an eyebrow. "Well, love," he replied, his British accent still remarkably clear, unlike the Captain's, which had been faint at best. "What you have there in your hand should do the trick all on its own. It was fashioned from the branch of a Nevernever tree. But, if you want to be extra prepared," the sailor said, pointing at a barrel securely bound to the center mast, "feel free to find something more to your liking." With that, he ran off towards the Jolly Roger's starboard side, grinning from ear-to-ear like a boy about to play with his friends.

A chorus of yells went up, and I beelined for the barrel. The lights were no longer dancing above Tiger Lily's boats, but coming towards us, illuminating a small army of braves—dark-skinned Faelings with razor sharp teeth, their bodies coated in war paint that seemed to curl sinuously over their skin, their hair made of feathers, wielding weapons fashioned from bone. I made it to the barrel as the first wave reached the sailors, and soon the clash of metal on bone sounded. Then the screams.

Guess the movies hadn't gotten everything wrong.

I fished around in the barrel, hunting through what turned out to be a ramshackle pile of iron knick-knacks. Scissors, coins, thimbles, crowbars, barbed wire...I froze. Barbed wire.

A malicious grin split my cheeks. Oh, yeah.

Perfect.

I nearly reached in and snagged it without thinking, but a voice in the back of my head screamed at me not to, and I jerked my hand away at the last possible instant. Right, barbed wire—the shit could slice up my hands something fierce if I wasn't careful. I scanned my immediate surroundings, looking for anything sturdy enough to grab it. Something leather maybe? I cursed. Nothing. But then, maybe I was thinking about this too hard.

Sure, I could open my own jars...

But this seemed like a job for a man—or, better yet, a vampire.

"Alucard! Come here!" I yelled, turning towards the skirmish, where Alucard was already busy taking on two of the braves. Alucard slid on his knees beneath the arc of a spear, using his wings to balance, and then popped up—improbably fast—to snatch his opponent by the throat and toss him into his companion. They landed in a pile on the far side of the ship, their bodies twisted up so badly I couldn't tell where one ended and the other began.

The vampire then half-ran, half-flew towards me. "What is it? Are you hurt?" he asked.

I waved that away. "No. I need ye to wrap barbed wire around me bat," I said, holding it out for him.

He blinked. "Why?"

"So they'll bleed more when I hit 'em," I replied, as if that were obvious.

The vampire's face broke into a frighteningly large grin. "I knew you'd fit in here," he said.

I grinned back, though a voice in the back of my head was screaming—something about my wrist. And something about pain. Lots of pain.

But I didn't have time to listen to it, so I squashed it down to a faint whimper.

I had pixies to pummel and braves to break.

CHAPTER 16

*T*he Fae natives soared down into the sailors in droves, impaling the less fortunate with their spears. Alucard and I took off towards the fighting the instant he finished winding the barbed wire around the thicker end of my bat, but we got caught up in a swarm of insects—outfitted with pulsing neon lights dancing in front of our eyes—before we could get close. I held up my hand, trying to wave them off, and it came away bloody.

"What the hell?" I hissed, stumbling backwards.

"This is not your fight," a tiny voice declared, less than an inch from my ear, like the buzz of a bee. I ducked away instinctively, heart racing. The pixie who'd spoken was as tall as my index finger, but proportionately sound—she was a leggy blonde with a short, feathered haircut that her kind had made famous, sporting a lot of black leather. She was also pink. Bubble gum pink, emitting a soft, rosy glow. I looked around and realized all the lights I'd noticed out in the fog had belonged to pixies; they hovered above our heads like technicolor stars. I noticed a few were pointedly staying away from Alucard, looking a little singed, which made me laugh.

"What's so funny?" the pink pixie asked, her voice dripping with derision.

"You, thinkin' just because it isn't me fight, that I'll stay out of it," I said. I swung my bat at her, as quick as I could, going for speed as opposed to power. She danced out of reach, screeching. The rest of the pixies began swirling about our heads, preparing to strike. "Alucard, light 'em up!" I yelled, then ducked for cover.

"That's not how my power works," Alucard said, leaving me hunkering down like an idiot, watching the pixies with narrowed eyes. I frowned. I wasn't sure how I knew, but I was certain he was wrong. As I stared up at the distracted vampire, his wild side on display, I realized he had no idea what he was.

And yet, somehow, I did.

Alucard was a Daywalker, sure, but the truth was that was more of a side effect than anything else—a symptom, you might call it. The fact remained that—no matter how dissimilar he was from his kin—Alucard was still a vampire. Nothing could change his nature. Other vampires, however, survived by consuming blood, using the lifeforce found in it to fuel themselves. But theirs was a liquid diet, no pun intended. Alucard's diet, on the other hand, had evolved; he fed on the energy nature provided, drawing in sunlight and converting it to power. In fact, his wild side was so dominant it burned the very air. But this was Fae air. The natural energy here was inherently less predictable, certainly, but also a hell of a lot more volatile. Powerful.

Powerful enough to be *used*.

I shuffled across the deck as the pixies launched an offensive, slicing at me with their slivers of bone. Except to shield my face with my arms, I largely ignored them. Alucard swatted several away, and they buzzed off, trailing smoke. I managed to reach him, at last, and took his hand in mine. His back arched, eyes fluttering in shock at the energy that passed between us, as if feeling it for the first time. I basked in it, his warmth washing over me like sunlight. I snapped my fingers in front of his face to get his attention. He blinked at me, close enough to kiss. "Have ye ever seen someone breathe fire?" I asked.

Kill first, kiss later.

Priorities.

Alucard snorted. "Sure," he replied, "my daughters are dragons."

Okay. Processing that later. "Fair enough," I said, spinning Alucard around to face the horde of pixies, most of whom had drifted away, content to leave us be so long as we didn't make a move towards the skirmishers.

"Whatever ye do, don't t'ink about it too hard. Just do as I say. First, take a deep breath."

Alucard did, sucking in a lungful of air, his cheeks bulging.

"And now let it out," I whispered. "Hard."

Alucard blew. Gouts of flame burst from between his lips, his power finding the currents of natural energy in the air and riding them, spewing jets of fire through the air, arcing out to tear into the pixies. Several of them screamed in agony, consumed by the blaze, falling to the deck like fireflies from Hell. Those who didn't end up smoldering on the deck fled, flying away as fast as they could.

All except one—the pink pixie. She dipped and dodged, pirouetting to avoid each tendril of flame, dancing closer, her tiny bone daggers dripping with my blood. Alucard finally ran out of breath and stumbled a little, woozy on his feet after exerting that much energy. I helped keep him upright—steadying him with one hand on his shoulder—until he was ready to stand on his own.

"How did you know I could do that?" he asked, panting.

"I just did," I replied, shrugging.

The answer seemed to satisfy him.

"Why are you helping them?" the pink pixie screamed, her voice no longer full of disdain, but full of rage. "Do you know what they've done?"

"Who are ye?" I demanded, jabbing the end of my bat towards her. She fluttered away, eyeing the barbed wire on my bat with disgust.

"That's none of your business," she said.

I considered that, then nodded. "You're probably right. Fine, ye wee, nameless sprite...time to die." I began swinging at her, casually, swiping slow and steady, causing her to flit about. I could tell she didn't want to fight us, not with Alucard standing nearby; he could light her up like a match if she wasn't careful.

"Alright, I'll tell you!" she yelled. "But you have to promise not to help Hook," she added, staring at Alucard as if imploring Death himself not to intervene.

I lowered the bat, scowling. Was I not scary enough to warrant a condition? "That's not how this works, sprite," I spat.

"Tinkerbell," she said, glaring at me. "My name is Tinkerbell. And I'm not a sprite!"

"Cher," Alucard drawled, the faintest hint of his usual self peeking through, "I don't know if I can handle any more of this storybook shit."

I grimaced. He was right; this was pretty insane. Captain Hook. Tiger Lily. Neverland. And now Tinkerbell. It was like we'd wandered into a story, except—looking around at all the violence, the braves and the sailors cutting each other to pieces, their blood seeping into the deck—it certainly wasn't a children's story. I shook that off, including the nagging sensation that I was forgetting something. Something important.

Survival—that's what mattered now.

"Alright, Tinkerbell," I said, "how about ye tell us what's goin' on? Why are ye and Tiger Lily attackin' Hook and his crew?"

Tinkerbell's eyes narrowed, and her dainty mouth hung open. "You can't seriously mean you're fighting for Hook without even knowing why?"

"Just answer me question," I demanded, "or me friend will roast ye alive. I've never eaten pixie before, but I'm willin' to bet ye taste like chicken."

"What's chicken?" Tinkerbell asked, brow furrowed.

"Nevermind that," I snarled. "Answers, now!"

Tinkerbell clenched her teeth. "We had a truce. Hook stayed on his side of the island, and we stayed on ours. No more fighting. But this morning, one of our scouts saw the Jolly Roger sailing the clouds over the mountains, preparing to cross into our territory. Preparing to attack us. So, Tiger Lily decided to strike first."

I started to put the pieces together, doing my best to shut out the sounds of sailors and Faelings dying behind us. From what Ryan had said, he'd recruited Hook to join Oberon's fleet. *That* was why Hook was sailing across the island. Hook wasn't planning an attack...he was leaving. Tiger Lily's reaction, while perfectly natural, was based on a false assumption. Unfortunately, her reaction was going to get a lot of her braves and Hook's sailors killed.

"We need to stop this," I said, turning to Alucard.

"That's not our job," Alucard replied. "And definitely not what we came here to do."

I scowled at him. Why *had* we come? I tried to remember, but couldn't. I shook my head, realizing it didn't matter. We were needed now. I wasn't sure why, but I knew I didn't want either side shedding any more blood— human or Fae. Especially not over a simple misunderstanding. "I don't care," I replied, finally. "This is wrong."

Tinkerbell snorted, rolling her eyes. "You sound like *him.*"

"Like who?"

Her lip curled up in a sneer. "Pan."

A voice cut through the din—Captain Hook's voice. "Come on, then, you savage!"

Tinkerbell glanced past us, her eyes wide, then zipped off toward the commotion.

Alucard and I turned to find the braves and sailors spreading out in a wide circle, stepping over the fallen bodies of their comrades as if they were nothing. In the middle, Hook stood, cutlass drawn, his iron hook poised in the air like the blade of a guillotine. Opposite him was a Faeling like none I had ever seen before. She was young, short, and fit, her body covered in smooth, rippling snakeskin hides. She had dark, faintly reddish skin, and her hair was pitch black—a mound of raven feathers spilling down her back. Lime green tattoos whorled over her eyes and mouth, her teeth bared and filed to points. She reminded me of a cobra—her every twitch promising death.

And yet, Hook struck first. He came forward like a fencer, lunging with the point of his sword. Tiger Lily spun, deflecting the strike with an animal's reflexes, her twin bone daggers licking the side of Hook's blade. And, with that, the dance began. Hook's strikes were quick and thorough, wavering between the precision of a duelist and the brutality of a pirate. He hacked and slashed, parried and riposted.

Tiger Lily, on the other hand, was pure savagery in motion. She dove to the ground to dodge one swipe, so flat the only thing keeping her from kissing it were her splayed fingertips. She leapt into the air to avoid another, defying gravity and the limitations of her body by clearing Hook and twisting her hips to land on her feet. Her daggers were like snakes, darting in and out, their tongues flicking along the edges of his sword, deflected from his body only by the careful positioning of his hook.

It was beautiful.

And wrong.

Hook's blade came down in a heavy-handed arc, a blow meant to drive Tiger Lily's daggers from her hands. Tiger Lily had dropped into a squat, clearly prepared to take the blow on her naked back if it meant thrusting her own blades into Hook's heart. I burst through the crowd before either could follow through with their strikes, bum-rushing Hook with my shoulder, hitting him hard enough to send him sprawling—using his body like a springboard to lash out at Tiger Lily with one foot, catching her across the jaw. She, too, fell back, though more from surprise than hurt.

"Enough!" I yelled. I raised my bat threateningly and spun in a slow circle, making sure everyone knew coming at me would mean pain—and lots of it. I was done playing. "Hear me! There is no need for this. Hook is leavin' Neverland!"

That declaration sent a shiver through the gathered crowd. The sailors, who had already known their destination, clenched their jaws, while the braves exchanged disbelieving looks. I rested the bat on my shoulder and glared out at them all, daring anyone to contradict me.

"You lie," Tiger Lily hissed.

"She does not," Hook interjected. He'd risen to one knee, and suddenly I could see the years on his face; he looked like a broken old man, the lines deep and engraved, his eyes tired and bleary with age.

"As if we would believe the words of Captain James Hook," Tiger Lily spat.

Hook raised his chin defiantly. "I swear it on my good hand," he said, driving his cutlass into the deck.

Tiger Lily's eyes narrowed. "You know what it means if you go back on your word this time," she said, her gaze anticipatory. "If I find out you're lying, I will peel the flesh from your hand until you beg me to let the Crocodile take it from you."

Hook sneered at her, but spoke softly. So softly only the three of us could hear. "I've grown tired of this fight, Tiger Lily. Our numbers are shrinking. Smee died five winters ago. We've been offered one last stand. You know," he said, standing, his back slightly stooped, "I hate to admit it, but I'd grown...fond, of this place."

"He's going to protect you all," a voice called out, interrupting whatever Hook had been about to say next. Ryan worked his way through the crowd and continued, "There's a storm coming. An ancient enemy of the Fae, who intend to make you all slaves. And Captain James Hook intends to fight on your behalf."

The sailors cheered.

"We are no one's slaves!" Tiger Lily snapped, once the hubbub had died down. But I could tell she was ruffled; the idea of Captain Hook doing anything altruistic clearly didn't sit well with her.

"I know, Tiger Lily," Hook said, his eyes flashing. "You never were, nor will you ever be."

Tiger Lily studied the older man, the expression on her youthful face hard to read, but—before she could respond—a cry went up from her braves. Several pointed. Another ship, far larger than the Jolly Roger, was approaching from the port side. Slate grey, with two smoke stacks spewing fire and belching smoke near the rear of the ship, it looked like an old cargo ship from World War I; the ship's side read *USS Cyclops* in faded letters.

"That's King Oberon's warship," Ryan yelled, twirling slowly to get everyone's attention. "Our escort. He won't be pleased at the delay, and so I suggest you all get out of here. Now."

I reached out and nudged the Faeling. "That ship's made out of what, steel?" I asked, whispering.

Ryan blinked. "Not the time, Quinn."

"Aye, but shouldn't that bother ye lot?" I asked, cocking an eyebrow.

"Steel has carbon in it. Enough that it doesn't repulse or poison us, the way true iron does. Still harmful as a weapon, but typically easy to ignore and recover from."

I frowned, considering the implications of that. I supposed in hindsight, Ryan's explanation made sense; if steel bothered the Fae that much, they would never be able to survive in the mortal realm.

It'd be like living in a nuclear wasteland.

Tiger Lily's hiss brought me back to the present moment, my bat at the ready, thinking she might attack anyway—but she seemed to understand the situation; one-on-one, she and her braves might have stood a chance of defeating Hook and bringing his ship tumbling from the skies. But against a behemoth like the *USS Cyclops*? Her braves would die. She dropped her daggers into a pouch at her hip. "Braves! Let's go!"

The remaining pixies—those Alucard hadn't roasted alive—came flooding back, brushing their fingers against the feathers each brave had for hair. Each of Tiger Lily's Fae warriors began to levitate off the ground, their moccasins barely brushing the wood, their tattoos fading before our eyes.

"Tiger Lily!" Hook called out, staring out at the massive warship as if he'd never seen anything like it.

The Fae chieftain spun around.

"I intend for this to be my last fight," Hook said, shifting his attention back to his lifelong enemy. "Which means I won't be coming back. I..."

Hook hung his head and reached for the handle of his sword, still stuck in the planks. He yanked it from the wood and slid it back into its sheath. "Could you tell Peter…"

Tiger Lily's gaze hardened, her jaw bunching. "Pan and I share no bond. Not anymore."

Hook grunted. "No, I suppose you wouldn't." Tiger Lily sniffed, ran, and leapt off the edge of the boat, soaring into the air with her arms outstretched—a pink light riding her shoulder. Her braves followed. Hook merely stood there, watching them depart, looking like a sad, broken, old man who'd already gone on his last adventure.

I felt Alucard settle in next to me, the heat of his body coming off—literally—in waves. "That could have been dangerous," he said, wrapping a hand around my forearm.

I yanked it free. "So?" Now that the fight was over, I was free to study the carnage. At least two dozen from each side had fallen, their bodies draped over the rails, over barrels, and curled up on the deck. The young man I'd spoken to earlier, the one I'd stopped to ask for help, was among them. His eyes were open, lifeless, his bloody teeth visible from where I stood.

What a waste.

At that precise moment, something—like an errant patch of sunlight—blinded me. I tried to blink it away, but couldn't. I frowned, raising my arm to shield my eyes. That's when I saw it: a silver light, pulsing on the far side of the foremast, far from everyone else. It flared again, as if urging me to come closer. "Wait here," I told Alucard, who'd turned his attention to the boarding party sailing across the clouds in a much smaller boat.

"Why?"

"Because I said so," I replied, before walking off.

Alucard's eyes narrowed, but he didn't argue. Which was good, because he was starting to get on my last fucking nerve. What I needed, I decided, was to let off some steam. Hell, I hadn't even gotten to try out my bat. Of course, there were other ways to find release…I froze halfway up the stairs, turning to glance back at the Daywalker, who'd crossed portside. Flames licked his collar and played along the slightly curled tips of his hair. Would it burn to kiss him? To run my hands through his hair? I felt the sudden, inexplicable urge to find out.

"As fun as that would be to watch, I wouldn't do that," a voice cautioned from only a few feet away.

I hefted my bat, snarling—prepared to strike—but there was nobody there.

"Over here," the voice called, a silver light poking out from behind a barrel. "Come closer."

I did, but cautiously. The light diffused somewhat as I approached, until at last I could make out the form of another tiny fairy—though she seemed remarkably different from the pixies we'd fought only moments ago. For the most part, there were subtler differences: how she held herself, the cool certainty in her eyes, the playful way she'd styled her hair...

Oh, and she was naked.

"Who are ye?" I asked, keeping my bat at the ready just in case.

"My friends call me Barbie," she replied, her voice high and clear, like a bell. "So you might as well do the same."

I frowned. "What do ye want?"

Barbie grinned. "To help you."

"By keeping me away from Alucard?" I asked, recalling her warning. I felt a sudden surge of anger; no one would be keeping me from anything, ever again. If I wanted him, he was mine.

It was that simple.

"Not exactly. Trust me, I would *love* to sit back and let that happen," Barbie said, licking her lips suggestively. "But you have other things to worry about right now, don't you?"

"I do?" I asked, scowling down at her.

"Why are you here?" Barbie asked, cocking her head to look at me.

"I..." I realized I didn't have an answer to that. "I don't know."

Barbie nodded, then stared pointedly at my wrist. "Does that hurt?"

I glanced down, wondering what the hell she was talking about. That was when I noticed the bracelet. It looked the same as it had before, still glowing with the same intensity—except the skin around it had changed; the flesh was blistered and bruised, even a little bloody where some of the blisters had popped and oozed. Strangely enough, however, I felt nothing. No pain. Of course, once I took a good look at myself, I could see that I should have been feeling a lot more pain than that; I was bleeding from dozens of tiny cuts all over my body. My shirt had been sliced to bits, and my jeans shredded. The handiwork of Tinkerbell and Co., I was guessing. But why didn't I hurt?

"What's wrong with me?" I whispered.

"Would you like my help?" Barbie asked.

I shook my head, my thoughts a jumbled mess. Now that I wasn't fighting, or stopping one, I wasn't sure what to do. How to feel. "I don't even know ye," I replied, feeling slightly dizzy, overwhelmed. "I don't know what I'm doin' here. What's goin' on?"

"Shhh, it's alright. Come on, I'll take you somewhere safe. Somewhere you can find answers," she added.

Answers. That's right. I needed those. I found myself nodding. "Aye, answers."

"Come on then," she said, waving me towards the front of the boat.

"What about Alucard?" I asked, turning slightly to find the vampire.

Barbie appeared in front of my face as if by magic, blocking my line of sight. "He'll be fine. But if you two stay together, you'll either end up screwing him, or killing him. Probably both."

I grinned. I had to admit, both options sounded pleasant...but they shouldn't have. I groaned, pressing my free hand against my scalp. "Jesus Christ, what's wrong with me?"

"Come on, just follow me!" Barbie yelled, taking off. I nodded and did as she suggested, sprinting away from the rest of the crew towards the bow of the ship. I found Barbie sitting on the bowsprit a moment later, kicking her legs. "You ready?"

"For what?" I asked.

Barbie grinned mischievously, then leapt out into the mist, her silver light disappearing from sight. "Jump, I dare you!" she squealed, laughing delightedly.

I was over the rail before I knew it, staring down at nothing but mist—a cloud bank so thick I'd mistaken it for fog. Part of me, the same part of me that wondered why I felt nothing, how I could so easily disregard the value of Alucard's life, screamed at me, warning me not to jump.

But she'd dared me—and I never backed down from a dare.

And so I dove into the clouds.

CHAPTER 17

The wind whipped past so violently I could barely keep my eyes open, tearing at my hair and clothes, nearly yanking the Fairyville Slugger out of my hands. But part of me refused to let it go; it was mine, and anything that was mine, I kept. I pinned the bat to my chest, ignoring the threat of the barbed wire, and tried to enjoy the ride. It wasn't hard; falling through the clouds without so much as a parachute felt like nothing I'd ever experienced before. I felt free, perhaps for the first time in my life. No memories washed over me. No thoughts. Just the pure bliss of being cradled by the sky.

And then—so suddenly it threatened to take my breath away—I broke through the clouds.

Sun as bright as I'd ever known it to be assaulted my eyes. I pinched them shut and turned away, blinking through tears until I felt them adjust to the light. I swung my face around, unable to look away now that I'd seen it—the island. It was fucking beautiful, the foliage a green so vibrant it was like seeing color for the first time, the water a crystal blue so clear I could see through it to the sand below, as if it were little more than a layer of glass. All the landmarks from the storybook were there: Skull Rock, Cannibal Cove, Mermaid's Lagoon, and more. It was stunning and completely, utterly ridiculous.

And it was getting closer.

Fast.

I felt something brush my back, like the tongue of a lover, sliding up my spine. I shivered, my body wracked with pleasure, and—when at last I could focus—the wind no longer felt like it was trying to molest me. In fact, the breeze was light and pleasant. The island grew closer, but incrementally, which meant I was no longer plummeting to my death. In fact, I found I could control how quickly I descended, not to mention my direction, with the slightest thought.

I was flying.

I was fucking *flying*.

"What's so funny?" Barbie asked, fluttering nearby, her silver glow surrounding us both, hugging our bodies. I realized it was her magic keeping us aloft, similar to how Tinkerbell's pixies had aided Tiger Lily's braves.

I shook my head as I considered Barbie's question. How could I begin to explain what I was feeling? I was flying over an island that shouldn't exist, defying gravity and logic at the same time...I'd never been happier in my life. I whooped and dove, turning somersaults in the air as I headed towards the island, eager to run and jump and taste and feel. Soon, Barbie's laughter joined my own.

"Come on! It's time you met the Lost People," she called a moment later, angling us towards a landmark I hadn't recognized—a towering medieval fort past Mermaid Lagoon on the island's far side. I zoomed after her, content to let her lead. So long as she let me fly by her side, I'd follow her anywhere.

Both the island and the fort—positioned on top of a flat mound the size of a soccer pitch—were much larger than I'd imagined; it took us considerably longer to get there than I would have thought. Up close, it was possible to make out the individual logs, so wide and thick they rivaled California redwoods, that had been stacked atop one another to create the massive, imposing walls. As we neared, I spotted a lookout in the closest tower, sighting down a long, cylindrical spyglass.

We'd been spotted.

"Don't worry," Barbie said, "they know not to shoot us down."

I grinned, not worried in the slightest. If they fired at me, I'd simply fly down and kill them. I swung my bat free, letting it dangle behind me as we soared over the walls. We angled our descent slightly, headed for the rear of the fort, where the majority of the dwellings had been erected—teepees formed of wood as opposed to animal skins, the timbers layered over one another to curve inward, secured at the top by thick rope. The whole place looked like a pyromaniac's wet dream.

Too bad Alucard wasn't here.

We could have had some fun.

Barbie landed first, balancing gracefully on the tip of a fence post. I followed, landing as delicately as I could manage; I ended up skidding forward on one knee, using my bat to prop myself up. I grinned, still high from the experience of flying. The instant I stood, however, everything changed. The bright, beautiful sun dimmed. The green of the trees faded.

And I hurt. I hurt a lot.

I fell to my knees, clutching my wrist. It ached and burned so badly it was all I could do not to remove the bracelet, to tear it off even if it cost me my hand. I whimpered, then screamed in pain, every movement bringing tears to my eyes, the lacerations on my body lighting up sequentially with each new muscle spasm. I scanned until I could see Barbie, who remained on the fence post, looking concerned...but not the least bit surprised.

I wanted to ask what was happening, but I was already falling. I dropped my bat, collapsed onto one side, and lay there until—mercifully—the pain receded.

But then so did the world.

*

*J*came to on a cot, my arm slung across a man's lap, paralyzed. I tried to sit up, to turn my head and draw away, but I couldn't so much as twitch a muscle. The air was bitter, acrid, and swelteringly hot. I started to panic, making small, whimpering noises in the back of my throat. I couldn't even speak.

But I could think.

I mean really *think*. I knew who I was—Quinn MacKenna, a black magic arms dealer from Boston. I even knew why I'd come to Fae; I'd hoped to find answers—trying to solve the mystery of who, or what, I was. I knew other things, too. Like the fact that I decidedly was not interested in killing a certain Southern vampire, and only moderately inclined to yank him into my bed. I liked watching cult classics, the occasional pun, and the familiar burn of a good glass of whiskey going down.

I knew I was not, however, a homicidal maniac, willing to kill anything that stood in my way.

Although, up until this moment, I knew I had been.

"I am sorry about the drug's effects, but you were in so much pain you were thrashing in your sleep," the man said, his face outside my field of vision. I watched as he dabbed his fingers into a worn, wooden bowl and applied its contents liberally to my wrist. The unguent was thick and red, like bloody pulp. He smeared it over my blistered flesh. "This salve was made from the heartwood of a Nevernever tree. We used to apply it often as boys to heal our wounds, during our war with Hook." He retrieved some more and began dabbing it across my other cuts, his fingers long and tapered—perfect for a musician. He ran one of those clever digits along my jaw, turning my head so I could look up at him. "Tinkerbell and her pixies sure did a number on you. They must have grown quite savage since I last saw them…or perhaps they were always like that, and I simply didn't realize it."

The man was about my age, but had the eyes of an immortal, haunted by a past his body couldn't contain. Aside from his eyes, however, everything else about him screamed youthful exuberance; he had tight, curly blonde hair and bow-shaped lips, a pointed chin, and the body of a dancer, lithe and athletic. He wore a thick, white cotton shirt and tan breeches.

"Who…" I asked, the single word as much as I could articulate.

The man smiled. "Don't worry, the effects will wear off soon. I'm Peter."

My eyes widened as the pieces fell into place. Neverland. The Lost People. "Pan…"

His smile dipped, and he shrugged. "Once, maybe. But it's just Peter, now."

But, when had Peter Pan become a full-grown man? What had happened to the Lost Boys? My head ached from trying to figure it all out, and my throat felt dry. "How…"

Peter chuckled. "You know, you're very inquisitive for someone who can barely talk. How…" he trailed off, repeating my vague question with an amused glint in his eyes. "How did you get here? Barbie brought you. She's one of the renegade sprites who came here looking for sanctuary, a deserter from King Oberon's army, and a friend to the Lost People. How did she know to bring you here? Your guess is as good as mine. I'm assuming she saw your wounds and realized you wouldn't last long, running around with Hook and his men. Your wild side had almost taken you over completely. Mortals from the human realm typically don't survive very long here for that very reason. Too reckless with their bodies, ignoring their limitations."

"How...does the water taste around here?" I asked, finishing my original question, my words only a little garbled.

"Oh...good, actually, although I have no comparison for it." Peter rose and fetched another bowl, this one with a ladle, and brought it over. He spooned a little water into my parched mouth, carefully. It tasted heavenly —so much so that I didn't even care some of it had spilled down the side of my face. Peter snatched up a bit of cloth and cleaned me up.

"Wild side...explain," I said, finding it much easier to speak now that my throat was no longer an Apocalyptic wasteland. For some reason, the thought reminded me of Alucard, who I vaguely remembered leaving behind. I cursed, inwardly—God only knew what that crazy bastard was going to do once he found out I was gone.

A silver light shot in as Peter prepared his reply, and suddenly I had a pair of very small—well, relatively small—breasts hovering above my eyes. I pinched them shut, unable to do much else since I couldn't exactly look away.

"Is she alright? She looks like she's still in pain," Barbie said.

"I think she's a little uncomfortable with your...assets, so close to her face," Peter said.

"Oh, right. Humans," Barbie said, clearly amused. The silver light receded, and I opened my eyes to find her sitting on Peter's shoulder.

"She wants to know about wild sides," Peter said, sounding reticent.

"So tell her!"

Peter sighed. "It's what happens when you come across into Fae. For some of us, especially the original Lost Boys, it came as natural as breathing. We were all raised here, although I was the first. The pixies took me in. They showed me how to fly, how to fight. Soon, the other boys came. It seemed like all the mortal realm's missing boys ended up here. I formed us into a tribe, hoping to give everyone a family...but we were a tribe of boys who felt no pain. Can you imagine?" He chuckled, but his voice held a note of sadness. "By the time Hook and his men came, few still remembered their homes or their lives from before. Taking on the Jolly Roger became just another game. That's all. And when Tiger Lily and her fellow Fae made contact, we simply added them to the mix. And—all the while—we were dying by the dozens. So many boys. So many sailors. So many pixies and Fae warriors. It was the grandest, deadliest game...and none of us felt like losers."

"What happened?" I asked, voicing the question that had been plaguing me ever since Ryan told me we were on the Jolly Roger, ever since I saw the years written across Hook's face. "What changed?"

"Time came to Neverland," Peter said. He rose and stepped out of view. Barbie remained in place, hovering, watching the man with curiosity. "A couple and a little boy arrived in Neverland. We'd never seen a man or woman like them before. Not together. We knew nothing of romance, or love. Nothing of parents. And the boy...we'd never seen anything like him, either. He was human, and yet so much more. He played with us, but he could do things no child should have been able to do—we showed him how to fly, and he showed us how to call the clouds. We taught him to fight, and he created swords out of shadows."

"The Manling born in Fae," Barbie said, her chest puffed up with pride. "Nate Temple."

I jerked a little in surprise, ears ringing as if I'd been cuffed upside the head. Nate...*Temple*? What in the actual fuck?!

Peter grunted. "That wasn't his name, then. We only knew him as Wylde." Peter laughed. "And boy was he that. But that's another story altogether. To fully answer your question, I think it would be best to *show* you." He came back into view holding my bat. "This is a nasty weapon. Cruel." He met my eyes with a disappointed look on his face, then tilted the bat and pressed its thick edge into the ground. "But a fairly useful cane. Can you walk?"

I frowned, then realized I did have *some* feeling in my legs. In fact, I could turn my head if I concentrated really hard. I struggled, but—after perhaps a solid minute—eventually sat up, my skin on fire. My wounds ached...but they weren't debilitating. My wrist, however, looked awful; the thick red paste had crusted over, and it looked like I'd delivered a baby one-handed.

I stared down at the bangle, wondering what had set it off this time. It'd heated up twice in the past—both instances resulting in time spooling backwards. But that had only been for an instant, nowhere near long enough to do this kind of damage—judging by the state of the wound, the bracelet must have been burning ever since I entered Fae. I held up my arm, trying to examine the bracelet, to see if it was dormant or still active, held at bay by the paste.

"It was warning you," Barbie said, flying in circles around my arm. "Trying to tell you to leave. That's what drew me to you. But don't worry, it won't hurt you here. Not in the Land of the Lost."

I frowned, sincerely hoping Barbie wasn't suggesting we were in an alternate dimension full of dinosaurs, proto-humans, and lizard people prepared to capture and kill us at any given moment. Neverland was hard enough to believe in as it was, and I had Peter-fucking-Pan standing not five feet from me. I swung my legs around and tested my weight, then took the bat from Peter, using it to keep myself from falling down face first. He was right; as a cane, it functioned pretty well.

"Come with me," he said.

Together, we left the hut, wandering out into the fort. A few men and women busied themselves here and there, not the least bit concerned to find an ichor-covered redhead in their midst.

"Women?" I blurted, too thrown to ask a real question.

"Sailors, mostly," Peter explained. "We took in anyone who didn't feel like joining up with Hook and his crew."

Oh, right. There *were* female sailors, after all.

Hell, I was somewhat sure Ireland had its own pirate queen, back in the Elizabethan era.

It turned out they hadn't taken me far from where I'd landed; I could make out the fencepost Barbie had settled on in the distance. Peter began walking, slowly, allowing me to keep pace, but not offering any help. I appreciated it. I'd always hated feeling weak, and having some strange man doting on me every second would have only made me feel worse.

"Where are we goin'?" I asked, a little concerned that I wouldn't be able to keep up, should Peter have something crazy in mind.

"To look at a tree," Peter replied, not bothering to turn around.

"It's a cool tree," Barbie said, without a hint of irony.

I sighed in relief. The truth was I'd come all the way to Fae, and so far, I didn't have much to show for it aside from a fuck ton of injuries and the faintest memories of bloodlust. Even my brief stint as a superhero—while thrilling—had required a free fall that should have killed me. Frankly, a little sightseeing—even if it was simply to see a tree—sounded damn good. Hell, compared to taking on an army of Fae braves led by Tiger Lily to avoid being detained by Captain James Hook, it seemed downright relaxing. "Lead on," I said, gratefully.

Peter chuckled. "Don't worry, we're nearly there. The tree is on the other side of the wall there," he said, pointing. "You can see the topmost branches of it from here."

I glanced up and realized he was right. Reaching out beyond the top of the fort's rear wall, the branches of a leafless tree loomed, smothered in ropes that dangled and swayed in the breeze. I stopped walking for a moment, marveling at the world above for the first time; high over our heads, the largest rainbow I'd ever seen lay draped across the sky. Each shift in color consisted of a band so thick I had to physically move my head to look at it, craning my neck to get from red to violet and back again.

It was breathtaking.

And then a section of it shattered in a crystalline explosion, and I jolted in horror, shock, and disbelief. I rubbed at my eyes, wondering if I was hallucinating. An entire section of the rainbow was gone.

In the gap of revealed sky, a wild, black horse—with wings seemingly made of pure shadowy smoke—galloped through the air. Its mane and tail consisted of long black and red peacock feathers, and a barbed, gnarled horn sprouted from its forehead. The sun glinted off silver hooves, and as it turned for another pass, fiery holes flashed where its eyes should have been. Then it took off for another brutal, physics-defying charge.

This time, shards fell from the sky as another crystalline explosion rang out when it struck, pieces like giant stained-glass window shards raining down and burying themselves in the distance, probably somewhere out to sea.

The creature neighed as it made one final pass, destroying the entire rainbow with the force of its assault. What little remained of the rainbow collapsed inwards on itself like a broken bridge, leaving nothing behind but a clear blue sky.

I realized I had been holding my breath when Peter let out a sigh from beside me. "That's the third time this month," he murmured.

"What the hell is that t'ing?" I asked with a shudder.

"Grimm," Barbie said, sounding highly amused. "Nate's horse. Hunts rainbows."

Seriously? How come everyone *but* me got a dope-ass ride?

I turned to eye the sprite. "Literally nothin' out of your mouth just now made any fuckin' sense, I hope ye know that."

Barbie giggled. "You two would probably get along. He has a potty mouth, too."

Peter tapped my shoulder. "Let's go, before it gets dark."

I glanced up at the sky, my hands clammy. I'd been so busy I'd lost track of time. What fresh horrors were out there, I wondered, lurking, waiting for the sun to go down so they could gobble us up? I glanced back down, realized they'd gone ahead without me, and rushed to catch up to Peter Pan and his stark-naked sprite companion—the three of us headed towards an improbably large tree covered in nooses, ignoring the exultant whinnies of Satan's Steed.

Basically, there was nothing else to see here, folks.

Nothing at all.

CHAPTER 18

*I*t wasn't until we stood directly in front of the ridiculously tall wall that I realized there was no gate on this side of the fort. In fact, looking around, I realized there were no gates at all—no exit signs either. In essence, a fire marshal would take one look at this place and have a fucking stroke.

"And how d'ye lot come and go?" I asked, cocking an eyebrow as I indicated the lack of egress.

Peter rested a hand against the nearest log, running his palm over the rough, sun-bleached wood. "At first, I wasn't sure about creating a true settlement. Walls were something adults put up, after all. But eventually I understood the necessity. Once we began to age, you see, it became harder to differentiate who was one of us and who wasn't. Hook began sending his youngest in as spies, claiming to be Lost Boys who'd run away from home. The game got complicated after that, the lines blurred. Over time, a few of the Lost ran off to become pirates, and a few of his pirates stayed behind to become Lost." Peter smiled. "That was the beginning of the end, really."

Barbie danced through the air to land on my shoulder. "You ready, Quinn?" she asked.

"Ready for what?" I replied, idly wondering when Barbie had caught my name. When Alucard and I had been talking, perhaps? Or had she been spying on me longer than that? I shook the thought away. So far, she and

Peter had done nothing but help me; the least I could do was give them the benefit of the doubt.

For now.

"For this," the sprite said, giggling. A silver aura enveloped me, and I levitated off the ground, the aches and pains of my wounds receding now that gravity was no longer tugging on them. I felt weightless, like I was floating beneath the waves. Unfortunately, the change in my atomic makeup didn't come with the sense of euphoria I'd felt earlier—it came with panic. I wobbled and spun slowly in the air, unable to control my body or my trajectory; I drifted like a damned bubble in the wind, with about as much say in the matter.

Eventually, I felt Peter's arm link in mine, and I desperately latched onto him like a drowning woman clutching a life preserver. He chuckled. "The walls aren't really walls, you see," Peter continued. "They're more like hurdles. Even the smallest of the Lost People can fly over them without trouble. Many of our children fly before they can crawl." He righted us and began towing me upwards.

Barbie was still giggling.

Punk ass sprite.

"So they're like a test, then?" I asked, trying to distract myself from the eerie sensation of floating through the air.

"More or less," Peter replied. "As I said, some of our boys switched sides. The walls weren't perfect. But you can't fly unless you've embraced your wild side, fully, which kept out most. Men like Hook—too old, too set in his ways. Unwilling or unable to change."

That made sense; I certainly couldn't see a man as rigid and intense as Hook soaring through the air with a smile on his face. Of course, for a man who rejected change—as Peter suggested—Hook had recently signed up for a relatively extreme one. "I can see that," I replied, "although I t'ink that may no longer be the case." I followed that up with a deep, calming breath, trying my best not to pinch my eyes shut until the ride was over. Where had the joy gone, I wondered? Before, I'd felt like a fucking eagle, strafing through the skies like a jet fighter—now I felt like a baby bird who'd fallen out of the nest.

"What do you mean?" Peter asked as we passed over the wall. He shifted, and the ground came up to meet us, slowly. Below, a flat, level path lined with multi-colored stones waited, leading all the way to the tree.

"I mean Hook's leavin' Neverland," I replied, relieved to find the ground so close.

Peter froze, halting our flight completely. My feet dangled only about ten feet from the trail below—so close, and yet so far. I swung around, prepared to give Peter a tongue lashing, but quickly realized there would be no point.

Because it wasn't Peter's face I saw.

Instead, he sported the face of a mischievous child, like a mask poking out from beneath the face of the man I'd so recently met, his once-tired, immortal eyes twinkling, his bow-shaped mouth cocked in a defiant smirk. Then, with an abruptness that made me feel like I'd dreamt the whole thing, the mask was gone. Peter met my gaze, and we continued towards the ground. "I had no idea he planned to leave," Peter admitted, as if nothing had happened.

"He's gotten old, Peter," Barbie said, trying to comfort the man. "He's lost friends. Not to a battle with the Lost Boys or Tiger Lily, but to old age. Your truce saved many lives, but you took from him what he valued most."

Peter grunted. "His war." He was silent for a moment, thinking. "Yes, I see your point."

"Well, I wouldn't worry. He found another war," I said, hoping to improve Peter's mood. Barbie's silver glow winked out at that precise instant, and I nearly fell as my body acclimated to its own weight. Was I really that damned heavy? I needed to do more cardio, I decided. Luckily, Peter kept his arm linked in mine until I was able to stand on my own.

Not his first rodeo, I gathered.

"Who's he fighting now?" Peter asked, stepping away. "Have the Queens begun another war?"

I shook my head, but Barbie responded before I could. "They're working together, with King Oberon," she said, a hint of anger leaking out at the mention of Oberon's name.

Peter frowned, his brow furrowed, and beckoned us to follow. "Why would they do that?"

"To fight a common enemy. The Fomorians, led by Balor One-Eye," she replied.

"Never heard of them," Peter remarked, back turned as we neared our destination. The tree, which had seemed impossibly large before, was even doubly so now that we were outside the fort and walking towards it; the base of the trunk stretched so wide that I had to turn my head to see from one side to the other to take the whole thing in. The limbs—swaddled in ropes of various sizes—ascended like bridges, stretching out into the distance until I could barely make out where they ended.

"An old enemy," Barbie replied. "Before your time. Before most."

I frowned, wondering just how much the sprite knew. It'd taken me a hell of a lot of research, not to mention an audience with the Winter Queen and a posthumous exchange with Jack Frost, to gather as much as she'd told Peter. What other answers might she have, if pressed?

"Worth fighting?" Peter asked, interrupting my thoughts, the pitch of his voice slightly higher, his back still turned to us. But I was willing to bet his mask was showing. Or, perhaps, not his mask at all—but the true face of Peter Pan.

"The Lost People would die," Barbie replied, matter-of-factly.

Peter tensed, but he kept walking. "I wouldn't discount us so easily, Barbie."

I was beginning to see that Peter was like a military commander. Always moving, always planning, always scheming, always... leading.

"If the Fomorians find a way into the Fae realm, we may all die," she replied, though she sounded not the least bit concerned. "The Fae were at the height of their power when they last faced the Sea People—and they fought in the human realm, where the Fomorians power was weakest. But even then, if it weren't for our generals, we would never have defeated them."

"Your generals?" I asked, intrigued. This was information I hadn't been able to obtain. Sure, there were plenty of legends out there about the Fomorians defeat, but they were vague—more mythical than factual—not to mention contradictory.

"You humans would probably call them gods," Barbie said. "You mortals have a bad habit of doing that—giving unnecessary titles to things you don't understand. But we knew them as our Lords and Ladies. Long before the Queens fought for dominion over the land, or King Oberon and his Wild Hunt terrorized the world, they ruled over us. Some are out there, still. Others sleep. When the Old Gods walked away for the sake of the ravished human realm, our Lords and Ladies did the same, out of respect."

I continued to crutch along as I processed everything Barbie had said, thrusting my bat into the dirt at a brisk pace to keep up with Peter—who was pensively silent as he moved effortlessly across the well-worn trail.

I'd heard several Fae mention the Old Gods before, specifically in reference to their mass exodus, but this was the first I'd heard of Barbie's Fae Lords and Ladies. In hindsight, though, her version of events made sense. The Irish had gods of their own, after all;

Dez had mentioned them more than once, telling me fantastic, unbelievable stories of the Tuatha de Danaan—the premier protagonists of Celtic mythology, sometimes called gods and goddesses...sometimes not.

Jack Frost, in his final moments, had named several.

"Lugh Silver-Hand," I said, mostly to myself, recalling the names I'd mistaken for the demented ramblings of a serial killer. "Clíodhna. Manannan mac Lir."

Barbie was nodding along, bobbing her head so forcefully it felt like a ball was bouncing on my shoulder. "Very good!" she replied, reaching out to lovingly brush my ear, causing me to shiver. "Of course, you can't forget the one who drove them into the sea," Barbie said, ignoring my protest, "she and her sisters were perhaps the greatest—"

"Father!" a little girl cried, high above our heads. I glanced up in time to see a girl of maybe six or seven dive-bomb off a tree limb, free-falling with a gleeful squeal. I reached out to catch her by instinct, although I had no idea what I hoped to achieve; she was falling far too fast and from too high for me to save her. But then, at the last possible instant, she snatched a nearby rope, used it to swing to another rope, and then another, until at last she landed. She had a bandana tied around her head like a pirate, one eye comically covered by an eye patch, a wooden sword slung in a band about her waist. She was up and on her feet before I could so much as blink, sprinting towards us with her arms outstretched.

Peter dropped to one knee and held his arms out wide, grinning. "Playing pirate again, Wendy?"

The girl giggled as she threw herself into Peter's arms, latching onto him like a damn koala bear, her face buried in his neck. He chuckled and rose with his very own human accessory, turning to me. "Quinn, I'd like you to meet my daughter, Wendy."

Wendy. As in *the* Wendy? I frowned. Surely it couldn't be the girl from the story? The one who'd helped Peter recover his shadow? That had been decades ago, and this little girl was Peter's daughter, not his wife. I shook my head, realizing I was being a jerk; Peter had one eyebrow raised, waiting for me to say hello.

"Aye, it's a pleasure to meet ye, Wendy," I said, as sweetly as I could manage.

Wendy poked her head around to look at me, a scowl on her face. But then her eyes widened in wonder. "Daddy, she has red hair," she whispered.

For some reason, that made Peter laugh. He pried her free and set her back down on the ground. "Sorry about that," he said to me. "Wendy here isn't very good with her manners, yet. Plus, she's got a reason to find your hair color fascinating." As if to prove it, he snatched the bandana off Wendy's head; hot orange locks spilled out onto her shoulders in massive curls.

Wendy glared up at her father. "Give that back, Daddy! It's mine. I won it from James, fair and square."

Peter held it out for her to take, then snatched it back as soon as she reached for it. It quickly became a game—her trying to snag the bit of cloth, while Peter danced out of reach or pulled it away. His grin spread as his daughter fought harder and harder to retrieve her bandana. Finally, after nearly a solid minute of his teasing, Wendy huffed, settled one bare foot into the ground, and lunged...only this time she didn't come back down. She soared upwards, the bandana in hand, whooping for joy as she flew circles around us.

"Pretty sure that's how she stole it from James, too," Peter remarked, wryly.

"James?" I asked, watching as Wendy floated on her back, retying the bandana across her forehead, letting gravity take care of her hair. I had to admit, I was jealous; she made flying look not only easy, but fun. I sighed inwardly, thinking how easy it would be to put my hair back in a ponytail if I could fly upside down.

"My son," Peter replied, interrupting my Faedream, his expression darkening somewhat. He glanced up at the sky, which had already begun to dim. "Right. We should hurry. Even with Barbie's light, it would be hard to show you what's inside the tree once it gets dark."

"*Inside* the tree?" I asked, arching an eyebrow.

"Can I come, Daddy?" Wendy asked, the fierce resentment of a moment before already long forgotten.

"No, I want you to head back to the fort, Wendy. You know you aren't supposed to be out here on your own."

Wendy rolled her eyes. "But no one's come out to play with me in forever," she whined.

Peter sighed. "Go find your mother and let her know we'll have a guest for dinner," he said, choosing to ignore her complaint.

Wendy brightened. "You're coming to dinner?" she asked, rotating to stare at me, her body parallel with the ground.

The gurgle of my empty stomach answered for me, but I decided to clarify just in case. "Aye, that sounds like somethin' I could use."

The little girl whooped once more and shot off, making a beeline for the fort. Peter, meanwhile, was busy shaking his head. "She has so much energy," he said. "But, unfortunately, no one her age to play with."

I frowned. "I thought ye had a whole settlement full of people back there?"

Peter nodded. "We do, but it's only us, now—the original settlers. There are no new Lost Boys or Lost Girls. They stopped coming around the same time we started aging. But come on, it'll all make more sense once you've seen it."

I frowned, not sure I liked the sound of that. Or the tone. But I opted to follow, if only to find the answers to the half-dozen questions I now had, like what had Peter meant when he said Nate's parents brought time to Neverland, and why was I only now hearing of it? And what was this second name nonsense? Wasn't Master Temple and King of St. Louis pretentious enough?

And what had the Temples been doing here in the first place? And—most importantly—where was I supposed to go from here? Obviously, Barbie had saved my life; all I had to do was look at the wounds I'd sustained to know that. And, based on her knowledge of the Fomorians, it was possible she could point me in the right direction. But I'd left Alucard, my guide, behind. Which meant, even if I knew which way to go to find answers, I had no idea how to get there...not to mention the fact that I had exactly zero leads on how I was ever going to get home. I sighed, deciding there was no use fretting about it now. I would worry more after we'd had dinner.

After all, everything was easier to handle on a full stomach.

Together, the three of us approached a door carved into the base of the tree, barely big enough for Peter and me to pass through, even with our backs hunched. I peered at the entrance, marveling at how comically small, nigh unnoticeable, it was—its seams so smooth I would have walked right past it if Peter hadn't shown me exactly where to look. He pressed a hand against a small knot in the trunk, and the door slid open with a low whoosh, like the doors of a supermarket.

"Welcome," Peter said, his voice playful once more, "to the Hangman's Tree."

CHAPTER 19

The Hangman's Tree.

The name brought up old, childhood memories of Dez—her feet propped up on an ottoman—reading beneath the light of a fire, her eyes sparkling as she spoke. The Hangman's Tree, I recalled, was the hollow tree Peter Pan and his Lost Boys had slept in, a perfect hiding place from Hook and his pirate crew. Of course, in my imagination that tree had always looked something like a sycamore—not the great-great ancestor of all trees in existence.

Once inside, both Peter and I were able to stand with little difficulty, having to duck only once or twice as he led me through a long, winding hallway connected to a series of rooms. Although it was dim, light poked in here and there, illuminating the chambers, many of which contained little more than scattered toys covered in dust and cobwebs. As we walked, we passed through a stretch of hallway in which shattered wooden swords hung from the rafters by knotted twine like beaded curtains from the 70s, each with a name carved into the handles—we had to part them slowly as we passed to stop them from swinging back at us.

It took everything I had not to read the names out loud, even knowing what they likely represented.

Fallen boys.

At last, we came to a large living area, of sorts—a tiered space with enough room to fit over a hundred people comfortably. The furniture was a moth-eaten mess, representing at least a dozen different epochs—couches and sofas that would have looked at home on the sets of period films, anything from the incredibly ornate Queen Anne style couches of the early eighteenth century to the retro Egg chairs popularized in the 60s.

To get to the middle of the room, we had to pass under a staircase carved out of the very tree, which wound upwards, spiraling so high that it disappeared from sight long before it actually ended. Ropes, knotted at ten feet increments, fell from the ceiling—or whatever you call the top of a hollowed-out tree. Peter grabbed one of those ropes and tugged, testing its reliability. He held out his hand. "Onwards and upwards," he said, grinning.

I cringed. "Is there no other way to get where we need to go?" I asked, jerking my chin towards the staircase—clearly the preferable option for us landlubbers.

Peter laughed. "If we had three days to wait for you to walk up all those stairs, I'd say sure...but I don't feel like waiting that long. Leave your cane here. We can collect it on the way back."

I muttered obscenities under my breath, but finally tossed my bat onto a particularly goofy-looking couch from the disco era, and took Peter's hand. This time, however, I was surprised to find myself not so much weightless as...lightened. Barbie flew above us, flitting about, keeping her glow to herself.

Peter smiled. "Alright, when I tell you to, grab hold of my ankle, and use the rope to steady yourself. Whatever you do, though, don't let go." He winked, then—before I voiced the dozen or so reasons why none of that sounded even remotely like a good idea—he tossed me up into the air.

Which made no fucking sense.

I hung there, suspended for an instant, wondering how the hell I was supposed to grab the ankle of the man below me, before I felt gravity slowly beginning to reassert its will—slower than I was accustomed to on earth. "Grab hold!" Peter called. I did, snatching at his ankle, realizing he'd already climbed up ahead of me as quick as a squirrel, one hand secure around the rope. Once I had hold of him, the sensation of being lighter returned. He checked to make sure I had a good grip, nodded, and took off towards the top of the tree, using the knots in the rope as handholds to speed up his ascension.

It was...exhilarating. Frightening, to be sure, especially knowing that the instant I let go of his ankle I'd likely plummet to my death, but honestly it felt a lot like agreeing to ride a roller coaster; sure, a gruesome death was a possibility, but the odds were slim so long as I didn't do anything stupid. Let's be honest...I'd done dumber things for cheaper thrills.

Together, Peter and I passed floor after floor of rooms, each containing beds of different shapes and sizes. From what I could tell, it seemed like there had once been dozens—perhaps hundreds—of children here. Far more than Peter's fort could support.

Hence the hanging swords.

At last, we slowed. Peter swung me back and forth with his leg, yelling down at me, "Grab the rope!"

I froze, not wanting to let go at first, but I finally gathered up enough courage to wrap myself around the rope, holding on so tightly I could feel the braiding press into my flesh. "Why couldn't we have just flown?" I asked, my eyes pinched shut to avoid looking down.

"Because then what would be the point of the ropes?" Peter asked, as if my question were somehow ridiculous. Peter shook his ankle loose, then swung around, snatching me by the waist. I yelped as he flew us over to the staircase. "Don't worry, just a few more steps from here," he said, laughing.

I followed the chuckling bastard, staring daggers at his back, doing my best not to look down; it wasn't that I was afraid of heights or anything... simply afraid of falling from them. A perfectly natural fear, if you asked me. "Wait," I said, pausing on the steps, "where's Barbie?"

"I'm in here," Barbie said, from the room up ahead, her voice surprisingly loud. I entered behind Peter, which is all that saved me from falling forward in shock; Barbie had gone life-sized. The sprite lounged on a fur-covered mattress, her nakedness on full display now that she was our height —well, Peter's height, anyway; she was still half-a-foot shorter than me. She crawled over on all fours, suggestively, her smile playful. "Maybe after he's shown you his, I can show you mine," she purred, gazing up at me with a serious set of fuck-me eyes.

I froze like a troll in sunlight.

"Your face!" Barbie finally shrieked, leaning back to clap her hands, cackling like a madwoman. "Peter, did you see her *face?*"

Peter coughed, trying his best not to laugh at my expense, though I could see it was costing him. "It's through there," he said, pointing to a curtain on the far side of the room.

"What is? Where are we?" I asked, pointedly ignoring Barbie, my voice laced with suspicion, cheeks still flushed from embarrassment.

"This is the room Wylde's parents stayed in," Peter explained. "We thought it would be funny to give them the top room, since they couldn't fly." Peter grinned at the memory. "But they didn't complain. I think we sensed it early on...how different they were from us. How disgusted they were by us...well, maybe not us, but our lives, certainly. We were filthy little demons who knew nothing of love, not to mention hygiene. We only knew how to fight. How to die well." He walked to the curtain and ran his fingers along the cotton. "What they did changed everything. After all this time, I'd like to think they meant well. But," he shrugged, "I suppose I'll never really know." Peter pulled the sheet wide.

Waning sunlight poured into the small recess Peter revealed, making the space easier to see. I took a step forward, peering into the gloom, but saw nothing out of the ordinary...if anything in Fae could be considered ordinary. "And what am I lookin' for, exactly?" I asked.

Peter pointed. "It's there," he said, indicating the furthest section of wood.

I frowned, but edged into the space, following Peter's outstretched finger with a sense of trepidation. I had a feeling that whatever I was about to see was either very dangerous, very grotesque, or both.

But what I found was neither.

Inside the wood was a small petri dish—like the kind scientists use when looking through a microscope—held in place so naturally it looked as if the tree had grown around it.

"Do you see it?" Peter whispered reverently.

"Aye, but...what is it?" I asked.

"Look closer," he suggested.

I did, peering at the glass container until, at last, I could make something out. Something so small I had to double check to make sure I hadn't imagined it. A speck, smack dab in the middle of the dish. I turned back. It was the only thing inside, or I would have mistaken it for contamination. "What is that?"

"*Time*," Barbie said, her head propped up in her hands at the edge of the bed, kicking her legs like a pin-up girl. "A single grain of sand, stolen. One tiny piece of a relic taken by Nate's parents."

"When they finally moved on," Peter said, "they left this behind. It took us ages to find it, to realize the Temples were the ones who changed our world as we knew it."

"I still don't understand," I admitted. "What does this t'ing do?"

"The relic they stole," Barbie said, "manipulates time. It was a gift, given to King Oberon, in case catastrophe ever again befell the Fae. Nate's parents pried loose that single grain of sand to bring time to Neverland."

"And, in the process," Peter added, "they pushed back the wild. Fae exists largely outside time, you see. The seasons change, but the Fae age so slowly that they don't even notice it. Fae itself changes even slower than that. Except here. Here, men and women grow old. Children grow up. The path outside marks the boundary that runs from the tree to the fort. If you step off it, or step outside the fort, your wild side will assert itself, once again."

I pressed my back against the wood of the tree, the gravity of what that meant threatening to hold me in place forever. If what Peter was telling me was true, I was safe here—safe to think and plan and reflect—but only here. The instant I left to find my answers, I'd become a slave to that...*other* me, the me who didn't even notice she was bleeding to death.

Basically, I was fucked.

"We should go," Barbie said, frowning. "She looks hungry."

Oh, Christ. In our rush to get up here, I'd forgotten all about the fact that we'd have to go back down. I hung my head, debating seriously for the first time whether I should have come to Fae, at all.

Peter studied my face, perhaps realizing it wasn't hunger written all over it, but resignation. "Don't worry," he said. "Falling down is a lot easier than climbing."

"Aye," I replied, my current mood resonating with the deep philosophical undercurrents of that statement. "It usually is."

"And my wife makes a killer stew," he added.

I nodded, my stomach reasserting itself with an audible gurgle.

Right. Food first. Fret later.

CHAPTER 20

*P*eter Pan's house was one of the larger dwellings within the fort, a teepee divided by thick, theater curtains that cordoned off three bedrooms from a communal living space, all of which Wendy eagerly showed me the instant Peter dropped me off at the door.

The bandana-clad child I had met earlier had changed into a nightgown, and her mother—a soft-spoken woman named Sarah—had done up half her hair in a pigtail by the time I arrived. Coincidentally, that was as far as the process got; Wendy ran around the house pointing out everything remotely interesting with one braid flying. Her older brother, James, busied himself by setting the table. After Wendy tired of showing me around, I was left to study the residence on my own.

It took me a minute, but I eventually realized what it was about the place that was nagging at me: the lack of manmade materials. Everywhere I looked, it seemed, I saw wood. Metal, plastic, and ceramic—which many common household items were made of—were represented, but in wooden form. It was odd, but appealing, in a rustic, backwoods kind-of-way.

"It's the Nevernever trees," James explained, watching me. The boy had dark hair and dark blue eyes, only partially obscured by a pair of glasses that were a little too big for his face. He was perhaps twelve, but acted much older, his expression seemingly incapable of hitting an extreme on either end of the emotional spectrum. "They grow uncommonly fast. If we don't keep cutting them down, they'd take over the whole settlement in a month. It's like the land wants to kick us out. Father says that isn't true, but I think he's wrong."

"Now, now, James," Sarah—clad in a green dress, her skin darkly tanned, with deep, honey brown eyes—said, patting his head as she headed for the kitchen. Once behind the counter, she began field-dressing a rabbit, peeling and tearing with savage efficiency without so much as a downward glance —her gentle attention focused on her son. "Quinn is our guest. Let's try not to start a fight with your father while she's here, alright?"

James nodded, then fixed his hair where she'd touched it, refusing to look at any of us until it was properly coiffed. "Alright, mother."

"Quinn!" Wendy called. "Come look at my dollies!"

Sarah gave me that sad, what-can-you-do smile that all parents end up giving their adult friends, at one point or another. Of course, I never much cared for that look, especially because I found the answer painfully obvious...

Don't have kids.

But, for a rugrat, I had to admit Wendy wasn't terrible; she was loud and demanding, but easy to please and hard to upset for longer than a few minutes at a time. James, by contrast, struck me as the moody type I'd hate to babysit—irritable and too smart to buy half the fabricated answers the adults parceled out.

Thirty minutes later or so, with the sun having only just fallen, Peter ducked through the open doorway with an armful of lumber. "It can get chilly at night," he explained, catching my curious expression. I scanned for Barbie, but she wasn't there, tiny or otherwise. I shrugged, figuring she was likely off doing whatever—or whoever—naked sprites did once the sun fell.

Peter dumped the logs in the corner, wiped his hands off on his pants, and sauntered over to Wendy and me. He hesitated, staring down at the expansive collection of dolls and stuffed animals, all of which I was now on a first name basis with. One, a teddy bear missing an eye that Wendy had dubbed Teddy Darling, seemed to snag his attention longer than the others. I noticed a haunted look in his eyes, but it was gone quickly.

"Peter, can you get the children washed up? Dinner's almost ready," Sarah called.

Peter swung away with an impish grin on his face. "Come on Wendy, let's get your brother." He began to creep forward, *Pink Panther* style, towards the curtain separating James' bedroom. Wendy followed, mimicking her father's prancing gait. It was adorable, and yet, at the same time, incredibly creepy; neither made any noise as they approached.

I meant that literally.

James, probably having heard his mother yell, swept out from his bedroom and headed straight for the wash basin, ignoring his father and sister completely. Peter spun slowly on his heel, staring at his son with comically wide eyes, but eventually gave up altogether when it was obvious James was in no mood for games—practically deflating as he assumed a normal posture. Wendy did the same, folding her arms across her chest.

"James, you're no fun," she huffed.

"Yeah, James," Peter said, now mimicking his daughter, arms folded across his chest, openly pouting.

James didn't seem remotely bothered by the criticism. He finished washing his hands, wiped them clean on a bit of cloth, and headed for the kitchen. "I'll help mother bring out the food," he said.

"I want to help, too!" Wendy said, chasing after her older brother.

Peter sighed as I came alongside, his arms falling in resignation. "One day I'll get that boy to smile," he said, with a wry grin. "If he ever laughs, I'll probably have to throw a party."

"Aye," I admitted, watching the somber boy as he helped his mother by stirring the stew, ignoring the heated demands of his little sister that he let her help.

"He can't fly, you know," Peter said, sounding tired. "Some days I wonder if that's why he refuses to play. If maybe he feels trapped here."

"He can't fly?" I echoed, arching an eyebrow.

Peter shook his head. "Too much of his father in him, I expect."

My eyes widened, to which Peter could only nod. "Remember when I told you about the pirates who came over to our side, hoping to spy on us?" Peter asked. "Well, Sarah was one of the first. She was older than most of the boys, but small enough that we didn't really notice. Not until she got pregnant, at least." He leveled his eyes at me, the weight of his gaze almost too much to bear. "James is named after his father, you see."

I felt my gut twist a little at the thought. That, or I was hungrier than I knew. James...Peter Pan's adopted son...the son of Captain James Hook.

Jesus *Christ*, what a legacy that poor boy had to carry. I shuddered, despite myself.

Peter nudged me a little, a sardonic smile tugging at his lips. "He doesn't know. Hook, either. Sarah's decision. I'd hoped they might reconnect themselves, one day...but now that he's left Neverland..." Peter shrugged.

"Is it hard, raisin' his son?" I asked, before I could stop myself.

"Of course not," Peter said, sounding surprised. "To me he's just another Lost Boy. He's *my* Lost Boy. I love him, just as I love Wendy."

I frowned. "And who is Wendy named after, then?" I asked, wondering if my earlier guess had been the right one.

A shadow passed across Peter's face. "A girl I knew, a long time ago. I expect she's dead, now. Her and her brothers." He shook himself, and his smile returned; I could see where his daughter got her resilience from. "Anyway, it's time to play the Eating Game. Are you ready?"

"The Eatin' Game?" I replied, dubiously.

"Daddy! Are we going to play? You mean it?" Wendy exclaimed, having overheard her father.

James groaned.

But, before Peter could so much as explain the rules, dinner was put on hold; Barbie rushed in, tearing through the open door like a bat out of hell, her silver glow so bright it caused us all to shield our eyes. "Peter!" she yelled. "There are goblins outside. They've asked for you! And Quinn," she added, glancing over at me, her expression fierce and protective.

Peter's jaw bunched as he glanced towards the door. He swung in a slow circle, studying his family, the people he'd sworn to keep safe, and then settled on me, eyes dancing.

I felt a chill run up my spine at the raw, unfiltered crackle of mayhem rising up from the depths of his soul, peeping through the window of his eyes.

"Let's go see what they want, then," he said, waving at me to follow him. "Wendy, we'll play when we get back. James..." he turned and eyed the boy. "If anything happens, keep them safe."

The boy's spine straightened, and he gave his adopted father a curt nod. "Yes, Dad."

Over his shoulder, Sarah gave Peter a look I couldn't decipher—something between pride and caution. "Be safe," she said.

Peter winked. "Always."

I hobbled after the man with my barbwire-wrapped, Fairyville Slugger in tow, fully anticipating a fight.

Or maybe I just wanted one.

CHAPTER 21

The moon—hanging so low in the sky I felt like I could reach out and prick my finger on its crescent edge—cast enough light that I could easily make out the goblin militia camped out in front of the fort by the main tower.

Ugly little fuckers, goblins. Green-skinned and grey-haired, they were essentially the Fae equivalent of pugs—their eyes bulging out at odd angles, breath struggling to find its way out, despite their cavernous nostrils and gap-toothed mouths. Still, for goblins, these bastards looked relatively well outfit-ted; they had matching crimson uniforms reminiscent of the Roman legions.

Together, Peter and I looked down on them from the nearest tower. After a few moments of study, Peter donned a thick, brown leather trench coat, strapped a wooden sword around his waist, and stepped out in full view, looking nothing like the mild-mannered family man I'd come to know; that arrogant smirk tugged at the corner of his lip.

This, I realized, was Peter Pan in his element.

A godling of war.

"So," he called out, his voice sounding ten years younger, "I hear you have something you want to say to me. I'm all ears."

A beautiful Faeling stepped out from between the goblins, standing much taller than his hideous companions, his hair loose and falling around his shoulders, obscuring his pointed ears. "We've come with a request from King Oberon," Ryan called out. "He asks that you hand over Quinn MacKenna."

Barbie, sitting on my shoulder, muttered a few choice words in a language I'd never heard before. She hopped off to stare up at me. "What would King Oberon want with you?" she asked.

I shook my head. I honestly had no idea. I'd never met the King of the Goblins before. Hell, until recently I hadn't even known he existed. My best guess was Ryan had something to do with it; who else would know to tell King Oberon anything about me?

Peter, pausing long enough to note my baffled expression, returned his attention to the Faeling below. "And if she doesn't want to go with you?" he asked.

Ryan frowned, then snapped his fingers. Two goblins, larger than the rest, came forward, carrying a man between them. At first, I didn't recognize him; his clothes were ragged and torn, his hair wild and unkempt. But, the moment he looked up, I knew exactly who he was, despite the gag tied around his mouth.

Alucard.

"Ye Faelin' bastard!" I yelled, stepping into the moonlight, pointing directly at Ryan. "Ye let him go right now, Ryan O'Rye, or I'll come down and shatter every bone in your body until the only woman who'll touch ye is a blind, ugly wench!"

Peter's eyes widened at my outburst. He leaned over, whispering, "Is this how you are all the time? Or are you feeling a little...wild?"

I huffed, but glanced down at my bracelet to be sure. Nope, this was all me. I gave Peter a flat, level look in response.

He made a placating gesture with his hands. "Alright then, thought I'd check, that's all."

"Your vampire volunteered," Ryan called up at me. "He said we could restrain him if we promised to find you. He was concerned. A little distraught, even. We saw you throw yourself from the ship, and thought you'd jumped to your death, until one of the sailors said they'd seen you talking to a sprite beforehand," he snarled, staring pointedly at Barbie, his eyes narrowed to slits. I'd never seen Ryan look so...menacing. For some reason that—more than anything—bothered me.

"Well, now you've found me. And I'm safe and sound. So let him go," I demanded.

"That wasn't the deal," Ryan replied. "King Oberon wants to speak to both of you."

"What does King Oberon want with her?" Peter asked, resting one hand on the hilt of his sword, which—I was pretty sure—had begun to wrap itself around his fist, as if the damn thing was alive, somehow.

"That's none of your concern," Ryan snapped.

Peter's eyes flashed, and that arrogant smile returned in full force. "I'd be careful, little Fae." He raised his hand, and four bowmen I hadn't even noticed sprung up, floating in mid-air, their arrows pointed straight at Ryan.

Ryan faked a yawn. "Please. If you fire," he said, "these goblins will storm this place and leave behind nothing but ash and bones." He leaned forward a bit, anticipatory, as if hoping Peter would call his bluff.

"On the contrary. They will all die," Peter remarked, coolly. "And painfully. All our weapons are made from the Nevernever trees grown in this place. Do you know what that means?"

Ryan's eyes narrowed, but eventually he jerked his head from side to side.

"The Nevernever trees have been drinking in the blood of men, children, and Fae for centuries," Peter explained. "They've gorged themselves for so long that now they can't stop." He leaned forward, grinning down at the Faeling. "They've grown used to the taste of us all, you see. The instant our weapons touch an open wound, they'll suck you dry."

He hunkered down, flashing his teeth. "It's a fun little game we play when we're bored. And my sword has a drinking problem."

A concerned murmur went up from the goblins. Ryan turned to chastise them, but I was too busy processing what Peter's claim meant to pay attention to what the Faeling had to say. My eyes widened in horror as I realized I held one of those weapons. I dropped my bat and danced away from it as if it were a snake. A vampiric baseball bat covered in barbed wire? Jesus H. Christ—I should have died ten times over by now, if that were true.

Barbie hovered in front of my face, appearing as if from thin air. "It's alright, Quinn. Take a deep breath. You need to calm down."

I did, realizing she was right. I was openly panting, and this was no time to panic. Besides, I was clearly fine. Maybe Peter was lying? Trying to scare

Ryan and his goblins off? "That's got to be it," I muttered to myself. "I'm covered in cuts and scrapes, there's no way I'd be alive now if he were tellin' the truth."

Barbie sighed. "Peter and I wondered the same thing. Once I saw you holding that bat on Hook's ship, I knew there was something special about you, even before I noticed the bracelet. I've never seen anyone bleed onto the wood of a Nevernever without being drained. Neither had Peter. In fact, when I told him, he didn't believe me. Not until he saw you himself, using it as a cane."

I glanced over at the man in question, who had the grace to look at least a little guilty. "I'd never have let it do any real damage," he said, "but I had to know. At first, I was hoping it might be the trees, but Barbie and I checked that theory while you were at my house." He drew a knife from his boot and pressed the tip to his thumb. A drop of blood beaded up, welling over his skin. He retrieved my bat and pressed his thumb against its base. Peter hissed, and the wood of the bat reddened. He held the shaft out to me, insisting I take it. I hesitated, but the pain on his face convinced me I had to, or he'd end up passing out. By the time he drew away, his hand was a shade of purple, the bones visible beneath his flesh. "And yet…" he waved his good hand at me, noting the fact that—despite all the minor cuts across my hands —the vampiric bat had no effect on me.

"You know none of us down here has any idea what's going on up there, right?" Ryan called, sounding more than a little put-off to have been ignored for so long.

Peter swung around. "You can't have her," he declared, shaking his bloodless hand as if trying to get feeling to return to it.

"Then we'll take her by force," Ryan replied, sounding eager. The goblins raised their spears as one, while four more men soared into the air to join the bowmen, these holding javelins in gloved hands.

"Will ye morons quit tryin' to see whose dick is bigger, already?" I yelled, too pissed off to be diplomatic about it.

Silence fell as all eyes swiveled to face me.

"Peter," I said, giving the boy who'd grown up my full attention, "they have me friend. I can't leave him behind. And I don't want any of your folk gettin' hurt on me account." I held up a hand before he could argue. "Besides, I need answers. That's why I came here in the first place. King Oberon may have those answers."

"Answers to what?" Barbie asked, landing on Peter's shoulder, looking concerned.

"To who and what I am," I replied, shouldering the bat. "To why I can hold this t'ing, and to what this bracelet means..." I trailed off, hoping Barbie might be able to supply me with at least a few answers; I'd planned to ask her later, but it seemed like later wasn't an option.

It was clear from Barbie's expression, however, that—while she wished she had the answers—she clearly didn't. Peter, meanwhile, looked disheartened. I wasn't sure whether that was because I'd denied him his chance to fight, or because he didn't want to see me go—both reasons I could understand. I reached out to grip his shoulder. "Will it make ye feel better if I promise to come back?" I asked.

Peter smiled, but it was a sad smile. "We all make promises we can't keep," he said. I frowned, wondering if he was thinking about Wendy—the girl he'd left behind, if the stories could be believed. Still, he wasn't wrong. This was a promise I'd be hard pressed to keep if I ended up dead in a Fae ditch somewhere.

"I swear it on me power?" I said, half-jokingly.

At that precise moment, a blast of cool air struck the side of the fort, the force of the gale nearly toppling us off the tower. Ryan and his goblins ducked for cover, coming up only after the blast of wind had stopped. Peter and I exchanged wide-eyed stares. He held out his hand. "I'll be waiting," he replied, his grin wide, no longer the least bit of doubt in his expression.

I shook it, choosing not to mention that the wind was likely a coincidence. Had to be a coincidence.

Whatever made him feel better.

"Alright," I yelled, waving to Ryan. "I'm comin'!" I frowned, then turned to Peter. "Now...how do I get down from here, exactly?" I asked.

A small dinghy lay capsized at the edge of Mermaid Lagoon. It'd taken nearly an hour to find it—longer than it had to, frankly, considering Ryan had insisted on tying me up, gagging me, and having Alucard and me carried. I'd been pissed, at first, but didn't mind it so much once it meant I didn't have to join the goblins marching up and down the shore, looking for their boat. I was still a little sore, though it seemed my wounds had closed thanks to the strange, red healing unguent Peter had liberally painted over all my wounds. Even after giving the order to have me tied up, Ryan had refused to touch my bat, which I found ironic considering he was the one who gave it to me—my guess was that Hook hadn't shared the secret of the Nevernever trees with his Faeling ally. Smart move. Instead, the Faeling had wrapped it in a cloak and handed it to one of the uglier goblins to carry.

The goblins had set Alucard and me down several feet from the edge of the water as soon as we arrived, forced to find their boat and then chase off the school of mermaids who'd apparently absconded with it; the goblins caught them moonbathing, lounging half-naked, their fins drifting lazily in the water, the scales of their lower halves glistening in the moonlight. I watched in fascination as the goblins went running after them, shouting obscenities—like chasing away a flock of pigeons. The whole affair was amusing, or would have been, if I'd been remotely in the mood.

I glanced over at Alucard, but the vampire didn't seem at all interested in exchanging eye contact; he'd averted his eyes from me ever since Barbie had sent me floating down to meet Ryan outside the fort. I wasn't sure if he felt guilty, or was pissed at me for abandoning him, or what—but I also found that I didn't much care. Now that I knew it was there, I could feel my wild side, threatening to take over—to disregard what I wanted in favor of reacting to whatever was happening in the moment. That other me was there in the back of my mind, insisting we break free, take back our bat, and slaughter the whole goblin tribe.

We could steal their boat, and use it to sail away from here, she insisted.

We could find our own adventures.

I bit my lip and concentrated on the dull, throbbing pain of my wrist. For some reason, doing so helped keep my wild side at bay, which I knew was a necessity if I wanted to survive. It wasn't so much that I thought my wild side's plan was flawed—minus the likelihood that I'd die long before I murdered all the goblins who'd been sent to retrieve me—as it was I thought her short-sighted; I'd meant what I said to Peter about King Oberon. If anyone had answers for me, it would be the Faerie King. I just had to hope he'd be willing to give them to me.

Or that I could find a way to take them.

"Get that boat flipped back over," Ryan yelled, imperiously. "And you," he said, pointing at the larger goblins, "get those two in the boat. Hurry it up!"

The goblin on the left swung around, pressing the tip of his spear against Ryan's throat. "I've had about enough of you bossing us around. You don't speak for us, *little Fae*," the goblin said, using Peter's derogatory term from earlier.

"I speak for King Oberon," Ryan replied, eyes narrowed.

"What comes out of your mouth isn't worth our King's shit," the goblin replied. "And I'm done putting up with yours. Get the prisoners in the boat, yourself." The goblin—a remarkably clever one judging by that exchange— lowered his spear and waddled off towards the boat with his companion, leaving Ryan alone with us. The Faeling's hands were balled into fists. He took a deep breath, and I watched the tension leave his body. He then turned and dropped to one knee, yanking our gags free.

"Quinn, please, no yelling," Ryan whispered, his eyes imploring me to stay quiet.

"Do as he says," Alucard added.

I glared at both of them, fully prepared to forego screaming if only I could get close enough to tear out their throats with my teeth. I took a deep breath. The pain in my wrist returned. "Ryan," I whispered, "so help me God if ye don't explain what's goin' on in the next five seconds..."

"Once I found out King Oberon wanted you two," Ryan said, his voice a low whisper, "I made a deal with your vampire friend here."

Alucard nodded, meeting my eyes for the first time since I'd been captured.

"I know King Oberon," Ryan continued. "He'll do everything in his power to recruit Alucard to his cause. But the Winter Queen herself has asked for you, Quinn. King Oberon can't deny her, since they're allies. I'm not even sure he'd want to, except out of spite. I honestly have no idea what's going on, but once you're on that warship, there's nothing I can do. So here's the plan we came up with..."

I blinked rapidly. Wait...Alucard and Ryan were working a con on the goblins? No wonder they were acting so strangely. I bit my tongue as I listened to the Faeling's plan, content to hear the Faeling out while he made a show of hefting us one at a time and carrying us towards the dinghy. By the time he was done, however, I was speechless and sure of only one thing: we were probably going to die.

And my wild side was totally onboard.

CHAPTER 22

$\mathcal{A}$pparently, the first step of their brilliant mutiny was for me to sit on a wet, rickety, water-warped bench.

It was excessively firm and far from ergonomic, and drenched, thanks to its brief soak in the crystal-clear waters of Mermaid Lagoon. Ryan, after laboriously transporting us to the boat, had placed Alucard and me back-to-back to support each other, our hands and feet tied to rungs that had no other discernible purpose than to restrain beings against their will. As the goblins piled into the boat, I had a brief moment to wonder how we could all possibly fit in the relatively tight space, but it turned out to be less of a problem than I'd anticipated; the goblins, weapons and all, huddled together like Tetris pieces, spread out around us like stones around a fire pit. Only Ryan and the two larger goblins occupied the center with us.

"Get us in the air," the grouchy, spear-wielding goblin barked at one of his lackeys, who punched a big, red button I would have pushed myself on principle—had I not been tied up.

The dinghy shuddered, the cough of an engine glugging below us, and suddenly we were airborne. Sleek silver wings shot out from either side, intricately carved, nothing like the metalsmithing I'd seen from goblins; their weapons were typically crude and garish. Jets of fire spewed out from their edges, propelling us forward. A moment later and we shot upwards into the sky, angled every now and again by the spear-wielder, who goblinned the helm by swiveling a mechanism shaped like an old-school window crank.

Once we were well on our way, Ryan cleared his throat. "Hand me the bat," he said, holding out his hand. The goblin carrying my bat exchanged looks with his companions, but—seeing as how he clearly didn't want to hold on to it either—gave it up without complaint. In fact, he practically sighed in relief. Ryan cradled the swaddled weapon, then carefully withdrew the bat from the confines of the cloak to the sound of barbed wire tearing through cloth. Once free, he held it aloft by the base, eyeing it up and down.

"Put that away before you hurt yourself," the helmsgoblin snapped.

In response, Ryan settled the bat across his knees, one hand hovering over the barbed wire. "Do you think it's true, what the Manling said?" he asked absently, studying the wood.

"Who cares?" the helmsgoblin replied, spinning the crank slightly to send us banking left, the island of Neverland far behind us.

"I was on Hook's ship for a long while," Ryan replied. "If the Manling was telling the truth, it means Hook was keeping the properties of this wood a secret from me. And, by extension, from King Oberon."

The helmsgoblin's eyes narrowed, picking up on the implications. "He'd have to answer for that."

"He would," Ryan said, meeting the goblin's gaze, the question on his face apparent.

"Alright, check it, then," the helmsgoblin said, shrugging.

Ryan nodded and—as planned—pressed the tip of his finger against one of the iron barbs. He hissed in pain, his eyes fluttering for a moment before he could even bring himself to press his finger against the wood. By the time he had his bloody digit prepared, he had the attention of every goblin onboard.

Which meant it was time.

I nudged Alucard as hard as I could—our signal—and closed my eyes to preserve my night vision. The vampire burst into flames. Or so it must have seemed to everyone else; I heard goblins curse and scream as they shied away from the monster in their midst. I could feel Alucard rising behind me, the ropes binding his hands and feet likely little more than a smoldering mess at his feet by now.

"Get him secure!" the helmsgoblin snapped, forgetting all about Ryan for the moment. Of course, that had been Ryan's plan all along—misdirection 101. Ryan slumped over, letting the bat fall into the middle of the boat, his skin faded and leathery, as if he'd been drained of every ounce of blood. The goblins at the front of the boat, several of whom had risen to deal with Alucard at the helmsgoblin's command, scrambled away, much as I had not too long ago—clearly not eager to donate their plasma anytime soon.

Selfish goblinses.

Fortunately, that meant Alucard had plenty of room to work with. Following the sudden fiery outburst, the vampire had already lashed out once, kicking two goblins overboard before they could so much as draw their swords. Unfortunately, the other goblins he squared off against were well-trained; they prepared their shields almost immediately, hunkering down with their blades out. Alucard crouched, searching for an opening. The helmsgoblin's large companion—perhaps realizing the lesser goblins might need backup—sneered, rose, and—in a very gutsy move—picked up the vampire bat. Hah. He took a practice swing, testing its weight, and grinned, one tooth poking out from between his gums—a regular Babe Tooth. Then he headed towards our side of the boat.

Well, that had decidedly *not* been part of the plan.

Time to improvise.

Still seated on the bench and attempting to appear meek and frightened, I leaned back as far as I dared, contracted my abs, and drew my legs close. I swiveled, incrementally, lining up my strike. I had one shot before Babe Tooth got close enough to do real damage, and I couldn't afford to miss. I took a deep breath and lashed out, kicking Alucard from behind with every-thing I had, sending him flying over the edge of the boat along with the three goblins he'd been squaring off against.

Their warbled screams faded remarkably quickly.

A meaty fist yanked me around by my hair, and I found myself looking up, teary-eyed, at the goblin with my bat. "Why you do that?" Babe Tooth growled, clearly less intelligent than the helmsgoblin, who was preoccupied with keeping the ship on course.

I mumbled something through the gag around my mouth. The goblin frowned, reached down, and tore the gag off—literally tore, making my cheeks ache. "Son of a faerie whore!" I cursed.

He tugged on my hair again, eyes dilating. "Why kick friend?"

"Because," I snarled, "me friend flies, and ye lot don't."

The goblin's single eyebrow furrowed as he tried to process what I was saying, but it turned out he didn't have to work that hard; Alucard had already found his way back. "Look out!" the helmsgoblin cried, but it was too late. Alucard came swooping in and tackled Babe Tooth by the waist— the impact forcing the goblin to drop my weapon as the vampire carried the big green fucker off into the night sky.

"Get into formation!" the helmsgoblin yelled. "Now!"

The remaining handful of goblins locked their shields together and faced outwards, creating a perimeter, a fence to shield them from the monster outside. Of course, that meant they'd forgotten about yours truly— always a mistake. I cut through the ropes binding my wrists and feet using the boot-knife Ryan had slipped me earlier. The Faeling, still prone on the deck, winked at me through the illusion he'd woven over himself to make it seem as though he'd been sucked dry.

I kicked him as I rose—to maintain the illusion that I hated him. And because there was nothing he could do in retaliation without giving the game away.

Just because we were fighting for our lives didn't mean a girl couldn't get in a little petty payback for a fake abduction.

"The woman's free!" the helmsgoblin screeched, clearly out of his depth now that he had both a renegade vampire *and* what appeared to be a batshit crazy redhead on his hands.

Like a flaming exclamation point for the helmsgoblin's panic, Alucard came blazing through the air from the port side like a comet. His laughter almost drowned out the helmsgoblin's attempt at reestablishing order.

"We're not far from the fleet! Keep him off us!" the helmsgoblin called out, then rose, brandishing his spear, prepared to take a jab at me the instant I moved. "Our orders are to bring you in alive, but I *will* kill you, if I have to," he threatened.

I hefted my bat in response while my wild side whispered sweet nothings into my ear canal. I opened up the buffer I had placed between us and felt my heartrate skyrocket as raw emotion and bloodlust bathed over me.

There was nothing remotely rational to be found within my wild side's seductive coos.

Simply the promise of undiluted mayhem.

And the one thing we agreed on, of course—that there was no way in Hell we were going to end up King Oberon's prisoners.

We are no one's prize, it said. I didn't realize I had echoed the sentiment out loud until I saw the mortified look on the helmsgoblin's face. I smiled wider, agreeing that *dead* sounded a hell of a lot better than *owned*. Which is why I ignored the helmsgoblin's last warning and swung at the nearest wing of our flying Fae-ship...

Bashing it to flying Fae-*shit*.

Suddenly, it was all any of us could do to hang on as the dinghy pitched violently to the right, clearly losing altitude. I wedged my boot in between the bench and the deck as the remaining goblins—off-balanced—flew past, tumbling end over end, the poor helmsgoblin the first to go. Ryan, I noticed, followed my lead, too concerned with actually dying to pretend any longer.

"What the fuck was that?" he yelled.

"Ye heard him, we were close!" I screamed back.

"So you decided to get us all killed instead?!"

I rolled my eyes. "Always such a pessimist," I mumbled. I wormed my way over to the edge of the boat and stared down, trying to make out the landscape below. I felt my jaw drop. Below, far below but getting closer, was a large body of water—as wide and far-reaching as an ocean. "Um, Ryan?" I called.

"What?"

"D'ye know of any bodies of water in these parts that are...well, red?" I asked.

"Did you say *red*?" he called back, a twinge of barely-veiled terror in his tone.

"Aye!"

The Faeling curses that flew out of Ryan's mouth after that were largely unintelligible, and definitely unrepeatable...even for me. At last, he responded. "Is it glowing?"

"Aye."

"Well, I'd love to say it was nice knowing you, but..."

Always so dramatic. "Are ye goin' to tell me where we're landin' or not?" I snapped. I turned my head, hunting the skies for Alucard, but couldn't spot him. I sighed, realizing that would have been too easy; it was far more likely he'd end up looking for us in the wrong place, what with the abrupt change in trajectory.

"We call it the Scarlet Sea," Ryan said, sliding up beside me, his tone fatalistic, at best—like a doomsayer, or a priest delivering one of the less upbeat sermons.

"Why?" I asked. The waters were fast approaching, and I knew we'd have to jump soon if we hoped to survive; the landing alone would kill us, at this speed. Well, me, anyway. For all I knew, Ryan could take a crash landing to the face and walk away without a scratch. It wasn't a theory I'd ever tested.

"Because it's red," he quipped.

"No, ye idgit, why are ye talkin' like we're about to die?" I asked.

"Because," he replied a moment later, "everyone who's ever sailed it supposedly does."

Oh, goodie, my wild side purred.

Challenge accepted.

I woke, floating on my back in a sea of arterial blood. Or, what looked like blood, at least; the liquid holding me aloft felt no different than any other bodies of water I'd been in. Thank God, it wasn't a thick, syrupy goop or anything—not that I would have been surprised in the slightest. The only difference was the color, the waves lapping against me a luminescent shade of cherry. I had a few moments to play back what had happened: dragging Ryan to his feet, tossing him overboard, my flawlessly executed cannonball dive, followed by a brief, painful memory of hitting the liquid surface. Then, nothing. I sighed. I must have misjudged things a bit and hit the water harder than I thought, hard enough to momentarily scramble my brain.

I drifted on my back, content to float until the concept of moving didn't make me want to puke. I felt bad for Lisandra—the wizard scientist I'd promised my corpse to after I finally kicked the proverbial bucket in exchange for a little help rescuing a colleague from a coma. At this rate, my brain was probably little more than an object lesson on the merit of concussion protocols. Hell, I'd been knocked out so many times in the last year, I was lucky I could still remember to brush my teeth at night or how to tie my shoes.

I shook off that dark thought and spun, treading water as I took stock of my surroundings. Water. A whole lot of red water. I scanned the immediate area, looking for remains of the dinghy—something I could grab hold of, at least—but saw nothing. Even my poor Fairyville Slugger had been lost at sea. I sighed. Assuming Ryan had landed far outside my immediate radius—which was likely since I'd waited until the last possible instant to leap from the damaged dinghy—that meant I was out here on my own.

I hated to admit it, but the stupid Faeling had probably been right—unless someone came looking, I'd likely die out here. Still, there were worse ways to go, right? I could explore in the meantime. The thought—so fresh after making peace with the likelihood of a watery grave—struck me as particularly odd. My wild side, again, trying to assert her dominance? Living entirely in the moment, not planning for the future. I snorted. Fine, why not? What would it hurt to let her lead, under the circumstances?

It's not like things could get any worse.

And so I let go, basically watching from the sidelines as I kicked, thrust my head under water, and dove down into the depths of the Scarlet Sea.

CHAPTER 23

I'd always been fascinated by what lurked beneath the water, even as a little girl. I used to watch documentaries of aquatic life as a teenager, my screen saver a stop-motion video of the heavily-trafficked, vibrant coral reefs. During Shark Week, Dez and I would camp out in front of the television, which was the only time she ever bothered watching cable; Dez vehemently decreed that reality television shows would lead to the degradation of our society. Still, none of that—not even the wonderfully diverse, multi-colored marine life found in the Great Barrier Reef—could compare to what my wild side found below the surface of the Scarlet Sea.

Palatial ruins, and dozens of stone edifices and monoliths so large they would take several dives to discern details like shape and scope, poked out from the depths, some rising uncommonly tall, the proportions too vast to be believed secondhand.

I also found the source of the Scarlet Sea's eerie glow—the depths were illuminated by a bright, fiery orb. Crimson light spread out from it like the rays of a tiny sun, making the ruins appear as if they were burning. Sadly, there was no aquatic life to speak of—although part of me was relieved not to have run into the Fae equivalent of a Great White. Still, I quickly found myself drawn to the perilous orb, kicking farther and farther down with each dive, trying to figure out how something so bright could burn under water for so long.

And burn it did.

I dove several times, using the debris below the water to propel myself, realizing the closer I got to the light, the hotter the water became. After my fourth descent, my skin felt fevered, as if I'd sat too long in a jacuzzi. After my seventh, I felt singed and raw. A voice in the back of my head complained, that we needed air, that we should rest for a while, but I simply couldn't do that; I needed to know what was down there, no matter what. And so I took a deep breath, the deepest I could manage, and dove for an eighth time, dolphin-kicking past the gargantuan face of some forgotten god carved on the side of a doorway, then through the outstretched fingers of a stone statue, and, finally, under the lip of the statue's shield—a disc as large as the Space Needle. I could feel my lungs burning, not to mention my flesh, but by the time I cleared the shield—the farthest I'd managed so far—I could finally see the orb for what it was.

I kicked forward with everything I had, fingers splayed, content to black out if I could just touch it...

And felt my hand brush open air.

Suddenly, I surfaced.

I came up gasping for air, my skin steaming. Overhead, a bloody sun hung in a dull ochre sky, its light brilliant and yet only faintly warm. I was still in an ocean, but the water that lapped against me was a dark, familiar shade of blue. A rush of vertigo hit me as I realized I'd passed from one world to another, somehow; the Scarlet Sea somewhere below me—or above me—held in place by some other source of gravity. But how? I shook my head, using the displaced sensation to reassert my true self, to take my mind back from my wild side, concentrating on my wrist—seeking out the pain like a lifeline.

But there was no pain.

I glanced down at my wrist and found nothing but the cool, metal bracelet; the salve Peter had applied had been completely washed away, and yet not a single scar remained. I checked my hands, arms, and shoulders— everywhere that I could see—and realized not only was I no longer covered in wounds, but all my old scars had been scoured clean. I felt baptized. Born again.

And...

I *hated* it.

My scars, no matter how ugly, no matter how conscious I was of them when out in public, were mine—no different than my green eyes, my red hair, or my accent. They were a part of me, an accumulation of life's harsher lessons. Without them, my body felt like the body of a stranger. I cursed, but —before I could bemoan their loss—I realized I needed to figure out where I was; my odds of survival depended on it. I kicked a small circle, exhaustion riding my shoulders like a lead blanket.

My wild side had overdone it, again.

Surprise, surprise.

Fortunately, that's when I spotted my salvation—a city floating like an island, drifting listlessly in the distance. I started swimming before I could even stop to think about it; if I stopped to consider how far away it was, I knew I'd never have the energy to make it. That's the trick with doing the impossible: the less you think about it, the better your chances. And so I swam, dragging my sorry, scarless ass through the water, propelling my body over the gentle waves until the city's spires were fully visible.

After what felt like an eternity—my arms aching, lungs on fire—I heaved myself out of the water and collapsed onto the harsh, unyielding stone surface of the island city. I lay there, unmoving, for so long I honestly felt like I forgot my own name, before finally drifting off, too exhausted to move or think.

*Y*ou know how nice it feels to wake up, comfortable, tucked away beneath the covers with sunlight drifting in lazily through your bedroom window on a day when you have nothing to do? How everything seems right with the world, and your only regret is that not every morning could be like this?

Now, imagine the opposite of that, with your covers on fire, your stack of favorite books smoldering, and your bed a heap of jagged gravel.

Then make it a little worse, somehow.

Do that, and you'll begin to have a smidge of an idea how it felt to be me waking up on the unforgiving ground of an ancient city in the middle of an unfamiliar ocean—a stranger in a strange land.

Of course, it didn't help that my figurative alarm clock was a harsh bright light beaming directly into my eyes, coupled with a vicious two-handed shake. I woke, startled, and scrambled back, scrabbling across the stone, my heart pounding. At first, I had no idea where I was, or even who I was—I felt like my mind had been thrust into someone else's body.

"Ye shouldn't be here," a man said in a menacing tone, his accent eerily similar to my own.

I struggled to rise, adopting a fighting stance, muscle memory taking over—the mechanics of preparing for a fight so ingrained I could, and sometimes did, perform them in my sleep. The instant I found my footing, however, a shadow fell over my face, chasing away the brutal sunlight, and I glanced up to see an obscenely titanic, vaguely familiar statue of a warrior with his hand outstretched, shield at the ready—his pinky toe big enough to sleep on.

Holy shit. Please tell me that statue hadn't woken me up.

"Ye need to leave. Now," a strange man—if man he was—said, drawing my attention back down. He appeared scrawny and feeble, bloody bandages wrapped entirely around his head to conceal his eyes and even his throat. Was he blind? His skin was like worn, leather hide—dark and spread too thin. Wisps of a greying beard dangled from his stubbled chin. Still, for all that, he gave off an ominous presence; his voice was full-throated and deep, his hands uncommonly large.

Of course, I was so relieved to discover it hadn't been the statue jostling me awake that I felt oddly compelled to shake one of them.

"I...I can't," I replied, stretching out my jaw, my tongue tasting odd in my mouth. "I don't even know how I got here..." I frowned, realizing that was true. I searched my memory, trying to mentally retrace my steps, but came up with nothing. Why was I here? And where was here? Someone was searching for me, weren't they? No, that wasn't right. I was searching for someone...

I glanced around, noting the eerily empty streets that led from the base of the statue into the city proper, a city full of spires. "Where is everyone?"

"Gone," the man replied. He reached a hand out to showcase the desolate city. "The Otherworld is no longer traveled freely. Ye bein' here is impossible. But don't ye worry, I'll send ye back where ye belong." The man moved faster than I could think, snatching my arm with a grip like an iron shackle. I didn't even have time to process how a blind man had managed to find my arm, let alone grab it; it was all I could do to struggle to get away, to pry myself free. But, no matter how hard I pulled, he hardly seemed to notice. Instead, he dragged me back towards the water and a vessel I hadn't noticed. It was a sleek, golden craft floating on the water, designed like nothing I'd ever seen before, with neither mast nor motor.

And, of course, the blind brute didn't stumble once, even though the path was uneven and littered with rubble.

"Let me go!" I demanded, lashing out with fists and feet, with no result; I might as well have been hitting driftwood. I snarled and swung a hammer fist down on the man's shoulder from behind, hoping to snap the man's clavicle. He grunted and flung me into the boat.

"Enbarr," he called, "get this one out of me sight!"

I was about to clamber out of his craft and make a break for it when the vessel surged forward, sending me falling back on my ass. I hung on for dear life as the vehicle picked up speed, only then noticing what was powering the damn thing: a damned horse. But like no horse I'd ever seen. The creature was a radiant shade of blue, for one thing, with a white mane that fell across its powerful shoulders like frothing surf, its tail cascading like a waterfall. Oh…and did I mention it was running on fucking water? In essence, while I was completely and totally freaked out and moments away from having a panic attack, I was relieved to learn my wild side and I agreed on at least one thing.

We wanted one.

Unfortunately, before I could so much as reach out and touch it, the water horse swung viciously hard to the left, the change in direction so sudden I went flying into the air, the ocean rising to meet me. Except I didn't hit water, at all. Instead, I passed through a shimmering Gateway and landed on the deck of a ship to the clamor of shocked voices, at least a dozen spears leveled at me, and—what's worse—the ugly mug of one very pissed-off looking goblin I thought I recognized.

"Babe Tooth!" I exclaimed, deliriously happy to see a familiar face after such a bizarre awakening. "Ye made it!"

I'd like to think his subsequent kick to my gut was more out of surprise than spite. Or a sign of goblin affection, perhaps.

But that was probably just wishful thinking.

CHAPTER 24

*T*urned out, the ship I'd landed on was the very ship I'd worked so hard to avoid: the *USS Cyclops*. I wasn't sure what sort of sick, cosmic joke was being played at my expense, but I wasn't a fan. Sadly, no one else seemed remotely interested in hearing me bitch about it; Babe Tooth and his goblin companions, wearing thick leather gloves, slapped me in irons before I could so much as regain my breath from the fucker's cheap shot. Of course, I couldn't blame them; the last time they'd underestimated me, I'd hijacked their boat and sent half their crew flying overboard.

Ah. Good times.

Babe Tooth dragged me to my feet as the rest of the crew returned to business as usual—whatever that was—the brief spectacle of a woman appearing out of thin air clearly not so incredible it warranted a break. Boston should hire the little goblin bastards out, I decided; as hard as they worked, Boston Landing could be built in a week. I was provided an escort of three goblins to lead me towards the rear of the ship, passing a series of workers lugging boxes and tying knots—typical sailor stuff, from what I could tell. Babe Tooth shoved me forward whenever I lagged behind to watch, which was often; my body felt like I'd gone ten rounds with Connor McGregor, and I wasn't exactly eager to get to our destination. Plus side, my body finally felt familiar, and my scars were back. Of course, so was the burning sensation around my wrist. At this point, however, I would have welcomed the sweet release my wild side offered—anything was better than feeling this broken.

Unfortunately, she didn't seem interested in coming out to play.

"Where are we goin'?" I asked, sounding pitiful.

Babe Tooth shoved me once more. "Walk."

"I am walkin', ye dumb brute. Where am I walkin' *to?*"

"Walk," he said, again. Clearly, Babe Tooth didn't understand the question. That, or he was just a dick.

I was leaning towards the latter.

The goblin pushed me again, like a schoolyard bully trying to assert his dominance, and I felt a hot surge of anger well up inside me. I slowed down, intentionally this time. Then, when Babe Tooth reached out to shove me once more, I spun—using the momentum of his thrust to slam my shackled wrists across his face. He ended up face down on the deck, cheeks smoking from contact with the iron, and I ended up with two spears hovering inches from my throat. Honestly—staring down at the small pool of blood nestled against Babe Tooth's hideously scarred cheek—I considered that a win.

"Enough!" someone yelled. I whirled and found Ryan O'Rye running towards me like a Hollywood movie star, fresh from the shower, his long, wet locks glistening in the sunlight. He snatched me by the arm before I could say anything and began dragging me across the deck. "I'll take her from here. She has a lot to answer for!" he insisted, sounding particularly self-assured.

The two goblins glanced down at their unconscious companion, shrugged, and sauntered off as if such things were commonplace. I watched them go, marveling at the Fae's exceptionally shoddy "if I take it, it becomes mine" prisoner transfer policy. Ryan waited until we were out of earshot before he spoke again, talking out of the side of his mouth, his expression stern. "What the fuck are you doing here?"

"Me?" I hissed. "What are *ye* doin' here? And why aren't ye wearin' a pair of these?" I asked, displaying my shackled wrists.

"You left me to die in the middle of the Scarlet Sea!" Ryan replied. "So I sent out a distress signal, and King Oberon's men picked me up. Thankfully, everyone assumed I went overboard with the other goblins, and that your escape was Rondak's fault."

"Rondak?" I asked.

"The ship's pilot," Ryan explained. "The one in charge."

"Oh, the helmsgoblin," I replied, nodding.

"The what?" Ryan jerked to a stop and looked at me. I mean, really looked at me—the way you look at the clinically insane, as if trying to gauge just how close they were to their next psychotic break. I glanced down at myself and frowned, realizing how I must look; covered in fading cuts, half my clothes torn away, my hair wet and matted, face as naked as the day I was born.

"What the hell happened to you?" Ryan asked, finally.

I frowned. "What d'ye mean?"

He shook his head. "I mean, you should be dead. We sent search parties out everywhere. It's been days. Your vampire kept asking about you." He glanced away, guiltily. "I didn't know what to tell him, so I stopped visiting."

"Wait, they have Alucard?" I asked, eyes wide. How the hell had he managed to get captured? Again!

"Yeah, I don't know what kind of benefits package you come with, but you should give that vampire a raise. He turned himself in on the condition we find you...again." Ryan gave me a flat, level look that suggested either Alucard was crazy, I was some sort of succubus, or both.

I sucked my teeth. "That's it, I'm goin' to kill him."

"So," Ryan said, ignoring my threat on Alucard's miserable life, "are you going to tell me where you were?"

I frowned. Where *had* I been? I remembered the Scarlet Sea, and diving among its ruins. Breaking through to the other side *a la* Jim Morrison. The city of spires in the middle of the sea. Being manhandled by that frail but ridiculously strong, blind bastard. The vessel with serious horsepower. I shook my head. "Aye, but we don't have that kind of time. Once ye get me out of these shackles, and get Alucard and I off this Godforsaken boat, I'll tell ye everythin'."

Ryan wouldn't meet my eyes. "I...can't do that, Quinn."

"And why the fuck not?" I asked.

"Because, if you managed to escape this time—and I were the last Fae you were seen with—King Oberon would hunt me down and have me skinned alive for weeks."

"Always so dramatic," I teased, nudging the Faeling.

Ryan arched one of his pristinely manicured eyebrows, glancing up at me meaningfully. "Where do you think Rondak is right now?" He pointed to our feet, then cocked one pointed-ear towards the ground, as if listening. I frowned, but followed suit. It was hard to hear over the general hubbub of the crew at work—goblin curses and shouts combining with the clamor of their boots beating against the deck—but eventually I caught the faintest echoes of what might have been a goblin squealing in agony.

Well, fuck—I guess King Oberon didn't play around. Unfortunately, that only made me more eager to find a way off this warship. "Ryan, I can't get shipped off to the Winter Queen," I said. "I just can't." Ryan opened his mouth to say something, but then a brilliant idea struck me. "What if we got ye back to Peter?" I asked. "He'd offer ye sanctuary, I'm sure. He's already taken in a few deserters, what's one more?"

Ryan glanced around as if making sure no one was paying us any attention, then shoved me into a recess provided by a stack of boxes. Hard. "Mother fucker!" I cursed. "What the—"

The Faeling clamped a hand over my mouth before I could finish, his expression cold and dispassionate, transforming his face from that of a leading man to that of a cruel villain. "What was her name?" he growled, releasing me.

"Ryan, what are ye—" I began.

"Her name!" he snarled. He took a deep breath. "The silver *bitch* you were talking to inside the fort. I want her name."

Why the hell did he want to know Barbie's name? And was that seriously the most important thing going on right now? I briefly considered telling him, if only to diffuse the situation and move on, but decided against it; if Ryan needed information, he'd have to earn it. Besides, no one came at me like that with questions and got away with it—not even an old acquaintance who'd done me a favor. Sadly, I didn't have a chance to tell Ryan as much; Babe Tooth—now Babe No-Tooth, still bleeding from his gums—had found us. He pressed a dagger up against Ryan's belly. Ryan glanced down at the blade, sneering. "I've got questions for this one," he said.

"No. King Oberon. Questions."

"He'll get his turn," Ryan replied.

Babe No-Tooth jabbed Ryan with the dagger, little more than a pinprick, but still. "King Oberon. Now."

Ryan slapped the dagger away and pushed past the goblin. "Fine. She's all yours." He glanced over his shoulder at me, face tight with barely restrained anger. "Enjoy the family reunion," he spat, then marched off.

Family reunion? What the hell was that supposed to mean? And since when did Ryan leave me to the proverbial wolves? Before I could dwell on any of that, however, Babe No-Tooth leveled his dagger at me and jerked his head. I stepped out from between the boxes, pleased to see the goblin had learned his lesson; he insisted I walk, but stayed far out of reach.

Still, even the pleasure of that brief victory quickly faded.

It's hard to stay cheery during a gallows walk, after all.

CHAPTER 25

The throne room aboard the *USS Cyclops* had clearly been erected after the ship found its way to Fae; the stairs leading up to the silver pyramid at the rear of the ship looked to be made of black glass, the structure glinting in the sunlight—reminding me far too much of things like virgin sacrifices and mummification. At the top of the stairs, for the first time, I stopped to consider exactly where we were. I could see a shit ton of ships—the fleet, I gathered—spread out as far as the eye could see. Some vessels like the *Cyclops*, were clearly salvaged from the human realm, while others, like the Jolly Roger, seemed to have been converted ages ago—their designs warped to reflect a wilder, more striking world. I spotted battle-ships and tugboats covered in animal hides, Norse longboats and Greek galleys loaded with catapults. Glancing down at it all, I realized the whole fleet seemed prepared to strike at any moment, which meant a fight was coming.

No, not a fight, I realized—fights were small, localized affairs meant to settle disputes.

This would be a war.

I turned and walked through the gilded throne room doors before my goblin escort could prick me with his dagger—euphemism not intended. Inside the pyramid-like structure, it was surprisingly dim, with a single beam of light illuminating a pathway that led to a rather unassuming, unoccupied throne: a white leather chair from IKEA. I frowned at the choice in décor, but marched dutifully forward. At this point, there was little I could do to prevent being shipped off to the Winter Queen, but the fact that he wanted an audience with me, first, meant I might have a shot at convincing him otherwise. Frankly, I had no idea what the Winter Queen had in store for me, but I knew I wouldn't like it; she didn't strike me as the type to handle rejection well.

And I'd basically left her at the altar the last time we'd met.

Once I was within perhaps a dozen feet of the throne, a white goblin emerged from the shadows—his skin covered in blotches like the spots of a dalmatian. He was tall, taller than Babe No-Tooth even, wearing fine leather hides trimmed in blue fur that offset his startlingly blue eyes. The newcomer ran a hand along the seams of the leather chair, seemingly engrossed in the sensation, before flicking his gaze to the goblin behind me. "Leave us," he commanded, the authority in his voice so obvious that there was no doubt who I was looking at.

King Oberon.

Babe No-Tooth was gone in an instant, the sound of the throne room doors slamming before I could so much as say goodbye. Not that I was inclined to.

I fidgeted with my shackles and glanced around, wondering if Oberon had any bodyguards lurking in the corners, Emperor Palpatine style, or if he was just that confident that I wouldn't find a way to beat him to death with the shackles he'd put me in. Unfortunately, it was impossible to tell. In the furthest corners of the room, the darkness was absolute.

"I really like what you've done with the place," I quipped. "Very *Stargate*."

Oberon pursed his lips. "You know, when the Winter Queen insisted I collect you and send you to her, I had no idea you'd prove to be such a pain in the ass."

I barked a laugh before I could help myself. I shrugged, too exhausted to bother with tact. "Aye, well, maybe next time you'll tell her to go fuck herself and leave me the hell alone."

"I expect I'll have to," Oberon said, surprising me. "Still, you're lucky I got wind of who you really were before I handed you over. I got the feeling she had plans for you."

"Who I really am?" I asked, cocking an eyebrow. He flashed me a knowing grin, as if we were sharing an inside joke, which made no sense.

And yet, I felt myself grinning in response. It suddenly seemed as if we'd known each other for years, the madness dancing behind his eyes all too familiar.

"Don't be coy," Oberon replied. "There's no need."

I frowned. "So ye aren't sendin' me to the Winter Queen?" I asked, still confused, but trying to hide it.

"Of course not. A higher authority intervened on your behalf," he said, teasingly, as if I knew exactly who he was referring to. But I didn't; I had no idea that was even possible. After all, who or what had more authority than a Queen of Fae in this realm? My incredulity must have shown, because Oberon's smile grew wider, his canines poking out. He cocked his head. "Come, Morrigan, there's no need to play games. Drop the act."

A faint buzzing filled my ears, and I stared at him, open-mouthed, literally struck speechless.

CHAPTER 26

A silhouette slipped out of the shadows to my right. "She is not Morrigan," the woman said, her Irish accent as thick and smooth as the black leathers she wore. She had her inky black hair pulled back in a tight ponytail, her skin pale as moonlight, her eyes so dark I could see my own startled face reflected in them. The only bit of color to her was her lips, a red so bright and vibrant it was like they'd been carved from the skin of a fresh apple.

"But, you said—" Oberon began.

"We lied," another woman interjected, seemingly materializing from the light. She wore a pale blue shift to match her eyes—the color of clear skies on a summer day. Her hair was flaxen, her skin sun-kissed and freckled. She had a warm, nurturing smile, but her eyes betrayed something altogether less pleasant, less predictable—like a storm about to break on a cloudless afternoon.

"I don't understand," Oberon growled. "Why would you lie to me?"

"Times change," the dark-haired woman said. "Allegiances shift. Ye were put in power to keep the Queens in check."

"But ye have forsaken your role," the blonde admonished, continuing where the other left off. "By joinin' together with the Queens to stop an enemy, ye have disrupted the balance of this realm."

Oberon's eyes glittered with anger. "I've done as I must. The Tuatha de

Danaan are no longer here to protect the Fae. What would you have us do? Accept our fate as slaves?"

The dark-haired woman's eyes narrowed, and I felt every hair on my body stand up all at once, my pulse spiking as adrenaline rushed through my body, as if being near her were enough to kick my fight-or-flight response into hyperdrive.

I ground my teeth. "Does someone want to tell me what the fuck is goin' on here?" I asked, no longer content to stay silent.

The blonde shifted her attention to me and smiled, gently. "We'll be with ye in a moment, niece."

I felt my heart skip a beat. Niece? What the fuck was she talking about? I opened my mouth to ask that very question when I felt the blonde's energy wash over me. My heartbeat began to slow, the tension in my body fading. I sighed, suddenly content to wait until they wrapped up their little chat. I had all the time in the world, after all. Didn't I?

Wrong, a voice whispered in the back of my head.

I shook off the various sensations warring within me and backed away from the trio, keeping all of them in sight, prepared to lash out should anyone make a move to touch me. I wasn't sure how or why, but the two women were clearly using magic, magic which ignored my field completely. The idea that anyone could fuck with my mood—my mind—sent a shiver up my spine.

"Tell me who ye are," I demanded, though I sensed the ridiculousness of that; I was still shackled, after all, and hardly a threat.

The two women exchanged glances. Oberon, meanwhile, looked tense, as if expecting a fight at any moment. Given the tone of their conversation up to this point, I wasn't surprised; the two women certainly hadn't sounded pleased with the Goblin King.

"I mean it," I said, again, glaring defiantly at them all.

"Well, it's nice to know stubbornness is an inherited trait," the dark-haired woman said, smirking.

"She looks like her ma, too, don't ye t'ink?" the blonde added, studying my face as though it were a painting and she was trying to determine the precise pattern of the brushstrokes.

I fought down the urge to lash out at their mention of my mother—a knee-jerk reaction I'd had ever since grade school. Instead, I took a deep, calming breath. "Seriously," I said, "I wish ye two would stop talkin' gibberish. I've had a long day."

"Oh, *you've* had a long day?" the dark-haired woman asked, eyebrow raised.

"Badb," the blonde chastised. "Don't tease the girl. It's not her fault we're in this mess."

The dark-haired woman, Badb, heaved a sigh. "Fine, ye talk to her, Macha. Morrigan always listened to ye more, anyway."

Macha, the blonde, snorted. "Except when she didn't. Remember the war with the Fir Bolg?"

"Who the fuck are ye?!" I yelled, interrupting the two women, my frustration boiling over completely. My shoulders slumped immediately following my outburst. I was tired. Tired of being in pain. Tired of having to repeat myself. Tired of being ignored.

Tired of fucking Fae.

And it didn't help that there were obvious similarities between us—the blonde's upturned nose and her sister's slightly lopsided smile.

Because that only seemed to indicate that this was not, in fact, some elaborate hoax. That they really were...

My aunts.

I perked up a second later, however, as something rippled in the air—a veritable heat wave. The two women turned to face me at the exact same moment, like marionettes, their gazes flat and unreadable. "We are the sisters," they said, in unison, the timbre of their voices harmonizing, echoing throughout the throne room. Frankly, it reminded me a lot of those little girls holding hands in *The Shining*, and I wasn't remotely okay with it.

"I'm Macha," the blonde said, her voice bright and clear—like the plucked string of a violin. She rested a hand on her chest. "Your mother was me sister."

"And I'm Badb," the dark-haired woman interjected, folding her arms over her chest, her raspy voice like autumn leaves rustling against one another. "Welcome to the family."

I shook my head, scowling, trying to grasp what these crazy bitches were telling me. The names rung a very distant bell. More fairy tales. Badb, Macha, and...Morrigan. The three sisters who, combined, represented *the* Morrigan—a deity and member of the Tuatha de Danaan. Perhaps one of the most powerful members, if the myths were true. Which meant, if what they were saying was true…

At that precise moment, pain—sudden and vicious—tore through my body. My bracelet, no longer content to simply irritate my skin, seared my flesh. I could smell it—the scent of cooked meat. I fell to my knees in pain, but found Macha there, kneeling beside me, peering down at the shackles. She waved a hand over them and they unlatched, falling to the floor with a clang. Macha's eyes went wide as she noticed the source of my distress.

"What is it?" Badb asked.

"Somethin' dangerous," Macha replied, guardedly, her melodic voice strained. She gritted her teeth and reached out, pressing a finger against the white-hot metal. In an instant, the pain was gone, and the bracelet had returned to normal—room temperature at most. Macha pressed her hand against my forehead as if I looked feverish, and I felt her magic wash over me once more.

I jerked back. "Stop it."

Macha sighed, but nodded.

"She always did t'ink she knew better than us," Badb said, staring down at the bracelet.

Macha shot her sister a look, which Badb ignored. "Not the time," Macha said.

Her sister shrugged.

Macha rose, drawing me up with her. I realized she was shorter than me —they both were. And yet, now that I knew to look for it, I could see the physical similarities between us. The slope of their cheeks, the cast of their noses. I frowned. "Are ye tellin' me that the Morrigan is…" I asked, my voice a hushed whisper.

"Was," Badb spat.

"Your ma, aye." Macha replied, glaring at Badb. "Although, technically, your ma was not *the* Morrigan. Morrigan represented one third of our power. She was extremely powerful in her own right, but only together are we truly unstoppable."

"I don't understand." I said, struggling with a whole host of questions, the most pressing of which loomed in my mind so large that I couldn't even begin to answer it on my own. "If she was one of ye, then why did she die?"

Oberon, who I'd completely forgotten about, hissed through his teeth, eyes wide. "Morrigan is dead?" The sisters, however, ignored him entirely.

"We didn't understand how it happened either, at first," Macha replied, meeting my gaze. "When we first began to realize Balor had returned, we sought each other out. Badb and I reunited and then went lookin' for your ma. We hadn't heard from her in a long while, however, and it took time."

"She was always runnin' off doin' t'ings we could never understand," Badb added, looking putout. "D'ye know how annoyin' it is to have a sister who can see into the future, but never explains herself?"

Macha grunted, clearly agreeing with her sister. "Later," she continued, "we learned she'd left our island for the Americas. That she'd given up her immortal form to bear a child. A girl."

"But, why would she do that?" I asked, struck by how ridiculous that sounded. "I mean, is that like a rule or somethin'? That to have a child, ye have to die?"

Macha shook her head, but clearly had no answers to offer.

"She wouldn't tell us why," Badb replied. "As usual."

"Wait, ye talked to her?" I asked. "When? How?"

Macha glowered at her sister, but smiled at me. "We spoke to our sister, aye. But not your ma. There is a fragment of her power out there, locked away in the Otherworld. She's nothin' but a ghost, compared to the original."

Someone who looked like my mother, but wasn't...a ghost, haunting windows. I felt a jolt of recognition. That was who I'd met. The goddess who'd given me the bracelet. The goddess who'd sealed away my power for the second time.

"Why now?" I asked, a sneaking suspicion dawning.

Macha frowned. "What?"

"What is it ye want?" I asked, skirting around her towards the door.

The sisters exchanged looks. "We need ye," Macha said, gently. "We have an obligation to stop Balor and his army, like we did before. But we can't without your ma's power."

That made me hesitate. "But she's dead," I asserted.

"Aye," Badb replied. "But she passed the power on to ye, that much is clear. Or else we would have felt her go."

"But this isn't just about power," Macha added. "It's also about family. It's obvious your ma wanted ye to find us. To join us."

"Oh, and how is it obvious?" I asked, the gnawing suspicion growing. These two had no idea I'd spoken to my mother's ghost—for lack of a better term. That I'd seen them before in my dreams—seen how she'd turned her sisters away, warning me in the process.

Macha smiled. "Well, your accent, for starters."

"Me what?" I asked, utterly thrown.

"Surely ye found it odd that ye talk the way ye do, given where ye were born and raised?" Badb asked.

I nodded, scowling. Of course I'd found it odd—I'd lived my whole life in Boston, getting teased and picked on for talking differently than everyone I knew. Hell, I'd even had to defend it to my teachers, many of whom claimed it was impossible for me not to learn the language of my peers...as if I'd chosen to speak this way. Assholes. "Aye, me accent...but—"

"It's like she wanted ye to find your roots, to return to the Emerald Isle," Macha interjected, eagerly, her own accent rich lilting.

"To find *us*," Badb added.

"To take your rightful place at our sides," Macha finished, with a flourish.

Bullshit. Total and utter bullshit. But at least now I knew for sure; my aunts were full of it. Not about the accent—although that sounded far-fetched at best. But the idea that my mother wanted me to side with them against Balor was blatantly untrue. If she had, she would have sent them to me directly. She would have told them about the bracelet. About my cage.

"I'm afraid I can't help ye," I said, finally.

Macha's eyes narrowed. "And why not?"

I shrugged. "Whatever power ye t'ink I have, I don't." I held my arms wide. "If I did, d'ye t'ink I'd even be here? That I'd let a bunch of filthy goblins take me prisoner?"

Macha frowned, considering that, then held out her hand, eyes closed. A moment later, she gasped, eyes fluttering, her face betraying the anger I'd always suspected was there, lurking beneath the surface.

"What is it?" Badb asked.

"Her power's been sealed away. No wonder we couldn't find her," Macha snarled.

"Sorry to disappoint," I said, grinning. "But I'm guessin' your sister wasn't the least bit interested in me helpin' ye, or she'd have told ye how to unlock the cage *she* created."

The two sisters stared at me, wide-eyed.

"Aye, now ye understand where we stand, ye and I." I glared at them both. "No one uses me. D'ye understand? No one."

"Oberon," Macha snapped, the Goblin King's name falling from her mouth like a meteor striking the earth. Oberon, who'd watched our little reunion with no small amount of interest, perked up, spine straightening like a butler who'd been caught slouching.

He sneered, clearly displeased to be addressed so casually—and at his instinctive bodily reaction to it. "Yes?"

"Escort Quinn to her cell. If she needs time to process, we'll give it to her. In the meantime..." she strode towards me, forcing me to retreat. But suddenly Badb was there, hands firmly on my shoulders, locking me in place with her magic; I began to sweat, feeling feverish. Macha approached with a snake-charmer's smile, leaned in, and planted a kiss on my cheek— her lips so cold they practically burned. "Let's see how long it takes for those walls of yours to come crashin' down," she said, enigmatically.

Badb rested her head in the nook of my shoulder from behind, delivered her own kiss—though this one actually did burn. I jerked away, but she slid closer, whispering in my ear, "Just know, every moment ye delay, Balor gets closer. He'll ravage your city, first. Mortals will call it a storm, but it will be like no storm they could have ever imagined. His army will hit Boston like a tidal wave and drown every last soul until he finds his way into Fae. He wants his eye back, and collateral damage means nothin' to him."

I felt a whisper of a premonition hit my gut; she was telling the truth. And, what's worse, I knew it for a fact. I'd been hearing about it for weeks, after all—the storm of the century, barreling towards the coast. Which meant Balor *was* coming, his hate so vast he'd cultivated a storm so fierce it could wipe away the entire eastern seaboard, his power at the center like the eye of a hurricane.

Ah, irony.

"T'ink about it," Macha said. "If ye want to save your city, ye will join us. Once ye do, ye can take your rightful place among the Fae. Together, we can fix this realm." She glanced over her shoulder at Oberon, whose mouth hung partially open in disbelief.

I frowned. I was a lot of things: morally ambiguous, a heavy drinker, a scrapper...but I wasn't, and never had been, a team player. And I certainly wasn't interested in a maintenance gig of that magnitude. Hell, back when I was a kid, I remember a few of my fellow classmates had insisted on becoming the next President of the United States, and even then, I'd thought they were crazy; who the fuck wanted a job with those kinds of stakes? Whether or not she realized it, of all the things Macha could have offered me, she'd picked the least appealing. "Alright, Your Majesty," I said to Oberon, shrugging Badb off. "Lead the way. I find the company here severely lackin'."

I left the throne room and the lure of power.

And I didn't look back.

CHAPTER 27

*O*beron hurried after me, pumping his little goblin legs to keep up as I descended the stairs. At the bottom, I briefly considered making a run for it—leaping overboard and swimming to freedom—but quickly realized it would be a lost cause; I'd be caught in no time and soaking wet for my trouble. So, instead, I waited for The Goblin King to catch up. Oberon stepped alongside, not the least bit winded, staring out at his fleet with a frown on his face. "Follow me," he said, eventually.

We moved freely across the ship, Oberon's lackeys so committed to their tasks that they barely took notice of their king as we passed by. Either he was known for walking about the ship, I decided, or he'd trained his underlings not to bow and scrape in his presence. Regardless, I appreciated the lack of fanfare; I sure as hell wasn't in the mood to be stared at. Frankly, I wasn't in the mood to do anything but be left alone.

"That was an unwise thing you did back there," Oberon said. "Refusing to cooperate, I mean."

"Aye, well, there's no Quinn in Team," I quipped.

"What?" he asked, glancing back up at me over his shoulder.

"Nevermind," I replied, with a sigh.

The Goblin King's head swiveled back around, and we continued on in silence. At last, we came to a hatch. Oberon reached down and pried it open, lifting the massive steel door with hardly any effort, and proceeded down a ladder into the belly of the warship. "They won't let you say no," he said, the instant I joined him at the bottom. Above our heads, lightbulbs flickered down a narrow corridor.

"I'm not interested in rulin' over anyone, least of all the Fae," I said, realizing I meant it with every fiber of my being.

"It's a thankless job, I'll admit," the Goblin King said, snorting. "But that's not what I meant." He waved me along, and we continued our trek.

"What *did* ye mean, then?" I asked, already fed up with our conversation.

"I meant they won't let you keep a third of their power," Oberon said, almost a full minute later. He halted, forcing me to stop as well. "They put on a show for you. Playing mortal. Macha, the fair Fae Lady, goddess of nature and order. And Badb, the Crow Goddess, avatar of war. What they offered you, however, was not power, but subjugation. They were your mother's right and left hand. But she was the brain. She called the shots, and they resented her for it, even then. Why do you think she left?" He turned to face me, his grin wild and savage beneath the glistering lights. "They will take from you the power they've always wanted, and you will have no way to stop them. That's why your mother kept you from them."

"And how would ye know?" I asked, dubiously.

"Because, she and I were close, once," the Goblin King replied. "You look very much like her, you know. Only taller." He stared up at me, leering. "Tall is good. I like tall."

"And what is it you're tellin' me this for, then?" I asked, scowling. "I don't suppose ye have an alternative in mind?"

Oberon shrugged. "If you joined me, we could save your city. Between your power, and my fleet, we could chase Balor and his army back into the depths from whence he came."

"And when the spray settles," I said, proceeding logically from his perspective, "with me at your side, ye would be able to rule over the Queens, as well." At last it all made sense; I knew why the Winter Queen had been so eager to find me—she must have figured out who and what I was early on. Through Jack, perhaps, or any number of agents she'd hidden within the Chancery. Had I agreed to her terms when last we met, she would have been able to supplant Oberon and her sister, the Summer Queen, to rule over the Fae unopposed.

With me locked away in a block of ice, no doubt.

"I'm no despot," Oberon claimed, raising a bushy eyebrow. "I simply wish to keep the Fae safe. To let them live according to their natures. I provide balance. Is that so wrong?"

I hated to admit it, but that didn't sound terrible. If anything, it sounded like the Goblin King was entitled to rule. But then—although I disagreed with my aunts' plan to "fix" the Fae realm in practice—there was something to be said for checks and balances. The Goblin King's leadership—or lack thereof—could lead the Fae down a dangerous, bloody path.

Of course, all that was a moot point.

Because I wasn't interested in taking anyone's side.

"I'll consider the offer," I replied, choosing diplomacy over honesty.

Oberon's eyes narrowed. "You won't leave this place without choosing," he asserted. "No matter how clever you think you are."

I shrugged. "Aren't ye supposed to be takin' me somewhere?"

The Goblin King spun on his heel. "To the brig, it is."

Ooh, a brig. That was exciting.

I'd never seen a brig before.

The brig was basically a cage, not much bigger than my bedroom, with thick, iron bars. Alucard met me at the gate in his normal form, hands wrapped around the metal so tight they groaned. "Quinn! You're alive!"

"Aye, I'm alive," I replied, glaring at the vampire. "Now, how about ye tell me why the fuck ye let them put ye in a cell?"

"He made a deal with me," Oberon answered for him. "He's my prisoner, to do with as I wish, so long as I keep you safe from harm. He swore on his power."

"Quinn, I—" Alucard began.

I sucker punched him in the gut through the bars, as hard as I could, before he could say anything else. The breath whooshed out of the vampire and he fell to his knees, clearly winded. "That's for bein' a fuckin' gentleman after I told ye not to," I snapped, massaging my knuckles.

I found Oberon looking up at me, eyes wide, when I turned around. He clucked his tongue as he retrieved a set of keys, shaking his head. "I take it back. Maybe it's best you and I don't join forces, after all."

"Why? Afraid I'll beat ye to death on the regular?" I asked, my blood still up.

"No," Oberon replied, "because it's possible you're as crazy as I am." He unlocked the cell before turning towards me, his form shimmering. Suddenly he loomed over me, horns like antlers sprouted from his head, his teeth and nails extending—everything about him immense and imposing. "There can be only one to lead the Wild Hunt, after all," the Goblin King said.

I eyed him as I stepped into the cage, skirting warily by. "Whatever ye say, Highlander."

Alucard snickered.

Oberon slammed the cell door shut, a mere goblin once more, glaring at us both. "Guards will be posted outside at all times. Don't bother trying to escape. There's no Fae here who will harbor you. To do so risks not just my justice, but the wrath of Macha and Badb."

"Bye now," I said, folding my arms over my chest.

The Goblin King spat onto one side of the floor, then walked back the way we'd come.

"And what did you do to piss him off, *cher*?" Alucard asked.

"Refused to hop into bed with him," I quipped.

"What?!" Alucard yelled, suddenly back up against the bars.

"Calm down," I said, placatingly. "It was an expression. I t'ink." I frowned, wondering if what Oberon had suggested included more than a joining of forces; I wasn't always the best at picking up on flirtation. I shuddered, hoping that wasn't the case. "Anyway, as much as I've loved our little Faecation, I t'ink it's time we got the fuck out of here."

"I think you mean *you* need to get the fuck out of here," Alucard amended, hanging his head. "I can't go anywhere."

"Why, because ye swore on your power?" I asked.

Alucard nodded. "As long as he keeps his end of the deal, I'm useless to you." He rapped his knuckles against the metal bars, producing a dull clang. "I couldn't break you out of this if I tried."

"Aye, that was fuckin' moronic of ye," I replied. "But not half as dumb as he was for makin' that the conditions of the deal."

"Why's that?" Alucard asked, glancing back at me.

I opened my mouth to explain, but snapped it shut as the sound of approaching footsteps echoed down the corridor outside. A moment later,

Oberon returned with two mugs of water, presumably for us prisoners. Once out of the hallway, the Goblin King's form wavered and—in an instant —a remarkably handsome Faeling stood in his place.

Ryan, no longer concealed by his glamour, tossed the mugs to the floor. "So?" he asked. "How'd it go with your aunts?"

"Your what?" Alucard asked, raising an eyebrow.

I glared at the Faeling. "I was thirsty," I growled.

Ryan shrugged. "Should've said something sooner. Like, right before I dumped out your water."

I sucked my teeth. "Does this have somethin' to do with why ye were ready to kill me earlier?" I asked.

"He what?!" Alucard said, whirling to face Ryan.

"Please stop talking," Ryan said, flicking his eyes at Alucard, who looked like he was about to have an aneurism.

I settled a hand on the vampire's back, patting it. "He's right," I replied. "Why don't ye have a sit down, ye wee, powerless mongrel?" I jerked my chin towards the corner of the cell and winked. "I'll let ye know if I need someone to jump in front of a sword for me."

Alucard looked a little hurt by my teasing, but I didn't care; the moron deserved a ribbing after risking his life over and over on my behalf. I was sick of knights in shining armor riding in on their high horses, fucking things up—first Jimmy, and now Alucard.

It's like I had a type.

The vampire huffed, but did as I asked, settling against the bars on the far side of the cell.

"Now," I said, giving Ryan the full weight of my attention. "Spill it."

The Faeling crossed his arms over his chest. "First, I want to know how you know her."

"Know who?" I asked.

"The silver sprite," Ryan replied, as if that should have been obvious.

I frowned, remembering Ryan's bizarre fascination with Barbie from earlier. "She found me on Hook's boat. She saved me life. Well, her and Peter."

"Holy shit, that was Peter Pan?" Alucard asked, eyes wide, then winced; the dirty looks Ryan and I gave him were so intense that he had to look away. He mimed zipping his lips and throwing away the key.

"So you never saw her before?" Ryan asked, gauging my reaction.

"No. Why, should I have?"

"I want her name," he replied, ignoring my question.

"And I want to go home," I said, crossing my arms, mimicking the Fael-ing's defiant posture.

"Then I suggest you take the offers you've been given," Ryan said, sneering in contempt. "Any one of them would see you back home in a heartbeat. Of course, we both know you're far too selfish to do that."

"What the fuck is wrong with ye?" I snapped, snatching at the iron bars in anger. But, before he could reply, pain—immense and immediate—sent me howling away from the bars of our cell. I cried out, tears in my eyes, and stared down at my hands. They looked singed, as if I'd touched a blister-ingly hot stovetop. Alucard had his arm around me in an instant, and I was in too much pain to shrug him off.

"Huh. Guess it's already begun," Ryan said. "You know, I could hardly believe it when they told me. My *friend*, Quinn, the Morrigan's daughter. You could have told me, you know." He sidled up and tapped the cage with the toe of his boot. "Soon you'll be just like us. Well, like *them*, at any rate. The Tuatha were before my time. But, no matter how this turns out, even-tually you'll have to leave your precious mortal realm behind, just as I did."

"Why?" I asked, staring down at my poor palms with tears in my eyes.

Ryan made an exasperated noise. "Because, they can't afford to leave you to your own devices, obviously. Gods aren't allowed to do whatever they want. You know that."

In hindsight, Ryan's logic made sense; I did know that. In the mortal realms, gods and goddesses could pick champions, but never interfere directly. I'm not sure if it was a written or unwritten rule—I'd never been privy to a cosmic library—but it was definitely the way things worked. Of course, that wasn't what I'd meant. "No, not that..." I replied, my voice tight with pain. "I meant why are ye actin' this way? Is it just because ye t'ink I kept t'ings from ye? I didn't. I just found out what I am, meself. That's why I came to Fae in the first place. To figure out what I am!"

"Whatever you say, Quinn," Ryan replied, but the tension in his shoul-ders lessened somewhat. "Listen, give me her name, and I'll go."

"Why d'ye want it so badly?" I asked, shrugging Alucard off to rise, the skin of my hands already returning to normal.

"Because she and her fellow renegades killed my father," Ryan snapped. I noticed Alucard's body language change out of the corner of my eye, but didn't dare look away from the Faeling. "When she chose to side with the Manling born in Fae over her own people," Ryan continued, "the silver sprite and her kind broke every bond they'd ever made. And, now that I know where she is, I intend to hunt her down and cut her to pieces."

My shoulders slumped as everything began to fall into place. A conversation from months ago, on the day of Ryan's departure, played in my head. I remembered how Ryan's father had supposedly died—taken down by pixies and sprites during one of the Goblin King's Wild Hunts.

Taken down on the orders of the Manling born in Fae.

Nate Temple.

Wylde.

Barbie's friend.

I glanced over at Alucard, who refused to look up, and realized he must have figured it out, too. Luckily, it seemed Ryan hadn't discovered the connection between Alucard and Nate. Yet. "You'll die if ye go after her," I said, finally.

Ryan's eyes narrowed. "You've always treated me like I was inferior. Like a kid brother you could boss around or beat up whenever you felt like it. But you don't know the first thing about me. About the Fae. About our vengeance." He sniffed. "You know what? I don't care what you decide to do. Just don't get in my way, Quinn MacKenna." And, with that, he turned on his heel and left.

Leaving me with one less friend.

"Could've at least given us the water," I mumbled.

CHAPTER 28

*O*ver the next couple hours, I filled Alucard in on everything that had happened to me since before and after we ended up separated from the dinghy—including what little I could remember of that fight, at Alucard's insistence; it turned out his memory of things since we'd crossed over into Fae was hazy at best.

"I can't explain why this is happening to me. The only major difference between my last trip to Fae and this one was I had Nate to guide me," he said, gritting his teeth as if hating to admit it. "But this time around, I don't know...it feels different. Not like I was on the outside looking in or any of that nonsense, but like everything sounded like a good idea."

"Your wild side," I offered.

"I guess so. Except before, I had direction." He frowned. "I mean, it was Nate's direction, but it was like all his goals became my goals, even if I went about things in my own way."

I scowled as I considered what Alucard was saying. I wasn't certain, but I had to admit it sounded a lot like Alucard had fallen prey to pack mentality. In essence, Alucard had given up his autonomy to the alpha—Nate. Frankly, I found it hard to imagine someone completely dominating Alucard, but being an alpha wasn't always about being the smartest or the strongest, often it was about confidence—the ability to say something and believe it with such assurance that everyone else around you ended up siding with you, whether they wanted to or not. And—while I'd only had two run-ins with Nate Temple and had wanted to junk punch the bastard in both instances—I had to admit the wizard exuded unassailable confidence like an expensive cologne.

And that kind of cologne could get you killed.

"Well, anyway, you're better now, right?" I asked, deciding not to voice my opinion on the matter; if Alucard wanted to play follow-the-leader with Nate Temple, he was welcome to it. So long as they stayed the fuck out of my yard.

He nodded. "As soon as I made the contract with Oberon. He took my power, but he took away the urges, too." He frowned, arms draped over his knees, back against the bars.

"I prefer ye like this, if I'm bein' honest," I replied. "Firefang was pretty damn close to gettin' himself shot."

Alucard snorted at my nickname for his wild side. "Bit possessive, huh?"

"Just a smidge," I replied, trying to get comfortable on the hard ground; my ass was falling asleep, and I couldn't risk touching the bars, since it was likely they'd end up frying me again. I glanced down at my bracelet once more, wondering if Macha had disabled it completely. It was obvious she and her sister had done something to me, as well. It wasn't simply my sudden iron allergy—although, as symptoms went, that did tend to stand out. But there were other, fairly noticeable, indicators I couldn't quite describe.

You know when you're about to get sick? How your body aches just a little, and you wonder if you did something to make yourself sore the day before? And then, how the mental fog sets in, making it harder to think than usual, like your brain decided to take the day off?

Well, this was pretty much the opposite of that.

I felt fucking grade A fantastic.

But I shouldn't have. The Fae realm had officially chewed me up and spit me out; I'd been cut up by pixies, goblin-handled, knocked unconscious, forced to swim through a sea of fire, thrown into and then off a boat, and—finally—hit with some of the heaviest emotional baggage I'd ever been asked to carry. I should have felt like shit. I should have felt like my whole world was one big lie. I should have been angry, and tired, and ready to kill anything that moved.

Hell, I'd even lost my *shoes.*

But, if I was being honest, I couldn't have cared less. All I really wanted to do was crawl up on top of the vampire in the corner and find out what he tasted like. Which I knew was a very, very bad idea. And so I sat on my hands, trying my best to be a good...whatever I was.

Fortunately, I didn't have to suffer for very long.

Because someone decided to crash the party.

On the far side of the room, the wall began to melt.

Steel, so hot it turned red, began to spill down towards the ground, replaced by a pure white light so bright it hurt to look at. At first, I wasn't sure what to expect—what fresh horror we were bound to face in the belly of Oberon's warship. I was betting on a Kraken, even though nothing about our current situation indicated that was the case; it was just that Oberon seemed like the douche who'd have a pet Kraken.

I held up my arm to block out the glare—glad, for once, to be behind bars. At least whoever or whatever was coming would have to get through iron to get to us, I figured. At last, the light dimmed, and I was able to stop shielding my eyes long enough to see what horrible fate was in store for us.

A woman I didn't recognize stepped through the gaping hole in the wall. She had red hair, like mine, although it was a shade brighter—the color of true flame—and braided so heavily it sat flush against her scalp. She was also wearing decidedly normal attire: combat boots, a pair of grey denim jeans, and a black t-shirt that read: Do You Even Kill, Bro? In fact, aside from her hairdo, the only thing about her that struck me as remotely Fae-like was the wicked-looking black bow she held. She swiveled that bow from side-to-side as she entered the room—clearing it with the profession-alism of a SWAT officer.

And I knew her.

"Huntress? Is that you?" Alucard asked, peering out at the woman in disbelief.

I frowned. "That's not the Huntress," I said uncertainly. The Huntress was a scary-ass Faeling with flaming eyes, who wore a pile of furs and a cloak of shadows and had a wicked-looking black bow.

Alucard raised an eyebrow at me, clearly in disagreement.

The redhead—who may or may not have been the Huntress—completed her circuit, glancing first at the vampire, then at me. "All clear," she called, keeping her voice down. As if on cue, a head was thrust through the opening. Not metaphorically, either; Cassandra—the headless horsewoman capable of opening Gateways into Fae, and one of the very few Faelings I still thought well of—held her own head in her hand, raising it high over the other woman's shoulder, her smile wide.

"Quinn!" she shouted, gleefully.

"Quiet!" the redhead hissed. She approached the cell, eyeing the iron bars with disdain. "Should've known getting you out wouldn't be that easy," she muttered.

"Why are you here?" Alucard asked, keeping his voice down so as not to alert the guards—wherever they were.

"I came for the girl," the redhead—who was probably the Huntress—replied. Her eyes flashed, spewing flame for just an instant, confirming her superheroine identity.

It *was* the Huntress. She looked rougher around the edges than when I had last seen her. Then it hit me. Her wild side.

Of course.

Turned out good ol' Hawteye was here to save the day.

"Wait, *the girl?*" I asked, both baffled and pissed off to be described so simply. "Why me? And how d'ye even know I was here?"

A third individual stepped into view from behind the Huntress. "I was keeping tabs on you," Robin Redcap said, his blood-drenched Red Sox ballcap hung so low I could barely see his face.

"On my orders," the Huntress added, peering through the cell's keyhole, although being extra careful not to touch it with any part of her body. "Turns out I was right to have you followed. Of all the moronic things you could have done, coming to Fae..." she snarled under her breath, still not looking at me directly.

I stared down at the redhead, still having trouble understanding what she was even doing here. I'd learned not too long ago, from both Othello and a bastard named Hansel—yes, *that* candy-smuggling Hansel from *Grimm's Fairy Tales*—that the Huntress had been watching me from the shadows and keeping me out of the Chancery's crosshairs, but I still had no idea *why*. As far as I had known, until she and a few other Faelings had come to my rescue a few months back, she and I had never even met.

But I'd been told she'd been guarding over me my whole life.

Or trying to.

Which meant her interest in me was still a mystery.

And I hated mysteries.

"Redcap!" the Huntress hissed, before I could interrogate her further. "Do you have anything that can eat through iron?"

Robin shook his head. "Not quietly. We don't keep stores of acid here."

"Why don't you ask the vampire to get them out?" Cassandra offered, eyeing Alucard up and down, her hands tilting her head so that it looked like anyone else cocking their head thoughtfully.

Creepy.

The Huntress frowned, then turned to Alucard, eyes narrowed. "That's a good point. Why haven't you gotten out on your own *already?*" she snarled, prepared to pounce on him for not offering his services earlier.

"Good to see you, too, Huntress. Um...could you do me a favor and not tell anyone about this?" he asked, too casually.

Huntress began tapping her foot, the sound oddly reminiscent of a murderer cocking a gun.

"I can't," he finally replied, frustration dancing in his eyes. "I had to swear on my power...to keep Quinn safe," he said, muttering the last few words so only I could hear them. I elbowed him in the gut.

"It's fine," I said, rolling my eyes. "He's havin' performance anxiety, that's all." I approached the edge of the cell, keeping a wary distance from the bars. "Robin," I said, keeping my voice low.

The redcap glanced up at me in surprise at hearing his name come out of my mouth. I didn't blame him for being a little startled; he probably knew I'd planned to gut him at my earliest convenience. The last time we'd met, I'd learned that he'd lied and nearly gotten me killed in the process. And he knew I had a reputation for holding grudges. But that wasn't important right now. What mattered was getting *out*.

Getting home.

Grudge match later.

"I need a knife," I said. "Preferably an iron one. Got anythin' for me?"

Robin's eyes widened in surprised. He opened his mouth, then closed it, and shook his head. "Weapons aren't allowed here. Especially not *iron* ones."

I cursed. Of course, that would be too easy.

The Huntress grunted, reached back, and drew a six-inch blade from a sheath at the base of her spine I hadn't even noticed was there. She held out the blade by the handle, clearly unwilling to touch it herself. "If you're planning on sacrificing the vampire, make sure you take his heart," she said, voice devoid of empathy.

"Really?" Alucard asked, cocking his head, nonplussed.

The Huntress shrugged. I chuckled, and shook my head. "No, we'll need him in a moment. But first, I need to do this." Then, before I could second guess myself, I slid my wrist savagely across the edge of the blade. And yes, before you ask, it hurt.

A lot.

A chorus of shocked noises greeted the action, and the Huntress immediately withdrew the blade, staring at me with wide eyes. "Are you insane?" she asked, although it was clear from her expression that the question was rhetorical.

I grimaced and dodged Alucard, who'd already stripped off his raggedy shirt to use as a tourniquet. That, or the sight of my blood on the floor had made him want to take some clothes off... I was banking on the former. "Maybe, but," I answered her, clamping one hand over my wound as the blood began to drip on the floor, joining the puddle already there, "at least now the dumbass fanger can get us out of here." I glanced back at Alucard. "Because, so long as I'm bleedin' out on this floor, I'm not *safe*," I said, meaningfully.

Alucard's eyes widened. He lifted one hand, and flames began to emerge from it, licking at the tips of his fingers. "*Cher*, you're a fucking psychopathic genius."

I shook my head. "No, I just really hated when it took a whole coliseum fallin' on Meg for Hercules to get his power back. Silly girl could have simply twisted her damn ankle and he'd have been good to go." I glanced around and realized no one knew what the hell I was talking about. "Oh, come on, ye Fae bastards, it's fuckin' Disney. Everyone watches Disney." I wobbled, the rapid blood loss making me dizzy.

The other members of Team Quinn shared a long look, and then disregarded me entirely.

Alucard helped lower me to the ground, then stepped up to the bars. With a savage growl, he yanked the metal apart, the noise deafening. The guards, shoddy though they may have been, would definitely have heard that. Things were a bit of a blur after that; Alucard picked me up and carried me through the portal, only to set me down on a chilly tile floor. A few faces hovered over me, and I heard Cassandra muttering as she strove to shut the rift she'd created. Someone snatched my arm and began applying pressure, halting the blood flow long enough to stitch it back together. Or try to, anyway.

"Something's wrong," Robin said, drawing the attention of the Huntress.

"What is it?" she asked.

"I've got the bleeding under control, but every time I try to sew up the wound, this happens." I felt something press against my arm, like being jabbed by a ballcap pen with the lid still on, unable to break the skin.

The Huntress cursed. "That's why she asked for an iron knife. Of course."

"What's wrong?" Robin asked.

"Silly Redcap," I said, feeling much better now that I'd had a few minutes to rest, "always slow on the uptake." I sat up, ignoring his protests and the half-dozen or so steel needles lying in a pile on the ground, each sliver bent nearly in two—having been unable to do much besides prick my flesh. Because apparently—along with the iron allergy—I'd become nearly impervious to steel.

You win some, you lose some.

I glanced over at the Huntress, who'd risen to her feet. "I'm guessin' me wound will heal on its own, aye?"

She gave me a curt nod.

"Glad to hear it," I said. I pried my arm free from Robin's grasp and took a good long look at our surroundings. They were eerily familiar, I realized; the walls were coated in precious stones, forming a mosaic depicting creatures—trolls and goblins and elves and sprites and many more—dancing from one wall to another. Dancing—no, *hunting* each other, I decided. Definitely hunting. I didn't know how I could have missed that my first time here, but, regardless, I knew the place.

The ridiculously gaudy bathroom outside the *El Fae*—a bathroom I'd used a few months back to change into a ridiculously gaudy dress as a condition for entering the infamous speakeasy run by the Faerie Chancery.

Which meant we were in enemy territory, more or less.

I spotted Alucard, still shirtless, standing watch behind Cassandra, who had finally sealed the portal, although not—apparently—before the guards had arrived; a pile of their severed hands lay at the vampire's feet along-side a small stack of broken weapons. I grinned, appreciating the grisly scene, wishing only that I could have sliced and diced a few goblins myself. I frowned at the thought. "Oy, Alucard! Where does your wild side go?" I asked, prompting the vampire to turn his attention to me. He stared down at my arm, brow furrowed as he took note of the already knitting flesh.

"It doesn't *go* anywhere," he replied, meeting my gaze. "Far as I can tell, anyway."

Ah. So I had a sex-crazed savage along for the ride at all times from now on.

Perfect. That was just perfect.

"We need to get you away from here," the Huntress interjected, taking me by the wrist. "Far away."

I jerked free. "How about ye tell me just who the fuck ye really are, first? For starters, ye can tell me why ye had the Max Cady impersonator over there track me down in Fae."

"Actually, that was me, dear," Cassandra said, winking and waving with her free hand, simultaneously. "The Redcap's been keeping tabs on you, but lost track of you after you and the vampire used your portable Gateway. Which is something I'd be *very* interested in knowing more about, once you two have finished your little row. But, anyway," she flicked her fingers at us, "as you were."

The Huntress glared at me. I glared back.

"Are either of them going to talk, or...?" Robin asked after a few moments of brittle silence, arms crossed.

"I can never tell with women," Alucard drawled thoughtfully, as if the two were watching a National Geographic show together about some fasci-nating foreign creature.

See the woman in her natural habitat...

"I'm not a woman," the Huntress snapped. "I'm Fae."

"I stand by my statement," the vampire replied.

"I'll ask ye one more time, what is it ye want from me?" I asked, ignoring the boys and their mindless banter.

Confusion flitted across the Huntress' face. "I don't want anything from you."

"Then why? Why the interest in me?" I asked, exasperated.

"Because your mother asked me to look after you," the Huntress replied, heatedly.

The bathroom was eerily silent for a moment. Then, somewhere in the bathroom, a showerhead turned on. Soon, a warbling voice joined the sound of spray, singing a discordant song in an operatic manner that made all of us wince. Apparently, we had company—although it was entirely possible they hadn't noticed us; the bathroom was uncommonly spacious. I shook my head and folded my arms. "Explain."

"We don't have *time* for this," the Huntress said.

"Make time," I countered.

She huffed. "Spoiled child! Fine. Before you were born, your mother came to me to request a favor. I owed her. She asked me to watch over you and keep you out of harm's way. There, are you happy?"

I took a deep breath, fighting against a whirlwind of emotions. Disbelief. Anger. Confusion. In the end, however, I settled on the biggest of them all: amusement.

I began to laugh. And I mean hard. Gut-busting laughter. The obnoxious, snot-bubble kind.

"What's so funny?" the Huntress demanded.

I waved a hand at her, barely able to breathe. "Have ye...seen me?" I asked, gulping in air. I held out my arms, which were still covered in tiny cuts, not to mention scar tissue and a fresh flesh wound running down the length of my arm. "Ye...had one job!" I doubled over again, the sight of her vicious scowl driving my mirth to new heights. "Nailed it," I added sarcastically.

Alucard coughed to cover a chuckle, earning a fierce look from the Huntress. He held up a hand. "Not to interrupt, but I noticed there aren't any urinals in here. Could we take this discussion outside the ladies' room, perhaps?"

"Fine," she snapped.

Alucard grinned and skirted around her, hands held up in mock surrender. "Much obliged." He headed towards the exit, while the rest of us made to follow him. Once I had control of myself, however, I realized that something wasn't right, although it took me a moment to realize what it was.

The singing and the shower had stopped.

A squeal, so loud it threatened to break sound barriers, erupted down the corridor to the left of the exit. Then, with a suddenness none of us could have anticipated, a great big, hairy foot came hurtling at Alucard, who'd turned towards the sound without thinking. The impact was jarring, like watching a career-ending hit, all of us wincing and shying away as one.

A heavyset ogress, wearing nothing but her birthday suit, stepped out into the corridor, looming over the vampire she'd booted into the jewel-encrusted wall. "No look." She poked him in the chest with her index finger, hard enough to crack the ribs of any Regular. "Bad man." She reached up, grabbed an industrial-sized towel that would have made an excellent blanket, and wrapped it around herself—completely oblivious to the rest of us. Then, without another word, she headed down another corridor towards the locker rooms, muttering in a basso grumble about how tired she was of being objectified.

Alucard groaned, the sound piteous, and fell forward onto the tile. "That really hurt," he ground out.

The Huntress sighed, stepped over him, and opened the door. "Alright, let's go."

I grunted, realizing—despite everything—that I rather liked her.

"You aren't planning on leaving him here, are you?" Robin asked, staring down at the crumpled mess on the floor.

"You're right," the Huntress said. "We should nurse him back to health with our copious amounts of free time."

Robin glanced around at us, as if trying to decide if she was joking or not.

Here he was, a killer of the highest order, facing the toughest decision of his life. His default setting was being challenged.

Never leave a bro behind.

Cassandra frowned and shook her head, one eye half-lidded. "Definitely kidding, I think."

I nodded. "Definitely."

Robin sighed. "Well, I can't just leave him here."

"I second that," the vampire wheezed.

"Then *you* take care of him," the Huntress said. "I'll let you know where to meet us."

Robin looked down at his new charge and nodded, but unenthusiastically, like he'd been told to clean his room or do the dishes. I reached down and mussed Alucard's hair. "Make sure he gets plenty of sunlight," I said.

"You want me to kill him?" Robin asked, sounding shocked.

"Just do as she says," the Huntress interjected. "Let's go." She stepped out, and Cassandra followed. I trailed them, glancing back only once to make sure Alucard's body wasn't completely crushed; that would be one hell of a waste.

After all, we liked that body.

CHAPTER 29

*T*he Huntress ushered us down the hallway beneath the light of the will-o-wisps hovering along the walls. "Cassandra, can you make another Gateway?" she asked, falling in step with the Dullahan, the headless horsewoman's official title.

"Into Fae?" Cassandra asked, one eyebrow raised.

"No, here in the mortal realm," the Huntress replied.

"Oh, sure. That's much easier," she said, our quick pace causing her head to jostle a little as she walked. "Where did you have in mind?"

The Huntress flicked her eyes at me. "St. Louis. She'll be safe there."

I halted in mid-stride, causing the other two Faelings to do the same. "Whoa," I said, crossing my hands back and forth to clarify how not okay I was with that idea, "that's so not happenin'."

"You agreed to leave," the Huntress said.

"I thought ye meant leave *here*," I said, waving a hand at the tunnel beneath the law offices of *Hansel, Hansel, & Gretel*. "Not leave the damned state."

The Huntress took a step closer to me, the top of her head threatening to brush against my chin. "The Fomorians are coming. Balor knows you're here, and he'll wipe out this whole city to find you. You need to go somewhere further inland, where he can't reach you."

"Why me?" I asked, flabbergasted.

"Because your mother was the one who defeated him the first time," the Huntress hissed. "He can't have her, so he'll settle for you."

I shook my head, struggling to understand. The one-eyed fucker was after *me* now? I thought he just wanted his damn eye back. And all because he had a grudge to settle with my dead mother? Seriously, if she weren't already dead, I'd strangle her, myself. "And what happens to Boston, if I do that?" I asked, trying to get back to the subject at hand. "What about the Chancery?"

"The Chancery's been evacuated," Cassandra replied in a soft voice, as if she couldn't quite believe it herself. "Well, mostly. There are a few stragglers," she said, clearly referring to the ogress who'd laid out Alucard. "But they'll be gone before the storm hits."

"And me city?" I pressed.

The Huntress at least had the guts to look me in the eye when she said it. "The city isn't my problem."

"Look here, ye—" I began, prepared to unleash a tirade.

"But," she interrupted, "it's possible that *if* we can hide you, Balor won't strike right away. Which means most will have time to get out. He's already delayed, sensing you weren't here. But he's coming, no matter what you decide. At least this way, the damage is minimal."

I ground my teeth, weighing my options. If what the Huntress said was true, then maybe St. Louis *was* my safest option. Of course, that would likely mean being at the mercy of The Wannabe King of St. Louis, Nate Temple—not exactly an ideal condition. Still, if Balor did follow, it might help to have a wizard with Temple's experience to fend him off. I could always change destinations and ask Callie for help, but somehow, I doubted she'd have the resources to take on something this big. Plus, I liked her. If I was going to put anyone in danger, Nate Temple was my Huckleberry.

"Fine," I replied, to the Huntress' obvious relief. "But I'm not leavin' without me aunt, Dez." I didn't care what the Huntress claimed about the city's inhabitants or their chances—Dez was coming with me. I wasn't about to gamble with her life. She'd hate it, I knew, but Dez could be pissed at me later. Once we survived. Besides, I had questions only she could answer.

Like who had my mother been, really?

The Huntress snarled in frustration, but knew better than to argue. "Can you make two Gateways?" she asked Cassandra. "One now, and another in fifteen minutes time?"

"Absolutely," Cassandra said.

"You'll have to drop me off outside," I said.

"Why?" the Huntress asked, eyes narrowed.

"Because I recently put wards around me aunt's place," I replied. "It was a two-for-one deal." In actuality, I'd requested the wards around Dez's place get put up first; I could handle myself, but the thought of anything happening to her was more than I could bear—even if she had lied to me all these years.

"Well then I won't be able to join you two on the first leg of the trip," Cassandra admitted. "I tend to draw a fair amount of attention, whenever I go out among Regulars."

"That's alright, we won't be long. Are you sure she's at home?" the Huntress asked.

"No, but if she isn't, we'll have just have to find her," I replied, matter-of-factly.

"When this is all said and done," the Huntress growled, "remind me to beat you senseless."

I snorted. "Hasn't anyone told ye? I'm the daughter of a goddess." Not surprisingly, saying it out loud like that brought a strange flutter to my stomach. I masked it well, though. "I don't fight below me weight class."

"You wouldn't be," the Huntress retorted, then blatantly ignored me.

Which was good, because I needed a moment to pick my jaw up off the floor.

Huntress was...a *goddess*? What the hell? Was this real life?

Cassandra, meanwhile, had prepared a Gateway, pretending to be oblivious to our bickering, though I could tell even she was a little startled by the exchange, especially considering for a moment there it looked like she might drop her head—though whether it was my admission or the Huntress' which had caught her by surprise, I wasn't sure. The rift opened up into a tiny alleyway between two buildings. The sound of rain and sirens greeted us, ominously.

"Let's move," the Huntress said, ducking through the Gateway, fully confident I'd follow.

I did, hardly making it through before I felt someone slap my ass from behind.

"Go team!" Cassandra said, as the Gateway shut.

I sighed and turned back, determined to quickly save my aunt, claim sanctuary in St. Louis, and plot the downfall of one old, evil bastard with an axe to grind.

As if it were going to be that easy.

CHAPTER 30

*T*he Huntress was waiting for me at the end of the alley, a grim
expression on her face.

"What is it?" I asked, sprinting through the rain in my bare feet, trying
my best to avoid the bigger puddles.

"Which house is hers?" she asked.

I frowned, then shoved past the Faeling. "Hers is the one in...the..." I
drifted off, staring out at the row of townhouses that lined Dez's block,
trying to make sense of what I was seeing. Black smog clogged the air,
barely affected by the falling rain—the clouds reflecting the strobe of the
fire engine's lights and the flames that smoldered from the second townhouse on the right. Dez's house. My house.

I took off, dodging the Huntress' attempt to grab me, bolting straight for
the gathered crowd of onlookers—many of whom were neighbors I knew
personally. I shoved past them, ignoring their shouts of surprise and recognition. My only goal was to get closer. Dez would be at the front of the
crowd, watching the house burn with a blanket wrapped around her shoulders. That's what they did with the survivors, after all. I scanned the area
immediately in front of me as I waded through the mob, searching desperately for that tell-tale blue blanket.

I knocked down a few people when they didn't move fast enough for my liking, the whole affair like one of those hazy dreams where nothing makes sense, and you can't think clearly.

I finally made it to the front, breaking through like a diver surfacing for air.

But Dez wasn't there.

Instead, a firefighter stopped me, his bright yellow uniform stealing my attention for a full ten seconds before I remembered what I was doing. "Dez!" I shouted, staring past the fireman. "Dez, where are ye?"

"Ma'am, you have to step back," the firefighter urged.

"No, I need to find me aunt, that's her house," I insisted, pulling desperately at his jacket.

He paused to look me up and down. "Jesus H. Christ, lady, are you okay?"

I glanced down, realizing I hadn't changed since returning from Fae. I looked like someone out of a horror novel, covered in cuts and scrapes, my feet bare, my once-white *Symposium of the Seas* tee shredded to pieces, and my pants torn up like something out of an Abercrombie catalog, revealing far more than I would normally be comfortable with.

I slowly shook my head. That didn't matter. None of that mattered. "D'ye find a woman in there?" I asked, yanking the man towards me, so savagely I completely tore off the sleeve of his jacket. "Where is she, the woman ye saved?"

His eyes were about as wide as they could get, staring at the impossible feat of me tearing off the sleeve of such a sturdy coat—one designed for about the most intense abuse one could imagine.

A blazing inferno.

And I'd done it with my bare hands, without any apparent effort.

"Joe, we've got something in here!" I heard another firefighter call out.

I released the sleeve and watched it flutter to the ground. "No...no...no, no, no..." I backed away, mumbling.

"Ma'am, it's alright," the firefighter said, placatingly, though he sounded a bit in shock himself. "Let's get you over to the ambulance, alright?"

"Don't worry, I've got her," the Huntress said, appearing at my side as if by magic, sliding one arm around my waist as if to guide me away.

I glanced past the firefighter's shoulder and saw two of his fellows step away from the wreckage, shaking their heads mournfully.

Something inside me...

Fucking snapped.

With a hoarse roar, I flung the Huntress away from me, watching in mild fascination as she soared over the crowd, colliding against the side of the ambulance with a loud crash and collapsing onto all fours on the pavement. I felt a twinge of guilt for that, but it was quickly swept up in a far larger whirlpool of emotions. I swung back towards the house and held out my hand, stepping forward, one thought repeating over and over again like a mantra in my brain.

I wasn't going to let this happen.

The firefighter tried to stop me, purely on reflex, but I sent him flying, too. No guilt this time, just determination. A familiar sensation began to register—the ache of my hot bracelet against the skin of my wrist.

I took another step, and time began to slow.

Firefighters, seeing what I'd done to one of their own, spun in slow motion, prepared to stop me by any means necessary.

Another step.

The bracelet began to shudder violently, and the firemen began rotating backwards, like those pieces on the old-school hockey board games you could spin in either direction.

Then, the rain began rocketing *upwards*.

The smoldering flames became brighter, at first, as the wreckage took shape. Beams flew back into place, the blackened wood brightening until the skeletal bones of the townhouse were visible. Scorched brick levitated, forming one facing wall. The door, a charred mess, sprung back into place. The bracelet, no longer able to handle the strain, fell from my wrist to splash onto the pavement in a chrome puddle, searing the concrete with a hiss of acrid smoke.

But I didn't need it anymore.

I could feel it now—my mother's magic, surging through me.

Time continued to wind in the opposite direction as I inched closer. The firetruck pulled away in reverse, followed by the ambulance—no longer dented—full of first responders. The flames shrunk, isolated to one room— the kitchen. If I could just go back a little further, I could find the source of the fire before it happened. Save the house. Pretend like none of this had ever happened.

But then, with an abruptness that left me gasping for air on all fours, the magic ran dry.

I felt like I'd been hollowed out, my insides removed. But still, I shuffled forward, staring with bleary-eyes at the flickering light from the kitchen window. Could I put it out? Maybe. I struggled to my feet, as tired as I'd ever been in my entire life. So tired I could cry.

Too bad I didn't have time for that shit.

I edged forward, picking up the pace once I got my feet under me, my adrenaline pumping hard enough to sustain me for a little longer. I hoped. Once through the door, I immediately began calling out Dez's name. The fire could wait; I needed to save Dez first. "Dez! It's me, Dez! There's a fire!"

A thump from upstairs shook the ceiling. I hurried to the flight of stairs, leaning hard on the bannister as I forced myself forward. Someone was up there. Dez, I was sure of it. I just had to find her. It wouldn't matter then how exhausted I felt, I *would* drag her out of here. I made it to the top of the stairs and slid along the wall towards her bedroom. But there was no one there. I groaned, exhausted, then retraced my steps. The guest room, I decided. She was probably working on one of her projects in the guest room—my old room, now converted into a workshop. "Dez!" I yelled once more as I shambled towards the end of the hall. "If ye can hear me, say somethin'!"

I fumbled with the doorknob, but found it locked. I snarled in frustration; I'd insisted on putting a lock on the inside as a teenager, against Dez's wishes. But it being locked now made no sense. Dez never would have locked the door, whether she was inside or not. Hell, she often forgot to lock the door to the damned *house*. "Dez! Dez, ye need to let me in!" I yelled, banging on the door with what little strength I had left. But there was no response. I stared down at the doorknob, willing it to unlock. To turn beneath my hand.

And then, shockingly, it did precisely that.

I almost fell as the door opened, leaning on it as hard as I had been. I steadied myself in what felt like a drunken stumble, glancing around to get my bearings, and was immediately overwhelmed with déjà vu. Posters, my posters, lined my purple walls. Beside the door stood my old dresser, the stereo system on it eerily reminiscent of the one I'd had as a teenager.

Holy shit, had I turned back time that far?

"I could have sworn I locked that door," a voice said, so deep and masculine it barely registered beneath the sound of the fire crackling away downstairs; the flames must have begun spreading, already. I whirled towards the sound—but of course the speaker was invisible.

"Dobby, what are ye doin' here?" I hissed, dumbfounded. What was he doing here? And what did he mean, he could have sworn he'd locked the door?

That didn't make any sense.

Dobby was my friend—why hadn't he let me in?

The spriggan—invisible thanks to a magic ring I'd inadvertently given him months ago—chuckled. I used the sound of it to track him toward the corner of the room, behind my old bed. And that's when I finally saw her. Dez, slumped against the bedframe. She was bleeding.

I stumbled towards her, fell, and finally crawled to her side. The window opened, and the sound of Dobby's horrible laughter faded as I heard him scrambling away. But it was a distant thought. I was too busy staring down at Dez to go after him. I snatched the covers off my bed and pressed them to the wound on her stomach, hoping to get the bleeding under control. Outside. I needed to drag her outside. The paramedics had been the first ones on the scene; they'd be here soon. They could help her.

"Quinn, is that ye?" Dez asked, her voice feeble.

"Aye, it's me," I replied, so glad to hear her voice I nearly broke down. "Don't worry, I'm goin' to get ye out of here." I started to try and lift her, but she was so heavy I had to stop. I needed a better angle. Leverage, I needed leverage.

Dez snatched my arm, drawing me back beside her, pain written all over her face. She took a deep breath. "Ye know...I always loved ye," she whispered in a weak sob.

I felt tears start to prick the corner of my eyes. I shook them off, searching the room for something I could use to get her up. "No, don't ye do that," I said, distractedly. "You're not sayin' your goodbyes, Goddammit."

She swatted my arm, weakly. "None of that, now. Ye swear too much, young lady."

I gritted my teeth, suddenly unable to speak past the lump in my throat. This wasn't happening, I decided.

I'd fix this.

I just needed to rewind time a little further. Get Dez out of the house. Find Dobby and crucify him before he could so much as lay a finger on her. I could do it.

I could.

I was...

A goddamned...

Goddess!

I could do *anything*.

And so I fucking *tried*.

I tried so fucking hard. But nothing happened.

Because...my bracelet was gone. I stared down at my scarred wrist, blinking rapidly, not knowing what to do, or how to use my powers.

I called out desperately to my wild side, urging it to take over and burn the world to cinders if it gave me the power to save Dez.

I promised her she could have anything. Anyone.

If it saved Dez, the entire city could fucking *burn*.

Hell, I would toss the first match...so long as Dez was holding my other hand.

But the demented whispers were gone.

"She said it would end this way, ye know," Dez said, staring out the open window. I blinked rapidly, snapped out of my impotent attempts to save her.

I sensed smoke drifting up the stairs, visible from the open doorway. "Your ma, I mean."

I gasped, too startled to say anything.

"She was always predictin' t'ings. The weather...which of our friends were goin' to end up together. T'ings like that. I could tell she knew more than she told us, though. She used to get sick at the oddest times, pulling the two of us out of missions at the last minute." Dez coughed, and a thin line of blood dribbled from her mouth. "Missions where t'ings went south," she said, oblivious to the red fluid on her chin.

Missions? Was she talking about her time with the Irish Republican Army? But why? She never talked about those days.

I reached out, dabbed the blood away with a corner of the blanket, and stared at it. For some reason, I couldn't stop staring at the blotchy stain, even as Dez continued speaking. "I never asked her about it. We were best friends, but there was a part of her I never knew. I was jealous when she ran off with your father, and even more so when she wouldn't tell me who he was. We fought. I said t'ings I shouldn't have, hurtful t'ings. And that's when she told me."

"Told ye what?" I whispered, letting the blanket fall.

"How I'd die," Dez said, her smile sad and thoughtful. "She said I'd never even see what did it, but that I'd end up in me daughter's arms. I used to t'ink I'd live forever, t'anks to that. Can't die in me daughter's arms if I never had a daughter, right?" She grunted, then coughed again, her face racked with pain. "But here we are, aren't we, me girl?" Dez said. She raised her arm, sliding it free from the blanket, and rested her hand against the side of my face.

This didn't make any sense.

I cupped her hand with mine, pinning it to my cheek. "Ye can't leave me," I moaned, shaking my head. "I don't care what she told ye, this isn't your time, ye hear me? She was wrong. She just said that to hurt ye..." I drifted off. "She was wrong," I whispered, tears splashing down my cheeks now.

"D'ye like what I did with the place?" Dez asked, her voice thready, eyes locked on the walls as she settled her head back against the bedframe, although it almost seemed as if she were looking at something far off in the distance. "I thought, if it reminded ye of home, you'd come visit more often..." A ghost of a smile played along her lips.

And, with that...she was gone.

CHAPTER 31

They found me cradling Dez's body, the smoke in the room so thick I couldn't see anything above my head except the dwindling light from the open window. I'd wrapped her up in the blanket, so she wouldn't get cold, closed her eyes, and slid a pillow beneath her head.

The pillow was charred on one side, so I adjusted it.

Didn't want her hair getting dirty. Couldn't have that.

Dez hated getting her hair dirty.

"There ye are. You'll die if ye stay here," Badb—covered in so much black leather she looked like she'd bathed in the ashes of the burning townhouse —said, her raspy voice interrupting my thoughts, sounding relieved to finally find me. As if they'd been searching a while.

I grunted. Of course I would. What kind of stupid fucking observation was that?

"That won't bring her back," Macha chimed in, looking immaculate in her pretty blue dress despite the smoke.

An idea struck me. I whirled around, my eyes—between the smoke and the tears—bloodshot and puffy. But I used them to plead all the same, giving them the same doe-eyes I'd used on Dez so many times when I was a little girl, to get what I wanted. "Can ye do it?" I asked, desperately. "Can ye turn back time and save her?"

The sisters frowned.

"That power was taken from the Tuatha, long ago," Macha said.

"Not even an immortal should hold dominion over time," Badb added. "It's too temptin' by far."

I hung my head. Even if I told them I had temporarily had that power, I knew nothing would change. If they didn't know how to access the power any more than I did, they had nothing to offer me. "Go away," I said, finally.

"Balor is comin' for ye," Macha said.

I shrugged. I'd be dead long before that happened; the fire would take care of that. The one-eyed bastard could do what he wanted with what remained—I'd have no stake in the game, at that point.

"He's already sent out his advance troops. Mortals are dyin' by the score."

"Go do somethin' about it, then, if you're so concerned," I said. "Or don't. Just leave me be."

"The one who did this is with him," Badb said.

Something stirred in the ashes Dez's death had left behind, and I slowly turned to look up at the dark-haired goddess. My aunt. "What d'ye just say?" I rasped.

"It's true," Macha said.

Dobby.

Dobby was with Balor. But...*why?* I shook my head. It made no sense. None of this made any sense. How had he gotten past the wards? And why had he gone after Dez? We'd had a minor falling out, sure, but killing my only family...I couldn't wrap my head around it. In the end, I suppose I didn't need to. I simply needed to wrap my hand around his spriggan heart.

And squeeze until it popped.

"I'm goin' to murder him," I said in an entirely too calm voice. I tried to stand, but ended up coughing instead, spittle soaking into the carpet as I fought to get the acrid taste of smoke out of my mouth.

"You'll never get close," Badb said. "Not without us."

My hair hung over my face, obscuring my vision—a wave of red clouding my sight. "If ye are lyin' to me, and he isn't there..." I began, locking eyes with each of them, "the t'ings I'll do to ye two will make ye wish you'd never been worshipped," I promised.

"We aren't lyin'," Macha said. "And I swear you'll get your vengeance. If," she added, holding up a single, leather-covered finger, "ye agree to join us."

I slid my hair over to one shoulder and stared down at the face of the only mother I had ever known, tracing the faint smile that tugged at Dez's lips.

The hint of a smile I'd never get to see again.

The smile that would herald destruction and devastation like the world had never seen.

And they said Nate Temple had a temper?

I was about to redefine the word.

"Where do I sign?" I asked.

CHAPTER 32

*A*pparently, my signature wasn't needed. Instead, the sisters held out their hands, clearly expecting me to take hold and fulfill whatever destiny they had in mind. I rubbed at my grimy cheeks. "Ye have to stop the fire, first," I said. "Dez was Catholic. She'll have wanted a proper burial." Frankly, such things made little difference to me, but—if Dez's Second Coming theory held up—it'd be great to see her walking about like her old self.

From my view down below, of course.

Because I had no illusions about where I was going to end up, after this; I already had the paint colors picked out for my room in Hell.

Macha and Badb exchanged looks. The dark-haired Crow Goddess nodded and headed for the hallway, while Macha closed her eyes and waved her hands about in the air. In moments, the smoke was funneled through the open window, as if suctioned out, leaving nothing behind but breathable air. The crackle of flames and heat from below died out a second later, and Badb returned.

"It's time," Macha said.

I glanced at Dez once more, then nodded. I climbed wearily to my feet and, this time, held out my hands for them to take. The sisters obliged. We stood like that, the three of us, for what seemed like at least a full minute. I frowned. "Do we have to chant somethin'? Or do we just wait until we feel it?" I asked.

"You're closed off," Macha replied, clearly irked.

"And?"

"And we didn't think you'd be able to block us out," Badb said.

"It doesn't matter," Macha insisted. "Badb, let's see if we can get her power to respond. Hit her with energy."

Cool, charged air—like a breeze on a stormy afternoon—washed along my right side, the side Macha stood on. A wave of dry heat blasted my left. It felt like I was standing between a refrigerator and a furnace, each fighting for dominance.

For control.

In a way, the sensations reminded me a lot of my brief interactions with other powerful beings.

Hemingway—the Horseman of Death.

Johnny Appleseed—the embodiment of life.

Even Alucard—with his stolen heat and sun-drenched vitality.

I frowned. What the sisters were doing wasn't going to work, I realized. They were each immensely powerful in their own right, but they were magnetic opposites—the way Hemingway and I had been, the first time we met—incapable of working in harmony without someone else steering.

I snorted, the play of air on my skin whipping my hair back and forth.

"What is it?" Macha asked.

"This," I replied.

And then I did the only thing I could think of to bridge the gap between the three of us.

I swallowed their power whole.

*P*ower.

It's a word heavy with implications.

There's implied power—that which gives people the ability to govern and lead.

And there's express power—the ability to exert our will on the world.

What I felt as Macha's cool, biting energy combined with her sister's brash heat within me was something else altogether, a power so vast it threatened to take me over completely.

The sensation reminded me, inexplicably, of one of my earliest memories, from when I was perhaps nine or ten. I'd been out with Dez on one of her Bible Camp retreats, skipping stones along the water with a few of the other children, when I'd spotted something floating on the surface. I don't remember why or how—probably a dare from one of the other children—but I'd leapt out into the water without so much as a warning. I didn't remember being rescued, or sitting by the fire that night. What I remembered was fighting to stay afloat, to keep coming back up for air no matter how much river water I swallowed.

The power I felt was like that—so immense it was all I could do to keep breathing. But—no matter how strong the current—I held tight to that memory, to all my memories, refusing to drown.

"How?" I heard Macha gasp, her voice inside my head.

"She's usin' *us*," Badb complained, the anger in her voice like sandpaper on varnished wood. "Ye said *we'd* be in charge, Macha!"

I sneered at the ridiculousness of that sentiment, as if this kind of power could be shared. I held out my hand and—with little more than a thought—saw a tiny raincloud form, little arcs of lightning dancing across my palm.

"What d'ye mean?" Badb asked, her question directed at me, as if she'd heard my thoughts.

Badb, the Crow Goddess—the avatar of war, to use Oberon's expression—didn't know, I realized.

But Macha *had* known.

She had to have known that the power couldn't be shared, and had assumed she could take it for herself, or else she never would have agreed to this.

She'd anticipated being able to manipulate Badb and me, to wield us like weapons. I could feel the nature goddess in my mind. Her resentment, her jealousy. Her desire to *finally* be the one behind the wheel.

"Why?" Macha asked, sounding defeated. "Why are ye the one the power chose?"

I wished I could explain it to her, but I couldn't—not in terms she could understand. Macha perceived power as an absolute thing. Something that the strong *had* and the weak *didn't*.

But that wasn't the case.

The power we three possessed, the power my mother had channeled to become the Morrigan, was as vast as the ocean itself. You didn't force the ocean to do your bidding. You sailed it, constantly adjusting—constantly adapting. Macha refused to do either; adaptation was anathema to her because it demanded something no goddess needed: courage. The courage to be wrong, to make mistakes, to grow. That's what had set Morrigan, my mother, apart from the other members of the Fae Court. She'd been courageous. Violent, passionate, cruel, sure...

But *also courageous.*

Suddenly, I saw her as my aunts had seen her. Their fierce, redheaded sister draped in shadow. Beautiful—but a distant, untouchable beauty, secure behind her mask.

"Had she only but shared a little of herself, we would have loved her," Badb said, sounding unaccountably sad.

"She didn't *want* our love," Macha spat, her voice ugly with disdain. "She only wanted our *power.* And now we've given it to her daughter, who has no idea how to use it."

It was hard to argue with that. Just because I could feel their power surging through me didn't mean I knew what to do with it. In fact, if I was being honest, it was taking everything I had to simply keep us afloat. If the power took control, I knew, we'd be lost to it; we'd drown, incapable of acting on our own. Incapable of stopping Balor. Incapable of seeking vengeance.

"So show me," I said.

Their reticence tugged at me, threatening to pull me under all on its own. They were goddesses. They'd been alive, impacting the realms for millennia. Who was I, the mortal, to ask them for help? To ask *them* to serve? Their thoughts were easy to read: better to drown than to give the power to someone unworthy of it.

But they had it wrong.

Because I wasn't asking.

No one, not even my aunts, were going to get in the way of my revenge. I reached down and thrust their heads below the waves inside our mind, pinning them there with my hate, my grief; if they weren't going to be useful, they may as well drown. I'd figure it out on my own.

I always did.

"Enough!" Macha sputtered, her outrage replaced by fear.

"We'll do it," Badb added, sounding cowed.

I released them. "Show me," I demanded again.

And so they did.

CHAPTER 33

*W*e—the three of us locked together in one body—*my* body— flew over the city, riding a current of air that bent to our combined will, soaring towards the tumultuous Massachusetts Bay. It'd taken me a little while to get the hang of it, but once I'd understood the basic mechanics, I'd realized commanding the air wasn't all that different than joy-flying with Barbie in Neverland had been.

Below, I could make out the enormous whirling pattern of the hurricane —no longer an abstract image on a television screen, a technicolor sawblade being prodded at by baffled meteorologists.

The sky boomed and cracked all around us, forks of lightning hammering down upon Boston, the thunder sounding like laughter from some malevolent god.

Frankly, it was worse than I could have ever imagined; the waves smashed against the city's harbor, tearing up wood and stone and steel, destroying homes, factories, and offices.

And they weren't alone.

There were creatures—built like Manlings, but considerably larger— riding the crests, wielding weapons fashioned from coral, only their torsos visible. Blue-skinned and broad-shouldered, hairless, they emerged from the water to lash out at the city's infrastructure, smashing and stabbing at random.

The Fomorians. The race of giants my mother and her sisters had once chased back into the sea—enemies so ancient that the Tuatha—Fae so powerful they'd once been worshipped as gods—had all but forgotten about them. Talk about a previous generation screwing things up for the rest of us.

Unfortunately, before I could share that little insight with my passengers, a coral spear came hurtling at us from below, so suddenly that—if Badb hadn't started screaming—I might have missed it. I shot my hand out, halting the projectile in mid-flight with a blast of air. Then, I let it drop to the ground below, its momentum completely stilled.

"I didn't know we could do that," Badb said, her voice echoing in my head like dry twigs rubbing together.

Clearly, she'd never seen *The Matrix*.

Which meant this would be fun.

I concentrated on riding the wind, plunging towards the Fomorian horde with all the confidence of The One—sans sunglasses. Granted, I wasn't yet to the point where I could go around breaking sound barriers as I sped between buildings and shit, but I had a decent handle on the straight shots, which was all I needed.

I beelined straight for the Fomorian who'd thrown the spear. Up close, he was even bigger than I'd originally thought—like Andre the Giant big. Fortunately, big in this case also meant slow; he was still winding up to swing at me with his blade by the time I hit him, inverting at the last moment to dropkick him in the chest.

A dropkick which—literally—tore him in half.

I landed among a veritable buffet of steaming blue viscera, mercifully unable to identify which organs were squishing between my bare feet. *Apples*, I told myself. *They're all just blue apples*. Badb was laughing, uproariously.

"Ye hit him so hard! That was fuckin' awesome!" she crowed.

"There's another behind ye," Macha warned.

I whirled in time to catch sight of another blue-skinned giant riding the crest of a wave, preparing to gore me with his spear. I took a deep breath, deciding it was as good a time as any to play with my new toys. I waited for the Fomorian to get close, his spear less than a foot from me, before deflecting it with a gust of wind. His arm went wide, leaving his body open. I pressed my palm against his chest and called down the lightning rumbling high above us. It answered on the first ring, pealing from the heavens down towards my hand.

It was just the Fomorian's bad luck that he was between the bolt of lightning and me.

I watched as the bolt struck the Fomorian's naked back in its hunt for my palm, electricity dancing across his skin, smoke instantly erupting out of his eyes and mouth.

I removed my hand, and he toppled into the water from whence he came.

I flexed my fingers open and closed. Was this the combined power of my mother's two sisters—the result of their fusion? Feeling the immense potential at my fingertips, I could understand what had driven so many to hate them and fear their combined might—the ability to wield the elements of air and lightning with absolute precision...all that was missing was the power to wield the darkness.

My mother's power.

According to my aunts' memories, only with her power in the mix were we truly complete. Truly unstoppable. But...how was I supposed to access it? Sure, I was controlling their powers, unifying them like a braided rope. But two strands wound together were about as effective as a stool with two legs—a thought which made me very nervous. Without the addition of the third power, were we going to suddenly collapse?

"It will come," Macha reassured me, drawing me back to the present moment. "When ye need it, it will come."

I cringed, preferring she hadn't been able to read the depths of my uncertainty.

Two more waves of Fomorians approached before I could dwell any further, carrying several riders prepared to avenge their fallen brethren, howling at me over the roar of the surf. I launched up into the air and settled down on top of the water, standing on the liquid surface as surely as if it were solid earth—the thinnest, sturdiest layer of air beneath my feet. I sighed, the shine of playing with my new toys already wearing off. I'd come here to find vengeance, and so far, all I'd done was murder a couple peons. What we needed, I decided, was to show them we meant business; I wasn't interested in picking off Balor's troops one-by-one, like plucking pawns off a chessboard.

I wanted the King himself to come out and play.

Because now there was a fucking Queen on the board.

Before the Fomorians could get any closer, I raised my hands—the air obeying so quickly in response that I felt my ears pop—and then I savagely flung them down. The air obeyed; the waves were immediately forced flat by the immense pressure. As was everything that had stood between the water and my blast of air.

The Fomorians.

Although more like blue applesauce, now.

The water was perfectly still for a few moments, as placid as the surface of an undisturbed lake.

I stepped around the corpses of the riders, and found the surviving Fomorians stepping back to open up a path for me—or perhaps attempting to circle around me, like vultures.

I ignored them and marched forward.

We found Balor One-Eye at the center of the storm, the waves supporting him as though he were sitting on a liquid throne. He was as large as the sisters remembered, a giant even among his own kind, a helmet wrapped like a lion's mane around his face. One eye socket sat empty, while in the other a blue stone glinted. It was easily twice the size of the fifty-six-carat blue diamond Geriatric Rose had dumped unceremoniously in the ocean at the end of *Titanic*. I had to admit I was surprised. Based on the myths, I'd assumed he'd be uglier—with one gaping hole in the middle of his forehead. But he wasn't—and there wasn't.

Had the myths been wrong? Or had they simply evolved over time, as myths so often did? I shook my head, realizing the longer I looked at him, the more fear—unfamiliar and unwelcome—I felt prickling along the edges of my consciousness. I was moments away from yelling at my chicken-shit passengers when I was assaulted by memories that were not my own.

Balor One-Eye and his army of ships approached our shores, their numbers so great they blotted out the horizon. The Fomorian warmonger led the charge, wearing seven patches, seven seals—a check against its power—over his malevolent eye.

A seal of wind, earth, water, and fire.

A seal of light and of darkness.

And, finally, a seal of iron.

We knew to fear it, but had not yet learned the true terror it represented.

He began removing those seals, one at a time, and we watched as the power of his eye grew and grew until his eye was unfettered by restraints.

And then...

Everything he looked upon withered and died.

Then we remembered how, after it was all over—after Balor killed Nuada, our King, and was slain by Lugh, Balor's very own son—we'd hidden the eye away, too frightened of its power to destroy it.

But it seemed he'd found himself another.

CHAPTER 34

I shook off the memories.

And yet, the fear remained.

"I see you have come to me," Balor said, his voice ridiculously deep and masculine—and strangely familiar. The light of his jeweled eye cast an azure glow that flickered across the water—as lovely a replacement as his old eye had been hideous. "I did not expect you to be so bold."

"We prefer the personal touch," I replied, the sound of our voices layered, one on top of the other. "Come on down here and we'll give ye the welcome ye deserve."

Balor cocked his head. "You sound different. And you seem taller."

"Upgrade," I quipped.

I could practically feel my aunts shaking their collective heads.

Whatever. Backseat drivers.

"This is not the Morrigan you faced in the past," a voice said, so similar to Balor's own that it took me a minute to realize the Fomorian hadn't spoken. "Morrigan is dead. This is her daughter's form." Dobby—several feet taller than when I'd last seen him, his body stretched, his once-comical features considerably less off-putting—stepped out from behind the throne. "Hello, my lady," Dobby said, with a slight bow.

I took a threatening step forward, but a wall of water appeared in my path. "Why?" I snarled, kicking up spray in frustration. "Why d'ye do it?"

Dobby glanced up at Balor.

"Tell her whatever you wish," Balor said.

Dobby nodded. "Quinn," Dobby began, flicking his eyes up at me, his gaze oddly dispassionate. "Do you know what a spriggan is?"

"Ye mean besides a soon-to-be dead Fae?" I replied, ignoring the sudden sense of alarm Dobby's words had triggered in my aunts; to be honest, I was getting really tired of experiencing emotions that weren't my own.

"Spriggans," Dobby said, ignoring my threat, "are a myth."

"What d'ye mean?" I asked, seething, prepared to leap the wall and end the miserable bastard. I wanted answers, but if Dobby wasn't going to give them to me straight, I figured I might as well kill him now and be done with it.

"I mean they do not exist. They are not a species within Fae. The truth is a spriggan is little more than a spoil of war. Long ago, you see, the Tuatha drove the Fomorians into the sea," Dobby said, ignoring Balor's warning growl. "But, before the war was over, the Tuatha stole a sizeable chunk of the Fomorian's power. Their shadows."

I felt a tremor of something—intuition, perhaps? "No, not the Tuatha," I said, gauging Dobby's reaction to see if my guess was correct. "The Morrigan."

Dobby sneered. "Indeed. Your mother, specifically. She fashioned Fomorian shadows into bodyguards. We became constructs, designed to protect Fae royalty. But, of course, we would never have agreed to that, so first, she stole our memories. Our autonomy. And so we remained, enslaved, shielding our oppressors from harm for centuries—not even aware our memories had been taken, and that we were protecting our jailers. But then, something changed, as it always does. The walls between realms thinned and border security was lax. That's when a lone spriggan, the oldest of his kind, wandered into the human realm."

I shook my head in denial. Not because what he said struck me as untrue, but because it still made no sense. Why had Dobby betrayed us? Ryan and I had given him a home. We'd kept him safe from the outside world, from the Chancery...and yet, hadn't he sought them out on his own, spying for them in exchange for his freedom? I frowned, remembering how cagey he'd been around some of the older Fae who might have recognized him. Had it all been a lie?

"But ye helped me," I said, trying to understand. "Ye protected me."

"Well, of course," Dobby said, as if I were being obtuse on purpose. "I needed you. If the Chancery found out a spriggan was running wild in the mortal realm, they'd have executed me immediately. But, for some reason, you were their blind spot. So long as I stuck with you, I was safe. At least until I no longer needed you."

"The whole time?" I whispered. "Ye were plannin' to betray me the whole time?"

Dobby waggled his hand. "I wouldn't think of it as betrayal. I simply did what I had to in order to motivate you. Feeding you enough information to keep you searching for answers was tough, I'll admit. But when I found out from your meeting with Hansel that you turned down the Winter Queen? I knew I'd have to do something drastic to get you to cut the umbilical cord. I was surprised to find you'd put up wards around your aunt's house, though. Took me a little while to figure out a way around *that*." And like a kindly father, he added. "I'm proud of you, my lady." Then he grinned, wolfishly.

"Why?" I growled, hands balled into fists. I wished I could say I wasn't hurt, that all I felt was anger—but it wasn't true. To know I'd been manipulated was bad enough, but at one point I had *trusted* Dobby. Felt *safe* around him. And now I learned it had all been a lie.

"Why what?"

"Why d'ye want me to embrace me power?" I ground out.

"Because you were the *key*," Dobby replied, as if that were obvious. "Once I realized you were Morrigan's daughter, I cast a spell on you. A spell to erode that awful seal your mother put on you. Remember?" Dobby raised his hands as if feeling the air, mimicking his actions the very first day I'd met him in Christoff's warehouse.

"Why would ye do that?" I asked, eyes wide.

"Well how else was I going to wake Balor up and tell him where to go?" Dobby asked.

My mouth hung open, too stunned to speak. For some reason, I recalled Jack Frost's voice as he stood over Lakota's body in that industrial warehouse a few months back, talking about a beacon. The signal calling to Balor and his men. The source that invited nothing but destruction and mayhem.

At the time, Jack hadn't told me what that beacon had been.

But...now I knew.

I'd been that beacon. My power had called the Fomorians to Boston.

It was all my fault.

"Besides," Dobby added, "we needed *the* Morrigan. All three of you."

"Needed us for what?" I asked, numbly.

"Enough talking," Balor said, rising from the throne, the water caving in on itself to leave him standing on a flat surface. The One-Eyed Fomorian stepped forward, and Dobby fell into his wake, folding in on himself until all that remained was a thin shadow attached to Balor's heels. I cursed myself for not killing the spriggan fuck while I'd had the chance, wondering now how I was supposed to tear a fucking shadow to pieces.

"Let's kill Balor, first," Macha said, "and go from there."

I grunted my agreement. Sounded good to me.

CHAPTER 35

*T*he one-eyed giant struck the first blow—calling to the water beneath my feet, liquid tendrils wrapping themselves around my legs, trying to drag me down. Luckily, my reflexes took over and I rocketed upwards before they could get a firm grip. I hovered high above the water, already feeling out of my depth. Despite the crash course I'd undergone, I was far from an expert when it came to wielding magic. Which meant I either needed to get better acquainted with my new abilities rather quickly, or I needed to win this fight fast with a cheap-shot; once Balor figured out he was dealing with a relative novice, I imagined my odds of killing him would steeply decline.

What I needed was something big. Something flashy, like what I'd done to the second Fomorian. But bigger. Much bigger. Something like…a thunderstorm. I could do a thunderstorm, right?

Then I looked up, and grinned.

Of course, I could do a thunderstorm. One was already right above my fucking head!

I threw my arms out wide and began to spin, slowly at first, but then faster. Soon, the sky above—already dark and foreboding—brightened as the first arc of lightning ripped across the sky. I concentrated, focusing on bringing the lightning straight down. A blast crashed into the ocean below. Then another. In an instant, dozens arced towards the water's surface, like someone had pressed the palm of their hand along the smooth curve of a plasma ball—each discharge linking to the other until the whole ocean glowed and frothed with charged ions.

Finally, exhausted and a little nauseous from spinning a couple hundred times in mid-air without stopping, I slowed. Surely, one of those blasts had hit the one-eyed bastard, I thought; his depth perception couldn't be that great, especially since his one good eye was, in fact, a fucking rock. Once I got my bearings, I scanned the surface, hoping to find his body floating belly up.

But of course I wasn't that fortunate.

In seconds, massive waterspouts—water tornadoes as wide as footballs fields—began to form. I could feel Balor's magic riding the air, causing an insane amount of turbulence as the towering behemoth funnels tore through the sky, the wind buffeting me so violently it was all I could do not to fall to my death.

Basically, we'd placed our bet, bluffing with the best of them.

And the fucker had raised.

I angled towards the ocean's surface, fighting against the air in a bid to reach the waves below.

"What are ye doin'?" Macha demanded. "The water is his element. We're better off above."

I didn't bother responding. She and I both knew it didn't matter whether I was up in the sky or swimming in the Godforsaken ocean; his magic was not only stronger, but better controlled, than mine. But I wasn't giving up— far from it. From what I could tell, my only chance at beating him was a head-to-head confrontation—something the giant bastard would least expect.

I realized, with a jolt of surprise, that no matter how badass Balor was...I wasn't exactly a featherweight. Frankly, if you got right down to it, this was no different than a bar fight. A grudge match.

And grudge matches? Bar fights?

Those were right up my alley.

I felt my aunts' doubts hit me like a physical weight.

I ignored them both. I wasn't an idiot; I knew it was a long shot, but—no matter what they said—the reality was I trusted myself more than I trusted the magic. Duking it out in the skies was all well and good, but I'd been scrapping my whole life, often against men who were bigger and stronger than I was. Picking a fight, at least, felt familiar.

"Balor!" I shouted, finding a place to land far from the whirling monstrosities he'd created. "Olly olly oxen free!"

His silhouette rose up from the depths a moment later, emerging slowly as if to increase the creep factor, his body eerily dry. "Are you ready to surrender?" Balor asked, finally, his feet firmly planted on the ocean's surface.

I snorted. Hell, I wasn't sure I even knew what that word meant. But, since he didn't yet know that about me, I flung myself at him.

I'd always heard actions speak louder than words, after all.

CHAPTER 36

*T*he fight, if you could call it that, was over in an instant. It turned out the sisters were right to doubt my chances, though not for the reason they thought; I didn't lose because I was smaller, slower, or even weaker. I lost because I'd forgotten all about the one thing that made Balor, Balor.

His Goddamned eye.

And so I hung, suspended in mid-air, held in place by the power of that precious stone—all my strategies, my plans to shatter kneecaps and snap limbs—completely unfulfilled. I felt resignation settle in almost immediately as the sisters realized what I'd known all along; we were the underdog in this fight, fated to lose.

"Now that we are done playing," Balor said, stepping up to me, "I want you to fashion me a door." He released me from the power of his eye, but took me by the throat before I could break away or lash out. He barely had to put any pressure for it to hurt; his hands were so big he held my neck between three fingers in a Force choke—like he found my lack of faith disturbing.

"We're not...fuckin' carpenters," I ground out.

"A Gateway," Balor said a moment later, having paused to glance back at his own shadow. Dobby, I thought, gritting my teeth and struggling to breathe. "A Gateway to the Fae realm," Balor said, more authoritatively this time.

"Oh, sure," I wheezed, fighting for air. "Would ye like us to…solve world hunger…while we're at it?" I managed between gasps.

Balor grunted. "Do not test my patience. If I must, I will snap your neck. There are others who will comply with my demand, even if you do not."

"Well, I guess…we're goin' to die, then, because…" I drifted off as voices in my head began yelling to get my attention. I raised a finger. "Hold please."

Balor scowled.

I focused inwards, talking to my aunts solely within my mind as my physical body choked beneath Balor's grip.

We can create Gateways into Fae? Seriously? I asked them.

Aye, Badb replied.

All of the Tuatha can do such t'ings, Macha added.

Internally, I snarled at them. *Goddammit. So, the big, dumb one-eyed bastard really does plan to use us to create a Gateway…*

And suddenly, I was struck by a truly brilliant idea.

Oh no, that's a terrible—Macha began.

I really don't t'ink ye—Badb chimed in, simultaneously.

Executive order! I snapped back, cutting them both off.

I came back to the real world and grinned up at the Fomorian warlord. "Ye should be careful what ye wish for, Dick Fury," I ground out, splitting my gaze between Balor and his shadow—Dobby. "I hope ye fuckers know a good shanty."

And, with that, I did exactly what the Fomorian had asked me to do.

I opened a Gateway into Fae.

CHAPTER 37

$\mathcal{K}$ ing Oberon's fleet—including the *USS Cyclops*—was right where we'd left it, each ship prepared to launch at any given moment. Which was exactly what I'd desperately counted on when I opened the Gateway in the first place. I ignored the immense pressure of Balor's hand around my throat and poured every ounce of my new power into the Gateway, expanding it, throwing it so high and wide its tip carved through the rainclouds above our heads. Impossibly bright sunlight from the Fae realm shone across the surface of Massachusetts Bay, and the merging of storm clouds and sun beams produced a double rainbow that arced over us like a comet.

"What have you brought me? A snack?" Balor asked, his grip tightening, making it impossible for me to breathe, let alone answer. But that was alright; I could die happy knowing I'd done what I could to even the playing field by bringing the fight to the Fomorians.

Plus—this way—Boston would be safe.

Balor's shadow writhed, and suddenly Dobby appeared at his side, staring at the armada on the other side of the Gateway—which had already begun creeping forward—with a disdainful expression. "It seems the denizens of Fae have come together to face you."

Balor snorted imperiously. "I see none of the Tuatha among them."

"Neither do I. You should release her throat, though," Dobby said, staring down at me with flat, emotionless eyes. "If she dies, the Gateway will close on us, and we will have to find another way into Fae."

Balor released my throat, tossing me into the water with a splash, my power too diminished to keep me from sinking. "She is nothing. Come." He marched forward, and soon the giant and his shadow faded from view.

I floated, coughing every so often, my throat burning. I wasn't sure what it was with men and choking me out, without permission, but I was getting pretty fed up with it. Sadly, it didn't seem like I'd have a chance to teach Balor a lesson in *safe words*; I was utterly spent. The energy I'd used to make and expand the Gateway had been far more than my body could handle. In fact, as I lay there, I could feel the other two slipping away—their combined power no more. In an instant, my aunts were no longer in my head, but beside me in the water.

"It's over," Macha said, a moment later. "We lost."

"Aye," Badb replied.

I twitched in irritation—their defeatist rhetoric nearly as irksome as Balor's self-assurance had been. No wonder neither had been capable of being the leader of our triumvirate. Still, they weren't wrong. Balor was simply too strong. At this point, the only way he'd lose was if he offed himself. I frowned, then began flutter kicking towards the Gateway, relying on buoyancy to do most of the work.

"Oy! Where are ye goin'?" Badb yelled.

I paused long enough to look back at them, treading water. "Ye two can give up if ye like, but I'd rather die," I replied, meaning every word. If I was being honest with myself, I realized, this had never been about beating Balor. Hell, even going after Dobby had been little more than an excuse to focus on something else, something other than grief.

What I'd really wanted, more than anything, was to feel *nothing*.

To crawl away and die.

But, after everything that had happened—after realizing this whole mess was my fault, one way or another—I couldn't just walk—well, *swim* away.

I could curl up and die later.

Right now, I had shit to do.

Besides, now that I was no longer plagued by my aunts' doubts and indecisiveness, I had a plan. Unfortunately, that plan hinged upon me finding my way aboard one of Oberon's ships on the other side of the Gateway—but one thing at a time. First, I needed to get closer. I turned and started swimming towards the fight that was about to erupt between the Fae armada and the Fomorian horde, when I felt something grab me beneath both arms, raising me up out of the water.

"So what's your plan, then? D'ye want us to throw ye at 'em?" Badb asked, holding my right side.

"I t'ink you'd make an excellent projectile," Macha added, on my left. "And they definitely wouldn't be expectin' it."

"Actually, could ye drop me off on that ship?" I asked, jerking my chin.

"The flyin' one?" Macha clarified.

"Aye, that's the one," I replied, grinning. "The Jolly Roger."

They tore through the skies, headed straight for the ship—and then blew past it. "Oy!" I yelled. "Where are ye goin'?"

"She did say drop her off, didn't she, Badb?" Macha asked in a tinkling voice, doubling back, only much higher up this time.

"That she did, Macha," her sister replied.

Oh. Of all the stupid fucking...

Except I never got to finish the thought, because suddenly I was falling from the sky. As the wind whistled past my ears, my torn clothing snapping in the wind, the pure, unadulterated chaos of my current situation struck me, and I felt oddly comforted. That might not make sense to most people.

But chaos was my element.

I quickly came within shouting distance of the ship full of Neverland sailors, only to find them pointing up at me in mild fascination—probably under the assumption that I was flying.

Please, I thought.

Anybody could fly.

But not everyone could fall...with style.

Unfortunately, it turned out neither could I; Hook's men had to fetch me from the rigging, in which I had—quite generously, I might add, considering the damage I might have done to the deck had I landed on it—ended tangled up in.

My aunts joined us *after* the crew brought me down, laughing so hard I thought they might die. Which would have been for the best since I was definitely going to kill them, once this was all over.

*C*aptain James Hook stared at me for a long moment after I'd finished explaining my arrival, my body still covered in rope burns. He looked surprisingly happy to see me, under the circumstances. Of course, that might have had something to do with the fact that I'd just admitted to opening the Gateway.

He held out his strong hand and slapped me on the shoulder, good-naturedly, as if I'd done something especially praiseworthy. "And it's a good thing you did," he finally said, smirking, looking perhaps ten years younger than when I'd last seen him. "The crew was getting restless. Lazy." The crew of the Jolly Roger certainly didn't seem lazy at the moment; they swung down from ropes attached to the masts, attacking the Fomorians from above like swashbuckling Tarzans.

We were constantly moving, which meant I was constantly stumbling as I proceeded to let Hook in on my plan, such as it was.

Hook, who never seemed to consciously adjust his balance and yet never lost his footing, rubbed at his jaw with his strong hand. "Sounds like a suicide mission," he admitted, once I finished.

"Aye, it does, doesn't it?" I replied, smirking.

Hook flashed a grin, shaving off another five years. "The crew'll love it." He spun away and marched off towards the helm, and soon we were flying towards the rear of the armada, to the surprise of many of the sailors onboard. My aunts, meanwhile, were staring at me like I'd started speaking in tongues.

"*That's* your plan?" Macha said, finally.

"The Manlin' with a death wish is right," Badb said. "This won't be pretty, and could wind up gettin' every one of the Fae killed. Once Balor has his real eye back, he'll be unstoppable."

"Oh, come on," I said, hugging the nearest barrel so I didn't go flying every two seconds, my wild side practically humming in contentment, "where's your sense of adventure?"

The two ancient goddesses exchanged exasperated looks and walked off. Haters.

*T*he Jolly Roger pulled up alongside the *USS Cyclops*, making it possible for me to leap from one vessel to the other. "Wait here," I called, the instant I was across.

Hook raised an eyebrow, but said nothing.

Good enough.

I sprinted towards the silver pyramid and the throne room within, praying the Goblin King was onboard. For my plan to work, I needed Oberon's help; he had access to information I couldn't find anywhere else, provided he was willing to part with it. My aunts had offered to come and shake it out of him, but I couldn't risk it; if Oberon suspected the three of us had joined forces, he'd never agree to help—especially considering my aunts' first campaign promise had been to boot Oberon and the Queens out of office at the earliest opportunity.

I took the stairs leading to the throne room doors two at a time, joining a host of goblin interns running to and fro with orders from the Goblin King. I'd almost made it to the top when it occurred to me that I'd forgotten one very important detail: Oberon's guards. And, who should I see guarding the throne room door—Babe No-Tooth.

Or, as was now a more appropriate moniker…

Babe No-*Hands*.

My guess was that he'd probably been on guard duty during Alucard and my escape. That, or he'd lost his hands in some sort of industrial accident since I'd last seen him.

Could have gone either way.

Regardless, someone really should have pointed out that he was pretty much shit as a guard, now that he had no hands.

"You!" Babe No-Hands shouted as I approached, pointing at me with his stumpy wrist.

See? Did he expect to bludgeon me into submission with his stumps or something?

But words can hurt, so I didn't belittle him about it.

Remember, actions speak louder.

"Me!" I shouted back, then pushed one of the stray intern goblins into the guard, sending them both flying off the top of the stairs with a crash. I craned my neck to look down at the poor bastards and realized both were unconscious. Maybe dead. I snatched up one of the interns by his ear, yanking him close and pointing. "Give that one a hand."

Then I shoved him away and ducked inside the throne room, feeling a little bad for tossing the first intern; hopefully, he hadn't been carrying anything too important. The throne room was chaos incarnate, with goblins milling everywhere, most of them little more than shapes in the darkness. I forced my way through the throng, shoving goblins aside like I was competing for the Heisman.

"What are you doing here?" King Oberon shouted, hopping up on his white leather chair—which actually made him a little taller than me.

The few goblins still in my way stepped aside, their eyes flitting between their king and me.

"I need to know where the Winter Queen is," I replied.

Oberon's eyes widened in surprise, then narrowed suspiciously. "Why?"

I sighed. This was the part of my plan I was the least fond of: telling the truth. "I want to take custody of Balor's eye and use it to kill him and all his minions," I replied, matter-of-factly.

The goblins began chattering away amongst themselves.

"Silence!" the Goblin King commanded. He waited until we could have heard a pen drop before speaking again. "Are you insane?" he hissed.

"Ye know," I replied, frowning, "I've had quite a few of ye lot askin' me that lately," I sighed.

"This isn't a *game*," Oberon snapped, hands balled into fists at his side. "If Balor regains the power of his eye, he'll lay waste to everything. Our realm, your realm. None of us will be safe."

"None of ye are safe, now," I replied, scathingly.

The goblins, as one, turned to face me, betrayed by their terrified expressions.

"What I'm plannin' isn't smart. Hell, it isn't even sane," I admitted. I stepped forward until the two of us were close enough to touch, and met the Goblin King's eyes, hoping he'd glimpse what lurked behind mine. That he'd be able to see my wild side—the savage creature within who refused to bow and scrape, who associated fear with fun, who would rather die than lose. "But, personally," I said, finally, "I t'ink sanity is overrated."

The Goblin King studied my face. "Fine, but I'm going with you."

"What? Why?" I asked, brow furrowed.

"Few reasons," he said, raising a finger for each, "one, if you go alone, she'll think you've come to kill *her*. Two, if you go alone, she'll probably try to kill *you*. And three, I'm the King and I do as I please," he replied, making a fist. "Take it or leave it."

"I'll take it," I replied, with a sigh.

What a royal pain in the ass.

CHAPTER 38

*O*beron stared up at me with an incredulous look on his face in response to my confession. "What do you mean you don't know how to create a Gateway?" he exclaimed, showcasing the massive rift between the two worlds with both arms. "What do you call that? Because to me, it looks like a giant fucking Gateway."

"Beginner's luck?" I offered, already regretting admitting to having created the Gateway. "Listen, I don't know how I did that. I just did it."

"You and your aunts, you mean," Oberon said, his tone shifting completely, catching me off-guard.

I winced, but didn't deny it.

"I thought so," Oberon said, his jaw bunching. "Which means, even if we survive this, my reign will end."

I snorted. "I wouldn't worry about me aunts takin' over Fae, no matter what they say. I've seen inside their heads. Both want the authority, but neither want the responsibility." I nudged the Goblin King playfully, something he was utterly unused to, thus earning me a fierce glare. "Now, how about ye show me how to make this damn Gateway? We're runnin' out of time."

As if to punctuate my remark, one of Oberon's Greek warships exploded at that very moment, sending gouts of flame soaring into the air. I grimaced. The trouble was—while Oberon's armada clearly had the advantage in a

215

straight fight—Balor's control of the waters made it nearly impossible for Oberon's sailors to do anything but stave off the giants as they navigated the whirlpools and waterspouts.

"Fine," Oberon said, snatching my hand. "I can teach you later. Let's go." I felt a tug on my belly button as the Goblin King stepped forward, whole landscapes within Fae blurring past. Some, like Neverland, I thought I recognized.

Hell, at one point I could have sworn I saw *Camelot* with its stone terraces and magnificent banners, besieged by the smoke of a thousand campfires.

Others were so bizarre I felt I could only have imagined them.

A forest of mushrooms as tall as trees.

A city in the sky connected by bridges.

At last, after several more steps, Oberon released me, and I found myself in the deep, dark cave I'd visited in what felt like a lifetime ago.

Where the Winter Queen had offered me a job.

"What the *fuck* was that?" I asked as a wave of vertigo struck me all at once, my knees threatening to buckle.

"Seven-league boots," Oberon said, smirking as he tapped one heel against the ground a few times. "Limited edition."

"I'm goin' to throw up," I said, propping myself up against a wall, bent slightly over.

"It'll pass. You'll be fine in a moment," Oberon said.

"No," a woman's voice said. "No, I don't think she will." I noticed something sharp had been pressed against my throat—an icicle as long as my arm, held by an old hag in stiletto heels.

The Winter Queen.

Oh, and did I mention the bitch had dogs now? Hounds as big as horses with glowing eyes prowled the shadows just outside the throne room, where we stood. Talk about a security upgrade.

"Nice to see ye again, Your Majesty," I quipped. "It's been too long."

The tip of the icicle sunk deeper into my throat, causing real discomfort this time. "What are you doing here?" she asked, though I was fairly certain no answer I gave her was going to convince the Queen to stop poking me.

"She's with me," King Oberon interjected, slowly removing the icicle from my neck, like someone adjusting the needle on a record player.

The Winter Queen stared haughtily down at Oberon, as if he were a child who'd just demanded he be treated like an adult. "And what are *you* doing here, Oberon? Shouldn't you be guarding our borders?"

The King and I exchanged looks. "Fae has been invaded," Oberon replied, choosing to leave out the finer details—like how I'd kicked open the door and gotten the party started. Probably for the best.

"And I need Balor's eye," I added, earning a glare from the Goblin King, which I promptly ignored. Granted, a more diplomatic approach might have been better suited to the situation, but I didn't have time to exchange pleasantries with the Faerie Queen on the off-chance I'd misjudged her.

The Winter Queen looked like she might explode, a vein appearing on her forehead like a crack in the ice, before marching off with a dramatic scream. "Return to your post, Oberon!" she commanded, heels punching holes in the ice-covered floors of her throne room. "Or else I will call off this truce and have your head for trespassing."

The Goblin King barked a laugh, only a few steps behind the Fae Queen, his boots unaffected by the slick floor. "You know as well as I do that if Balor defeats my fleet—which he will at this rate—decapitation would be a preferable outcome. I suggest you hear the girl out."

"You think I should give her the very eye I've been charged with hiding from Balor? So she can *bring it right to him?*" The Winter Queen exclaimed, whirling back around, her face outraged.

"And who charged you with that, again?" Oberon asked, his eyes glinting beneath the light of the strobing fish dancing above our heads—the only source of light to speak of.

"The Tuatha," the Winter Queen snapped. "As if you didn't know."

"Yes, but which one?" Oberon asked, taking a step forward, peering up at his fellow royal with an impish expression on his face. "Which of the Fae Court raised you above the others, on the condition that you never use the power of Balor's eye for your own gain?"

The Winter Queen's eyes flicked to my face, then away again. "It doesn't matter. She's dead."

"Aye, she is," I replied, skirting around Oberon until I was close enough to the Queen to see the pulse in her neck jump. "But her daughter," I said, picking up on Oberon's not-so-subtle hints, "is right fucking here."

The Queen eyed me up and down, skeptically. "That's not possible," she said.

"Drop the act," I snapped. "Ye knew all along who I was. That's why ye brought me here and offered me a place at your side, months ago."

"You did what?" Oberon growled, his face tight with anger.

"Easy there, Lyin' King," I said. "Ye did the same, not twenty-four hours ago."

"He what?!" the Queen exclaimed.

I sighed, quickly realizing my aunts may have been right to question the current state of Fae politics; if the ruling class was this divided, this cutthroat, I doubted the ruled were having their needs met.

"Enough!" I barked, before either could start in on the other. "I've come for the eye, and I mean to have it."

"Over my dead body," the Winter Queen snapped.

"That," I snarled, "can be arranged." At that precise moment, I felt something inside me give way. Not my wild side; she and I were totally on the same page at the moment.

Get the eye.

Bludgeon Balor.

Dismember Dobby.

Save Boston and the Fae.

No...this was a subtler sensation than anything my wild side had to offer. Of course, I might have overlooked it altogether if it weren't for the fact that—clearly—I wasn't the only one who'd picked up on the change: both the Queen and Oberon had drawn back from me, simultaneously, the whites of their eyes visible.

Oberon recovered first, coughing as if to clear his throat. "I suggest you do as she asks," he supplied.

"Are you telling me she sided with *you*?" the Winter Queen demanded.

The Goblin King smirked, clearly content to let her think so. In fact, that's probably why he'd insisted on coming with me—anything to advance his own agenda. Of course, it was possible I was being uncharitable. Either way, I didn't have time for their political bullshit.

"I side with no one," I replied, taking a threatening step forward, the ice beneath my feet crackling. The two royals recoiled, shuffling backwards. "The actions I take," I continued, "are me own. Always. If either of ye ever t'ink that—even for a moment—you're ever goin' to convince me otherwise, you're dead fuckin' wrong. And by the time ye take your last breath, you'll be *certain* of it." I took another step, and suddenly the luminescent fish above our heads froze in place—the abrupt change making the two royals jump. "I'm Quinn MacKenna, Morrigan's daughter, and *I am not to be trifled with.*"

The Queen whimpered, drawing my attention—but soon it was held by something else altogether: the face I saw in the smooth, reflective surface of her icy throne. My eyes were the first thing I noticed—emerald green and glowing, even the sclera, like moss-covered ponds beneath the summer sun. Next was my hair, a curtain of flame that framed my face—a face sculpted by hands that knew nothing of imperfection. I looked so beautiful...and yet so very, very cruel.

I closed my eyes.

And took a deep, calming breath.

A moment later, I opened them. The fish had resumed swimming, the play of their carefree light enough to distract me for a moment. I took another breath—glancing at the throne's reflective surface once more to make sure I was my old self—before turning my attention to the two royals, who watched me like I was a bomb that might explode at any moment. "Well, now," I said, smiling reassuringly, "I'd very much like ye to bring me Balor's eye, if ye would."

The Queen jerked her head fitfully. "I'll...be right back."

The Goblin King said nothing, though it was clear from his wary expression that he and I weren't hitting up the batting cages together anytime soon. Not that I blamed him; even I wasn't sure I was safe to be around, at this point. Oh well, I decided—guess I'd have to pick somebody else's brain regarding Gateways. Fortunately, I had a few experts to choose from.

Networking, people.

It's all about the networking.

CHAPTER 39

The Winter Queen returned with a box swaddled in cloth—the iron stench it carried making my nose rankle. Unfortunately, she also seemed to have recovered at least a portion of her previous attitude; she held the box out only partway, as if waiting for me to come collect it. I rolled my eyes and moved to take it from her—if being petty made her feel better, so be it.

"In exchange for this," she said, withdrawing the box just out of my reach, "I would like your...assistance."

I sucked my teeth. "Perhaps I wasn't clear last time—"

"You were," she interrupted, nervously. She took a deep breath. "But nothing in Fae is gained without an equal and worthwhile exchange. Surely you, *as Morrigan's daughter*," she said scathingly, "know that much."

I bit my tongue to stop from lashing out. She was right, although I hated to admit it; the Fae treated favors like currency. It was the only barter system that mattered to them. Which meant, if I wanted to take Balor's eye, I had to offer something of equal value in return. Of course, as a stranger in a strange land, I wasn't exactly familiar with the exchange rate. "Assistance with what?" I growled.

"For far too long, Fae has been terrorized by an outsider. In exchange for Balor's eye, I want you to see that the outsider pays for his crimes against our people. Against *your* people," she clarified, meeting my gaze.

I frowned, the truth of that addition hitting me over the head like a hammer. Jesus *Christ*, was I really one of them? A Faeling? *Me*? I cursed inwardly as I realized she was right; the Fae—who I'd always thought of as *other*, somehow—were technically my people, now. Of course, with that realization came a whole new host of questions, ranging from the reasonable to the ridiculous. What classification of Fae was I? Was I immortal? One of the Tuatha? Did antihistamines work on iron allergies?

But then I asked myself one that stopped me in my tracks...

Was I even human?

"Was it something I said?" the Winter Queen asked, glancing sidelong at Oberon.

"I think it just occurred to her that she's one of us," the Goblin King replied, studying my face.

"She isn't one of *us*," the Winter Queen hissed. "You saw that little power display, you know what that meant. She's clearly one of the Tuatha de Danaan. A Lady of the Fae Court. A goddess..." She looked me up and down, as if noticing my attire for the first time, her gaze lingering on the tacky, gay cruise ship logo splayed across my tattered t-shirt. "Well, the potential is there, at any rate. Anyway, do you accept?"

"Accept what?" I asked, finding it hard to focus; I was still a little busy coming to terms with the fact that I'd have to mark *Other* down when I filed my taxes from now on.

"The conditions I've given you," she said, exasperated.

"Wait, ye want me to track someone down? Was that it?" I asked, replaying her request in my mind.

"I want you to find the Manling born in Fae," the Winter Queen said, her eyes blazing with a cool, sadistic light that had nothing to do with the fish. "And I want you to end his miserable life."

I did a double-take "Nate Temple? Ye want me to kill Nate Temple?"

She nodded. "He's taken everything from us. Wiped out hundreds of our race. The loyal Fae tremble at the very mention of his name, and he has become a rallying cry for those who despise our rule. He cannot be allowed to live. As one of the Tuatha, it is your duty to protect us."

I glanced over at Oberon, wondering what he'd have to say on the subject—but, aside from looking vaguely constipated, I couldn't tell where he stood.

Kill Nate Temple in exchange for Balor's eye, huh? I scowled, weighing my options. I had to admit, I'd killed my fair share of Regulars, Freaks, and Fae; pulling the trigger didn't bother me nearly as much as it used to. But I'd never assassinated anyone before. Most of my kills had been in self-defense, or at least morally justifiable. Taking out Nate Temple—even if I had no idea who he was—would be a difficult task, ethically, not to mention practically. I mean, the bastard *was* a wizard—perhaps the most powerful one alive, for all I knew.

Lightweights didn't typically run around declaring themselves royalty, after all.

But then, of course, there was the fact that I could think of at least a half-dozen people who would never forgive me for trying—people I actually cared about...or at least didn't despise.

Namely, my one true friend...

Othello.

No, I realized—not even for the sake of vengeance could I agree to hurting her.

And Callie probably wouldn't take too kindly to it, either. I'd always gotten the impression they were dating. Or on the verge of dating. One of those *were they*, *weren't they* situations that everyone else seemed to be able to see so clearly, no matter how aloof the two of them were on the matter.

Frankly, I thought she could do better.

"I can't do that," I replied.

"Can't, or won't?" she asked, eyes narrowed.

"Probably the latter, but definitely the former."

The Queen sneered and drew back with the box. "Then no eye."

"But," I countered, meeting the Queen's gaze, "I will promise to track him down. To hold him accountable for what he's done and see he never does it again. To stop treatin' this realm like his own personal battleground whenever he..." I drifted off before I could finish that sentence. Christ, hadn't I just done the same thing by opening up a Gateway into Fae, banking on Oberon and his armada to help solve the problem I'd created?

Was I really no better than Nate Temple?

Ugh. I needed a shower.

"I accept," the Fae Queen said, "on the condition that, should he fail to live up to your ideals, you go after him in earnest. With the intent to kill."

I could tell from the smug expression on her face that she fully expected Nate to ignore me—to continue doing as he pleased, despite the damage it caused. In fact, from her perspective, the moment I agreed to this deal, a clash between Nate and me would be inevitable. And I had to admit, she might be right. But I had to try; it was possible Nate—like me—had simply gotten too embroiled in his own shit to notice the effect he had on the world, on both worlds. Maybe all he needed was a gut check—someone to act as his conscience, if only to make him realize the Fae were worthwhile, living beings.

And the only person who could do it was me.

God help us all.

"Deal," I said, holding out my hand.

We were so fucked.

CHAPTER 40

I collapsed on the deck of the *USS Cyclops*, dry-heaving, cradling the cloth-covered box to my chest to make sure I didn't accidentally drop it and inadvertently kill us all.

"It really isn't that bad," the Goblin King said.

Unfortunately, I was too busy fighting off the nausea that came with traveling by seven-league boots to argue with the goblin. Of course, no matter what he claimed, there was clearly no reason to ever do that shit again. Strictly Ubers and Gateways for me from now on.

Maybe hiring a driver—I was still ruminating on that one.

I took a deep breath and rose wearily to my feet, glancing out across the water to see how the battle was faring.

It wasn't pretty.

The gouged bones of ships bobbed everywhere I looked—their wooden guts spilled out into the water, stretching out along the horizon for as far as my eyes could see. A few ships remained, but only the smaller, nimbler vessels—the ones capable of avoiding the literal *waves* full of Fomorian warriors and Balor's magic.

As I watched, the blue light of Balor's jeweled eye abruptly pulsed, flashing against the side of a schooner full of elves in an arc of azure flame. The boat split neatly in two as swiftly as ripped paper, blue flame licking at its entrails as pointy-eared sailors dove into the sea—only to be immediately slaughtered by Balor's troops waiting patiently below.

I had to admit to a momentary sense of panic—if Balor was this powerful with that strange replacement stone in his eye socket, how deadly would he be with the one I held in my hands?

Suddenly, the box felt like a lead weight.

An anchor.

Oberon grunted, studying the scene with far more composure than I would have expected, as if he'd anticipated finding most of his fleet wiped out upon his arrival. "Well," he said, hiking up his pants, "you know what they say…if you want something done right, hire a professional." I opened my mouth to point out that wasn't how the saying went, but before I could get a word in edgewise, Oberon seized the nearest goblin intern—most of whom had gathered behind us the instant we arrived, like we were food and they were a horde of starving, feral cats. "Sound the retreat!" he barked.

The goblin intern—a portly creature with a pot-belly—jerked his double-chin and bolted towards the front of the ship as fast as his stumpy legs could carry him. I snatched the Goblin King by the shoulder. "Listen, I don't want any more Fae to die, either," I said, imploringly. "But ye can't expect me to get anywhere near Balor without your fleet to distract him. Ye can't retreat."

The sound of a bell tolling interrupted me before I could say anything else. At the front of the ship, a giant church bell—its frame built into the deck—swung back and forth, the rope beneath held by the surprisingly quick goblin intern. Almost instantaneously, a swarm of pixies burst forth like fireworks spitting off into the sky, headed for the remaining boats in droves.

Oberon shook me off, glaring at the contact. "I'm not," he replied, enigmatically, before marching towards the ship's portside. I hurried after him, glancing back only once to make sure Hook's Jolly Roger was still in play. Thankfully, it remained where I'd left it. I spotted Hook still standing where I'd left him, more or less, watching the battle through a spyglass, but my aunts were nowhere to be seen. I sighed, grateful that at least that part of my plan was still intact.

When I finally caught up to the Goblin King, I found he'd claimed another goblin intern—held by the throat this time, a good foot above the deck—and was commanding him to tell the ship's captain to get us airborne. Five minutes ago. I frowned, feeling foolish for having forgotten all about the fact that the USS *Cyclops* had met us in the skies above Neverland. I wasn't sure about the warship's mobility, should Balor decide to throw one of his waterspouts at us, but it certainly helped to have the higher ground.

In a manner of speaking.

The intern took off the instant Oberon dropped him back to his feet. The Goblin King swept the ship with a calculating glare, assessing the situation. Then he took a deep breath and blew it out. "Alright," he muttered, "time to call in the big guns."

The big guns? What the hell was *that* supposed to mean?

"I thought *we*," I said, hoisting the box as evidence, "were the big guns."

The Goblin King snorted as he marched across the deck, clearly expecting me to follow. "Of course not. You really think I'd let you run out there and risk everything? You're the bait. The only reason I agreed to take you to the Winter Queen was to get what I wanted," he muttered, waving a hand in the direction of the box I clutched.

I jerked to a stop, blinking at his retreating back.

A single purple pixie beelined towards us while I tried to process what Oberon was saying, the wee creature halting inches from the Goblin King's face, saluting smartly. "All the captains have been notified, my Lord!" she declared, her voice so high-pitched it sounded vaguely like a mouse squeaking.

"Excellent," Oberon replied with an efficient, dismissive nod, before continuing on.

I double-timed to catch back up with him, furious that he had been playing me. "What the fuck d'ye mean I'm *bait*?" I hissed, as soon as we were relatively alone.

"His eye," Oberon said, glancing at the box in my hands. "He'll have sensed it by now, and—with the fleet retreating—I expect Balor is feeling especially confident. I doubt he's feeling patient, after spending centuries below the seas." Oberon pointed through the still-open Gateway I had made, indicating the line created by the waters of Fae colliding with the waters of Massachusetts Bay. "But, once he passes that threshold, both he and his army will be vulnerable. I simply needed him to think he'd won."

Then he began walking again, seemingly unconcerned about my opinion. I scowled after the Goblin King, realizing everything he'd done up until now—especially by helping me—had been to advance his own agenda; he'd seamlessly integrated my proposition into his own plan...whatever that was. I hurried after him, not the least bit happy to discover he'd helped me under false pretenses—but not particularly surprised either. Maybe even a little bit impressed.

"Why would that matter? I thought ye didn't want him steppin' foot in Fae?" I asked, heatedly, pointing out the fact that Balor was, most definitely, about to do just that.

In fact, at the moment he seemed to be *literally* stepping on a Viking longship full of Fae sailors, snapping it in two as he tore the dragon figurehead free, studying its craftsmanship—not remotely concerned about the sailors being massacred by his nearby troops.

"Ordinarily, no," Oberon murmured, dispassionately watching Balor's casual act of destruction. "*Especially* if he had his eye. But these are *Fae* seas," he said. "Balor won't find them so easy to bend to his will."

I scoffed. "Oh, I don't know. Looks to be havin' no problem so far. Even without his eye," I growled.

He ignored that, sighing with annoyance, like I was some pesky child at his hip, tugging on his shirttail. "There are creatures below that do not bow to him, creatures far older than he." He met my eyes this time, glancing over his shoulder, and I caught a mischievous twinkle in those haunting depths. "Far older than even *me*." The Goblin King halted alongside a massive foghorn mounted along the ship's hull, its bizarrely curved frame like a boat-sized boomerang.

The foghorn itself was a seemingly infinite spiral, like a Nautilus shell.

"My Lord," a goblin intern called, approaching from the front of the ship. "Balor's army has given chase to the retreating ships, as you predicted!"

"Excellent," Oberon whispered, eyes gleaming, that twinkle I'd caught seeming to catch fire with an inner light. "Alright, someone get the straps off this thing!" he yelled to no one in particular, pointing up at the topmost portion of the horn—at least ten feet in the air. Several goblins standing nearby eyed each other, waiting for one of their number to make a move, but none did.

"Ye have to single one of 'em out," I suggested, remembering my lifeguard training from my very first summer gig. "Ye have to point and say somethin' like 'ye with the red shirt' if ye want it to get done."

Oberon frowned thoughtfully, and then looked around. He pointed. "You with the ugly face! Get those straps off."

"I don't t'ink that's bein' specific enough…" I muttered under my breath.

But apparently the distinction made sense to the creatures gathered, because the goblins parted to make way for an ogre I'd mistaken for a pile of seaweed-covered boxes, who rose, yawned, and trudged over. The ogre studied the straps for a moment, as if deciding how best to remove them. Before the Goblin King could offer a suggestion, however, the ogre reached out and tore the straps in half, the leather snapping in two beneath his hands.

Oberon squeezed the bridge of his nose, taking a slow meditative breath, as if silently reminding himself that no, he *shouldn't* kill the ogre for being an idiot. But I was instantly distracted as gravity took over and the horn's flared bell tilted towards the water, falling in with a humongous splash that drenched a few of the goblins near the ship's railing. Suddenly, the ridiculous shape of the thing made a little more sense; the mouthpiece stood at approximately mouth height—for a goblin, at any rate—while the vast majority of the rest managed not to brush up against the ship's hull. Oberon strode up to the mouthpiece, wiped it clean with a handkerchief he fetched from his pocket, and blew.

Truth be told, I flinched, expecting a cacophony of sound, but all I caught were the audible cracks of tremendously large bubbles as they surfaced and popped. Oh, right. Because the horn was underwater, I realized.

Wait, why was the horn underwater?

The Goblin King stepped away and put his hands on his hips, chest puffed up. "That should do it."

"Should do *what?*" I asked, baffled.

Oberon grinned and pointed out at the water behind us, where a dark shadow began to spread along the horizon line, darkening the surface of the sea in an impossibly huge swathe. The Goblin King turned to his sailors and began fist-pumping, yelling one word over and over again.

"Kraken! Kraken! KRAKEN!"

Soon, all the other goblins were screaming it, too, saliva stretching from their pointed teeth as their eyes grew wild with anticipation.

So the son-of-a-bitch *did* have a Goddamned Kraken.

I fucking *knew* it!

CHAPTER 41

We were airborne by the time the Kraken's shadow darkened the sea beneath us, which meant we got a great view of just how gargantuan the creature was as it made for Balor's front lines. I couldn't put an exact measurement down, or even an imprecise one, because I had nothing to compare it to.

Basically, it was so fucking big that I found my brain momentarily short-circuiting as I tried to map out the evolutionary biology of the damned beast using creatures I *knew* existed. Squid. Octopus. Giant Squid. Kraken?

I shook my head.

All I knew for certain was that I was more than happy to be up here and not down there.

Since the goblin intern's report, the Fomorians had charged through the gap in the hundreds, rolling across the water like a cresting wave of giant, murderous blue surfers.

Of course, what concerned me most wasn't Balor's troops. Sure, there were more than enough of them to cause damage—perhaps even invade Fae —but without their leader they were simply another race of relatively terri-fying creatures in a realm full of relatively terrifying creatures. And so I scanned the waters below, looking for that tell-tale flash of blue light, but saw nothing, not even as the Kraken's shadow cruised beneath Balor's army.

Where the fuck was he?

I gasped suddenly as tentacles—as big and thick around as giant sequoias and covered in glistening silver scales—exploded up from the water like rockets.

And...

Began *decimating* Balor's army in great, big, berserker swings.

I blinked, trying to take in the screams, explosive geysers, and thunderous *booms* as the Kraken's tentacles pummeled anything in its vicinity—which was a big fucking vicinity.

This was...Whac-A-Mole on steroids.

The difference in scope made the Fomorians—giants themselves—look like nothing more than ants scurrying from the wrath of a malevolent child. They tried to escape, but the waters of the Fae seas suddenly seemed to refuse to move as quickly, thickening just enough to make the Fomorians incredibly easy targets. Oberon, standing beside me, looked appropriately smug. I couldn't blame him; he'd manipulated the situation perfectly.

We watched the carnage for a solid minute, both speechless.

But then it was Balor's turn to wield the mallet.

Oberon's smirk vanished, replaced by open-mouthed horror as a deceptively thin beam of blue light shot out across the water, flitting across each of the Kraken's tentacles, severing them one-by-one.

The Kraken screamed—a sound so piteous and uncanny it threatened to drive us all to our knees.

The severed limbs toppled into the water like calving glaciers, causing immediate forty-foot swells before the dismembered calamari slowly floated back up to the surface, the silver scales alone worth a king's ransom. The Kraken fled, drawing its remaining limbs back under the water, trailing golden ichor that altered the surrounding waters and now left them looking as though they'd been made of molten gold.

Combined with the broken pirate ships, dead sailors, and dismembered silver tentacles, it looked like a treasure hunter's wet dream.

Pun intended.

"Damnit!" Oberon cursed, slamming his fist—suddenly much larger, claws clenched tight against his palm—down on the railing, splintering the wood. "What in Fae is that infernal light?"

"Balor's eye," I replied, realizing Oberon had yet to see the leader of the Fomorians up close.

The Goblin King, nearly as tall as I was now—taller if you counted the wicked-looking rack of antlers that had emerged from his head—flicked his gaze to the box in my hand.

"No," I replied. "He found a replacement. No idea where or how, but it's powerful." I didn't bother explaining beyond that; I really had no idea what the eye was capable of at this point, other than what I'd seen. Regardless, it seemed as though Oberon's strategy—clever though it had been—had failed.

"How are we supposed to defeat something like that?" Oberon asked, his voice tinged with despair.

I grunted. The Goblin King was right; no matter what the Fae tried—between his magic and the power of his bejeweled eye—Balor's might far exceeded their own. Frankly, I knew exactly how that felt. But then, that's why I'd made a deal for the real thing; it was time to fight Balor with Balor.

I sniffed, once, then marched off.

"Where are you going?" Oberon yelled.

"To do what I should have done the moment I got here," I called back, holding the box up in the air for him to see.

A string of goblin curses erupted behind me. "That's suicide!" he shouted, finally.

I glanced back over my shoulder. "And?"

The Goblin King had balled up his fists, eyes blazing. "And...we'll cover you," he snarled.

I winked. "Who's a good goblin?" I muttered, under my breath. "Ye are, aye ye are, Obie."

Hook helped me across to the deck of his ship, which hovered in the air alongside the USS Cyclops. "Took you long enough," he quipped. "For a minute there I thought we'd miss out on the fighting altogether. Anyway, did you get it?" he asked.

I held up the box, still swaddled in cloth. "Aye."

"You know, after seeing what happened to that monster, not to mention those ships," Hook said, glancing out at the gilded sea, now cluttered with the shattered remains of ships and the glimmering limbs of a wounded Kraken, "I'd rather not see the Jolly Roger join the festivities."

I frowned. "Does that mean ye want to back out?" I asked.

Hook snorted and looked me full in the eye. "Please. No, it means I'd rather we end this without my ship in pieces."

I grinned. "Ye know, for a villain, you're alright."

Hook frowned. "*Who* says I'm a villain?"

Thankfully, my aunts approached before I had to comment, strutting across the deck as if they owned the place. I turned at their arrival, wondering what they'd been up to while I was away, but was too surprised to ask once they stopped in their tracks, staring at me like I had something on my face. "What is it?" I asked, reaching up to brush my cheeks.

"Somethin' is wrong with ye," Badb replied.

"She means somethin' is *different*," Macha said, choosing the more diplomatic adjective.

I frowned, wondering what they meant. Did it have something to do with why Oberon had refused to look me in the eyes? With the strange face I'd seen reflected back at me in the Winter Queen's throne room? I shook my head, realizing it ultimately didn't matter. Soon, Balor would be close enough to turn his attention to the skies, and I didn't want to see what that replacement jewel of his could do to a pair of ships moored in the sky like sitting ducks. We needed to *move*.

"I got the eye," I said, changing the subject entirely.

The sisters took a healthy step back.

"That's...nice," Macha said.

"Good luck with that," Badb replied.

I turned from one to the other, blinking in confusion. "Seriously? I need your help if I'm goin' to use it," I snapped, exasperated. "I have no idea what this t'ing can do, or how to wield it."

"Unleashed, his eye will kill everythin' in its line of sight," Badb said.

Macha shrugged and nodded, as if Badb had told me all I needed to know.

"Aye, but I need specifics," I said, testily. "Like what's its range? Its area of effect?"

The two looked at me like I was speaking a different language.

"I need to know how close I need to get," I replied, speaking slowly, as if I were talking to someone hard of hearing.

"Oh. Close," Badb replied.

"Aye," Macha said. "The closer the better, I'd say."

I fought the urge to strangle my dear old aunties, the only family I had left.

"Don't worry," Hook said, resting his good hand on my shoulder and squeezing. "I can get you close enough to count the teeth in his mouth. Just don't blame me if he uses them to chew you up and spit you out."

"I hate all of ye," I ground out. "I hope ye know that."

"I'll take that as a yes," Hook replied. "All hands! Let's go!" he barked suddenly, standing so close his command made me jump. I stared daggers at his back as he headed towards the helm.

"Ye seriously plan to go through with this?" Macha asked.

"Ye know dyin' won't bring her back?" Badb said, after a moment's silence. "The woman you mourn, I mean."

I hung my head. Jesus, where had *that* comment come from? As if I needed any *more* emotional baggage right now.

"We were inside your head, too, ye know," Macha said, reaching out to lift my chin. "We knew from the beginnin' what ye were hopin' might happen. That ye sought vengeance, but also oblivion."

I looked away, my face flushed. Not from embarrassment, but from exposure; the idea that they'd been privy to my innermost thoughts made me feel incredibly vulnerable. But—after taking a moment to collect myself —I turned back. "T'ings have changed," I admitted.

And it was true.

I still felt like my heart had been torn out of my chest, but now that I'd had a little time to process, I realized I had too much to live for to throw it all away. I had promises to keep, answers to find, and friends to save.

Dying now would be incredibly inconvenient.

Besides—on the off-chance Dez was waiting there on the other side—I couldn't risk it.

She'd fucking murder me.

The sisters studied my face, then nodded as one—the symmetry of it still creepy as hell. "Alright, then we'll help you," Macha said.

"Although I still t'ink this is a *monumentally* stupid idea," Badb added.

I scowled. "T'anks, I t'ink."

"Don't mention it," Badb said, with a wave of her hand.

I sighed.

Ain't family grand?

CHAPTER 42

*T*ogether, we soared over the wreckage in the Jolly Roger, dodging the desperate attempts to bring us down by the small faction of Balor's remaining army—their coral spears whistling past as the Jolly Roger flew by. Tired of sliding all over the deck, I'd tied a rope around my waist and attached myself to the rear mast near the helm. It wasn't ideal, considering it limited my mobility, but at this point I was more focused on finding Balor than helping out the crew; since severing the Kraken's limbs, the light emitted by his jeweled eye had been conspicuously absent. Did the damned thing need to recharge, or was he simply content for us to come to him before making his next move?

A glance behind was all I needed to reassure myself that the *USS Cyclops* still trailed us—a steel titan in the skies, approaching like a dark cloud. I wondered, idly, why none of the other ships in Oberon's fleet had been able to fly as these two could. Was it the pixies? As far as I'd seen, only the Goblin King's ship had them onboard. And I knew that's what powered the Jolly Roger—at least according to the story. Still, it seemed a little miserly on Oberon's part, hoarding the power of flight for himself. But then, given the Goblin King's unscrupulous nature, it made sense; it was easier to rule from a position of strength. Delegation was a double-edged sword like that, after all.

"There he is!" Badb pointed, bringing me back to the task at hand.

I swung around, following the line of her arm, and finally spotted the bastard. He stood at the threshold between the mortal realm and Fae, arms casually at his sides as if waiting for us to approach. I gripped the railing, wondering what the hell he was playing at—but then I saw it. Beyond the Gateway, perhaps a mile out to sea, a wave was coming. And not just any wave. This was a wave so large it would pour through the Gateway like a flood, wiping out everything before it, including us.

I watched as Balor raised his arms and saw the breaker climb even higher behind him, the tip of the swell now well out of sight beyond the arch of the Gateway. Too late, I realized his plan. He'd drawn us close for this very reason; the USS Cyclops was far too bulky to climb fast enough to avoid it, and the Jolly Roger—which was even *closer*—would only survive if we took immediately to the clouds, but by then it wouldn't matter. We'd be the only ones left, and Balor would have little trouble blowing us out of the sky the moment we descended.

"What's the plan?" Hook yelled, clearly coming to the same conclusion. We had to decide now, before the wave got any closer, whether to climb or run. Badb and Macha exchanged looks, while I desperately tried to find a third option.

"Head straight for the wave," Macha yelled.

"Do suicidal tendencies run in your family?" Hook asked, gaping at me with wide eyes.

"Wouldn't know," I replied. "I only met 'em today."

Hook's eyes widened still further. Then he cursed. "I really hope you know what you're doing," he muttered, spinning the wheel, angling us straight for the fast-approaching wave.

Macha ignored the conversation and strode forward, her hair and dress whipping about in the wind.

Except...neither were blowing the direction they should have been. It was like she stood in a pocket of air all her own, a bubble that swirled about her like a personal whirlwind.

"Showoff," Badb said, folding her arms over her chest.

"What's she doin'?" I asked.

"Clearin' the way," Badb replied, jerking a thumb towards the wall of water looming before us.

The wave reached the Gateway at the same exact moment we did. I cringed and braced for impact, but...

There wasn't one.

Instead, the wave collided with the edges of the Gateway and we—the Jolly Roger and its crew—flew right *through* it, surrounded by a tunnel of water that corkscrewed around us as though we were the tip of a power drill. I stared up in fascination at the revolving water, then back down at Macha, who was rotating her hands in slow motion, clearly manipulating the air with enough force to forge a path for us to fly through.

The crew, realizing we weren't going to die, began cheering.

And then, so suddenly I gasped, we were out. Hook, clearly having expected instant annihilation as well, jerkily spun us around, instinctively banking us towards Balor from behind, like a skidding car.

Fast and Furious: Neverland Drift.

I held tight to the rail, the shift in momentum threatening to throw me overboard, despite the safety rope tying me to the ship.

"My turn," Badb said, cracking her neck, somehow perfectly balanced. She stepped out onto the deck and patted Macha—whose shoulders now drooped from exhaustion—on the back. I frowned, wondering what Badb intended to do now that we were past the wave. But, before I could ask, she raised her arms towards the sky, her fingers curled like claws.

A thunder clap ripped above us, so loud it shook my bones, like a bass beat at a rock concert. I had to shield my eyes as lightning tore down from the sky, heading right for us, changing paths at the last instant—channeled directly through Badb's arms, which were now aimed at Balor's unprotected back.

It seemed we'd snuck past the warlord without his noticing.

And now he was going to pay.

Except the Fomorian warlord spun around at the last possible instant, his jeweled eye blazing as a shield of blue light materialized before him. The lightning crashed against the barrier in an explosive spiderweb as the errant arc sought a way through, so bright I couldn't stand to look at it. But, even without looking, I knew it wouldn't find an opening; we'd already tried hitting him with enough voltage to run a city block for a week, with no results. I frowned. Badb wasn't stupid. Socially inept, maybe, but not stupid. She knew the lightning wouldn't kill him...but it would blind him.

If only I could get close enough.

"I can give you one pass!" Hook yelled over the sound of crackling electricity, banking the ship in a slow circle.

I shook my head. "It won't work unless I can hit him from the side!" I called back. I wasn't sure if Balor's replacement eye was strong enough to defend against the power of the original, but I couldn't risk wasting my chance. If I unleashed the power of the eye in my hand and it failed, Balor would have little trouble tearing our ship apart and retrieving his prize. Sadly, it didn't look like we had a choice; Badb's lightning was fading, fast.

And, with it, our chances of distracting Balor.

At least, that is, until I saw what was screaming through the skies towards us from Boston's harbor—or, should I say, *who*. I rubbed at my eyes, not believing what I was seeing. But, no matter how inconceivable, I'd have recognized that fierce set of fiery wings anywhere.

Alucard, my vamp in ragged armor.

As he drew closer and Badb's lighting died down completely, I realized there was something different about him. He appeared...wilder, somehow, more savage, with concentric golden rings spinning around his torso, jets of molten flame trailing from his eyes, his robes an even darker shade of red at the hem.

Alucard rocketed forth, so fast the Fomorian warlord didn't have a chance to turn, and hit Balor from behind with the force of a Mack Truck, sending the Fomorian skipping across the water's surface like a chucked pebble.

The gloriously vengeful Firefang hovered above the waves and glanced up at us imperiously, which was probably why he didn't see the Fomorian warlord's fist emerge from below the water at a hundred-miles per hour.

I was pretty sure he felt it, though.

Alucard was blasted back by the blow, soaring into the sky like a ball knocked out of the park by Big Papi in his prime.

Balor, who seemed a little singed—at most—kept his glittering sapphire eye fixated on the tumbling vampire, his immediate attention riveted on the only threat who had, so far, managed to do more than merely annoy him.

Which meant we had a chance. I gritted my teeth anxiously, calculating how best to sneak up on the Fomorian before my window closed.

Hook, meanwhile, stared down at the combatants with the easy temper of a man who'd seen his fair share of pitched battles. He reached up and tugged on his hat, then bellowed, "Crew! Let's show that blaggard what for! Prepare the cannons!" Before I could say anything, crew members began hurrying below deck, scurrying out of sight. Hook waved me over, steadying the ship long enough for me to meet him at the helm. "We'll fire everything we have at him," he said. "Give him a fight on two fronts. That should give you the time you need."

"To do *what?*" I asked, still trying to figure out how I was supposed to get close enough to hit the bastard from his *blind* side—because nothing about cannon fire struck me as particularly subtle.

Hook grinned and pressed a bag into my hands. I frowned and opened it, then stared at its contents in total confusion. "Ye want me to throw glitter at him?" I asked, cocking an eyebrow.

"What's glitter?" Hook asked.

"This!" I said, holding up the pouch full of twinkling, technicolor tinsel.

"No," Hook drawled, as if I were the one who was hard of hearing, "that's pixie dust. I stole it, ages ago. Now, I suggest you pour it all over yourself, think some happy thoughts, and get your ass down there!"

I blinked several times, opened my mouth and then closed it with an audible *click*. "So, you're tellin' me that—to save all of Fae, not to mention me city—I have to give meself a glitter shower?" I rehashed.

"Pixie...Dust," Hook said, then mouthed the words for me, signaling the cadence with his iron attachment. "Say it with me...*pixie...dust.*"

I snatched up the bag and stalked off, shaking my head, ignoring the Captain's baffled expression. Of course I knew what pixie dust *was*, but the idea of rubbing myself down with sparkles was some Dorian Gray shit. Couldn't saving the day come with something more dignifying?

"Pixie dust," I muttered, stomping my bare feet.

Hook could call it whatever he wanted.

The shit still looked like glitter.

CHAPTER 43

I wobbled awkwardly in the air, trying my best to think happy
thoughts. That part was important, wasn't it?

Because it sure as shit wasn't working well for me. I felt like a drunk
seagull.

"For the dust to work, I have to be fuckin' happy?" I snarled at the open
air around me, struggling not to flip upside down as I heard someone who
sounded suspiciously like Macha laughing in the distance. I ignored her,
ignored the fact that my life was in shambles while I tried to think of happy
shit.

Like life before I met my aunts, for example.

Those had been good times.

Whether it was the thought itself or simply focusing on something other
than the flight, I found I was no longer cartwheeling through the air. The
truth was I had no idea if Hook had been fucking with me regarding the
whole happy thoughts business—but I couldn't exactly take chances. Off to
my right, he and the crew of the Jolly Roger were busy firing down on
Balor, each fucking boom of their cannons fucking with my flying Zen.

Cannonballs the size of watermelons spewed from her sides, raining
down on the Fomorian, who—I hated to admit—was living up to the hype;
he deflected each projectile with towering water pillars, their change in
trajectory making them as much a hazard to Alucard—who had returned,

and was currently doing his best to trade shots with the warlord—as they were to Balor.

Which left me, Quinn "TwinkleFae" MacKenna, free to ungracefully roam the skies, unmolested, clutching the box containing Balor's eye as though I were preparing to drop an atomic bomb. Now able to remain at least mostly upright, I still sucked as a pilot. The harder I tried to direct my flight, the further off-course I ended up. Granted, all I needed was to get close enough to Balor to open the box while his attention was elsewhere, but at this rate I doubted I'd make it before either the Jolly Roger ran out of ammunition or Alucard ran out of juice.

Either way, we were probably fucked.

What the hell had I been thinking?

I felt something slither inside me, reading my thoughts, sensing my needs. I shuddered, the familiar sensation of my wild side creeping into my consciousness making it hard to concentrate. I tried to focus, but then a dark, desperate thought occurred to me.

Why not...let *her* take the reins? My wild side, unleashed.

She, at least, knew how to fly.

I shook that thought off. It wasn't so much that I didn't want her taking control—it was that I feared what that might mean. We needed to stop Balor, obviously, but this battlefield was especially chaotic. What if she got distracted by the Fomorian cannon fodder who remained on the other side of the Gateway, or began dry-humping Alucard?

At least with me at the helm, the priorities were clear.

But with her...who knew what she would consider most pressing?

I ground my teeth, willing myself towards the water, but nothing happened.

Let go, a voice whispered. I jerked in alarm, almost dropping Balor's eye into the Fae seas far below.

Give in.

I tensed again, but this time it was internal. Because the voice...it came from *inside* me. In my *mind*.

Trust yourself, the voice purred, sounding amused.

Wait, trust myself?

I frowned, dipping a little as I considered what that meant.

Trust myself...

So suddenly the thought threatened to throw me into a dive, it hit me...

I'd been thinking of my wild side as something separate all along, like a creature I could cage and let loose at will. But she wasn't. She was *me*, as surely as the reflection of that cruel, beautiful goddess I'd seen in the Winter Queen's throne room was *me*. I wasn't creating barriers by thinking of them as *other*, I was killing off parts of my...

Self.

The truth—and I was beginning to see it clearly, now—was that they wanted what I wanted, even if we took different paths to get there.

I took a deep breath, let it out slowly, and did exactly what the voice in my head had suggested.

I let go.

CHAPTER 44

A moment later, I tore through the skies, whooping in delight as I flew circles around cannonballs that seemed to sluggishly drift through the sky on their path towards Balor. The instant I'd let go, my doubts had evaporated, and seconds had become minutes—giving me plenty of time to cross the divide between where I'd left Hook and where Balor stood, the power of his bejeweled eye slowly slicing a furrow in the air that Alucard was narrowly avoiding—twisting in mid-air with one wing cocked, the other straight out, leaving a trail of fire in his wake.

Almost like I was watching an underwater battle where everything was a fraction of the speed.

Well, everything except *me*.

I landed on the ocean's surface, light as a feather, perhaps twenty feet away from the Fomorian. His back was turned. I approached him, slowly, carefully unfolding the cloth to reveal the iron box within as I went. Beside me, water sprayed in a slow arc from one of the cannonballs striking a liquid column—the droplets distinct enough to count. I ducked them and returned my attention to Balor.

But it wasn't Balor I was facing, now.

It was Dobby.

The spriggan had emerged in his shadow form like a spider, tendrils arcing out towards me in a lazy wave. I danced around them, laughing,

242

hopping over one like a jump rope, and limboing beneath another, until at last I was within striking distance. By the time I looked back at him, Dobby's face had begun to form out of the shadows, his eyes wide in surprise. Balor, meanwhile, had begun to twist at the hips, to bring the light of his eye to bear, but it was too late.

Far too late.

I sank beneath the waves, angling the box so that the exposed eye would stare at nothing but its owner and a dark, desolate sky, and cracked the lid of the box. Pain lanced up my arm the instant I touched the iron—but by then it didn't matter.

I watched with wide eyes as a pale, sickly light unlike any I'd ever seen screamed outwards like an exploding star, kissing upon Dobby's face, then Balor's back, and finally through to the sky above.

The spriggan was the first to feel its effects—his impossibly large eyes sunk deeper and deeper into a cavernous face, his lips peeling back against his gums—every inch of him withering until even his shadow was eaten up by the flash of light from the exposed eye in my hands.

He screamed in sheer agony.

I almost closed my eyes to fully savor the beautiful sound, but I couldn't afford to look away; I wanted to be able to look back and enjoy *both* memories.

Balor was next. The warlord broke down incrementally until the weight of his own head snapped his brittle neck in two, and his dry, shriveled flesh fell off his bones.

Beyond, the clouds wisped into nothing, vaporized by the power I held in the palm of my hands.

I slammed the box shut as time reasserted itself.

If it burned me this time, I didn't even notice.

CHAPTER 45

*A*lucard—no longer bathed in golden light but looking fairly scrumptious anyway—met me on the deck of the Jolly Roger. I had a small, threadbare pirate blanket wrapped around my shoulders in an attempt to vanquish the incessant chills that were racking my body and making my teeth rattle; closing the iron box and sealing away the virulent power of Balor's eye had chased away both my newfound power and my wild side, for some reason, leaving me stranded in the freezing Atlantic until Hook and his crew had found me and brought me onboard the flying vessel. Unfortunately, the abrupt loss of my magic had also shut down the Gateway entirely, leaving Oberon's fate, and that of the remaining Fomorian warriors, up in the air for the time being.

As if by magic—and by that, I meant totally by magic—the moment Balor had died, the dark storm clouds and choppy waters had all but disappeared. Which left the ship hanging out among the remaining wisps of white cloud cover on a sunny afternoon above Boston harbor.

My aunts—between our short-lived fusion and the individual powers they'd exerted getting me close to Balor—appeared equally drained, albeit dry and looking far worse for wear than I did. At this point, I'd basically embraced my inner hippie; no shirt, no shoes, no problem. Well, practically no shirt, anyway, since it was basically a tattered ruin, and my blanket little better than an ancient doily. I caught Alucard sneaking a peek the instant he came over, and so—with the grace of a shambling, homeless hermit—I kicked him in his shin.

Which hurt me a lot more than it hurt him, I think, because all he did was laugh.

"Can I help ye?" I asked, scowling up at him. Seeing the sun glinting off his eyes and the slight breeze rustling his hair like a damned slow-motion shampoo commercial, I realized I didn't even know what day it was, or how long Alucard and I had been gone.

"I thought that was my line, *cher*," Alucard drawled, drawing me back to the present.

I scowled. "Don't t'ink I'm just goin' to run into your arms because your knight-in-shinin' armor routine actually proved useful for once."

"Wouldn't dream of it," he replied, sardonically. "Does that mean you don't want me to dry you out?" He held out a hand, channeling the heat of the sun in his palm so that it bathed me in warm, soothing light.

"Ye can stay," I murmured in a pious tone, accepting his hand. "For now."

"I almost didn't step in, you know," Alucard said, absentmindedly, his thumb tracing slow circles in my palm that threatened to make my toes curl. One look into his distant eyes let me know he wasn't even consciously doing it.

The bastard.

"Oh?" I asked, cocking an eyebrow.

"The Huntress was pretty damn clear about our chances of survival if we tried to help," he replied. "And she was right. That son-of-a-bitch was something else."

"So what changed your mind?" I asked, waving his hand off now that I was no longer freezing to death. I kept my tattered doily over my shoulders. One, because I was tired of flashing people by accident. And two, because my assets weren't the only things I hoped to keep prying eyes away from.

"Hook's ship," Alucard answered me. "Once I saw it bust through that wave, I knew you'd be onboard. No one else I know is that…brave."

"Ye were goin' to say stupid, weren't ye?" I said, narrowing my eyes.

"No," Alucard said, shaking his head vehemently. "Nope. Never."

I snorted. "It's alright, it was stupid. Borderline suicidal."

"Well, regardless, you saved a lot of lives with that stunt you pulled, *cher*. I hope you know that," Alucard said, bent over so we were at about the same eye level.

I glanced away, cheeks flushing. Partially out of embarrassment, but also because Alucard had no idea what I'd had to agree to in order to pull that stunt off—that soon his friend Nate and I might end up on one hell of a collision course. I wondered, morbidly, which side he'd pick if things went to shit.

Oh well. Problems for another day.

When I finally looked back, I noticed Alucard's attention had turned to the crew of the Jolly Roger, many of whom had gathered near the ship's helm —probably the only ship in Oberon's fleet to have come away with most of its personnel intact, I figured. Captain Hook, it seemed, was preparing to give a speech of some kind. Something inspirational about survival, I assumed— lauding the achievements of man over nature, praising the grit they'd shown during the battle. The heart, the bravery. How good had triumphed over ev—

"Crew!" Hook bellowed, raising his namesake in the air, its iron edge gleaming. "Hop off your lazy asses and get my ship seaworthy. We're going home."

"Quite the motivational speaker," Alucard murmured.

"It's all in his delivery," I added, dryly.

"What's that?" Hook asked, coming down the stairs towards us.

"Just admiring your way with words, Captain," Alucard replied.

Hook scowled at the vampire, hand and hook folded behind his back. "You know, I was like you, once. In my youth. Had a real smart mouth."

"Oh?" Alucard asked, standing upright once more, looking amused. "And how did you cure such a horrible malady?"

Hook pursed his lips in a thin line, before finally holding up his metal appendage. "I lost my hand." The Captain's eyes gleamed wickedly. "I'd be careful, boy, or *someone* may cut off something *you* value."

"Now, now, gentlemen," I said, putting myself firmly between the two men before they started dueling. I tapped them both firmly on the chest since they still hadn't broken eye contact with each other. "Men as devil-ishly handsome as ye two shouldn't talk so much."

Alucard smiled, then scowled. "Hey!"

Hook did likewise, then glanced over at Alucard. "Are all women this rude nowadays?"

Alucard snorted. "More than I'd like."

"Good thing I'm going home, then," Hook said, grinning.

Now it was my turn to glare at the two men; I'd always hated how they did that—beat their chests one minute and bro'd out the next, usually at a woman's expense. Whatever. At least they weren't bickering anymore. "Are ye sure ye want to go back?" I asked, turning my attention to more serious matters, like a responsible adult.

"I am," Hook said, his grin dimming.

I frowned, recalling his promise to Tiger Lily. If he went back, he'd have to surrender his other hand. That, and he'd already made it clear that he found Neverland tiresome. Why go back? "D'ye not have anywhere else to go?" I asked, finally.

Hook shook his head, and then shrugged. "It's my home. I wasn't sure until I left, but now I know. If I die there an old man, with no hands, in my sleep...well, so be it."

Jesus, talk about morbid. Still, I envied the man. At least he knew where his home was. After everything that had happened since my trip to Fae, I truly had no idea where I actually belonged. Boston had always been my town, but I wasn't sure if I could handle being there without Dez. Granted, I hadn't visited her nearly as often as I should have between work and my obsession with finding the answers to my past, but it had always been reassuring to know she'd be there waiting for me whenever I needed her. In a way, *she'd* been my home. Without her, I wasn't sure what that word even meant for me anymore.

"Speaking of," Alucard interjected, studying my face, "I think it might be a good idea for us to head on back. Quinn here looks a little...tired."

I glared at him. "Listen here, Firefang," I began in a warning tone, "if ye don't start sayin' the first t'ing that comes to your mind from now on, I'm goin' to deck ye."

Alucard ran a hand through his hair with a frustrated sigh. "Except if I say the first thing that comes to mind, I *know* you'll deck me."

I snorted. "Probably."

"Damned if ye do," Badb rasped, her leather squeaking as she approached.

"Damned if ye don't," Macha finished, curtsying.

Alucard cocked an eyebrow. "And you two are?"

Oh, right. Introductions. Cue Quinn, stage left.

"These are me aunts," I answered, before they could introduce themselves. "The would-be dominatrix is Badb. The *Sound of Music* extra is Macha."

The two women exchanged baffled looks.

"What's a dominatrix?" Badb asked, arching an eyebrow, sounding mildly intrigued.

Alucard coughed into his hand. "Well, it's a pleasure to meet you both," he replied, before I could explain. Then he shot a seemingly casual glance my way, though it was laced with undertones. "I'll...give you all some time alone to chat. I'm sure you have some catching up to do." He turned to Hook. "Captain, why don't you show me that thing you wanted me to look at." He threw one arm over Hook's shoulder and began forcibly ambling away with the man.

"If you don't get your arm off me this instant, I'm going to..." the rest of Hook's response was inaudible, but I noticed Alucard quickly withdrawing his arm and leaning in to speak softly to Hook.

"Ye defeated Balor," Macha said, drawing my gaze away from Alucard. "Somethin' we were unable to do."

"Though I'm still curious how ye managed it," Badb grumbled.

"What she *means* to say," Macha interjected, "is that your ma would've been proud."

"T'anks," I replied, though perhaps with less enthusiasm than their praise deserved. The problem was, I'd never known my mother. In my mind, she'd always been some mythical figure. Now that it turned out she actually *was* one, all I could do was wonder what she'd been *thinking*—having me, pawning me off on Dez, and then leaving me with this powerful legacy and no instruction manual to speak of. If I was being honest, I couldn't care less what my mother—Morrigan—thought. I'd done what I had for me, and for Dez.

The only *real* mother I'd ever known.

"What will ye do now?" Macha asked. The question, which should have sounded casual, came off as anything but.

"She wants to know if you'd like to join us," Badb said, resting a hand on my shoulder. "We're headed back to the Otherworld to recover. Neither of us have used that kind of power in centuries. We thought ye might like to come."

A brief flash of memory momentarily overwhelmed me—the astonishingly sure-footed blind man I had briefly met in the city of spires, before he had chucked me into a boat drawn by the most stunning creature I'd ever seen. The Otherworld. That's what he'd called his strange island.

I had to admit, the offer was tempting.

Especially the idea of seeing a blind man about a horse...

But I couldn't; I had things to do.

"Maybe some other time," I replied, finally.

Macha rested her hand on my other shoulder. "Ye should know that the Tuatha are not meant to live in the mortal realm forever. One day, ye will have to accept your role among us, whatever that may be."

I arched an eyebrow. "Meanin' what? That I don't have a choice?"

The sisters drew back. "Maybe ye do," Macha chimed, studying me. "Perhaps that's why your ma kept ye from us. So you'd have a choice. But power draws power."

"Which means," Badb added, her husky voice heavy with implication, "ye may want to accept what ye are, *sooner* rather than later."

"And what *am* I?" I asked, holding my hands out in supplication.

Macha took my hand, and I felt the briefest twinge of her power whisper over my pebbled skin. "That's easy," she replied.

Badb took my other hand, flooding me with her energy. "You're our niece."

In eerie unison, they winked, and then stepped away, directly into a freshly-opened Gateway, disappearing before I could so much as say goodbye. I stared after them, trying to come to terms with how I felt, but couldn't. I'd been on an emotional roller coaster for so long, I realized, that I didn't even know if I was going up or down. Or what to do when the world wasn't topsy-turvy.

Alucard, seeing that I was alone, headed over. "Well how 'bout it, *cher*? You ready to go home?"

I took a deep breath and let it out slowly. "Aye, why not?" I replied, feeling strangely torn over the simple, four-letter word.

Home.

Overhead, a horrifying whinny sounded, drawing the attention of everyone onboard. I knew that sound...suddenly, a black, winged horse from the darkest depths of my nightmares burst through the clouds, charging directly at the double rainbow that lingered in the sky, his single horn glinting, eyes gleaming with lethal intent.

The Goddamned murdercorn I'd first seen in Neverland.

"Oh, for fuck's sake," I said, rubbing the bridge of my nose.

"Looks like Grimm's going for a double," Alucard drawled, grinning.

"Get me out of here," I said, sighing, trying to ignore the joyous neighs from above as the creature stomped and stabbed to his black heart's content.

"As you wish," Alucard replied as he hooked one arm around my waist and pulled me close.

For once, I didn't complain.

CHAPTER 46

*A*lucard took to the clouds, flying so high above the city that we'd easily be mistaken for something other than what we were—not that it mattered. Realistically, the jig had to be up after the battle on Massachusetts Bay. I mean, I'd created a Gateway the size of Wal-Mart that bled over into a whole other dimension—who could possibly explain that away? Then again, the masses had bought the government's insanely feeble explanation for a wildlife preserve suddenly emerging on the Brooklyn Bridge... so what did I know? Either way, I didn't mind; the flight was peaceful, the relative solitude more than welcome after the past few days.

Christ, had I even *slept*? No wonder my emotions were spiraling out of control; other than briefly passing out from exhaustion and trauma, I'd basically run at breakneck speed from one crazy scenario to another without so much as a breather. Which meant, if I really wanted to sit down and sort my shit out, I desperately needed some sleep.

Otherwise, I was bound to crash at the worst possible moment.

Fortunately, by the time Alucard set me down outside my apartment, I was damn near ready to fall over and nap on the pavement. Hell, thinking about my bed was making me salivate. I slid away from the vampire, slapped my cheeks a little to wake myself up for the daunting trek to my apartment door, and headed towards the entrance.

"You gonna say goodbye, *cher?*" Alucard asked. "Or is this you inviting me up?"

Oh, right. Manners and shit.

"Aye," I replied, then whirled, blushing as I realized that I'd answered the wrong question. "I mean, aye, I'll say *goodbye*," I stammered.

Alucard chuckled. "You going to be alright up there, all by yourself?"

I scowled at him. "D'ye t'ink I can't take care of meself?"

Alucard shook his head. "No, I *know* you can do that. What I mean is..." he rubbed the back of his neck. "Well, the Huntress filled me in on what she saw when she got to your aunt Dez's place. All jokes aside, I thought I'd offer...well, whatever you needed." He glanced up at me, his eyes so earnest it almost hurt to look at them. "So, again...will you be okay? By yourself, I mean?"

I looked away, fighting off the absurd urge to cry. I hated crying, ever since I was a little girl. It always made me look like a tomato—my face and eyes all puffy and red beneath a mound of burgundy locks. In my mind, crying was something you did on your own, in the privacy of your own room, with the childhood teddy bear you kept locked in a very secret, very well-hidden place. Still, Alucard was making it awfully hard on me; for some reason, his sympathy made it all real—*too* real.

Dez was *gone*.

And I was all *alone*.

I shook my head, sniffing once. "I'll be fine," I replied. "I just need some sleep."

Alucard nodded, apparently deciding that—if I could pretend to be fine —he could pretend he believed me. He skirted around me and held the door open, like a true Southern gentleman. I had to admit, that act alone damn near sealed the deal for me. Maybe it wouldn't be terrible, inviting him up. I could use the company, after all. And as distractions went, I had a feeling he'd be a good one. Hell, him being a vampire didn't even bother me anymore; it had been a while since I last thought of him as *just* a vampire.

But there was one problem he wasn't yet aware of—a big one.

I didn't screw men I might have to kill.

No matter how much fun it would be, or even how much I enjoyed our witty banter, Alucard was on Team Temple. Hopefully—one day—that wouldn't matter, but today it meant he was potentially on an opposing side. A side I had to keep things from. A side I might have to lie to.

And so I brushed hurriedly past, without so much as a goodbye. Manners…maybe one day I'd learn some.

CHAPTER 47

*T*urned out, my door was locked.

But, not *just* locked, it was also *warded*.

To keep out anything that wasn't human—*anything*.

Including me, apparently. I'd tried to will the door open using the very abilities which kept me out and, when that didn't work, I seriously considered running straight through the wall like Juggernaut—the price of patching it up potentially worth the reward of sleeping in my own bed.

But I didn't.

Because I was an adult, Goddamn it.

Sadly, that meant—since I'd left Alucard, my one available mode of transportation, without saying goodbye—I was forced to find someplace *else* to go. Someplace that wouldn't kick me out for looking like a refugee, didn't require any money since I'd lost my wallet when my bug-out bag went down with Narcissus' passenger ship, and—preferably—had lots and lots of free booze.

Because, after the shit I'd been through, I was fully prepared to drink myself to death.

Sadly, where I ended up met only two out of my three conditions—Christoff's bar.

The building, which he still owned despite having been missing for so

254

long, was easy to break into—unlike my fucking warded apartment. Unfortunately, while the empty pop-up bar provided a warm, dry place to stay without having to pay a dime, all the liquor had been cleared off the shelves, leaving only a dusty bar top, a few stools, and a mirror I refused to look in lest I run from my own reflection.

And that's where the Huntress found me, face down on the bar, using the ratty blanket I'd gotten on Hook's ship as a pillow, afraid to fall asleep and tumble off my barstool, but equally afraid that if I stayed up too much longer I might actually die. I'd heard you could do that, you know—die from lack of sleep.

Her boots cracked savagely against the floor, shocking me upright.

"Knew I'd find you here," she said, slipping onto the barstool beside me.

I scowled. "No ye didn't. Not even *I* knew I'd be here," I muttered. "Welcome to the saddest hellhole in the universe," I complained, pointing at the empty, dusty shelves. "A bar with no booze."

"Well, I knew you'd be here *after* I tried literally every *other* place I could think of," the Huntress clarified, a ghost of a smile on her lips as she appraised me from feet to doily.

She didn't look very impressed, but then I didn't feel very impressive as I glared back at her, trying to make sense of what she was doing with her face.

Was that…a *smile*?

"Who are ye, and what have ye done with the Huntress?" I asked, truly wondering if I weren't hallucinating the woman's presence. I glanced in the mirror, just to be sure, and nearly fell off my barstool. Sitting beside me was no longer the spitfire woman I'd argued with just a few hours before, but the legendary Hawteye, herself—a creature with blazing eyes, covered in the furs of her numerous kills, and sporting a cloak of shadows. I spun back and found the redhead gazing at me with a passive expression.

"Do you really want to know?" she asked in a soft, cautious tone, her eyes flicking to the mirror briefly.

"Do I really want to know *what*?" I replied, one hand on my chest, trying to slow my racing heartbeat.

"Who I am."

I frowned. "Wait, are ye offerin' to tell me?"

"When I thought Balor was coming, I told you we didn't have time. But you killed him. So I've got some to spare. Maybe a half-hour's worth," she said, leaning forward on her barstool to pluck a bottle off the shelf that hadn't been there before.

My jaw dropped at witnessing the world's greatest bar trick. Like an Irish Jesus. Ashes to ashes, dust to Scotch.

Then I saw the *brand*.

A dusty bottle of...

"50-year-old Macallan," I whispered reverently.

Huntress nodded. "Thirty minutes should be enough time for us to finish this, I think."

She thought we could split a bottle of Scotch that cost thirty grand in a *half hour*?

Dear sweet baby Jesus...if I were into women...

"How," I whispered, licking my lips, "d'ye do that?" I finally asked, watching as she poured us two glasses—which had also appeared out of thin air.

"Do what?" she asked absently, her smirk decidedly less horrifying, now.

"Ye know," I said, mimicking grabbing a bottle that didn't exist. "That."

"Oh. Practice."

"Teach me," I pleaded, resting my head in the crook of my arm, afraid to blink and realize this had all just been a dream. She passed me my glass, but ignored my request. I sighed and took a sip. "Holy shit," I said, sitting up a little, the insidious burn working its way luxuriously down. "This even *tastes* like the real t'ing. Or what I dreamt the real t'ing tasted like, anyway," I said, worshipping the Scotch before me. I'm not crying. You're crying.

The Huntress nodded. "That's because it *is* the real thing." She took a liberal sip.

I slowly turned to face her, wondering if being locked out of my apartment just may have been the luckiest moment of my life. "Seriously? Where d'ye get a bottle of 50-year-old Macallan?" I asked.

"I stole it," she replied, grinning fiercely.

Of course she did. I took another sip and lay back down, blocking out the sunlight by pressing my face into my arms on the bar top. "I want to be ye when I grow up," I mumbled.

A silence settled over the bar, so heavy it suddenly felt like I was the only one in the bar. I frowned and looked up to find the Huntress staring down at me, her expression unreadable, utterly still. "Was it somethin' I said?" I asked.

"Your mother," the Huntress began, "was a goddess among the Fae."

I sat up. "Aye, she—"

The Huntress pressed a finger to my lips. But—before I could bite it off —she continued, "Your father was not." She raised a hand. "I don't know who he was. She never did tell me. But he was mortal, of that I am certain."

I struggled with the implications of that, trying to figure out what that made me. Half Fae? Half goddess? Half human? What? I opened my mouth to ask those very questions, but found my glass pressed against my lips, the Scotch seeping down my throat, the Huntress' finger tipping the glass further and further back.

"This means you will face a difficult decision," the Huntress said, staring into my eyes over the bottom of my glass. "One I am uniquely familiar with. You see, I was mortal, once." She settled back, retrieving her own drink, content to leave me be now that she had my full attention. "I trained warriors. Heroes and villains. Legends, many of whom have faded from memory. I also bore a daughter."

I arched an eyebrow. The Huntress didn't really strike me as the maternal type. But maybe that was simply me projecting—although on second thought, anyone who used the phrase *I bore a daughter* probably wasn't going to be nominated as mother-of-the-year anytime soon. "What happened to her?" I asked, before I could help myself.

"She died. A long time ago. She took her own life after being spurned by a man who was supposed to love and protect her," she said, clenching her teeth. She took a deep breath and polished off the rest of her glass, then began pouring another. "Your mother saw to it that he died."

"She did *what?*" I asked, eyes widening.

"Don't act so surprised," the Huntress said, unperturbed. "As if *you've* never killed someone who wronged you."

Well, I mean, yeah. But still...damn.

"In return for her avenging my daughter, I agreed to look after you. And yes, before you start, I know I've done a fairly terrible job of it. Up until the last couple years I was...preoccupied. And I'm sorry for that," the Huntress said, eyes haunted at the unspoken memory. "But things have changed. You're no longer a child. No longer protected by your mother's magic. And

I'm no longer… preoccupied. Soon, I suspect, you will have to choose your path."

"What does that even *mean*?" I asked, shaking my head, my hands trembling with frustration. The Huntress sounded just like my aunts—great at explaining problems, but shit at offering solutions.

"It means you, unlike so many of us, can decide your own fate," she said, topping me off in the process. "Will you walk among the mortals, with—but not *of*—them, as your mother did? Will you make your home in Fae as a goddess, ruling those who would worship you? Or will you retreat to the comforts of the Otherworld, among those who would accept you as one of their own, but never understand what drives you?"

I lay my head back down, overwhelmed by the options—none of which sounded particularly appealing. "I just want me old life back," I whispered. "I want Dez back. I want to be Quinn MacKenna, *just* Quinn MacKenna. And I want to be able to *get into me damn apartment*."

"Wait, why can't you get into your apartment?" the Huntress asked.

I pursed my lips, but finally told her.

"Wow, and I thought I had shitty luck," she said chuckling.

I glared at her, but then let out a sigh. My eyes settled on the Scotch, and I felt a flicker of a grin as I turned to look back up at her.

"Oh, I don't know. Me luck isn't too bad," I said, lifting my glass to hers.

"I can drink to that," she smiled.

It went down even smoother than before, and the silence stretched. But it was a comfortable silence. A companionable silence.

"Are ye goin' to tell me who ye are *before*, or after I kick your immortal ass for bludgeoning me with more problems to think about?" I growled, only half-joking.

The Huntress grinned and clinked her glass against mine again. "Scathach," she replied, downing her Scotch and patting me on the back. "My name is Scathach. Now, let's go break into your apartment so you can get some sleep. You're going to need it if you want me to train you."

I nodded woodenly, convincing myself that I really didn't want to ask her anymore questions right now. I snatched up my blanket, feeling significantly less battered with at least five grand worth of Scotch in my stomach. I turned to the Faeling who'd once been a mortal woman—the soon-to-be trainer of yet another legend.

"Bring the Scotch," I told her, and then marched out to the sound of her laughter and the clinking of her gathering our glasses.

The sound was like an Angel's laughter.

The glasses, not Scathach.

Her laughter was downright *horrifying*.

CHAPTER 48

I dreamt.

Only this time, I knew I was dreaming, just as I knew where I was. I stood on an invisible floor, the light of an unfamiliar galaxy glittering beneath my feet. Familiar, otherworldly windows hung on either side of me for as far as my eyes could see, hanging in thin air. This time, however, what called me was not what lie behind the windows, but the creature who guarded them.

My mother's ghost.

She approached in a white gown, her eyes on fire, as if fated to watch everything burn for eternity. I knew how that felt. It'd been a week since Dez's death. Her body had been recovered by the EMTs and ruled a homicide, perpetrator unknown; I'd been questioned, but turned loose. We'd had the wake a few days ago. Old family friends had reached out, each expressing sympathy. But none of that mattered. Closure was a lie, and now everywhere I looked I saw a charred, lifeless world.

"You should not have sought me out," she said.

"Ye should have told me who ye were from the beginnin'," I countered.

A crinkle appeared between her eyes, then smoothed. "It does not matter. You survived your mistake."

"Me mistake?" I hissed. "Ye mean takin' on the creature ye left alive to terrorize not just the mortal realm, but Fae as well?"

"Balor was slain," she replied, matter-of-factly. "His Fomorian kin drug his body into the sea, and he was destined never to be seen or heard from again."

"And yet!" I said, exasperated.

"Time has begun to unravel," she said, stepping around me to walk along the corridor, seemingly ignoring both me and the obvious inconsistency between fate and reality. "Your mother foresaw this. Someone, or something, has corrupted the balance."

"What d'ye mean, *she* 'foresaw this'—aren't ye her?" I asked.

"Your mother?" she asked, glancing back at me. "No. I have her memories, but not her emotions. I know *what* she did, but not *why*. She separated me, long ago, in her bid to live among mortals."

"What are ye, then?"

"That's not important."

"It is to me," I insisted, hands balled into fists at my side. "I need to know t'ings. T'ings she would have known. I need ye to *be* her," I whispered, finally.

"What questions do you have?" she asked, finally. "Ask them, and I will do my best to answer. But then, we must discuss your role in what's to come."

I started to ask what that was supposed to mean, but held back before I got off track. She said I could ask my questions, and I had several. Of course, at the moment, only one really mattered. "Why Dez?" I asked, at last.

"You'll have to be more specific," she replied dryly.

"Why Dez?" I repeated. "Why her? Why pick someone mortal, someone fragile? Why pick her if ye knew she was goin' to die in me arms? How could ye do that to your best friend? How could ye do that to me?!" I finished, practically screaming at her by the time I was done.

She studied me with my mother's face—the face in the painting that now hung in my living room, the painting of Dez and my mother. "The mortal woman your mother chose was an ideal candidate. A former member of the Irish Republican Army. Fierce. Protective. Loyal. Religious. Of all the possible options, she was deemed the most suitable. That, and—because she was mortal—she was especially susceptible to the spell."

"The...*spell*?" I asked, disgusted by the clinical evaluation of Dez's qualities as a human being, but baffled by the mention of a spell.

"The spell your mother wove."

"Me cage, ye mean?" I asked.

"No, that was something she and I created, together. A way to keep you from attracting the wrong attention too soon. I had hoped the bracelet would act as a release for your powers, but—"

"Me powers?" I could feel a migraine beginning to burst behind my eyelids—which was exceedingly shitty, considering this was all supposed to be a dream. "Wait, are ye sayin' those t'ings the bracelet did...that was *me? Not* the magic bracelet?"

"Of course it was you. The bracelet was simply a totem. A release valve, for if you unknowingly accessed your power." She glanced down at my wrist pointedly. "*When* you unknowingly accessed your power."

"But, I thought..."

"That it was your *mother's* power?" She scoffed, shaking her head. "Morrigan held no authority over time. That's what I have been trying to tell you, it—"

"Wait," I said, crossing my arms, refusing to let her off the hook before she answered all my questions. "The spell. Tell me about that, first."

"Surely, you noticed it yourself."

"Of course not, or I wouldn't be askin' ye," I replied, scathingly.

She frowned. "The spell your mother cast was on you and your caretaker. A bonding spell that used your mother's voice, her pattern of speech, to make certain Dez would take care of you."

"To...what are ye sayin'?" I closed my eyes, struggling to understand. "Ye mean..."

"Your accent. It was anticipated that your caretaker would bond more closely with you if you shared the same dialect, and so your mother forged a link between you and your caretaker. We could not risk her turning you out, or failing to look after you, after all."

I took a halting step back, then another, trying to wave off what she was saying. It wasn't true. It couldn't be. Dez had loved me. Hadn't she? It couldn't all have been because of some stupid spell. Could it? Giving me an accent solely to forge a bond between us. That was...*unbelievably* callous.

Had Dez loved me...*only* because of my accent?

I ground my teeth, locking the treacherous thought away, fighting back the urge to scream in frustration; I was so sick of being manipulated. So tired of having my trust—already so hard to earn—betrayed.

"If that is the end of your questions," she said, "then it's time we—"

"Get out of me head," I hissed.

"I'm not in your head, you're in my realm, within the Other—"

"Fine," I snapped. "Then I'll go."

"No, you must—"

But I was already gone.

CHAPTER 49

$\mathcal{A}$fter the day Dez died, I knew my world would never be the same. Strangely enough, however, the rest of the world seemed to have moved on without so much as a backwards glance. The storm that had threatened to devastate Boston—which, it turned out, was dubbed Hurricane Ripley…believe it or not—got hardly any coverage. Instead, the city was quickly flooded with UFO chasers, many of whom swore to anyone who would listen that a ship had come down from the sky over Massachusetts Bay, which explained why the storm caused such minimal damage compared to the projections. I had to admit, their grainy photographic evidence did look vaguely alien—unless you knew what you were looking at.

I'd have to let Hook know he was famous, the next time I saw him.

And I *would* be seeing him—and the other denizens of Neverland—before long. I'd promised Peter I'd return, after all, and I always kept my promises. For now, however, I figured it was best to keep my distance from Fae. Let things cool down a bit. Thanks to the Huntress—or Scathach, if you preferred—I'd learned that Oberon's ship had survived the massive wave Balor hit them with, and that the remaining Fomorians had been rounded up and imprisoned. I had no idea what would happen to the seafaring giants, but frankly, I couldn't have cared less.

Caring in any capacity was hard for me to come by these days, though, if

I was being honest. I'd already fielded dozens of house calls from old acquaintances from the neighborhood, each offering me some little anecdote, in case I'd forgotten what a great person my own aunt was. Eventually, I stopped answering the damned door.

Unfortunately, the one person I'd have loved to talk to was unreachable; a phone with a message had been waiting for me in my mailbox, accessible once I got a new set of keys—a message from Othello. Well, two, to be exact. The first was a handwritten note that read: Dear Quinn, hope you had fun in Fae. Figured you would lose your phone. Or break it. So here's a replacement. XOXO Othello.

It was sad how well she knew me.

The second was a voicemail she'd left on the new phone, explaining she'd found a lead on Christoff's whereabouts and would be in touch. I hadn't heard anything else from her since, but it really hadn't been long. Besides, I knew better than anyone that Othello did things on her own time. All the same, it would have been nice to talk to her.

Hemingway, too.

As the Horseman of Death, it struck me he might be uniquely qualified to give me some advice on how to grieve. And, if I was being honest with myself, a very small part of me secretly hoped he might have enough juice to let me see Dez—even just one last time. I needed to know—to find out if what my mother's ghost had said was true. The thought that Dez might not have loved me without the influence of magic tore at me from the inside; I rarely slept and, when I did, I had horrifying nightmares.

Of course, I could blame at least some of that on Scathach. The Faeling had a sadistic streak, for sure. She routinely stopped by in the wee hours of the morning to bang on my door, forcing me to join her on some errand that inevitably turned out to be a training lesson; two days ago, she had forced me—at sword point—to spend three full hours trying to start an industrial-sized lawn mower.

At the time, she had neglected to tell me there was no gas in it.

The next day, she informed me I now knew how to draw a bow.

And *that* day was even *worse* than the lawn mower lesson.

She was like Mr. Miyagi from Hell.

Despite the aches and early wakeup calls, however, I had to admit I appreciated her dogged insistence I brush up on my fighting skills. With my newfound strength and resilience, I couldn't exactly train at the dojo; I might accidentally kill somebody—or worse—out myself. Plus, it helped to discover some of the limitations I should expect. Things like the various ways iron can affect the Fae. How much damage their bodies could take. What their recovery rate was like.

Unfortunately, Scathach's experience didn't extend to magic. She could train me to fight and use unfamiliar weapons, but had no advice when it came to refining my metaphysical abilities. At this point, however, I'd have settled for simply having access to my magic; since my fight with Balor, I hadn't felt the barest whisper of power. No matter how hard I tried or what ridiculous incantations I muttered, I couldn't so much as get a quarter to spin in slow motion. It was almost like my magic—such as it was—had fled altogether.

But I could sense something lurking deep inside me.

Like a light peeking out beneath a closed door.

Which, given the fact that I'd promised the Winter Queen I'd have a serious discussion with Nate Temple, really sucked. Because if there was one thing I'd learned as an arms dealer, it was that it was best to negotiate from a position of strength. At the moment, I wasn't even sure he'd listen to me, let alone take me seriously. Which meant I needed to learn how to use my magic, and fast.

Of course, if that failed, there were always the eyes.

That's right. Eyes. Plural.

Before Hook and his crew had fetched me, I'd managed to paddle over to Balor's corpse and pluck the jewel from his skull, only to secure it and Balor's original in the blanket they'd given me—keeping both out of sight, hoping everyone would be too overjoyed to have survived to care about either artifact. Luckily, I'd been right, although I had a feeling someone was bound to come asking for them sooner or later.

Which was sort of the point.

After all, while I had no idea which path I'd choose—human or Faeling or goddess—I did know what I was: a black magic arms dealer who was damn good at her job.

Besides, it never hurt to get back to the basics.

Well, it *could*.

But pain and I were old friends...and I could use one of those right about now.

VIP's get early access to all sorts of Temple-Verse goodies, including signed copies, private giveaways, and advance notice of future projects. AND A FREE NOVELLA! Join here: www.shaynesilvers.com/l/219800

Quinn returns in MOSCOW MULE. http://www.shaynesilvers.com/l/324655

Turn the page to read a sample of **OBSIDIAN SON** *- Nate Temple Book 1 - or* **BUY ONLINE (It's FREE with a Kindle Unlimited subscription)***. Nate Temple is a billionaire wizard from St. Louis. He rides a bloodthirsty unicorn and drinks with the Four Horsemen. He even cow-tipped the Minotaur. Once...*

TRY: OBSIDIAN SON (NATE TEMPLE #1)

*T*here was no room for emotion in a hate crime. I had to be cold. Heartless. This was just another victim. Nothing more. No face, no name.

Frosted blades of grass crunched under my feet, sounding to my ears like the symbolic glass that one would shatter under a napkin at a Jewish wedding. The noise would have threatened to give away my stealthy advance as I stalked through the moonlit field, but I was no novice and had planned accordingly. Being a wizard, I was able to muffle all sensory evidence with a fine cloud of magic—no sounds, and no smells. Nifty. But if I made the spell much stronger, the anomaly would be too obvious to my prey.

I knew the consequences for my dark deed tonight. If caught, jail time or possibly even a gruesome, painful death. But if I succeeded, the look of fear and surprise in my victim's eyes before his world collapsed around him, it was well worth the risk. I simply couldn't help myself; I had to take him down.

I knew the cops had been keeping tabs on my car, but I was confident that they hadn't followed me. I hadn't seen a tail on my way here but seeing as how they frowned on this kind of thing, I had taken a circuitous route just in case. I was safe. I hoped.

Then my phone chirped at me as I received a text.

I practically jumped out of my skin, hissing instinctively. "Motherf—" I cut off abruptly, remembering the whole stealth aspect of my mission. I was off to a stellar start. I had forgotten to silence the damned phone. *Stupid, stupid, stupid!*

My heart felt like it was on the verge of exploding inside my chest with such thunderous violence that I briefly envisioned a mystifying Rorschach blood-blot that would have made coroners and psychologists drool.

My body remained tense as I swept my gaze over the field, fearing that I had been made. Precious seconds ticked by without any change in my surroundings, and my breathing finally began to slow as my pulse returned to normal. Hopefully, my magic had muted the phone and my resulting outburst. I glanced down at the phone to scan the text and then typed back a quick and angry response before I switched the cursed device to vibrate.

Now, where were we?

I continued on, the lining of my coat constricting my breathing. Or maybe it was because I was leaning forward in anticipation. *Breathe,* I chided myself. *He doesn't know you're here.* All this risk for a book. It had better be worth it.

I'm taller than most, and not abnormally handsome, but I knew how to play the genetic cards I had been dealt. I had shaggy, dirty blonde hair—leaning more towards brown with each passing year—and my frame was thick with well-earned muscle, yet I was still lean. I had once been told that my eyes were like twin emeralds pitted against the golden-brown tufts of my hair—a face like a jewelry box. Of course, that was two bottles of wine into a date, so I could have been a little foggy on her quote. Still, I liked to imagine that was how everyone saw me.

But tonight, all that was masked by magic.

I grinned broadly as the outline of the hairy hulk finally came into view. He was blessedly alone—no nearby sentries to give me away. That was always a risk when performing this ancient rite-of-passage. I tried to keep the grin on my face from dissolving into a maniacal cackle.

My skin danced with energy, both natural and unnatural, as I manipulated the threads of magic floating all around me. My victim stood just ahead, oblivious to the world of hurt that I was about to unleash. Even with his millennia of experience, he didn't stand a chance. I had done this so many times that the routine of it was my only enemy. I lost count of how many times I had been told not to do it again; those who knew declared it *cruel, evil, and sadistic*. But what fun wasn't? Regardless, that wasn't enough to stop me from doing it again. And again. And again.

It was an addiction.

The pungent smell of manure filled the air, latching onto my nostril hairs. I took another step, trying to calm my racing pulse. A glint of gold reflected in the silver moonlight, but my victim remained motionless, hopefully unaware or all was lost. I wouldn't make it out alive if he knew I was here. Timing was everything.

I carefully took the last two steps, a lifetime between each, watching the legendary monster's ears, anxious and terrified that I would catch even so much as a twitch in my direction. Seeing nothing, a fierce grin split my unshaven cheeks. My spell had worked! I raised my palms an inch away from their target, firmly planted my feet, and squared my shoulders. I took one silent, calming breath, and then heaved forward with every ounce of physical strength I could muster. As well as a teensy-weensy boost of magic. Enough to goose him good.

"*MOOO!!!*" The sound tore through the cool October night like an unstoppable freight train. *Thud-splat!* The beast collapsed sideways onto the frosted grass; straight into a steaming patty of cow shit, cow dung, or, if you really wanted to church it up, a Meadow Muffin. But to me, shit is, and always will be, shit.

Cow tipping. It doesn't get any better than that in Missouri.

Especially when you're tipping the *Minotaur*. Capital M. I'd tipped plenty of ordinary cows before, but never the legendary variety.

Razor-blade hooves tore at the frozen earth as the beast struggled to stand, his grunts of rage vibrating the air. I raised my arms triumphantly. "Boo-yah! Temple 1, Minotaur 0!" I crowed. Then I very bravely prepared to protect myself. Some people just couldn't take a joke. *Cruel, evil,* and *sadistic* cow tipping may be, but by hell, it was a *rush*. The legendary beast turned his gaze on me after gaining his feet, eyes ablaze as his body...*shifted* from his bull disguise into his notorious, well-known bipedal form. He unfolded to his full height on two tree trunk-thick legs, his hooves having magically transformed into heavily booted feet. The thick, gold ring dangling from his snotty snout quivered as the Minotaur panted, and his dense, corded muscles contracted over his now human-like chest. As I stared up into those brown eyes, I actually felt sorry...for, well, myself.

"I have killed greater men than you for lesser offense," he growled.

His voice sounded like an angry James Earl Jones—like Mufasa talking to Scar.

"You have shit on your shoulder, Asterion." I ignited a roiling ball of fire in my palm in order to see his eyes more clearly. By no means was it a defensive gesture on my part. It was just dark. Under the weight of his glare, I somehow managed to keep my face composed, even though my fraudulent, self-denial had curled up into the fetal position and started whimpering. I hoped using a form of his ancient name would give me brownie points. Or maybe just not-worthy-of-killing points.

The beast grunted, eyes tightening, and I sensed the barest hesitation. "Nate Temple...your name would look splendid on my already long list of slain idiots." Asterion took a threatening step forward, and I thrust out my palm in warning, my roiling flame blue now.

"You lost fair and square, Asterion. Yield or perish." The beast's shoulders sagged slightly. Then he finally nodded to himself in resignation, appraising me with the scrutiny of a worthy adversary. "Your time comes, Temple, but I will grant you this. You've got a pair of stones on you to rival Hercules."

I reflexively glanced in the direction of the myth's own crown jewels before jerking my gaze away. Some things you simply couldn't un-see. "Well, I won't be needing a wheelbarrow any time soon, but overcompensating today keeps future lower-back pain away."

The Minotaur blinked once, and then he bellowed out a deep, contagious, snorting laughter. Realizing I wasn't about to become a murder statistic, I couldn't help but join in. It felt good. It had been a while since I had allowed myself to experience genuine laughter.

In the harsh moonlight, his bulk was even more intimidating as he towered head and shoulders above me. This was the beast that had fed upon human sacrifices for countless years while imprisoned in Daedalus' Labyrinth in Greece. And all that protein had not gone to waste, forming a heavily woven musculature over the beast's body that made even Mr. Olympia look puny.

From the neck up, he was now entirely bull, but the rest of his body more closely resembled a thickly furred man. But, as shown moments ago, he could adapt his form to his environment, never appearing fully human, but able to make his entire form appear as a bull when necessary. For instance, how he had looked just before I tipped him. Maybe he had been scouting the field for heifers before I had so efficiently killed the mood.

His bull face was also covered in thick, coarse hair—he even sported a long, wavy beard of sorts, and his eyes were the deepest brown I had ever seen. Cow-shit brown. His snout jutted out, emphasizing the golden ring dangling from his glistening nostrils, and both glinted in the luminous glow of the moon. The metal was at least an inch thick and etched with runes of a language long forgotten. Wide, aged ivory horns sprouted from each temple, long enough to skewer a wizard with little effort. He was nude except for a massive beaded necklace and a pair of worn leather boots that were big enough to stomp a size twenty-five imprint in my face if he felt so inclined.

I hoped our blossoming friendship wouldn't end that way. I really did.

Because friends didn't let friends wear boots naked...

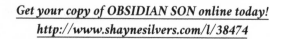

Get your copy of OBSIDIAN SON online today!
http://www.shaynesilvers.com/l/38474

Shayne has written a few other books without Cameron helping him. Some of them are marginally decent—easily a 4 out of 10.

*Turn the page to read a sample of **<u>UNCHAINED</u>** - Feathers and Fire Series Book 1, or **BUY ONLINE (FREE with Kindle Unlimited subscription)**. Callie Penrose is a wizard in Kansas City, MO who hunts monsters for the Vatican. She meets Nate Temple, and things devolve from there...*

(Note: Callie appears in the TempleVerse after Nate's book 6, TINY GODS...Full chronology of all books in the TempleVerse shown on the 'Books by the authors' page)

TRY: UNCHAINED (FEATHERS AND FIRE #1)

*T*he rain pelted my hair, plastering loose strands of it to my forehead as I panted, eyes darting from tree to tree, terrified of each shifting branch, splash of water, and whistle of wind slipping through the nightscape around us. But… I was somewhat *excited*, too.

Somewhat.

"Easy, girl. All will be well," the big man creeping just ahead of me, murmured.

"You said we were going to get ice cream!" I hissed at him, failing to compose myself, but careful to keep my voice low and my eyes alert. "I'm not ready for this!" I had been trained to fight, with my hands, with weapons, and with my magic. But I had never taken an active role in a hunt before. I'd always been the getaway driver for my mentor.

The man grunted, grey eyes scanning the trees as he slipped through the tall grass. "And did we not get ice cream before coming here? Because I think I see some in your hair."

"You know what I mean, Roland. You tricked me." I checked the tips of my loose hair, saw nothing, and scowled at his back.

"The Lord does not give us a greater burden than we can shoulder."

I muttered dark things under my breath, wiping the water from my eyes. Again. My new shirt was going to be ruined. Silk never fared well in the rain. My choice of shoes wasn't much better. Boots, yes, but distressed, *fashionable* boots. Not work boots designed for the rain and mud. Definitely not monster hunting boots for our evening excursion through one of Kansas City's wooded parks. I realized I was forcibly distracting myself, keeping my mind busy with mundane thoughts to avoid my very real anxiety. Because whenever I grew nervous, an imagined nightmare always—

A church looming before me. Rain pouring down. Night sky and a glowing moon overhead. I was all alone. Crying on the cold, stone steps, an infant in a cardboard box—

I forced the nightmare away, breathing heavily. "You know I hate it when you talk like that," I whispered to him, trying to regain my composure. I wasn't angry with him, but was growing increasingly uncomfortable with our situation after my brief flashback of fear.

"Doesn't mean it shouldn't be said," he said kindly. "I think we're close. Be alert. Remember your training. Banish your fears. I am here. And the Lord is here. He always is."

So, he had noticed my sudden anxiety. "Maybe I should just go back to the car. I know I've trained, but I really don't think—"

A shape of fur, fangs, and claws launched from the shadows towards me, cutting off my words as it snarled, thirsty for my blood.

And my nightmare slipped back into my thoughts like a veiled assassin, a wraith hoping to hold me still for the monster to eat. I froze, unable to move. Twin sticks of power abruptly erupted into being in my clenched fists, but my fear swamped me with that stupid nightmare, the sticks held at my side, useless to save me.

Right before the beast's claws reached me, it grunted as something batted it from the air, sending it flying sideways. It struck a tree with another grunt and an angry whine of pain.

I fell to my knees right into a puddle, arms shaking, breathing fast.

My sticks crackled in the rain like live cattle prods, except their entire length was the electrical section — at least to anyone other than me. I could hold them without pain.

Magic was a part of me, coursing through my veins whether I wanted it or not, and Roland had spent many years teaching me how to master it. But I had never been able to fully master the nightmare inside me, and in moments of fear, it always won, overriding my training.

The fact that I had resorted to weapons — like the ones he had trained me with — rather than a burst of flame, was startling. It was good in the fact that my body's reflexes knew enough to call up a defense even without my direct command, but bad in the fact that it was the worst form of defense for the situation presented. I could have very easily done as Roland did, and hurt it from a distance. But I hadn't. Because of my stupid block.

Roland placed a calloused palm on my shoulder, and I flinched. "Easy, see? I am here." But he did frown at my choice of weapons, the reprimand silent but loud in my mind. I let out a shaky breath, forcing my fear back down. It was all in my head, but still, it wasn't easy. Fear could be like that.

I focused on Roland's implied lesson. Close combat weapons — even magically-powered ones — were for last resorts. I averted my eyes in very real shame. I knew these things. He didn't even need to tell me them. But when that damned nightmare caught hold of me, all my training went out the window. It haunted me like a shadow, waiting for moments just like this, as if trying to kill me. A form of psychological suicide? But it was why I constantly refused to join Roland on his hunts. He knew about it. And although he was trying to help me overcome that fear, he never pressed too hard.

Rain continued to sizzle as it struck my batons. I didn't let them go, using them as a totem to build my confidence back up. I slowly lifted my eyes to nod at him as I climbed back to my feet.

That's when I saw the second set of eyes in the shadows, right before they flew out of the darkness towards Roland's back. I threw one of my batons and missed, but that pretty much let Roland know that an unfriendly was behind him. Either that or I had just failed to murder my mentor at point-blank range. He whirled to confront the monster, expecting another aerial assault as he unleashed a ball of fire that splashed over the tree at chest height, washing the trunk in blue flames. But this monster was tricky. It hadn't planned on tackling Roland, but had merely jumped out of the darkness to get closer, no doubt learning from its fallen comrade, who still lay unmoving against the tree behind me.

His coat shone like midnight clouds with hints of lightning flashing in the depths of thick, wiry fur. The coat of dew dotting his fur reflected the moonlight, giving him a faint sheen as if covered in fresh oil. He was tall, easily hip height at the shoulder, and barrel chested, his rump much leaner than the rest of his body. He — I assumed male from the long, thick mane around his neck — had a very long snout, much longer and wider than any werewolf I had ever seen. Amazingly, and beyond my control, I realized he was beautiful.

But most of the natural world's lethal hunters were beautiful.

He landed in a wet puddle a pace in front of Roland, juked to the right, and then to the left, racing past the big man, biting into his hamstrings on his way by.

A wash of anger rolled over me at seeing my mentor injured, dousing my fear, and I swung my baton down as hard as I could. It struck the beast in the rump as it tried to dart back to cover — a typical wolf tactic. My blow singed his hair and shattered bone. The creature collapsed into a puddle of mud with a yelp, instinctively snapping his jaws over his shoulder to bite whatever had hit him.

I let him. But mostly out of dumb luck as I heard Roland hiss in pain, falling to the ground.

The monster's jaws clamped around my baton, and there was an immediate explosion of teeth and blood that sent him flying several feet away into the tall brush, yipping, screaming, and staggering. Before he slipped out of sight, I noticed that his lower jaw was simply *gone*, from the contact of his saliva on my electrified magical batons. Then he managed to limp into the woods with more pitiful yowls, but I had no mind to chase him. Roland — that titan of a man, my mentor — was hurt. I could smell copper in the air, and knew we had to get out of here. Fast. Because we had anticipated only one of the monsters. But there had been two of them, and they hadn't been the run-of-the-mill werewolves we had been warned about. If there were two, perhaps there were more. And they were evidently the prehistoric cousin of any werewolf I had ever seen or read about.

Roland hissed again as he stared down at his leg, growling with both pain and anger. My eyes darted back to the first monster, wary of another attack. It *almost* looked like a werewolf, but bigger. Much bigger. He didn't move, but I saw he was breathing. He had a notch in his right ear and a jagged scar on his long snout. Part of me wanted to go over to him and torture him. Slowly. Use his pain to finally drown my nightmare, my fear. The fear that had caused Roland's injury. My lack of inner-strength had not only put me in danger, but had hurt my mentor, my friend.

I shivered, forcing the thought away. That was *cold*. Not me. Sure, I was no stranger to fighting, but that had always been in a ring. Practicing. Sparring. Never life or death.

But I suddenly realized something very dark about myself in the chill, rainy night. Although I was terrified, I felt a deep ocean of anger manifest inside me, wanting only to dispense justice as I saw fit. To use that rage to battle my own demons. As if feeding one would starve the other, reminding me of the Cherokee Indian Legend Roland had once told me.

An old Cherokee man was teaching his grandson about life. "A fight is going on inside me," he told the boy. "It is a terrible fight between two wolves. One is evil — he is anger, envy, sorrow, regret, greed, arrogance, self-pity, guilt, resentment, inferiority, lies, false pride, superiority, and ego." After a few moments to make sure he had the boy's undivided attention, he continued.

"The other wolf is good — he is joy, peace, love, hope, serenity, humility, kindness, benevolence, empathy, generosity, truth, compassion, and faith. The same fight is going on inside of you, boy, and inside of every other person, too."

The grandson thought about this for a few minutes before replying. "Which wolf will win?"

The old Cherokee man simply said, "The one you feed, boy. The one you feed..."

And I felt like feeding one of my wolves today, by killing this one...

Get the full book ONLINE! *http://www.shaynesilvers.com/l/38952*

MAKE A DIFFERENCE

Reviews are the most powerful tools in our arsenal when it comes to getting attention for our books. Much as we'd like to, we don't have the financial muscle of a New York publisher.

But we do have something much more powerful and effective than that, and it's something that those publishers would kill to get their hands on.

A committed and loyal bunch of readers.

Honest reviews of our books help bring them to the attention of other readers.

If you've enjoyed this book, we would be very grateful if you could spend just five minutes leaving a review on our book's Amazon page.

Thank you very much in advance.

ACKNOWLEDGMENTS

From Cameron:
I'd like to thank Shayne, for paving the way in style. Kori, for an introduction that would change my life. My three wonderful sisters, for showing me what a strong, independent woman looks and sounds like. And, above all, my parents, for—literally—everything.

From Shayne (the self-proclaimed prettiest one):
Team Temple and the Den of Freaks on Facebook have become family to me. I couldn't do it without die-hard readers like them.

I would also like to thank you, the reader. I hope you enjoyed reading *DARK AND STORMY* as much as we enjoyed writing it. Be sure to check out the two crossover series in the TempleVerse: **The Nate Temple Series** and the **Feathers and Fire Series**.

And last, but definitely not least, I thank my wife, Lexy. Without your support, none of this would have been possible.

ABOUT CAMERON O'CONNELL

Cameron O'Connell is a Jack-of-All-Trades and Master of Some.

He writes The Phantom Queen Diaries, a series in The TempleVerse, about Quinn MacKenna, a mouthy black magic arms dealer trading favors in Boston. All she wants? A round-trip ticket to the Fae realm…and maybe a drink on the house.

A former member of the United States military, a professional model, and English teacher, Cameron finds time to write in the mornings after his first cup of coffee…and in the evenings after his thirty-seventh. Follow him, and the TempleVerse founder, Shayne Silvers, online for all sorts of insider tips, giveaways, and new release updates!

Get Down with Cameron Online

f facebook.com/Cameron-OConnell-788806397985289
a amazon.com/author/cameronoconnell
BB bookbub.com/authors/cameron-o-connell
🐦 twitter.com/thecamoconnell
📷 instagram.com/camoconnellauthor
g goodreads.com/cameronoconnell

ABOUT SHAYNE SILVERS

Shayne is a man of mystery and power, whose power is exceeded only by his mystery...

He currently writes the Amazon Bestselling **Nate Temple** Series, which features a foul-mouthed wizard from St. Louis. He rides a bloodthirsty unicorn, drinks with Achilles, and is pals with the Four Horsemen.

He also writes the Amazon Bestselling **Feathers and Fire** Series—a second series in the TempleVerse. The story follows a rookie spell-slinger named Callie Penrose who works for the Vatican in Kansas City. Her problem? Hell seems to know more about her past than she does.

He coauthors **The Phantom Queen Diaries**—a third series set in The TempleVerse—with Cameron O'Connell. The story follows Quinn MacKenna, a mouthy black magic arms dealer in Boston. All she wants? A round-trip ticket to the Fae realm...and maybe a drink on the house.

He also writes the **Shade of Devil Series**, which tells the story of Sorin Ambrogio—the world's FIRST vampire. He was put into a magical slumber by a Native American Medicine Man when the Americas were first discovered by Europeans. Sorin wakes up after five-hundred years to learn that his protege, Dracula, stole his reputation and that no one has ever even heard of Sorin Ambrogio. The streets of New York City will run with blood as Sorin reclaims his legend.

Shayne holds two high-ranking black belts, and can be found writing in a coffee shop, cackling madly into his computer screen while pounding shots of espresso. He's hard at work on the newest books in the TempleVerse—You can find updates on new releases or chronological reading order on the next page, his website, or any of his social media accounts. **Follow him online for all sorts of groovy goodies, giveaways, and new release updates:**

Get Down with Shayne Online
www.shaynesilvers.com
info@shaynesilvers.com

facebook.com/shaynesilversfanpage
amazon.com/author/shaynesilvers
bookbub.com/profile/shayne-silvers
instagram.com/shaynesilversofficial
twitter.com/shaynesilvers
goodreads.com/ShayneSilvers

BOOKS BY THE AUTHORS

CHRONOLOGY: All stories in the TempleVerse are shown in chronological order on the following page

PHANTOM QUEEN DIARIES

(Set in the TempleVerse)

by Cameron O'Connell & Shayne Silvers

COLLINS (Prequel novella #0 in the 'LAST CALL' anthology)

WHISKEY GINGER

COSMOPOLITAN

OLD FASHIONED

MOTHERLUCKER (Novella #3.5 in the 'LAST CALL' anthology)

DARK AND STORMY

MOSCOW MULE

WITCHES BREW

SALTY DOG

SEA BREEZE

HURRICANE

NATE TEMPLE SERIES

(Main series in the TempleVerse)

by Shayne Silvers

FAIRY TALE - FREE prequel novella #0 for my subscribers

OBSIDIAN SON

BLOOD DEBTS

GRIMM

SILVER TONGUE

BEAST MASTER

BEERLYMPIAN (Novella #5.5 in the 'LAST CALL' anthology)

TINY GODS

DADDY DUTY (Novella #6.5)

WILD SIDE

WAR HAMMER

NINE SOULS

HORSEMAN

LEGEND

KNIGHTMARE

ASCENSION

FEATHERS AND FIRE SERIES

(Also set in the TempleVerse)

by Shayne Silvers

UNCHAINED

RAGE

WHISPERS

ANGEL'S ROAR

MOTHERLUCKER (Novella #4.5 in the 'LAST CALL' anthology)

SINNER

BLACK SHEEP

GODLESS

CHRONOLOGICAL ORDER: TEMPLEVERSE

FAIRY TALE (TEMPLE PREQUEL)

OBSIDIAN SON (TEMPLE 1)

BLOOD DEBTS (TEMPLE 2)

GRIMM (TEMPLE 3)

SILVER TONGUE (TEMPLE 4)

BEAST MASTER (TEMPLE 5)

BEERLYMPIAN (TEMPLE 5.5)

TINY GODS (TEMPLE 6)

DADDY DUTY (TEMPLE NOVELLA 6.5)

UNCHAINED (FEATHERS... 1)

RAGE (FEATHERS... 2)

WILD SIDE (TEMPLE 7)

WAR HAMMER (TEMPLE 8)

WHISPERS (FEATHERS... 3)

COLLINS (PHANTOM 0)

WHISKEY GINGER (PHANTOM... 1)

NINE SOULS (TEMPLE 9)

COSMOPOLITAN (PHANTOM... 2)

ANGEL'S ROAR (FEATHERS... 4)

MOTHERLUCKER (FEATHERS 4.5, PHANTOM 3.5)

OLD FASHIONED (PHANTOM...3)

HORSEMAN (TEMPLE 10)

DARK AND STORMY (PHANTOM... 4)

MOSCOW MULE (PHANTOM...5)

SINNER (FEATHERS...5)

WITCHES BREW (PHANTOM...6)

LEGEND (TEMPLE...11)

SALTY DOG (PHANTOM...7)

BLACK SHEEP (FEATHERS...6)

GODLESS (FEATHERS...7)

KNIGHTMARE (TEMPLE 12)

ASCENSION (TEMPLE 13)

SEA BREEZE (PHANTOM...8)

HURRICANE (PHANTOM...9)

SHADE OF DEVIL SERIES

(Not part of the TempleVerse)

by Shayne Silvers

DEVIL'S DREAM

DEVIL'S CRY
DEVIL'S BLOOD

9 781947 709157